~ ~-04

# Shades of Black

# shades of
# BLACK

*Crime and Mystery Stories
by African-American Authors*

**Edited by**

# Eleanor Taylor Bland

BERKLEY PRIME CRIME, NEW YORK

A Berkley Prime Crime Book
Published by The Berkley Publishing Group
A division of Penguin Group (USA) Inc.
375 Hudson Street
New York, New York 10014

This book is an original publication of The Berkley Publishing Group.

First edition: February 2004

Library of Congress Cataloging-in-Publication Data

Shades of black : crime and mystery stories by African-American authors / edited by
Eleanor Taylor Bland.
p.   c.m.
ISBN 0-425-19402-7
1. Detective and mystery stories, American.   2. American fiction—African American authors.
3. African Americans—Fiction.   I. Bland, Eleanor Taylor.

PS648.D4S527 2004
813'.0872089287'0896073—dc22
2003062955

# Copyrights

# Contents

# Preface

*Lerone Bennett Jr.*

While researching and writing history books, I relax by reading murder mysteries, which keep the pot of my mind simmering and which remind me of what sleuth Larry Cole called real history. During these periods, and the periods in between, I read all of the great masters of the craft, Christie, Allingham, James, Hugh Holton, Chandler . . . Wait a minute! Back up! Hugh Holton?

Yes, Hugh Holton, Chicago police captain and creator of Deputy Police Chief Larry Cole, and also Chester Himes, Walter Mosley, Grace Edwards, and other African-American masters who have not received proper recognition for their contribution to this genre. Within recent years, primarily because of the Freedom Movement, which changed the color of almost everything, including the color of some police chiefs, writers like Mosley, Eleanor Bland, and my colleague Chris Benson are reaching a wider audience. They are also reminding us that mystery writers from Sir Arthur Conan Doyle to Dame Agatha Christie assumed a natural order in which all police chiefs and police captains were White. But that's another story or rather another part of the same story, for there is still a tendency to relegate African-American writers to a lower order of the realm.

This anthology warns against that conceit and invites us to a reevaluation of major and neglected talents who added multiple dimensions, including the why-dunit and the race-dunit, to the traditional and limited whodunit.

Hugh Holton is particularly relevant in this connection, because he spoke not from the library but from the precinct. A full-time police officer and the highest-ranking police officer writing mystery stories at the time, he provided a new perspective and spoke to us from a fully realized world that included murderers living in penthouses and murderers stalking the street.

I don't think there is a finer rendition anywhere of urban police and detective rituals than in Holton's novels. Nor, I think, is there a finer rendition of the *structures* of crimes that create drug addicts, criminals, and crime-fighters the same way Detroit assembly lines turn out cars. Where else can we find a Martin Luther King Jr. march (in his novel *Criminal Element*) defining and anticipating the paths of a rogue cop or a more perfectly drawn portrait, in a crime scene setting, of a Black man rising from the cotton fields to Congress. But I don't want to make this too heavy. For Captain Hugh Holton didn't write essays; he wrote mystery stories that included structure, atmosphere, layers, *the whole,* because he knew that a good mystery story, like any other piece of art, is a world that includes, at least by implication, everything. More than this, Hugh Holton knew that his task was not to preach or teach but to *show* the world and to make us freely re-create it and assume responsibility for it.

I have always preferred the traditional whodunit that gives you the clues and challenges you to identify the murderer. It can be said that Holton's art is greater than that, for he tells you who the murderer is and how he did it and then makes you sit on the edge of your seat as layer after layer of explosions and revelations hold you enthralled until the last page.

On this level, and on others as well, Captain Hugh Holton was a rare talent who bore witness to a world that most of us deny but that none of us can ignore without diminishing art and freedom. In addition to all that, Holton, like Himes, the progenitor of the African-American police procedural, Mosely, and other writers featured in this anthology, was a great storyteller who increased our understanding of Black, White, and Brown humanity.

# Acknowledgments

I did not become a mystery writer because I was a longtime fan. I discovered detective fiction in 1988, about two years before I began writing the Marti MacAlister mystery series. The only other African-American mystery writers I was aware of at that time were Chester Himes and Walter Mosley, neither of whom I had read. I had no idea of the long and significant history of African-Americans in this genre. I am deeply indebted to Frankie Y. Bailey and *Out of the Woodpile: Black Characters in Crime and Detective Fiction* for what I know now that I didn't know then.

I had read *The Conjure Man Dies: A Mystery of Dark Harlem,* written by Rudolph Fisher and published in 1932, but I did not know that prior to that, W. Adolph Roberts had published several mystery novels, including *The Haunting Hand* in 1926. *Native Son,* by Richard Wright, published in 1940, continues to be a major influence in my writing, but as a woman writer I did not know that in 1900, Pauline Hopkins published the short story "Talma Gordon," a locked door mystery, in *Colored American Magazine.* Nor did I know that by 1907 short stories were being published by J. E. Bruce, or that other early African-American writers of mystery fiction include Alice Dunbar-Nelson, John A. Williams, and Sam Greenlee.

There is a rich tradition of African-Americans who wrote cozies and thrillers and every other mystery subgenre. Although not all of these writers had Black protagonists, those who did included the social and political issues of their time. They added a significant dimension to our rich and varied literary tradition. We are all deeply indebted to them as well as enriched by them.

In keeping with our literary traditions, history, and heritage, this smorgasbord of short stories includes writers whose work you know and love, writers who are published in other genres, and a few writers who are being published here for the first time. Their stories vary from cozy to suspense; their protagonists vary in age from young adult to senior citizen and include a wide variety of sleuths as well as varied locales. Alternative viewpoints on social and political issues, our own unique perspective of the world we live in, and even an element of fantasy and science fiction are included. In short, we have brought to this work what is representative of who we are as writers, and as African-American writers.

# INTRODUCTION: WHAT A DIFFERENCE A DECADE MAKES

*Eleanor Taylor Bland*

In 1992, Gar Anthony Haywood and Walter Mosley were the only two African-Americans publishing mystery novels. Percy Spurlark Parker, who published a mystery novel in 1974, was publishing short stories.

Before that year was over, Barbara Neely and I published our first mysteries. Four years later, in 1996 fifteen of us gathered at the University of Minnesota in St. Paul-Minneapolis, at the invitation of Archie Givens Jr., to attend a three-day Black Mystery Writer's Symposium in conjunction with Bouchercon XXVII. Today we have approximately forty-six African-Americans who have published mysteries. And, I hope, we're still counting.

In my opinion, the most significant contribution we have made, collectively, to mystery fiction, is the development of the extended family; the permanence of spouses and significant others, most of whom don't die in the first three chapters or by the end of the novel; children who are complex, wanted, and loved; and even pets. We have brought our mothers and fathers, or grandparents, and other relatives and friends to our work in a unique—often humorous, frequently reverent, and sometimes brutally honest—tribute to who they are, all they have survived, and what they have given. As writers of fiction we have added a new depth and dimension to members of the opposite sex. Women write about caring and compassionate men who are also strong and self-sufficient. Men write about women who are independent and intelligent and also affectionate, giving, and accurately strong.

We write about sleuths who are gumshoes—both hard core and relatively benevolent private investigators—police officers, former police officers, FBI agents, attorneys, forensic scientists, domestic workers, bail bondsmen, doctors, a drug addict, an ex-convict, journalists, historians, educators, political and community activists, concerned citizens, and citizens trying to mind their own business.

We write about things common to everyone, and things uniquely our own, such as '50s doo-wop music groups; life in Los Angeles in the '50s and '60s as well as the present; blues from the 1960s to the new millennium; lynching and the death penalty from 1912 to 1922; the Underground Railroad; and Black genealogy. References to religion and a religious context to right and wrong are not unusual. Problems of color, what shade of Black you are, is also referenced. We give visibility, context, and dimension to issues, dilemmas, and society that are often invisible to others.

We write about familiar places like L.A., Boston, Baltimore, Philly, New Orleans, Northern California, Colorado, Maine, Missouri, and Virginia, as well as less familiar, more stereotypical places like Newark, Harlem, Detroit, Chicago, and Washington, D.C., small towns in particular and the South in general, from our own unique perspectives.

I have withheld the identity of the authors of these works, because I am hoping that you will go to your independent booksellers, libraries, chain stores and—based on your own interests and curiosity—find out who these authors are. I am also hoping that such forays will open up to you the entire, exciting world of African-American Mystery Fiction. Keep reading . . .

# SINCE YOU WENT AWAY

*Frankie Y. Bailey*

John Quinn set the take-out bag he was carrying on the kitchen table. "Have you considered giving it a decent burial?"

"It's not dead," Lizzie Stuart said, not looking up from the drooping, yellow-leaved plant she was trying to extract from its pot. "It's just sick . . . I gave it too much water, and it needs more sunshine . . . and more room to spread its roots."

"Or you could just buy another plant," Quinn said, his silver gray eyes reflecting his amusement. He held out the card in his hand. "Before I forget again . . . I got this in the mail last week. This isn't something we want to do, right?"

Lizzie glanced up from her task. "What isn't?"

"This." Quinn held the card closer. "A fund-raiser. A murder mystery evening aboard a train."

Lizzie shook her head. Her gaze returned to the plant. She eased it up and toward the larger red pot. "I don't think so, Quinn. I don't think that I could get into the spirit of trying to solve a pretend murder for the fun of it."

"I'll send them a donation."

"Definitely a better idea. If we went . . ." Lower lip clasped between her teeth, she settled the plant into its new pot. "Before the night was over, a real corpse would probably turn up."

Quinn laughed. "I think we'd be safe on that count, Lizabeth. The homicide rate aboard trains is quite low."

Lizzie nodded toward the plastic bag of potting soil. "Would you pour that, please, while I hold it up? And for your information, my grandfather had a murder aboard one of his trains."

Quinn tilted the bag, distributing the soil around the plant. "Really?" he said.

"Yes, really. Paper towels, please."

He set the bag down, tore off a handful of towels from the roll, and passed them to her. "You were saying."

Lizzie brushed the loose soil from the counter into the trash bin. "It isn't really a date-night story, Quinn."

"Tell me anyway."

"I'm starving. What'd you bring?"

"Chinese. Shrimp and cashews. Chicken and vegetables."

"Let me wash my hands, and I'll get the plates. Do you want wine? Or there are a couple of bottles of beer in the refrigerator."

"Beer's fine." He opened the refrigerator and took out a bottle. "Tell me the story about the murder."

Lizzie set the plates on the table. "All right, Chief Quinn. If you insist. But don't blame me if this little tale casts a blight over our romantic evening."

"I think our romantic evening can survive, Professor Stuart."

Lizzie spooned rice onto her plate and reached for the shrimp and cashews. "I didn't have lunch," she said. "This happened in March 1946, shortly after the end of World War II. The demobilization of the troops was still going on, but civilians were traveling again, and things were beginning to get back to normal. This particular train was en route from New Orleans to Chicago, but it had stopped at the station in Lexington to pick up passengers. My grandfather was waiting by the steps of his sleeping car to greet the new arrivals when he heard his name called . . ."

. . .

"Good evening, Mr. Walter Lee Stuart."

Walter Lee turned at the sound of the husky voice. He grinned, his white teeth flashing in his ebony face. "Good evening to you, Miss Peaches," he said, tipping his cap to the tall, reed-thin woman in the coral suit and matching high heels. "How's life been treating you?"

Miss Peaches smiled and brushed back her shoulder-length hair with her free hand. "Never better, Mr. Stuart, never better. Congratulations on your news!"

Walter Lee shook his head. "Now, how did you hear about that? I just heard it a couple of days ago myself."

Miss Peaches tilted her head. "I know things, Mr. Stuart. You give your wife Miss Peaches' best, you hear?"

Now, he wasn't likely to do that, Walter Lee thought. In her "delicate condition," Hester Rose wasn't up to receiving a message from Miss Peaches.

He watched as Miss Peaches sauntered over to the train window that one of the hooting, grinning soldiers had lowered. She reached into her basket and handed the soldier and his friends pieces of her homemade gingerbread. Miss Peaches' own personal contribution to the war effort for the past few years, and now to the demobilization.

"Hey, Miss Ginger Peaches," one of them called to her, using the name she was sometimes known by. "That's who you are, ain't it?"

"That's me, honeychile. None other."

A woman, white and proper, glanced in Miss Peaches' direction, looked startled, and veered away from her. The woman almost trotted toward Walter Lee. Running for safety? "I believe I'm in this car," she said, in a voice that was more pleasant than he had expected.

He glanced at her ticket. "Yes, ma'am, the conductor will be through to collect your ticket later. I'll show you to your room."

"I can find it, thank you."

She hurried up the steps, gone before he could speak. He was about to follow her to make sure she did find the right room, when Zach Garfield popped out onto the platform.

Zach glanced over at Miss Peaches. "Lord, look at that."

Walter Lee said, "Miss Peaches looks real nice this evening. Real spring-like."

"Spring-like! That he-she makes me wants to puke."

"Live and let live, young Zachary. And hadn't you better get yourself back to the kitchen? You know you ain't supposed to be out here."

"I needed some fresh air," Zach said. "Not that I'm getting any with that going on over there. I thought they had laws—"

"They do have laws," Walter Lee said. "But Miss Peaches don't hurt nobody. She works as an orderly at a hospital during the week. Been working there since she was a teenager. If she wants to dress up on Saturday—"

"Hey, Walter Lee." The hail came from Marvin, one of the redcaps. He was pushing a cart containing several suitcases. "This lady's in your coach."

Changing his expression to eagerness to be of service, Walter Lee moved to welcome the woman. He was caught off guard by the slow, lazy smile that she gave him. He touched his fingers to his cap.

"Yes, ma'am, let me show you to your accommodations."

She adjusted the little black hat that set atop her own shimmering blonde hair and pulled the fur collar of her jacket a bit higher against the nip in the evening air. "I'm meeting someone," she said. "My friend. But I'm running late, and I'm sure by now he must have just about given up on me."

Her voice still had more than a trace of Kentucky backwoods. Not as citified as she'd like people to think with that outfit, Walter Lee thought.

"I don't think he would have given up on you, ma'am," he said. "So far, only two gentlemen traveling alone come aboard my car at this station. One of them was a major, and he—"

"No, that couldn't be him." Something had flickered in her eyes, was covered up with a smile. "My friend Johnny wasn't in the Army. Flat feet."

From the corner of his eye, Walter Lee saw Zach Garfield make a movement. Zach had been 4-F too. Bad knees.

No shame in that. But it was no use trying to tell the boy that.

"Well, why don't I show you aboard, ma'am," Walter Lee said. "We have a few more minutes before—"

"Ruby, baby, there you are!" A man darted through the crowd. In his late twenties or early thirties and chubby, already balding, he reached out to stroke her arm. "I was afraid you were going to miss the train, honey."

She smiled at him. "So was I. But here I am."

Walter Lee said, "Ma'am, sir, if you'd care to board . . ."

The man signaled to his own redcap. "Get the bags on board, boy."

"If you and the lady will go on ahead, sir," Walter Lee said. "We'll be right behind you."

The woman linked her arm with the man's. "First-class service all the way, Johnny. Just like you said."

"Nothing's too good for you, Ruby, baby."

His eyes still eating Ruby up, Johnny started up the steps and almost bumped into Zach, still standing there. "Watch out, boy!"

That temper that Walter Lee had warned him about showed for a second on Zach's face, but he held his tongue. "Yes, suh," he said, stepping back and to the side.

"Please, pardon us," the woman said, sending her smile in Zach's direction.

He stood there, staring at her.

The man looked from one of them to the other. His face flushed red. "I said, watch yourself, boy. Come on, Ruby, honey."

"Anything you say, Johnny," the woman said, her voice amused.

She was teasing old Johnny some, Walter Lee thought. Except he was too busy pushing his chest out and playing big man to notice.

As he followed the couple on board, Walter Lee shot Zach a look. He liked the boy, but he had no patience with his manner. Zach might think he was better than his kitchen job and the white folks who thought colored men weren't fit for nothing but to serve them. But as long as he was wearing the uniform, he might try to do what he was being paid to do.

Not that Zach was likely to be around much longer. The way he was going, he was gonna get himself fired as soon as a passenger complained or one of the spotters the company put on board wrote him up.

"Yes, sir," Walter Lee said as he opened the door of the first room. "Here we are. And ma'am, you're right in here."

"Oh, Johnny," Ruby said, hugging his arm. "You really know how to treat a girl right."

"This is just the beginning, honey," Johnny said, sticking out his chest some more. "Just the beginning."

"Let me show you how everything works, ma'am and sir," Walter Lee said.

When he had gotten them settled, he went back to check on the other passengers who had come aboard at this station. The widow—a pretty girl, in her twenties, looking like she was weighed down by her grief. Well, that was to be expected when her soldier husband's casket was up there in the baggage car. She had her son with her. But the boy looked like he was more than she could handle. Couldn't be more than six or seven, and not likely to pay attention to his mama telling him to behave himself.

There was a minister and his wife in the room next to them. The flashy kind of slick-as-grease minister who preached hell and brimstone from his pulpit—and could probably shoot crap and drink moonshine with the best of them. Odd that him and that little whey-faced wife of his would be traveling first-class. Probably traveling on money they borrowed from the collection plate.

But the other passengers who had gotten on didn't look like they'd be any trouble. The major was still in his uniform, not long back from the front, judging by the look of him. His hands still trembling a little. Still limping.

The spinster schoolteacher who had given Miss Peaches that look was in the room next to him. At least, that was what Walter Lee had decided she was—a schoolteacher. Her brown hair pulled back in a bun and glasses perched on her nose. Wearing a plain brown dress that covered her body—and that was about all that could be said for it. It was a shame when a woman who could have done something with herself just gave up like that.

'Course they did say that there was a man shortage now because of the war. That would explain why a beautiful woman like that Ruby was set-tling for old Johnny. Probably making do with him until he got her to Chicago where she could do better.

Walter Lee paused as he passed the open door of the room on the end. The young man inside was on the floor on his hands and knees peering at something.

"Anything I can help you with, sir?"

The young man—rounded face and rosy-cheeked—sprang to his feet. "No, thank you. I was examining the room's design. It's very efficient. Good use of space."

Walter Lee nodded. "The company would be pleased to hear you say that, sir. Sure there's nothing I can get for you?"

The young man shook his curly brown head. Then he stepped forward and held out his hand. "Dwight Kent. I'm a cartoonist."

Walter Lee looked at the slender, long-fingered hand held out to him. He clasped it with his own. "Pleased to meet you, sir. Walter Lee Stuart. Just call me if you need anything."

The young man nodded. "Thank you, that's very good of you."

Walter Lee stepped back and into the corridor. He was grinning as he turned away. Now, that one was still newly hatched. Wonder where he'd come from?

"Your hair smells funny, and I don't like your ugly dress."

The woman Walter Lee had named "the schoolteacher" raised her gaze from her book to the boy hovering over her chair. "You are testing my patience, young man."

She said it in a voice that was calm but firm. It was that rather than his mother's weak, "David, please don't say things like that. Leave the lady alone," that made him back off.

When their eyes happened to meet, the schoolteacher gave Walter Lee a brisk nod. Then she turned her attention back to the book on the table in front of her. *Anna and the King of* something or other, Walter Lee had seen when she came in the lounge carrying it.

"George," Johnny called out, snapping his fingers. "Over here. Bring me another bourbon."

No point in telling the man that his name wasn't George. He was one of them kind that called any porter who worked for the company after George Pullman. "Coming right up, sir. May I get you something, ma'am," he said to Ruby.

She smiled and shook her head, but she was watching the boy, David, as he climbed up on a chair to peer out the window.

She got up and went over to kneel down beside him. "What do you see out there?"

"Can't see nothing," the boy said. "It's dark."

He jumped down from the chair. "I'm hungry, Mommy."

His mother looked up from the knitting that was lying untouched in her lap. "David, when we were in the dining room, you wouldn't eat."

David jumped up and down. "I'm hungry."

Walter Lee turned from setting the bourbon on the table in front of Johnny and spoke before the man could get out the harsh words he saw forming on his lips. "I'll be glad to get him something from the kitchen, ma'am."

"Thank you," she said, more tears in her eyes.

Nerves. The woman was nothing but a bundle of nerves. That was plain to see. No wonder the boy was acting up. Children could sense it when grown-ups aren't feeling up to being in control.

He brought the boy the sandwich he had asked for and a glass of milk and persuaded him to sit down in front of one of the small tables to eat.

The boy pulled the sandwich apart. Crumbled up one slice of bread, then started licking at the peanut butter and jelly on the other slice.

Ruby'd come and sat down across from the widow. She was chattering on, trying to get the widow to talk. Walter Lee glanced over at Johnny. Johnny was nursing his bourbon and watching Ruby.

The major was watching her too. Not that she wasn't the kind of woman who drew men's eyes. But it seemed to Walter Lee that the major was watching her kind of odd. He had come into the lounge and sat down in the chair that young David had climbed up on. For a few minutes, he had been staring out the window into the darkness, with his back turned on the others. Then he had suddenly turned in his chair and started staring at Ruby.

That had been about the time Ruby said to the widow, "I know how it is, honey. I was engaged to someone during the war."

Her friend Johnny had frowned at that.

"He was wounded," Ruby said. "They sent him home to a hospital here, and they did all they could. The doctors and nurses . . . but he . . .

well, he died later." Ruby sighed. "But you have to go on, you know. You can't just let yourself get down and stay that way. You've got your kid." She smiled. "I always wanted a kid."

The schoolteacher looked up from her book. "Children are a considerable responsibility. You're young and pretty. Do you really want to be tied down?"

Ruby turned to look at her. "If I met the right man—"

"And presumably you thought you had when you met your fiancé," the schoolteacher said.

"I knew I had," Ruby said. She shook her head. "But the war screwed up a lot of lives, didn't it?"

Johnny said, "Hey, you, still got me."

He said it like he wanted to sound like he was making a joke. But he sounded hurt. Like a little boy, Walter Lee thought.

Ruby laughed and jumped up from her chair to go to him. "Of course, I have you, honey. I was just talking about the past." She bent and kissed his cheek. "But that's over and done. We're going to Chicago to have ourselves some fun."

"Porter, may I have a scotch and soda, please," the major said, his voice hoarse.

It was the first time he had spoken since his "good evening" when he'd come into the lounge. Heads turned in his direction. He flushed and turned to look out the window again.

"Coming right up, sir," Walter Lee said.

When he brought the drink over to the major, he noticed again the tremor in the man's hands. Could be shell shock. Some of the soldiers coming back had that.

He should be grateful himself, Walter Lee thought as he had many times before. He'd been a year or two too old to be called up. So he'd stayed here safe at home, his body and his mind still whole. No man's blood on his hands.

"Porter, may I have a cup of tea," the schoolteacher said, breaking into his thoughts.

"Yes, ma'am, I'll get you a cup from the kitchen."

It went on like that for the next hour or so. Other passengers passed through the lounge, stopping on their way to the observation car or coming back through from the dining room. But it was the passengers who had gotten on in Lexington that lingered.

Even the minister and his wife came in.

"Good evening, folks," the preacher said, before he was halfway through the door. His voice, rich and deep, filling the lounge. "We thought we'd come out and be sociable."

He glanced over at the bar that Walter Lee was standing behind. "Think I'll have a nightcap, porter. Something for my digestion."

"A glass of sherry, Byron," his wife said. "A glass of sherry would be nice. I'd like one too."

The preacher nodded at Walter Lee. "Two glasses of sherry. Your best."

"Yes, sir," Walter Lee said, reaching for the bottle. Well, at least, the man wasn't a hypocrite. Come right out and had his self a drink. Let his wife have one too.

His wife glanced around, settling on a seat by the widow and Ruby, who'd gone back to sit with her. "Eunice Harcourt," she said. "That's my husband, Byron. Who are you ladies?"

"Ruby Jeffries," Ruby said, looking amused again.

The widow tucked her knitting into her bag as if she was thinking she might need to make a run for it. "Joanne Burton."

Eunice nodded. "We saw you arrive . . ." She paused. "With the casket. Your husband?"

The widow's hand fluttered to her throat. "Yes. I'm taking his body back to Chicago. His family . . . they want him buried there."

Eunice leaned closer. "And none of them come down to help you? They shouldn't have left you to—"

The widow stood up. "They . . . I told them I could manage. Excuse me, please. David, come . . . it's time for your bedtime."

David puckered up his face for a moment, as if he was going to argue. But instead, he jumped up from the floor and ran over to take her hand.

Walter Lee's gaze went to the major, as the man came to his feet. "If there is any way I can be of service, ma'am," he said to the widow.

She paused, looking like she wasn't sure what to say. Then she shook her head. "Thank you . . . there's nothing."

"Why don't you come on back and join us after you get him tucked in," Eunice Harcourt said. "You don't want to sit there alone in your room."

But the widow didn't come back. Johnny and Ruby and the preacher and his wife ended up playing cards. And what would his Hester Rose say about that? Walter Lee thought, grinning to himself. A preacher in his collar playing cards.

'Course, they weren't playing for money, so maybe that made it all right.

The major made a half movement, as if he was going to stand. Then he groaned and fell back into his chair. Before anyone else could move, the schoolteacher was on her feet. "What is it?" she asked him, bending down beside his chair.

"Cramp. Cramp in my leg."

Without as much as a by your leave, she had his pant leg up and was rubbing at his leg and telling him to try to relax it. A few minutes later, he settled back, looking pale but not like he was hurting anymore.

"Thank you," he said.

"You're welcome."

"How did you know what to do?" the preacher's wife asked her.

"My mother used to have trouble with her legs," the schoolteacher said. She sat down at her table again and picked up her book.

By then Dwight Kent, the cartoonist, had come into the lounge. He asked for a cup of hot chocolate. Walter Lee had to go out to the kitchen to get that. When he got back, Dwight had his big pad out, and he was sitting there in the corner, drawing.

When Walter Lee put the cup down beside him, he saw that Dwight was sketching the preacher on his pad. Not line for line. Just strokes of his pen that caught the man—the way that collar he was wearing didn't go with his mouth or his dark eyes that were sliding looks in Ruby's direction. Dwight made it almost look like two little horns were just beneath the preacher's thick black hair.

Walter caught himself before he chuckled out loud. But Dwight had seen Walter Lee sneaking peeks at his work. He flipped the pages of his pad backward so that Walter Lee could see the other drawings he'd done in the same quick stokes. Ruby looking like an angel, except for the smile on her full lips. And the preacher's wife looking like a little brown mouse with its nose wiggling.

And there was Johnny, looking like he was about to bust out of his shirt and jacket. Full of his self as could be.

Dwight winked at Walter Lee and turned in his chair so that the schoolteacher was in his line of vision. Walter Lee picked up an ashtray and fiddled around nearby so that he could see what Dwight would draw.

The boy should be ashamed of himself—and he ought to be ashamed of himself for looking, Walter Lee thought when Dwight gestured him over.

He'd drawn the schoolteacher with her hair down and flowing about her shoulders and her glasses in her hand. She was smiling, like she was looking at some man and telling him to come and get her.

But, then, the boy had seen what Walter Lee had. The schoolteacher had given up on herself too easy.

Still she wouldn't approve if she saw that drawing. Walter Lee gave Dwight a shake of his head and went back to his bar.

Walter Lee saw Dwight glance at the major. Drawing him too, most like.

He didn't get to see the sketch of the major until the preacher's wife said it was getting late and the card players agreed that it was bedtime. The major limped out behind them. That was when Dwight brought his pad over.

Without a word, he flipped to the major. Walter Lee almost winced. This one was cruel. There in the strokes of Dwight's pen was a man, face half in shadow, eyes wide with fear. Hands clenched.

Before Walter Lee could speak, Dwight flipped the page. Walter Lee laughed out loud. There he was himself. But instead of his cap, Dwight had drawn him holding a top hat like magicians used—pulling a rabbit from that hat.

"Why you'd draw me like that?" Walter Lee said. "How'd you know I like magic tricks?"

Dwight smiled and shook his head. "It just occurred to me when I was watching you dealing with all of them."

Before Walter Lee could say anything, the door opened again. It was Ruby. "Porter, I meant to ask about when we get into the station in the morning—"

She broke off, her eyes on the pad. "What's that?"

"I'm a cartoonist," Dwight said.

"Can I see?" she said, smiling and reaching for the pad.

She laughed as she flipped the pages, delight on her face. Until she got toward the end, then her smile faded. "You shouldn't have drawn the major like that," she said.

"That's what I saw when I looked at him," Dwight said.

"The soldiers who fought . . . the man I was engaged to . . ." She shook her head. "Things happened to them. Not just to their bodies."

She stared down at the drawing of the major, and then she began to flip back through the pages. Not laughing now.

Walter Lee glanced at Dwight. The boy's eyes were glinting, his lower lip curled.

Walter Lee cleared his throat. He didn't like the boy as much as he'd thought he did.

"What did you want to ask, ma'am?" he said to Ruby.

She had paused over another one of the drawings. She was frowning. "There's something about . . ." She looked up, her eyes going from Walter Lee to Dwight. "It . . . was nothing important. I'll ask you in the morning."


Walter Lee was sitting in the men's washroom polishing the shoes the passengers had left for him to shine, when the brakes screeched and the train jerked. He was thrown from his chair as the train came to a stop.

Lord, they must have hit something on the track.

He jumped up and grabbed his jacket.

In the corridor, the doors were opening, passengers asking what had happened. He went down the line, calming them down and making sure everyone was all right. Then he hurried toward the door separating the sleeping quarters from the lounge. He needed to find the conductor.

He didn't have far to go. Mick O'Malley was in the lounge, his solid two hundred pounds of muscle planted between two men, Zach Garfield and Ruby's friend, Johnny.

She was there in a chair.

"You killed her, you nigger bastard!"

Zach Garfield was standing with his back pressed to the wall, his eyes dark and wide against skin that looked chalky. "I didn't. God, I told you I didn't!"

Mick O'Malley's hand held Johnny back, as he tried to rush at Zach.

"I saw how you were looking at her when we got on the train!" Johnny said, his fists clenched, his face red.

Walter Lee pulled his gaze from the men and looked down at the woman slumped sideways in the armchair. She was still beautiful. But she wasn't laughing anymore. A knife—a large kitchen knife—was sticking out of her chest.

Help us, Jesus, Walter Lee thought.

"Talk fast," Mick O'Malley said to Zach.

"I told him what happened," Zach said, his voice shaking. "I heard a noise, and I came to see what it was. And I found her like that."

"You're lying!" Johnny said.

"We'll hold him for the police," Mick O'Malley said. "Until we get to Chicago. I'll not have a lynch mob on my train."

His words were as much for the passengers that had began to crowd into the room as for Johnny. They were mumbling. Staring from Ruby dead there in the chair to Zach with his back against the wall.

"I'm going to lock him up in the storeroom in the kitchen," O'Malley told the passengers. "I'll put a guard on the door." Then, to Walter Lee, "This man here . . ." he gestured with a nod at Johnny. "Pulled the emergency brake to signal for help. We'll be back under way in a few minutes."

"Yes, sir," Walter Lee said.

He turned to the passengers behind him. "Ladies and gentlemen, we . . . there's nothing you can do here. If you would please go back to your rooms—"

"Don't you be telling us where to go, nigger," a man's voice said from the crowd.

"Then *I'll* tell you," Mick O'Malley said. "Get back to your rooms and stay there."

They went back with curses from the men and wails of fear from the women. Walter Lee thought he heard the preacher asking the Lord's assistance.

He'd be willing to bet that they all were locking their doors and would keep them locked until the next station. They wouldn't be ringing for their colored porter tonight.

And that was good because he had some thinking to do.

Walter Lee wondered in passing what instructions Mick O'Malley would give to the kitchen crew. Would he lock them up somewhere too, to make sure none of them tried to let Zach free? Or would he trust them?

Hard to tell what O'Malley was thinking right now. He'd left Walter Lee in charge of his car. But by the time they got to Chicago, all the colored men who were in the vicinity might have gotten named in Ruby's death. And, however, it came out for the rest of them, Zach was in a world of trouble right now.

Walter Lee went back to the men's washroom and began to collect the shoes that had been scattered across the floor when the train came to a stop. Whatever happened, the passengers were going to want their shoes back and polished in the morning. He could think while he shined.


When he knocked on Dwight Kent's door, Walter Lee was prepared to have the young man look at him suspicious. Instead, Dwight opened the door, smiled, and made a sweeping gesture of his arm for Walter Lee to enter. "I was hoping you'd come," he said, shutting the door.

Now, Walter Lee was the one feeling suspicious. Not that he had been sure this was the best idea he'd ever had, even before he knocked. "Why is that, sir?"

Dwight Kent nodded. "We need to confer don't we? About the suspects. I've been watching them, and you've been watching them, and if we put our heads together—"

"So you don't think Zach did it?" Walter Lee said.

"I asked myself why he would kill her." Dwight looked up toward the ceiling. "Unless, of course, he was tying to rape her, and ended up killing her when she fought back. But from what I could see, there wasn't much of a struggle. And you would think she would have screamed loud enough for somebody to hear if she was being attacked . . . unless he stopped her from screaming . . . but he didn't have any bite marks that I could see . . . and, anyway, that stuff about colored men lusting after white women all the time . . ." he stopped talking and looked at Walter Lee. "But you've already thought all this through, haven't you? Not that you probably had to think about it as much as I did."

"No, I didn't have to think about it long," Walter Lee said.

"So you've come to confer, haven't you?" Dwight smiled. "That must mean you don't think I did it. Well, I don't think you did either."

"Thank you, sir," Walter Lee said. "But what I need . . . if you wouldn't mind . . . is to have another look at those drawings you were doing—"

Dwight nodded. "I thought of that too. She reacted to one of them when she was flipping back through the pad. But I couldn't see which one it was, could you?"

"No, sir. But I thought if we looked at them—"

They spent the next half hour looking and trying to see what it was that had made Ruby say, "There's something about . . ."

"She must have meant something that reminded her of something," Walter Lee said.

"Or something that wasn't right about one of the sketches," Dwight said from his lounging position in the other chair.

"But all your drawings aren't quite right, sir," Walter Lee said. "I mean they—"

"They're caricatures," Dwight said. "And, sometimes, I can be a little mean."

Walter Lee nodded. "Yes, sir, like with the preacher and the major."

Dwight held up the pad. "But I did flatter our middle-aged spinster."

"Yes, sir, you made the schoolteacher look pretty. Except she looks like she—"

"Well, she'd probably like to."

"Uh-huh, sir. But we aren't getting anywhere with—" Walter Lee closed his eyes. He'd had a thought and lost it. He tried to find it again, to grasp what it was.

"What?" Dwight said. "You've got something haven't you?"

Walter Lee pointed at the sketch. "Her hair," he said. "David, the widow's little boy, said her hair smelled funny."

"Maybe he meant it didn't smell as nice as his mother's."

"Yes, sir, maybe. But have you ever been in one of those beauty parlors. I don't know if they're the same for white women as for black. But when you walk in there, it smells . . . like hair frying and chemical smells, like in the labs they have in high schools. Women put stuff on their hair to straighten it or to change the color. What if, the schoolteacher—"

"Had dyed her hair that dull brown?"

"Yes, sir. And put on glasses. And that ugly brown dress. What if she wanted to look like a spinster schoolteacher?"

"When she's really something else? What? A spy left over from the war?"

"Or somebody Ruby . . . Miss Ruby . . . might have recognized if she looked like she usually did."

"But if she was someone Ruby knew, even with her hair dyed and glasses—"

"But what if she didn't know her that well, sir? What if she was just someone she would have seen in passing somewhere else?"

"You've got something in mind, haven't you?"

"Yes, sir, but I don't know . . . it was just when the major had his cramp . . . and the way the schoolteacher made a beeline away from Miss Peaches when she saw her and—"

"Miss who?"

Walter Lee shook his head. "I'm just thinking this through, sir. But what if . . ."

When he was done, Dwight laughed. "That's some theory. And you haven't really identified the motive."

"The motive? You mean why, sir? Well, I don't know about that. I'm just trying to think how some of these things might tie together. 'Course it could have been one of the others. The major acts kind of strange. Still got the shakes. And the preacher was watching her." Walter Lee shook his head. "I'm just saying suppose, sir."

Dwight nodded. "So now we have to figure out how to test your theory."

"Yes, sir, and that could be trouble. Especially if I'm wrong." Walter Lee rubbed at his chin. "And I'm wondering whether I should say anything to the conductor. But I'm feeling kind of uneasy, because he ain't come to speak to me about this."

"Better leave him out of it then." Dwight grinned, "But I'm in."

"Yes, sir," Walter Lee said, and kept to himself his opinion that Dwight didn't have a whole lot to lose. He was playing a game. But his help was welcome.


The train would be coming into Union Station in less than an hour. The conductor had instructed Walter Lee—still without saying much about what had happened—to do his best to make things as normal as possible for the sleeping-car passengers. Bring their shined shoes and breakfast to their rooms if they didn't care to go to the dining room and be served. Keep them as content as possible until the police could board the train to take Zach away. They'd be wanting to question the passengers too, so there would be some delay in getting people off.

But Walter Lee knew time was running out. If the police thought Zach did it, the passengers would be questioned only about what they might have seen or heard. And then they would be gone.

If he was going to do it, it would have to be now.

Taking a deep breath, he knocked on the schoolteacher's door. She hadn't come out of her room to go to the dining car or rung for service. She might still be sleeping, but he doubted it.

When she opened the door, she was dressed in another ugly dress, this one with a little jacket. Her hair was in that bun.

"I need to speak to you, ma'am," Walter Lee said.

"Yes?" she said.

"Inside, please, ma'am. This . . . you wouldn't be wanting anyone else to hear this."

She looked at him, her eyes calm behind the glasses. Then she stepped back. Walter Lee stepped into her room.

It was not unusual for him to be in a passenger's room. He made their beds. He cleaned up after them. They seem to think nothing at all of being half-dressed in front of him, both the men and the women.

But this was different. He was trying to hold the upper hand here. And it could go bad wrong. He glanced toward the door that he had left slightly ajar.

"Ma'am, I know," he said.

"You know what?"

"I know you killed her."

She stared at him. "If this is a joke—"

"No, ma'am. I know you killed her, and I can prove it."

"How can you prove something that—"

"Miss Peaches, ma'am. You were scared Miss Peaches was going to recognize you."

"I don't know what you—"

"She works as an orderly at the hospital, ma'am. Dressed like a man during the week. And she would have known you were one of the nurses from the hospital. If she'd seen you, she would have known you were dressed up for something too—"

"I don't know what you—" Her eyes glinted behind her glasses. "I had no reason to kill that young woman—"

"Not that much younger than you, ma'am. I bet you look a whole lot younger when you're dressed like—"

"Get out of here," she said. "I don't wish to continue this ridiculous—"

"We don't have to, ma'am. I'll just go tell them—the conductor and the police when they come on board—and let them ask you about it. Check up on you."

Walter Lee turned toward the door. He heard the screech she gave, before she landed on him from behind. She jabbed at him with something sharp. He twisted around and saw the scissors in her hand. He held up his arm in front of his face as she came at him again. He shoved her away, as she stabbed at him. But she came back, shrieking, jabbing with the scissors. He was down on the floor, flailing his arms to try to keep her away.

He heard voices on the other side of the door. They were tying to open it, but he was against it.

He could feel the blood in his eyes. He caught his breath and rose up, shoving her away. She came after him again.

But now, they were inside, pulling her away. She was still screaming like a wild thing.

Walter slumped back against the wall.

They held her—Dwight and the conductor, Mick O'Malley—until she settled down. She whimpered. "I sat by his bedside willing him to live, and he did . . . but all he wanted was her. She came, and she looked at him, and there was revulsion in her eyes, and he saw it. And I could feel the pain he felt. And I tried to comfort him. But she was all he wanted. When she stopped coming, stopped pretending, he let himself die. Because of her." Her head hung down, her hair falling around her face. "She said he drove her away. But she didn't love him. I did. I did . . . even broken and scarred . . . I loved him."

Dwight bent down and pressed his handkerchief to Walter Lee's shoulder. "There's your motive," he said. "Good work."

"Yes, sir," Walter Lee said.

Before he passed out, he wondered if the company would replace his uniform or if he would have to buy another out of his pay.


"I told you it wasn't a date-night story," Lizzie said, reaching for their empty plates. "Do you want some coffee?"

"I'll make it," Quinn said, following her over to the sink. "And actually, Lizabeth, it was the perfect date-night story."

She turned, eyebrows raised in her tawny face. "How so, Quinn?"

"Because," he said, drawing her into his arms. "That little tale of love and murder reminded me of how lucky I am to have you."

"Yes, you are, aren't you? Of course, I'm rather lucky to have you too."

"Before we get too mushy, why don't we go—"

"That's a splendid idea."

# THE COOKOUT

*Jacqueline Turner Banks*

"Don't leave me with him. I'm warning you!"

Stacey's mother stopped packing clothes and turned to face her. "Excuse me?" Frances Barron considered herself a good mother, an easy mother. She'd given her daughter a lot of slack in recent months, but even the mild-mannered Frances had her limits.

Stacey forced a smile. *But I'm not going to apologize,* she told herself. "I just mean it's not fair," she said aloud, in her most whiny teenage voice. "Why do I have to stay here with him? He's your husband, not mine!" *And you could have done a lot better,* Stacey silently added.

Frances stopped her packing again and sat on the bed. She patted the spot where she wanted Stacey to sit. Stacey joined her. "I'm going to ask you one more time, baby, and I want you to tell me the truth. Has Phil ever touched you or done anything to make you think . . . you know?"

Stacey thought about what her mother was asking. She wished she could lie and say Phillip had molested or tried to molest her, but she knew, ultimately, that that lie would involve too many people. Her mother would probably want to take Phil to court, or worse, she might want to get them all into counseling. Maybe her mother would tell her brothers, inciting Stacey's uncles to come over and beat, maybe kill, Phillip. That would be fine, but she wouldn't want any of her beloved uncles to do time because of her.

"No, it's not that, nothing like that; I just hate having him here. It was good before him, we had fun before your husband ruined everything. And every time that fool gets a few beers in him and somebody makes him mad . . ."

"You know that's just an act. He couldn't hurt a fly," Frances interrupted.

Stacey remembered the day, about nine months earlier, when her mother called her into their bedroom. She had "the gun" in her hand. It was a .22 that Phillip waved around whenever he got really angry. "I want to show you something," Frances had said. Her mother pulled the gun's trigger while pointing it at the television screen. Nothing happened, it didn't even click. She tried the trigger again and again, but the results didn't change.

"See, honey, this gun doesn't work. There's a part missing. I just don't want you to be afraid when Phil goes off and starts acting crazy. He said he used to carry this when he was younger. I guess it's hard being a little guy. This gun made him feel like a big man. He said he used to call it his equalizer."

Stacey grunted and left the room. She wasn't interested in any stories about Phillip's tragic life—not that day, not ever. Why her mother had married the little fool was beyond her.

"I'll only be gone three days. I'll be back just as soon as Grandma is stable and your Aunt Regina gets there. Try to get along with him. He means you no harm, you know that. He's from the old school, he doesn't know how to talk to today's kids."

Stacey nodded, and her mother smiled. *I was agreeing that he doesn't know how to talk to people,* Stacey said to herself, *that's all.*

· · · ·

"Well, it's just the two of us," Phillip announced when he returned from the train station.

"What a firm grasp of the obvious!"

Phillip looked at her and frowned, his shiny bald head falling into natural groove lines that extended down his forehead and from ear to ear across his face. Half the time he had no idea what the girl was saying. "What do you mean?"

"Nothing."

"Do you want me to go rent videos or something?"

He tried to grin, and wondered if she noticed that his big yellow teeth seemed too big for his mouth.

"No," she answered. She didn't look at him.

"We can go out for dinner?"

"No thanks."

"Are you going to cook?" he asked, still not sure if they were having a conversation. With her it was hard to know.

"Will you barbeque?" she asked him.

Phillip winced. That was the last thing he expected to hear her ask. He wondered would he ever come to understand this child. *I try, I really do,* he thought. "You know I love the Q," he said trying to impress her with his hip lingo.

"Yes, I do know that," she replied, still not meeting his gaze.

"Do you need to go to the store to get that stuff you eat?" He asked, his hand already in his pocket.

"No, I have what I need, and there's some pork ribs in the freezer for you. I'll go thaw and marinate them. When it's ready, I'll bring it out to the front yard."

Her mentioning of the front yard brought a scowl to his face. He liked their new condo; plenty of room inside, new appliances—a new start for the three of them. But whoever heard of a house with the green space in the front? In the area that should have been their little backyard was a walkway and a carport. Behind the carport was one of the busiest, noisiest streets in the neighborhood.

It was a beautiful day, and Phillip felt good. For the first time, he felt as if he was getting somewhere with Fran's spoiled daughter. He smiled, remembering when his buddy Clarence had called her a BAP, black American princess.

It took three trips inside and back to get everything set up the way he liked. Barbequing was a ritual, one that he enjoyed. There was ice in his cooler and four beers chilling. The beer on his preparation table was already nice and cold. The tongs, potholder, and water bottle were in place. He was a slow reader, and it took him all day to get through Sunday's paper, but the front page and sports section were on the table, ready. On his last trip, he remembered his cigarettes and lighter. Normally he would have gotten the phone, but, with the girl home, he knew there was little chance it would ring for him. When it did ring, she always got to it first.

Phillip thought about calling Clarence and a few of his other buddies over for a game of dominoes, but he fought the urge. This day was for getting to know the kid.

He sat down and read the paper while he waited for her to come out with the meat and her food.


About ninety minutes and four beers later, Stacey joined him on the front deck. She sat in the chair next to his, her mother's chair. The only items in her hands were an emery board and a bottle of midnight mauve nail polish.

"Where's the meat?"

"What meat?" she asked.

He turned his head in a manner that reminded her of a confused dog. "The meat I'm suppose to be out here barbequing, girl."

"I changed my mind. And don't call me girl!"

"What?"

"What what?"

"Are you trying to say you didn't thaw the meat?"

"I ain't trying to tell you nothing, but what you said is true. I-did-not-thaw-the-meat," she said it slow and carefully like he was a limited child. "And before you ask, I didn't marinate it either—that's what I changed my mind means!"

Phillip was a simple man. Her words left him speechless. He finished his beer as he paced inside the house. He reviewed everything that had happened since he returned from the train station. There was nothing in his experience that could explain what had set her off. He knew he wasn't the brightest bulb on the Christmas tree, but he knew damn well he hadn't done or said anything wrong this time. "Somebody should have beat her little ass a long time ago," he said to himself as he paced. He looked at the kitchen wall clock. Frances wouldn't be arriving at her grandmother's house for at least another hour. He went to the cabinet where he kept his good stuff. *She asked me not to drink while she was gone, but she probably asked her daughter to act like she had some sense too.*

He poured about two fingers in a glass. Just a touch. The thought briefly crossed his mind that his wife might have wanted him to avoid drinking beer in her absence too, but he shook it off. She knew beer was little more than a soft drink as far as he was concerned.

He stood at the dining room window and looked out at Stacey. She was poking around with his fire. She didn't seem to be putting it out or stoking it. The damn girl was just playing around with his coals. The nerve, he thought. He knew why she didn't respect him. Frances denied it, but he knew. At age fifteen, the girl stood five nine in her bare feet. Two inches taller than him. He figured she had him by at least twenty pounds too.

*But make no mistake about it, baby girl, your mother didn't marry no punk.* He decided he would go out there and tell her about herself. Phillip took a step and caught himself. *No,* he reasoned, *I don't have to play games with kids. I'll just leave. Maybe go see a movie or something.* He turned around and reached for the telephone so he could call the movie line. It was gone. He looked out on the deck. *I'll just be damned, she's got my telephone out there.*

He stopped briefly in his bedroom before returning to the deck. "Look, bitch," he started.

She stood before he could say another word. She towered over him. "Don't call me bitch!"

He stood rooted to the three feet that separated them. He was determined not to put his hands on her. He'd never struck a woman, and he wasn't going to start with the child of the woman he loved and the only one who ever loved him. "That's what you are. A little spoiled bitch. I'm a man, Stacey . . ."

"You're not my man, and you better not touch me!"

"Touch you?"

She called him a stream of names he didn't want to remember, because it would hurt Frances too much to hear him repeat them. She left him no choice, he removed the gun from his waistband.

With his back to the street he looked at her. "This seems to be the only thing you little thugs respect nowadays." He waved the gun as she knew he would.

They both heard the siren. He thought it was coming from the main street, they ran up and down that drag constantly.

From her perspective, she saw them approaching cautiously. Both uniformed officers were waving their free hands at her. She knew they were telling her to move, but they were waving in opposite directions. One seemed to be beckoning for her to come to him, and the other seemed to be telling her to move to the side. She stood still.

She knew she would never forget the shocked look on his face when one of them spoke.

The police said something. Later, they said the one who shot first told Phillip to lower his gun. She had to testify that she heard the words, but she didn't. The only thing she remembered hearing were the gunshots. They sounded so different than gunfire in the movies and on television. They didn't sound as real, but later her ears hurt.

Phillip Barron had been buried a month when Frances appeared at the precinct. The month had taken its toll on the petite woman. That toll was seen in the bags under her eyes and the slow, wary, way she walked. She asked for homicide and was directed to offices on the second floor.

"She killed him," she told the young detective who'd asked her to have a seat. "She killed my husband."

She looked ten years older, but the detective remembered her. "Mrs. Barron. We know about your husband," he said carefully. His mind quickly calculated whom he should call to get some help for the poor woman.

"No, you don't understand! My husband was murdered! She used the police to murder him, and I can't live with it anymore." She exhaled deliberately as if she'd been holding her breath. "There's got to be something sick in her. Something dangerous. I can't sleep with her in my house anymore."

The detective sat back in his chair and picked up his pen. "Okay, I'll take your statement."

"The first thing you should know is my daughter is a strict vegetarian. Whenever we cooked out, she would grill either soy burgers, mushrooms, or tofu. None of that stuff was in the house. I know . . . knew my husband. The idea to cook out had to be hers, and he would have asked her if she had the food she wanted him to grill. She knew it would never get to that point. My daughter didn't go to the store, and neither did . . . Phillip. I love my daughter, detective, but I can't live with her anymore. She killed him."

The detective asked a few questions, and Frances answered them honestly, without passion.

"If what you say is true, Mrs. Barron, there's still one factor your daughter couldn't have predicted. She couldn't have known the responding officers would shoot her stepfather."

Frances laughed without mirth. "That was as predictable as Phillip getting his .22. He was a black man waving a gun, detective. You're old enough to know the outcome of that."

The detective thought about what she was saying. He had to admit, he didn't often hear of a black or brown man living to tell his story if the police arrived to find him armed. They would have to bring the juvenile in for questioning. "Why are you coming to us now?" he finally asked.

Frances opened her purse and took out a gun. She carefully set it on his desk. At a glance he could see it was a .357.

"I didn't know he had this. I found it last night. It works. If he had wanted to hurt her or anybody else, he could have. He was just a little guy trying to make her listen, and she killed him."

# DOUBLE DEALING

*Chris Benson*

Funny thing about a murder scene. Hang around long enough, you're a suspect. Only the cops, the paramedics, the medical examiners, the reporters, only they are above suspicion. Most of the time, anyway. Life was like that in Little Beirut. That's what they called the place, Woodridge, a depressed, angry, four-square-mile, armed-camp-of-a-community. Little Beirut. A South Side neighborhood at war with itself. A place where the cops couldn't even finish cleaning up one killing before you'd hear shots coming from the next block over. Like dueling murder scenes. Funny thing about a murder scene. People in Little Beirut were nowhere to be seen when a crime was committed, but they came *out* of nowhere to watch the aftermath. Like vultures to raw meat, we were all drawn to a bloodbath. Death sustained us. And we were all guilty. Everybody. One way or another. Everybody who might have seen it coming and did nothing to stop it.

So we all stood around on sagging greystone stoops and fractured sidewalks, looking suspicious just standing there like that, watching Ant, face-down in the street, at the edge of the curb he used to own. It was two in the morning in the thirty-five hundred block of South Woodridge. Two in the morning, and I had never seen it so bright there, so lit up. Two in the morning, and the place was jumping like two in the afternoon. Nobody seemed like they had anywhere else to go, nothing else to do. No-body seemed like they wanted to leave. Maybe it was because they knew what you can't help knowing when you live in "The Root" long enough to know anything. What you know is this: standing around might have made you look suspicious, but leaving was even worse. Leaving could make you a target. Move, and you'd attract attention to yourself. Like you were running from something. Run, and they'd chase you down. And once the chase started, it was all over. Inevitable. No escape. Not from the cops. Not from the thugs. Made no difference who was chasing you, really. They were all driven by the same instincts. The cops, the thugs. So if you left too soon, five-O would think you had seen something, and the bangers, well, they would think the same thing, and they'd all want to come after you because of it. For different reasons. For the same reason. Seemed like everybody on the block knew that. Which is at least one rea-son why we all just hung there. Like a neighborhood lineup. In suspense while the story developed right there before our eyes, checking all around to figure out who might get cuffed. Funny thing about a murder scene. Everybody feels like the killer's right there in the crowd. Watching. Wait-ing. Wondering. So everybody there is suspicious. And everybody there is a suspect.

Maybe it was because I had just jumped out of bed, fifteen, twenty minutes earlier. Maybe it was because I was scoping everything—down to the smallest detail—the way I always did. But the whole street seemed to be moving in slow mo'. Blue and red lights flashing like strobes. All the while the police and the paramedics and the medical examiner and the re-porters, they were all doing their thing. Checking the body, shooting pic-tures, interviewing potential witnesses, marking the asphalt. And the rest of us, well, we just watched as they did all this and as Ant's blood slowly ran down the gutter, making it hard to get the chalk mark just right. It was all unfolding right there in front of my stoop. All around, there was a low and constant murmur rising from the crowd. Both sides of the street. Be-fore the night was over, everybody would have a theory. They always did. My only hope at that moment was that I had covered my tracks.

"Punk-ass muthafucka."

I had been so caught up in studying Ant's body, that I never saw him coming. But there he was, Russell Carver, standing at the foot of my stoop, hard against the wrought iron gate, heavy lean on his crutches. He had taken a bullet one night in a messed-up holdup. Took it in the back. Doctors over at County left the bullet in there. Too close, they said. Too dangerous. So, for whatever life he had left, Carver would live it on crutches.

"What was that?" I asked.

He looked up at me, standing three steps above him. " 'Punk-ass muthafucka.' " He was damn near breaking his neck, punctuating each word with a whiplash-of-a-nod. "That's what they said 'fore they popped his ass."

There was a power surge. Adrenaline flow. Couldn't tell whether it was anticipation, or fear. But the blood rush seemed to force my words. "So, you saw it?"

Carver caught himself. He had a bad habit of running his mouth too much. Which is why he was on crutches. Ant had told me that much. Carver turned toward the "Gator" across the street, gazing at the tinted windows like he was looking for somebody looking at him from behind a two-way mirror.

"Naw, man, I didn't see it." Carver spoke the words so distinctly, much more clearly than he ever said anything I was around to hear. It was like he wanted everybody on the block to be able to read his lips. Or at least the man on the other side of the tinted Gator glass. Carver turned back to me. "I didn't see shit."

I checked him for a beat, pulled out the Marlboros, lit one. Didn't see it, but he heard it. Life was like that in The Root. Life, *and* death. I turned, gazed at Ant's body just on the other side of the curb, imagined him standing there, the way he was, so full of life, just one week earlier.


"That's funny, yo."

I looked over at the curb ahead as I walked down Woodridge, headed toward my raggedy-ass greystone apartment building. I saw the skinny sixteen-year-old, who always seemed to be there, at the curb, in front of my stoop. So, there he was again, turning away from another window of yet another car pulling off after closing one more deal. He put the wad of bills in his loose pocket and smiled in a way I hadn't seen since I moved into the neighborhood at the beginning of the month. It was still hot, mid-September hot, late afternoon, late summer hot, and all I wanted was to get inside, get out of the uniform. All I wanted was to avoid a long conversation with a curbside drug dealer.

I stopped at the wrought iron gate to my place. "*What's* funny?"

"Bus driver," he said, "walking home from work. The shit's just funny, that's all. Seems like if anybody should get curbside service . . . knowmsayn? Maybe even keep it overnight."

I nodded. "And, so, where would I park a bus around here, if they let me drive the motherfucker home?"

"Well, I don't know," he responded, without a pause, unfazed. "Maybe we could work something out right here at my spot, yo." He glanced down at the ground he had claimed. "Maybe a little barter. You know, you let me set up my office, transact my business inside your bus, I let you park rent-free. Everything's negotiable."

Life was like that in The Root. No straight lines. Just angles. "Sounds like you got it all figured out," I said, intrigued.

"Got *that* right." He pointed to his head, gave me a wink. "Mind like a computer."

I was struck by how glib he was, how knowledgeable for a boy who seemed to be stuck in a groove. Limited to an entire life right there in Little Beirut, right there on his spot, his whole world on drive-by mode, pulling up to his curb, twenty a pop. What a waste.

"Noticed you just moved in, yo." He smiled again, that disarming smile that might make you forget for a deceptive moment that he was just another common thug standing there in his baggy jeans, muscle shirt, do-rag, checking the intersection a half-block away, like he had just seen something he was *supposed* to see coming a half-block away. "I'm Ant," he said, turning back to me, with a special kind of confidence that suggested he knew just who he was, what he was doing, where he was going at every moment of his short life. He was about five nine, just a growth spurt away from the manhood he might never see. A life on the brink. Medium brown skin, kissed by the summer sun. Innocence and treachery balanced on a razor's edge.

I nodded. "D."

I tried to push open the wrought iron gate, fumbled with the grocery bags, and he stepped to me, trying to help. I didn't really *want* help. He eyeballed me. I felt something drop into one of the shopping bags, but I didn't look down. I locked onto his gaze, as he pushed open the gate and turned to walk across the street. As it turned out, I made it into my vestibule just in time, just before the unmarked car screeched to the curb, stopping Ant in his tracks. I kept moving up the stairs and into my apartment, where I could watch the scene from the safety of my living room window. Ant, up against the car, searched by a linebacker-of-a-detective. Big, Black, bold. Bad enough to work this block all by himself. But Ant was unaffected by it all. I moved away from the window, knowing without knowing just why Ant felt no pain. I checked the shopping bag. Ant had dropped his nine millimeter and a wad of cash inside. I just stood there looking down into the bag for a thrill of a moment.


Don't know why I felt the need to go out for cigarettes that night. Something told me I'd live to regret it, or regret I'd lived it.

"What up, D?" It was Ant, rushing me up the walk to my stoop. "Got my shit?" I knew what he meant was, "You *better* have my shit, and hurry your ass giving it up."

When we got to my apartment, I paused. What would he do once he got his gat back? Was he going to let me walk? I took the chance, let him in.

I pulled the shopping bag out from behind the couch, handed him the gun, the cash. "How did you know what was coming?"

He flashed that smile of his. "You talking about Moore?" he said, referring to the cop stop. "Detective Maurice? Shit. When it comes to danger, yo, I got eyes in the back of my head."

He didn't count the money. Just sort of weighed it in his hand. Must have been all right, because he peeled off a couple of bills, dropped them on my table, stuffed the rest in the pocket of his baggy shorts. Just then, as he was turning to leave, something caught his attention. On the table. It was a big manila envelope on a stack of other mail.

Ant took a long hard look at the top envelope, then eyed me, checked me from head to toe. Nothing in my eyes. I knew they wouldn't give me up. No reaction, but my mind raced while he did the full-body scan. In that split-second eternity he did a flash inventory of my persona; the darkness about me—my eyes, my skin, my short dreads with just a hint of early gray. He seemed to pay special attention to the uniform. What was he thinking about me? He was standing close now, so close he had to look up at me. I was standing over him at six feet. But that didn't affect him since he had that equalizer back under his belt again. And just like that, while I tried to figure it all out, he tapped the envelope.

"A'ight, D." He held a beat. "Be cool, yo."

I watched from the windows as Ant hit the street. At that moment, the black Navigator drove up, parked on the other side. The dark tinted glass slowly lowered on pace with Ant's step. There in the driver's seat was Terrell Reynolds, snug inside his high-powered cocoon. Terrell Reynolds. "T-Rex." Predator-in-Chief. Unofficial mayor of Little Beirut. Ant quickly took the huge wad of bills from his pocket, handed it to T-Rex, said something, I don't know what, but something that made T-Rex look up at my window. Maybe I was just paranoid. Maybe I had good reason to be. Ant had made me. I knew it. But, had he given me a pass? Or had he given me up to T-Rex? He had read the outside of that envelope he picked up, the one that was addressed to me at the job. And, because he had read it, he knew that my job was not with the Transit Authority.

"That's exactly why I didn't like this assignment for you in the first place." Brian Jennings was pacing his office as he spoke. He was like that. Agitated. Always. Stressing. Never really mattered what he was dealing with at the time. Made me wonder how he could deal with such high-pressure issues for a living. Life on deadline. Life cut short in the process. "What if you're wrong about his reaction? What if the kid is plotting something on you right now? Blowing this, this . . . *undercover* thing you're trying to pull off." As he spoke, he turned deeper and deeper shades of red, which was about as much color as I had ever seen on his pale face. "I don't know what you're trying to prove, Dash."

That's what they called me. David Steven Hunter was my name, but the people who knew me well enough knew better than to call me any of that. Dash was all the name I needed for a fast-track life, a life in perpetual motion.

Guess he was right. I was taking a huge risk. But that's what I did. For me, the reward was in the risk, hidden there, waiting to be cracked open. I just sat there for a reflective moment, turned away from Jennings, gazed through the wall of windows of his office, looking out at the cubicles and the late afternoon insanity of our world, the world we had chosen—a world on deadline. I pulled out the Marlboros, lit one.

Jennings looked at me like I was crazy. Maybe I was. Just another crazy Black man raising his blood pressure. "You know you can't smoke in here," he said.

I took a long draw, slowly blew out the smoke. "The way you've been talking, I feel like I'm a condemned man. So, what, you going to deny me a last smoke?"

I took another hit off the cigarette, watched as the medical examiner bent over Ant's body. Looked like the bullet had torn through the back of his head, exploding on impact. Couldn't tell exactly from where I stood, but it looked like the shot was fired point blank, like somebody just ran up behind him, held the gun straight up, knowing one shot would do it. I wondered if Ant had suffered. If he knew what hit him. If he even knew it was coming. His words came back to me: "When it comes to danger, yo, I got eyes in the back of my head." Guess this time he blinked. Right away, these thoughts were pushed aside by another one. I looked down at Carver, still leaning up against my gate. Did he or anybody else know that Ant was on his way to my place when he got capped? What would happen if they started piecing it all together, found a reason to search my place, found all the rocks I was holding?

I hesitated at the door, checked him through the peephole. He was alone. I thought about what he had seen the day before. The envelope. Considered what he might have figured out, what he might have come back to my place to carry out. Thought about that nine millimeter tucked down in his waistband. Thought about Jennings and his warning earlier that day. Finally, I realized that in The Root, death doesn't knock first. So, deep sigh, twist of the locks, I opened up, let Ant in.

"Damn, Dog." He walked in like he owned the place, carrying some rolled up papers. "Took you long enough. You scared of something?" He held the deadpan for a heartbeat. Then there was that fresh-faced smile again. But I wasn't about to let him disarm me. Not yet.

"Got anything to drink . . . David Steven Hunter?"

I checked him, knowing now that he must have known more than just my full name. "Okay, cool, you got a little information on me." I pulled a Coke out of the refrigerator. "So, what does it tell you?"

He grabbed the Coke, laughed, plopped down on the living room couch. "Oh, I got more than just a *little* information on you." He popped the can, and it sounded more like a gunshot in his hand. "But we're getting a little ahead of ourselves, yo. You're not asking the right questions. I mean, like, *damn,* I thought you were a re-fucking-porter, man. Don't all the best stories start with the right questions?"

"Okay," I said, backing the shit up, wondering where all this was coming from, where it was going. "Sounds like there's something you want, like there's something you're looking for."

He nodded, pursed his lips. "That's better. Now you're getting there."

"Well, thanks for the reporting lesson . . . *yo.*"

He turned real serious. "That's one of the things I want to talk to you about."

"Reporting?"

"Ripping the covers off the shit."

I sat in the chair facing him. "Bad day in The Root, Ant?"

He smiled again. "Fact is, this was a pretty good day."

"No shit?"

He nodded. "Yeah, good day. Sold a few rocks. Went down to Springer's."

"The funeral parlor?"

"Right. Picked out my box."

"Your casket."

"Mahogany, yo." He waved his hand across the air, conjuring up the image. His fantasy funeral. "Satin lining, whole nine, Dog."

"And *that* made it a good day?"

He checked me, ditched the little boy demeanor. "Hey, gots to be ready for wha'ever."

That was it. Self-determination in Little Beirut. You lived without options, but at least you could choose the way you went out.

"Then," he went on, "day got even better. When I got to school, I went straight to the library. Computer room."

I don't know why I had figured him for a dropout. Maybe it was those crazy hours he spent on the block. Should have known, though. He clearly was smart enough to have had some kind of agenda. And I was about to find out just what it was.

Ant began to unroll the papers he was carrying, slowly, carefully, like they were part of some precious, ancient scroll. It was a printout from the *Trib*'s website. My story. Part of the series I had done on local hookers. Working on the edge of The Root. I had hung with them. The hookers. Paid them for the time, for the interviews. Won a regional award for it, too.

I was impressed by Ant's resourcefulness. "How did you—"

"Told you," he pointed to his head, the way he had done before, "mind like a computer. Guess I just forgot to tell you that I know how to work with them, too. Looked your shit up." He tapped the paper on the coffee table between us. "I read the whole series." He narrowed his eyes. "That shit was cold-blooded. Malicious. Intentionally bad, yo. I mean, bad on purpose. When I read that story I . . . you know what . . ." He leaned forward, arms on his knees. "I saw myself."

"Reporter or pimp?"

He shook his head, chuckled. "So, you telling me there's a difference?" He slid to the edge of the couch. "Look, here's the thing. I don't want to be world famous in Little Beirut, yo. What you do is bigger than one tired-ass neighborhood. What you do makes a difference. *I* want to make a difference. I want to be known for the way I lived, not the way I died. I mean, hell, twenty years from now, somebody's going to be pulling up your shit on the Net. And where will I be? In that box I just picked out, probably."

He sat back, arms spread across the back of the couch. "Then again, maybe not. Doesn't have to be that way. I don't really want to go out like that. Don't want to keep doing this shit, Dog. Ain't my flow, understand what I'm saying?"

I stroked my moustache, all the way down the goatee, doing that slightly nervous, mostly thoughtful thing I did sometimes. "So . . . this is all leading to . . . what exactly?"

There was that smile again, slowly moving across his entire face. It was like he was seeing everything happen just the way he had envisioned it before he knocked on my door. Before he walked up my stoop. Hell, before he even left his high school computer room. "What story are you working on, now? I mean, all that Transit Authority shit." He checked my uniform again. "What is it, 'hos on the bus?' "

I laughed. "Yeah, right. Special investigation for H-B-ho." Then I told him the truth. Or, as much as I *could* tell him. Another installment in my series of lifestyle profiles. This one was on Little Beirut. The uniform was just a cover, the only thing my brother, Isaiah, had left me. An emblem of what had driven us apart. The thing he had to settle for, after I drained the family till to chase my dream in J-school. I thought about all that, and felt the uniform tighten all around me, like a boa constrictor. Maybe that's why I was letting this kid come into my life. Maybe he was like *my* kid brother who took a wrong turn, never made it back. Then again, maybe he represented something else. Ant had said he saw himself in my work. Maybe I was seeing my work in him. *Myself* in him, really. The way things might have been for me, if I hadn't gotten the hell out of my own Little Beirut. Maybe he was right. Maybe I really *could* make a difference. Maybe, sitting there in my dingy little living room on South Woodridge, right in the bosom of The Root, maybe we were both at the crossroads. Trying to figure which way to go.

"Well," Ant said, as he began to flash his trademark smile, "if you're looking for a hot story here in Little Beirut, yo, I got the bomb for you."


"And how do you plan to verify what he's telling you? I mean, how do you know he's not setting us *all* up? The paper, or even worse, you." Jennings was like that. Always played by the rules. And the basic rule of reporting called for double-sourcing. If your mother tells you she loves you, check it out.

"Cross-checking police files, court records for a lot of it," I said. "Also picked up a few new sources. Amazing how many inmates want to get their stories in print. Anonymously."

He eyeballed me. "That's what worries me. Or have you forgotten—"

"That's not going to happen again. I won't let it," I insisted, as I remembered what I had hoped I could forget. All that I had revealed in that hooker series. All that I had placed in jeopardy because of it. All that my lust for the story, for the truth, had cost a young unsuspecting life. And what had we gained? People dug the stories, I took home another trophy, and the Sisters were still walking the streets. All but one.

"And you're sure that's the only thing he wants out of all this?"

"That's it," I considered Ant and the deal he had struck. Back there at the crossroads. A kid smart enough to read the signs. Dead end, or freedom's trail. And I was his ticket.


"Poor baby."

I turned, looked behind to see Gladys Sampson standing at the top of our stoop. I wondered what had taken her so long to come out since I had been there for about twenty-five minutes already—twenty-five minutes that seemed like a lifetime.

"I watched that little boy grow up." She set her heavy frame down on the concrete bench by the front door. "Always figured if anybody could get out this hellhole, it would be Antwon. Poor baby."

The pain was heavy in that husky voice, but nowhere else, it seemed. Like she was surprised and not surprised all at the same time. Like all the hope she had ever felt for Ant was only some distant longing now. Like she had given up hope of anything, really, years ago. Like now she was only witnessing the inevitable outcome of a life where all your expectations are one day ripped from your soul the way your most precious and irreplaceable possessions might be snatched from your purse in the chill of some lonely late-night corner.

I looked down at Carver, who turned back toward the street. We knew she really wasn't talking to us anyway. I dropped the cigarette butt on the stoop. Stepped on it only to feel the back of my head getting singed. I turned to see Mrs. Sampson glaring at me. I kicked the butt down off the steps out onto the sidewalk. She looked back at the murder scene. I took out the pack of Salems. Lit one.

"Why do you always do that?"

I looked across my dining table at Ant, put out the match, blew out the smoke.

"Do what?"

"Smoke like that." He looked at the two packs on the table. "Marlboro, then a Salem. Back to back. Wha'sup with that?"

I laughed, shrugged. "Don't know, really. Maybe it's just the yin and yang of my fucked-up world," I said, knowing by now that he knew what that meant. "It's like the extremes of my life. Hot and cold. Sweet and sour. Bad and . . . worse."

He just shook his head. "Bad habits like that keep people like me in business."

"Yeah, well, not for long." I took another puff.

He checked me, nodded. "Yeah, right. Not for long. So, everything's set, right? Internship, on-line edition? That's the *dealio*, right?"

"Bet," I said. "Solid." Just a shot. That's all he wanted. Chance to prove himself. That, and some heavy-duty mentoring from me. I wondered what I could possibly teach a kid who had seen so much life already. Wondered what I would *owe* a kid who was showing *me* so much of the life he had seen.

I didn't know why I kept feeding his fantasy about becoming a reporter. Was I just using him to get my story? I didn't think so. Seemed like, after several sessions, we were bonding. Not father and son. I was only thirty, not old enough to be his father. Except, well, maybe in Little Beirut. But it wasn't like that, really. No, I was more like a big brother, he was more like the kid brother I had lost, and it scared me. We were developing the kind of connection you should never have with a source.

I got up, checked the window. Saw the Gator, other side of the street. Then I saw that unmarked police car, with the detective, Moore, the one who had been fucking with Ant the other night. He was just cruising. It was like Moore was challenging T-Rex by trespassing on his ground, and like T-Rex was challenging Moore by standing his ground.

Ant stood to leave. "You know the drill, yo."

With that, he pulled a rock from his pocket and I threw down a twenty. We had decided this was the best way to make it look good, all these trips to my crib. He snatched up the money, dropped the drugs into the cigar box. I gazed down at the growing rock pile. Felt the rush of the moment. Thought about what Ant had said on another visit. "Not my flow."

Not mine either, Ant. Adrenaline, that was my drug of choice. That's why living in The Root was my high. And my low.

The story was progressing beautifully. But I still found myself sitting in Jennings's office, trying to convince my editor that I could make it work, that it was worth giving me more time. In just a few days, Ant had given me the profile of the whole neighborhood. The people, the culture, the deals. And how he had gotten his start, his initiation in the Imperial Viceroys. It was only a year ago, when T-Rex and his chief lieutenants wanted to go to a rap concert. They let young Ant hold their stuff. He sold it all while they were at the concert. Turned in all the money. Earned their trust.

Things started going south in the last few months, though. Somebody was muscling in on T-Rex. Viceroys were getting set up, arrested. Some were getting killed. T-Rex was fighting back. Only way he knew how. Low-down, dirty. He had fixed up a suspected informant with a "hot batch," a rich mixture that made the guy OD. No one even knew whether the guy had talked in the first place. But everyone knew he wasn't talking anymore. And that's the only thing T-Rex wanted everybody to know. Made me worried about Ant. He kept saying he could handle it, that everything was still cool with T-Rex. I wasn't sure. It was on in Little Beirut. Tension was high. And I was caught all up in it. The tension *and* the high. The thrill of what

Ant and I were able to find out over those few days—between his street connections, his Internet skills, and my work with inmate sources and official documents. It was all part of some drug chain that led all the way up from Miami. It's just that nobody knew the phantom who was running things on our end. T-Rex was getting edgy. Caught between cops like Moore, and all the rest of the vicious thugs. Time was running out. I was depending on a kid who was street smart. But still just a kid.

"And that is the point, isn't it?" Jennings cut me a piercing look.

I really didn't have a good answer. Somehow, in the upside-down world of The Root, it had all made sense.

Finally, after a painful pause, Jennings spoke again. "Have you called your wife recently?"

I thought about Dakota. "You a family counselor now?"

"No, I'm a supervisor who sees a bunch of phone messages piling up, and I wonder about the *pressure* piling up and how you're ever going to get your job done."


"Nice." Ant checked out the signed, numbered print on my wall. Bearden.

I thought about Dakota, how she had opened up a whole new world to me, then shut me out of hers. Wondered how things were going with her down at the gallery. Couldn't bring myself to call. Thought about that, how I hadn't talked to her since I moved out. Little Beirut wasn't just my cover now. It was my home. It was my purgatory.

"So, you're not gonna use this stuff about Carver." Ant looked at the file folders on the table where I had sorted the background material from the things we would definitely include.

"You mean when he—"

"When he was loud-talking that Korean in the store—"

"After taking the cash, when he should have been getting the fuck out of there."

"Right. Gave the clown time to go for his gat, pop his ass," Ant said. "Says a lot about this place, yo. The hard lessons we all have to learn. How fast life can move away from you. How you have to think fast to keep up."

I considered it all, the take on life from this young urban philosopher.

"Yeah, well, we'll see. But, some of the best color never makes it into a story."

He weighed it for a minute. "Like with the hos?"

"You mean, the hooker series?"

He shrugged. "You know what I mean. Anything you didn't stick in that one?" He cut a wicked smile.

"Some stuff, yeah." I thought about my talk with Jennings and how there are always consequences with each story. People whose lives are changed and sometimes not for the better.

"Some stuff with this Peaches, I bet. I checked her picture, yo. She's banging, Dog. So, look, you can tell me, since we're partners and shit. She put it on you?"

I just let that hang there for a suspenseful moment. Thought about how Dakota had asked the same thing. In so many words. "First thing you have to learn if you're going to keep good sources," I said, "is that you've got to keep some shit tight. Confidential."

"Cool." He beamed. "So, I won't tell."

I thought about it and started talking. It was more like I *had* to than wanted to. It was like my confessional. I told him what Peaches had told me. There was somebody out there running their whole game. Somebody over the pimps, calling the shots, setting the rates, turning in the competition to the cops. He was even claiming freebies with some of the girls. Power trip. She had heard he was "a real monster motherfucker."

I looked Ant dead in the eye. "That's what they called him. 'MoMo.' That part never made it into the series because I couldn't get confirmation. No second source. Not long after the series ran, they found Peaches in a South Side alley. She was banged up pretty bad. I paid the hospital bill, got her out of town, set her up. But she'll never look like that picture you saw in the paper. Never again." I looked down at the table. "She said it was a bad trick. Everybody knew better. I sure did. It was MoMo, paying her back for talking to me." I looked back up at him again. "You were right on the money, Ant. What I do makes a difference. All the difference in the world."

· · ·

"No telling where his no-account mother is." Gladys Sampson was still hanging in there with us. "You'd think a boy like that, out at two in the morning like that, I mean somebody should care about what's happened. Shame. Real shame."

"Yep, real shame, all right," Carver chimed in. "Boy shouldn't been running his mouth so damn much."

I didn't want to ask, but I couldn't stop myself. "Running his mouth about what?"

He turned, slowly, to face me. "You ain't been in The Root long, Dog, but you been here long enough."

I took another hit. "For what?"

"To know the one thing you need to know."

"And that is . . . ?"

He turned away from me, gazed down at Ant again. "That there's some things you better off *not* knowing."

"Everybody takes chances," Ant said. "I take a chance every time I step out in the street, doing what I do and all. Peaches knew what she was getting into, what she was putting on the line when she started talking to you. She knew it just like she knew what she was getting into first time she stepped off the curb, into some trick's ride." Then he smiled in a way that showed he still held on to some measure of hope, despite everything he had seen, despite everything he had revealed to me. "We're reporters, yo. No risk, no reward. Hell, I'm taking a chance talking to *your* ass."

I nodded. "You mean T-Rex?"

He ditched the happy face. "I mean, how do I know I can trust you, D? This phantom drug king motherfucker. I mean, he could be anybody." He narrowed his eyes to laser focus, as if he was trying to pierce my consciousness. "Could be you, for all I know."

My eyes tried to conceal what my mind was flashing. Was this a joke? Was it an elaborate scheme? I thought about Jennings again. Had he been right? Had the kid flipped the script on me? Was Ant setting me up? For sure this kid was double dealing. What I couldn't be sure about all of a sudden was exactly who the trick was in this game of deception. T-Rex, or me? Shit! The more I thought about it, the more I could see all the moves in some game this kid could have put me in. What the fuck had I gotten myself into? Just as all the alarms were sounding in my consciousness, Ant took it down a notch. He gave up that smile again. Only thing was, now I found little comfort in it, now I was back on guard.

"Yo, man, I gotta bounce. Before T starts wondering what's taking me so long up here." He stood up, reached into his pocket, and I reached into mine.

"So, let's see now," he said, almost as an afterthought, dropping another rock into the cigar box, snatching up another twenty. "How much do reporters make, anyway?"

I snorted a laugh. "Probably not as much as you're making off me right here."

"Damn." He held a beat. "Well, do *they* buy drugs, too?"

We both laughed. But he laughed the most. Left me wondering if the joke really was on me.


One of the detectives wearing rubber gloves bent over Ant's body, pulled the nine millimeter from his waistband. But the real chill for me came next. It was Ant's cell phone.

"Bet *that* don't make it to the evidence room," Carver said, spitting the words more than speaking them. "Cops . . ." He shook his head. "Nothing but gangbangers with a badge, yo."

That wasn't the part I was concerned about. I knew what Carver couldn't possibly have known. Just a push of the "redial" button and they would know the last call Ant had made.


Seemed like a dream at first. Then I thought Ant had somehow let himself into my apartment. It was all a blur as I sat up listening to his voice. Then it hit me.

"Come on, D, pick up," he said.

It was the answering machine. Before I could pick up the phone, he started saying what he had called to say.

"I'm coming past the crib, yo. Wake your tired ass up. You are not going to believe this shit. The phantom drug dealer, man, it's MoMo. Now we gotta figure out who the fuck *that* is."

I checked the clock. It was one forty-five. I tried to call him back on the cell, but there was no answer. So, I just rolled over listening for the door. I closed my eyes, thought about Ant and what he was putting on the line. I thought about how I had doubted him, suspected him, feared him. For a minute. And how now I had come to care about what happened to him. And how I didn't want to. Everybody I ever cared about got hurt. Dakota, my brother Isaiah, Peaches. Besides, this was an assignment. I had work to do.

I must have drifted off again. Thought I was dreaming when I heard the pop of a gunshot. Same sound you would hear in The Root a half-dozen times a night. But this time, the reality started setting in, slowly, and I opened my eyes again, and I thought about it, trying to clear my head of dreams and nightmares. This time it seemed different from all the other times. This time, the gunshot was a lot closer to home. My home. Not on the next block or some far away block in the neighborhood. Then I heard the sirens, heard them getting louder and louder, screaming down my street. That's when I jumped out of bed, looked out the bedroom window onto Woodridge Street, and saw the first of the squad cars to pull up to the curb outside my building, next to the body. Ant's body.

As I watched the detective examine the phone, push the redial button, there was the sound of a gunshot. Thought I was dreaming again, until I realized there were screams from the crowd. It spooked me. I had been watching that phone so intently that it seemed the cop had pushed some weird-ass sound effects button that triggered everything, like a recording, of what I had heard in my sleep. As it turns out, the sound came from the next block over and about a half-dozen cops started running toward my building, heading for the gangway to take a shortcut to the crime scene. The screams of more sirens started up in the distance and made their way to our neighborhood.

. . .

It wasn't long before word started drifting from the next block that there had been another murder. This time it was nine-year-old Sloopy Taylor. Already, word was that it was all gang-related. Sloopy had been hooked up with the Imperial Viceroys and had put it to Ant. Then somebody offed him to keep him quiet. That's the way of the world in The Root. Soon some of the cops started making their way back to our street. A couple went straight to the Gator, tapped on the window, made T-Rex get out for questioning. Just then, another cop made an appearance. It was Detective Moore. He walked right by us through my gangway from the other block, started talking to the cop holding Ant's cell phone.

Carver turned toward me. "Shit, I know I'm out now."

"What's up?" I asked, thought about how Moore had been stalking Ant, T-Rex.

"I do not want to be in the same time zone with that monster mutha-fucka."

My body went cold.

"Show a little respect, young man," Mrs. Sampson snapped.

"No, wait a minute. Say that again," I said.

"Don't you dare," Mrs. Sampson said.

I moved down the steps as Carver started to hop away on his crutches. I grabbed at his arm, spoke softly, firmly. "What did you call him?"

He jerked his arm away, almost fell in the process. "Monster mutha-fucka," he said, almost in a whisper, partly out of respect for Mrs. Sampson, but mostly, I knew, out of fear of the cop. Maurice Moore. MoMo.

Carver started hobbling off. But it was too late. Funny thing about a murder scene. Stick around too long, you're a suspect. Try to leave too soon, the chase begins.

"Hold up." MoMo pointed straight at Carver, stopping him in his tracks. He looked back at the phone as the other cop pushed a button again. Then they both looked in my direction. MoMo made his move.

Most of the other cops were distracted, still across the street, still interrogating T-Rex, who looked like he was unfazed.

"What's your rush, niggah?" MoMo was talking to Carver, but he kept looking back and forth between him and me, like he was holding us both, frozen in place.

"I ain't doing nothing," Carver said.

"Yes, you are," MoMo said. "Looks like you trying to leave without asking permission." Then he looked at me. "What's your name?"

I looked away, down the street, trying to avoid the inevitable. Just then, I caught the eye of one of the reporters on the scene. He was from the *Trib,* a former intern of mine, interviewing people a couple of doors down. Worse yet, he started making his way to me.

"I *said,* 'What's your name?'" MoMo was like a pit bull, and I felt like he was clamping his jaws down on my leg, like I couldn't get away.

"D," I said.

He stepped to me. "Don't fuck with me," MoMo said. What's your *whole* name, bitch."

It was obvious what he was looking for. A match to Ant's caller ID. I knew the script. They would use that to get a search warrant for my crib, bust me for the drugs, maybe more. MoMo was going to need a scapegoat. I turned, saw the *Trib* reporter coming. Knew I couldn't get away. Run inside, and this rogue cop would come in after me. Hot pursuit gives you an excuse for a whole lot. Bust into my place. Or worse. Shoot me. Say I made the first move. I had no place else to go. I'd never make it past him and all the other cops on the block.

Just as MoMo started inching up the steps to get in my face, the other cop, the one with Ant's cell phone, walked closer to the stoop. "What's going on, Mo?"

"Think we got something here." MoMo was looking me dead-on, like he was reading me, doing a brain scan. As he stared me down, slowly reaching across his broad chest for the gun in the shoulder holster, all his muscles seemed to flex through the tan colored polo shirt. Everything was tensed. He was poised to pounce.

I was frozen in place. Not as scared as I was anxious. Trying to figure the angles, plot a way out. He had killed Ant because he knew Ant knew too much, killed little Sloopy just to cover it all up. He had to know that Ant wasn't in this by himself. My name was on the caller ID. Now all he needed was the confirmation. That, and an excuse. There was nothing he wouldn't do. I held a dead-on stare at his eyes, knowing that I'd see something just before he made a move. Hoping I would, anyway. Figuring I would figure something out.

Somehow, I caught the *Trib* reporter in the corner of my eye. He had made his way to the foot of my stoop, looked like he wanted to come closer.

"Dash?" He checked the situation, stopped. "It's me, Geoff."

"Be cool," I said.

"That's right," MoMo said. "Mad cool."

I was careful not to even flinch and give MoMo an excuse to turn me into some fucking accident. So, I just stood there, perfectly still, eyes locked onto his eyes.

Apparently, Mrs. Sampson was looking at something else. "What's that on your shirt, son?"

That's when I saw it, too. The confirmation. "It's blood, Mrs. Sampson."

"Shut the fuck up," MoMo said, as he whipped the gun up in position, pointing it dead in my face.

"I'm David Hunter," I said, mostly to the other cop, my only hope, now. I turned back to MoMo, a glimmer of recognition in his eyes, but no feelings. He knew who I was now—from the hooker series—and knew what I knew. I kept talking to the other cop. "That's probably my name you're looking at there. I'm from the *Trib*."

"I can verify that," Geoff said from the foot of the stoop, next to the other cop.

"Did I ask you, muthafucka?" MoMo snapped his head in Geoff's direction, slowly turning back to me.

I kept talking to the other cop and noticed the ones across the street were starting to check us out, move in our direction. "That kid was helping me with my investigation. Of this man," I said with a nod toward MoMo.

"Mo," the other cop said. "What's up with this?"

I kept on. "This detective has been moving in on the Viceroys. Now he's trying to protect his turf. I think if you get this shirt tested, you'll find out that splattered blood matches Antwon there. Maybe Sloopy in the next block."

With that, MoMo extended his arm, bringing the gun just inches in front of my nose. "On your knees, bitch."

The cop with the cell phone moved closer to MoMo. Couldn't tell at the time whether he was going to pull him back or back him up. Apparently, MoMo couldn't tell either. He turned quickly, almost like he was threatening the other cop with his gun. That's when the police walking across the street caught the whole thing. Couldn't believe it. MoMo freaked. He hopped over the railing of my stoop, landed in the gangway ready to make it to the next block. That's when Carver did something I never would have expected. He swung one of his crutches around and let it go in MoMo's direction, snagging him between the legs, tripping him up. Just long enough.

Without even pausing to think about whether any of this made sense, but just long enough to think about how it might make sense to Peaches and Ant, I flipped over the railing and down feet first onto MoMo's back. I heard a crunching sound and a grunt as he flattened out on the pavement. But I didn't stay there for long. Somebody tackled me from behind. Another cop, who caught me in a choke hold. And that was the last thing I remembered before my whole world started a slow fade to black.


I gazed through that window in Jennings's office. Head bandaged, doing the post mortem on my story and everything Ant and I had uncovered. A huge scandal meant a huge story, and I was the last one standing, the only one who would be there to hear the applause. The tributes. The award ceremonies. A journalist's dream. And all I could think about was my recurring nightmare. There was MoMo. Finally in custody, facing a fate worse than death: caged up with so many other animals he had trapped. MoMo. Maurice Moore. Running his own game, his own gang from inside the police force. Prostitution. Drugs. Dirty cop. Double dealing. But, hey, was I any better? After all, hadn't I violated some public trust, getting involved in the story I was covering? Lying to get at the truth?

I thought about Ant and the hope I had created in him and how it all came crashing down around him. His own dreams like shrapnel, cutting deep into his soul. Thought about the plans he had made for his life and the irony of how he had fulfilled a part of that plan after all, and how, in the end, I had helped him carry it out, serving as a pallbearer at his funeral, gripping that box he had picked out.

Funny thing about a murder scene. Stick around long enough, and a big part of you dies, too.

# MURDER ON THE
# SOUTHWEST CHIEF

*Eleanor Taylor Bland and Anthony Bland*

Detective Marti MacAlister wasn't sure what had awakened her. Perhaps it was the cessation of the train's gentle rocking. The last thing she remembered was leaving Colorado. Now there was nothing but desert outside. Rock formations were outlined against the night sky. She was traveling coach with her son, Theo, and her stepson Mike, both eleven. The only lights were along the floor. Nobody moved about. She listened for a few minutes, but heard no distinctive sound other than a soft, nasal snore. After a few minutes of no movement and near silence, she decided that a trip to the rest room was in order.

A tall, African-American conductor stood at the foot of the stairs, blocking her path. "Sorry ma'am. This section of the train is off-limits until the ambulance arrives."

She hesitated long enough to look into the small compartment reserved for the handicapped. The doors were closed. The lights were out. She could see the four seats on one side of the aisle. They were empty. There were only six seats in all. Three elderly couples had boarded in Kansas. One of the women had talked loudly and nonstop while they were upstairs. They had been moved down here earlier in the evening.

"Where are they?" she asked. "Those three couples?"

"We moved them again, ma'am."

"Where are we?"

"About midway between Raton and Albuquerque."

Marti debated showing the man her badge, but decided against it. Whatever the problem, it didn't seem urgent. She went upstairs, retrieved a backpack the boys had filled with pop, snacks, books, and Lord knew what else, and walked back three cars to the lounge. It had been crowded early when the movie was showing, but there were only two people there now.

"I can tell you right now she's dead," the young man said. He looked to be in his early twenties and had his hair pulled back in a ponytail fastened at the nape of his neck. "Otherwise her mouth would still be going."

"The train is quiet now, ain't it?" a woman agreed. They weren't sitting together, and the woman had to be at least ten years older than the young man. Marti recognized them because they had been assigned to the same coach. "They took 'em all downstairs, thank God," the woman said. "Now the whole downstairs is off limits, and they're not there. Musta taken them off the train."

"And took them where? In what?"

"One of them probably offed Big Mouth and the rest of 'em are being held somewhere for questioning."

"I sure hope Big Mouth is the one who's dead," the young man said. "The way she was going on about peanut butter, I thought I was going to puke."

Marti thought that given the age of the three couples, it was more likely that if one of them had died, it happened without outside assistance, and the others were being given some privacy. She rummaged through the backpack until she found a bottle of water, took out her journal, hesitated, then took out the boys' journals, too. She usually respected their privacy, but all they were writing about was a train ride. The trip was half over, and she hadn't even opened her journal yet, and they had agreed to share what they wrote when they reached Los Angeles. She took out a pencil. Except for crossing the Mississippi, she couldn't remember much, other than the three elderly couples. Reading the boys' journals might help her think of something to write.

"The Peanut Butter People," Mike had written. "What a fun time we are having listening to these old people talk about peanut butter. Did you know it got stuck in your dentures and made them come loose and flop around in your mouth? Did you know it has SALT!!!!! That is bad, bad, bad, if you are old, old, old. And it does not have enough dietary fiber, which is good if you are old. More about this when we get back home and Momma Lydia makes us some peanut butter cookies and helps us eat them."

Marti had tuned out most of what the couples had discussed and tried not to focus on the woman's voice, which was high-pitched with a Midwest accent. She opened her journal and made a few notes, outlining what she remembered about the flat Kansas landscape.

"You gonna tell us what's going on?" the young man with the ponytail asked when a female attendant walked through the car.

"Nothing to tell," the woman said. "Someone's sick. Town's a ways from here. Soon as they get 'em into an ambulance, we'll leave."

"'Em, Him." the woman said as soon as the attendant was out of earshot. "I told you it wasn't big mouth." Marti noticed a slight slurring as she spoke.

"She said 'em," Ponytail said, "Like in them, not him. It could of been her. Bet it was."

"Nah. People like her don't die. They just get more annoying. I bet it was the nice little old lady who hardly talked at all."

Marti took out Theo's journal.

"Mrs. Lindstrum doesn't listen to anyone. All she does is talk. Everything she says is more important than anything anyone else is saying, especially Mrs. Borzak. When Mrs. Borzak was trying to explain ways to eat peanut butter because it was good for you, Mrs. Lindstrum just kept interrupting her. Mrs. Borzak bakes peanut butter cookies a lot and gives them to her husband. He says they taste awful, but he eats them anyway. She doesn't like him very much."

It had been dusk when the three couples boarded the train in Dodge City. Mrs. Lindstrum spoke in a voice two octaves above soprano. She led the way to the front of the car and told everyone else where to sit. That done, she directed the conversation, cutting off anyone who dared change the subject. At first Mike and Theo had been amused, but they soon became annoyed. Marti had suggested that they write about it in their journals, but had to bribe them first with a trip to the club car for pizza.

Theo had written, "Old people need to have more to do than eat and talk. They are getting on my nerves. Their jabbering is uncontrollable. They sit around and have stupid conversations. I don't care what kind of cereal they like, or why bran is good for you, or why they eat fake eggs. Now Mrs. Lindstrum is ordering everyone to put on their sweaters because SHE is cold. AND THEY ARE ALL DOING IT!!!!!!!"

Marti tried to remember what Mr. Lindstrum looked like and could not. She couldn't remember hearing any of the men speaking either. She got the impression that the couples had known each other for years and wondered if they had always interacted this way or if things had changed over time. She read Mike's journal.

"Hup, two, three, four.
got one sweater get five more.
Put them on and do it quick,
I am cold and you must pick
a place where you can sit and mind.
I'm in charge and you're behind.
The worst thing when you get old,
is doing just what you are told."

"We're just sitting here," Ponytail complained.

"Yeah, and the club car isn't even open," the woman said. "The least they could do is open the club car. Too bad the old biddy isn't here to boss the attendant around."

"I bet we are miles and miles from a city or even a town. There is nothing out there but sand, snakes, and rocks. Man, we might be here for hours."

"I knew when they got on that they were trouble. Miss Mega Mouth leading the way, Miss Prissy in the middle, and Miss Mouse bringing up the rear."

Marti thought that was an interesting description, more so because she couldn't relate it to any of the women other than Lindstrum. She made three entries in her journal. Miss Mega Mouth, Miss Prissy, and Miss Mouse. She decided to try to match up the names and the husbands with the nicknames. Miss Mega Mouth had to be Mrs. Lindstrum. She drew a blank with the other two.

She wondered if this woman, or if anyone, had noticed the men. When she and the boys went to dinner, they had been across from and seated just behind the three couples. That was the only time she had gotten a good look at them. Mrs. Lindstrum was so skinny the bones in her wrists looked like knobs. Her hands had a bluish tinge, and the veins stood out. Her hair was so thin her scalp showed. She looked sick. Maybe that was why she was so bossy and waspish.

Then there was the woman in the blue velveteen jogging suit with the rhinestone trim on the collar. Was she Miss Prissy? According to the boys, the third woman was Mrs. Borzak. Marti wasn't sure she would describe Mrs. Borzak as Mousy. She butted in every time Mrs. Lindstrum took a breath and probably could have talked as much, given the opportunity. When she wasn't butting in, she was clearing her throat. Her cough was distinctly phony. Marti did recall the man bringing up the rear. He shuffled along, dragging his feet. His shoulders were hunched, his hands crippled.

She opened Mike's journal again and found the entry for dinner.

"Fiber folks! Get your Fiber here! Fiber! Eat that broccoli! Whole grain toast for breakfast! Bran cereal for lunch! And—ta-da—fruit, fruit, fruit and eat the skin!!! Oranges too? Bananas? Yuck!! Oh, and if that doesn't work, get some Metamucil!"

Marti had to smile. If she hadn't found the woman's voice so annoying, she would have been amused by them, too.

Theo had written: "Fiber means a lot to old people. Mrs. Lindstrum says 'using it' is very important. I think she means going to the bathroom, but I'm glad she didn't say that while we were eating. Mrs. Lindstrum must be very worried about her health. She took a bunch of herbs and vitamins, and she has this special salt shaker that she uses on her food. Mrs. Borzak grows whatever is in it in her garden. That must be why Mr. Borzak put it on his food, too. The other man didn't want any. He said it tasted like grass. Mrs. Borzak made him have some anyway. It must be something healthy, because everyone who had some looks sick. They are all going to Kingman, Arizona, because Mr. and Mrs. Lindstrum have a condo there. They have one in Florida, too. The Lindstrums and the Borzaks have been friends for a long time, and they go there every year. This is the first time the other couple is going. I hope it is not too far to Kingman."

"Damn!" Ponytail jumped up. "I'm going to go see what I can find out," he said. "This is worse than being in jail."

The woman sat there for a few minutes, said, "God, I need a cigarette," and went down to the club car.

Marti flipped through the boys' journals, looking for something the men had said, or some description of what they looked like. There wasn't anything. She tried to remember who had been sitting beside each woman at dinner. The man with the arthritic hands had been sitting with the lady in the blue jogging outfit, who, although she wasn't young, looked a lot younger than he did, and seemed to be in much better health. Then there was the gentleman with the steel gray hair and deep blue eyes and a faint expression of amusement on his face. He didn't pay much attention to Mrs. Lindstrum and gave the impression that he was either tolerating or humoring her. He was sitting with Mrs. Borzak, so Marti penciled him in as Mr. Borzak with a question mark beside his name. She still couldn't remember what the third man looked like.

The woman came back upstairs and sat down with a loud sigh. "Damn. We'll be here all night, and they won't even open the damned club car."

A few minutes later, Ponytail burst in. "Told you!" he said. "It was one of the women."

"You said it was Big Mouth."

"And I still say it. At least we know for sure it wasn't one of the men. And, we know that she's dead."

"How come you're so sure about that?"

"Did you hear anyone suggesting mouth-to-mouth resuscitation, or CPR? No. They just got everyone out of that compartment. And they had to open the door and take them outside to get them to another car. Why would they do all of that if someone wasn't dead?"

"Maybe you're right. I usually take the bus, so I don't know what they'd do." She was quiet for a moment, then said, "Actually, I didn't think Big Mouth was so bad. It's just that she wouldn't shut up."

"That and she didn't have shit to say."

"That too, but she kind of took charge, know what I mean? Like Miss Mousy was trying to aggravate the hell out of her, and Miss Prissy was sitting there like she was better than everyone else, but Miss Mouth, she was in charge. I like a woman who's in charge."

They both went downstairs.

Marti looked outside. The sky was clear and dark. There was no pollution. There were no jet stream trails. The stars were not hidden behind clouds. She wondered if someone was dead, if Ponytail knew what he was talking about, or exaggerating something he had overheard. When the female attendant came in and sat down, Marti leaned forward and said, "Long night tonight."

"We'll make up some of the time," the attendant said. "Once we get going, there won't be nothing for a while but rails and desert."

"Too bad about that old lady."

"Hah. Too bad for us. She's out of here. Cardiac arrest. Not that any of her friends feel too bad about her passing. Must be their age. By the time you get that old, you must be used to having your friends die."

"How's her husband holding up?"

"Hah. If he's as rich as he is good looking, he'll be just fine."

"But he's old."

"Not as old as she was."

"Is he that nice-looking guy with that thick gray hair. Tall, quiet."

"Yup. Surprised me, too. They were on their way to *her* condo. Would have been picked up by *her* limo driver. Everything was paid for by *her* credit card. Annoying when someone brags all the time like that. Too bad they didn't fly, but her doctor said no more airplanes, something about blood clots. Maybe that's what killed her."

"Too bad they didn't have a sleeper," Marti added.

"Oh, her husband and the lady with the blue outfit insisted that they go coach. Can't say why."

The attendant stood up, cupped her hand over her eyes, and looked outside.

"Will we be here much longer?"

"Another hour at least. You want anything? They've got coffee on in the galley, but don't tell anyone."

Marti thanked her and opened her journal. She would write about what was going on now. Theo and Mike would really be surprised when they heard about it. She looked at her list, added Miss Money Bags beside Lindstrum's name, erased Mr. Borzak's question mark and added Mr. Lindstrum—attractive, younger man. She decided that Miss Mouse was Mrs. Borzak, but put a question mark beside that. Miss Prissy she left blank. That done, she returned to the boys' journals.

With typical flourish, Mike wrote "Toilet lock!!! Use your toilet lock!!! Don't go to the doors on the side!!! The side toilet's are too small!!! Go to the door in the center!!! The bathroom is bigger there!!!! You won't get stuck trying to get out!!!!! And don't try to wait until you get to Kingman!!!"

Theo had written, "I think the conductor got tired of listening to them talking about their trip to the bathroom, because he helped them get their things and go downstairs. I am glad they are gone. It is nice and quiet now. He closed the door to the room they are in. Now they can talk the whole trip and not bother anyone."

When the female attendant came back with a cup of coffee for each of them, Marti asked, "How's that poor man doing who's got the arthritis?"

"Mr. Felton?"

"Yes."

"Lord, he looks like he's on his last leg, too. And he's taking at least half a dozen prescriptions, not to mention drinking that nasty looking bottle of homemade stuff his wife makes him drink. I hope he doesn't die before we reach Kingman. That's way in Arizona, and we haven't even been able to make it out of New Mexico."

As soon as the attendant finished her coffee and left, Marti wrote Mrs. Felton beside Miss Prissy and added her husband, and his description— crippled and sickly—to her list. The third man had to be Mrs. Borzak's husband, but Marti still could not remember anything about him. Beneath the names she added, salt shaker with home grown herbs and a bottle of homemade tonic.

She flipped through the boys' journals again to see if they had made note of anything about the husbands. Theo had written, "Poor Mr. Borzak. He stutters. That must be why he never says anything. Every time he tries to say something, Mrs. Borzak tells him to be quiet. She ordered the lasagna for him for dinner, but he kept saying st-st-st. I think he wanted the steak. Mrs. Borzak wants to be the boss of everybody, but Mrs. Lindstrum won't let her."

Ponytail jumped up, walked the narrow distance between the rows of windows without bumping into the seats, and said, "Will we ever get out of here? They should have brought in a flight-for-life helicopter."

The woman consulted a train schedule. "I wonder what time the bars open in Albuquerque?"

"Hell if I know. Now that another one of them's gotten sick . . . I hope there's room for all of them in the ambulance."

"You mean they might not all get off here? Do not even think it."

"Where are all of them going to fit in one ambulance, with two of them sick?"

"If one of them is left behind, I will never take the train again. At least on the bus . . ."

"You'd be stuck in the desert with a stinking bathroom and no water fountain."

The woman didn't answer.

Marti wanted to ask who else was sick, but decided to stay out of the conversation. Instead, she looked through Mike's journal seeking an entry about a man who stuttered. It wasn't hard to find. Mike had written "MR. BORZAK!!!!!!" then, " 'd-d-d-d-don't g-g-g-give me any m-m-m-m-ore of that.' Mrs. Borzak FINALLY let him say something, but she made him drink that yucky looking tonic anyway. It has stuff floating in it!!!!"

Marti flipped back though the entries and added Grandma's tonic to Mrs. Lindstrum, Mr. Borzak, and Mr. Felton. All of the sick people. She checked the entries again. The three of them were using the shaker filled with homegrown herbs also.

"The least they could do is put on a movie or serve sandwiches or something," Ponytail said.

"And serve drinks, like they do on planes."

"If whoever it is wasn't dead when they called for an ambulance, they're damned sure dead by now."

"This is no place to have an emergency," the woman agreed. "I thought the club car would be open all night."

Typical alcoholic, Marti thought. One-track mind. Annoyed, she began to wish that she had taken the plane.

The female attendant came back, and was bombarded with questions. When Ponytail and the woman couldn't get anything out of her, they sulked at the other end of the car. The attendant sat next to Marti.

"Damn," she said in a soft voice. "Like I like sitting here any more than they do."

"I heard someone else is sick," Marti whispered.

"Mr. Felton. He's not really complaining. Just says he doesn't feel good. No chest pains or anything, thank God. I don't know how to use the defilibrator. But his wife is almost hysterical. 'You can't be sick, you can't be sick. Not now, Howard, my God, not now. You are not sick, do you understand me, Howard? You are not sick.' She is really upset, pacing, checking her watch, just frantic. Having her friend die like that and now her husband complaining, it's just too much for her. Poor man keeps asking her for his tonic, but she insists he's had enough and doesn't need any more. Gave him one of those tablets you put under your tongue though. Poor woman is just beside herself with fear. And her so pretty, and him so old. Folks sure do surprise you sometimes."

"Hey!" Ponytail called. "You know what time this ambulance is coming?"

"Like maybe before daybreak," the woman added.

The attendant stood up to leave. "They're on their way."

Marti looked at the meager entries in her journal, added nitroglycerin beside Mr. Felton's name, and decided to see what else she could mine from what Mike and Theo had written. This time she began at the beginning, looking for entries she had skipped.

Mike had written, "Sick people here. Calling all sick people!! Doctor

Lindstrum is in!!! Line right up!!! Don't listen to your doctor! Do what Dr. Lindstrum says!! Chest pain, Mr. Felton? Heartburn. Don't take that digitalis! Drink Grandma's tonic!!! Chest pain, Mrs. Lindstrum. Heart trouble. Take that digitalis. Dr. Lindstrum!! Calling Dr. Lindstrum!!! Don't do anything your real doctor says."

Marti noted who was taking digitalis and looked for a similar entry in Theo's journal.

"Mrs. Lindstrum must really be sick. Maybe that is why she's so thin and looks so pale. She has a bad heart, blood sugar, (what is that?), hypertension, anemia, bunions, and an ingrown toenail. Mr. Lindstrum said she has halitosis too, and flatulence. Mrs. Borzak told her to just keep taking that tonic her grandmother used to make. She said her grandmother lived to be a hundred and three and drank it every day. I hope Mrs. Borzak brought enough since it's made from stuff she grows in her garden. They only have cactus in Arizona." Then, "Mrs. Lindstrum should stop talking long enough to listen to her husband. This is the third time he's told her to take her digitalis. He keeps telling her she forgot. She must be absentminded, too. She can't find the other stuff she is supposed to take, Coumadin. He says she doesn't need any of that anyway."

Marti added, "chest pain—no digitalis" beside Mr. Felton's name and chest pain—digitalis, no Coumadin beside Mrs. Lindstrum's name. As she reread what she had written, flashing lights could be seen in the distance. By the time the ambulance arrived, flanked by two police cars, she was certain that Mrs. Felton was dead and Mr. Felton and Mr. Borzak were sick because of what their spouses were giving them, or not allowing them to take. She went downstairs to advise the officers to confiscate Mrs. Borzak's tonic and her special salt shaker. She was also going to tell the paramedics to make sure that Mrs. Lindstrum, Mr. Borzak, and Mr. Felton were tested for homegrown poisons. She looked out the window. Mr. Felton and Mrs. Borzak were standing close together. There were two gurneys, each with a shrouded body. Mrs. Felton was kneeling beside one and crying. Marti could hardly wait to begin writing in her journal. Wait until Theo and Mike found out about this.

# THE SECRET OF THE 369ᵀᴴ INFANTRY NURSE

*A Poplar Cove Mystery*

*Patricia E. Canterbury*

In 1991 the ZICA Creative Arts and Literary Guild, a collection of writers and artists in which I am a member, decided to begin pulling colors, numbers, and phrases from a "hat" that would begin the first sentence of a poem, short story, or novel. When the number "3" was pulled, I knew that I wanted to write about triplets, but I wanted them to be best friends not siblings. I developed three best friends in a small, coastal village in the late 1920s. I had the townspeople call the girls the Triplets. The eleven-year-old Triplets solve mysteries in the Poplar Cove Mystery series. I have written three middle-grade novels, *The Secret of St. Gabriel's Tower* and *The Secret of Morton's End. The Secret of Sugarman's Circus* is currently seeking a publisher and will be available in 2004. In each book of the series, I attempt to tell a portion of African-American history, for example, Juneteenth, Buffalo Soldiers, and in this short story, a taste of the 369th Infantry Division. I was thinking of writing an adult murder mystery for Eleanor's anthology, but she e-mailed me and said, "I'm so glad that you're going to submit a children's mystery." So I decided, or rather, the Triplets decided, to add "The Secret of the 369th Infantry Nurse" to their adventures.

. . .

It was a few days before Armistice Day in 1928, and most children, animals, and things in general were enjoying the quiet that enveloped coastal towns just before sunset in the early fall. This sense of calm also covered the small *"colored"* village of Poplar Cove, California. Poplar Cove, brightly decorated in red, white, and blue ribbons, was one of three close-knit towns (the others being Grant's Cove and Marshall Cove) that hugged the northern California shoreline in the early twentieth century. The town lost five very special men in the Great War, and it and others in the TriCove area rotated the celebration of the end of the war with lots of fireworks, a parade, picnics, and a dance. This year it was Poplar Cove's turn to host, and the town had outdone itself in decorating every structure on Main Street. The ribbons usually went up on All Hallow's Eve and remained in place until Thanksgiving. The quiet nestled among the leaves and waited for adventure. Adventure would happen a few hours later in the image of Mrs. Lana Sue Barton.

While most children were content to read books and play in their yards with their siblings and friends, three of Poplar Cove's more interesting young inhabitants were busy minding other people's business. These individuals were eleven-year-old best girlfriends that were so close that the townspeople nickname them the Triplets. The Triplets prided themselves in their role as "junior deputies," a name that the sheriff had given them the year before in a misguided attempt to keep them out of police business. The Triplets, however, took every opportunity to *help* Sheriff Brown manage not only police business but the business of the town as well. So when their school friend, Three, short for Eli Shaw the Third, walked past them deep in thought, the girls seized the opportunity to find out the reason for his frown. Not that Three smiled a lot, in fact he was a rather solemn child, but on this particular morning he was more sorrowful than normal.

"Something must be wrong with Three," Amber Walker said, her foghorn voice startling a few heron that rested in the nearby Monterey pines.

"He looks fine to me," Jessica "JJ" Johnson replied, as she pulled an old straw hat over her freckled forehead. She and Robyn Jones, the third member of the Triplets, looked outside the Jefferson Five and Dime and Ice Cream Parlor where they had just completed their second ice cream cone. Eating ice cream together was the third best thing the girls enjoyed. First, of course, was being together, and second was putting a mystery into every little gathering. Getting up and going outside into the warm autumn weather, the girls followed Three into the park into the middle of the Main Square.

"Three. Three, wait up," Robyn called. "What's the matter? You look like you've lost your best friend."

"Oh, hi," he mumbled, looking down at his dust-covered cowboy boots. "It's Grandpa. He received a letter a few days ago. He hardly ever receives any mail. I just know that it's bad news 'cuz the few times he has received letters it's always been that someone he knew was very sick or had died. When I . . . when I . . . I asked to see it, he . . . he . . . just walked away from me like I wasn't there. He even *smelled* the envelope. Now, why would he do that? He hasn't mentioned it since, but I see it sticking out of his shirt pocket. Grandpa's never kept any secrets from me before." His voice cracked as he tried to suppress a sob. He turned quickly, but the Triplets saw the tears in his eyes. He walked under the Poplar Cove water tower's brightly draped pillars. One of the red, white, and blue ribbons blew in his face. He glared at it, pushed it away, then ran down Calhoun Street toward the Old Mill Road.

"I've never seen Three so unhappy. You know he thinks the world of his Grandpa. What could have been in that letter that Mr. Shaw wouldn't show him?" Amber asked.

"Grown-ups have all kinds of secrets. Maybe it's a surprise for Three's birthday," Robyn answered.

"Three's birthday was in May. Besides why would Mr. Shaw smell an envelope with information about a present for Three?" Jessica added, enunciating each word as she tried to keep her lisp from regaining its rich hold on her words.

"Then we'll just have to find out what was in the letter, who wrote it, and let Three read it," Amber said.

"Oh, and just how are *we* going to get, much less *read,* a letter that belongs to Mr. Shaw?" Robyn asked.

"We'll just have to think of something. After all, Mr. Shaw fed us soup when we escaped from Miss Swanson," Amber said, remembering last year's mystery with the Triplets' substitute teacher. "He likes us. We can go over to the Shaw's place to see if Three wants to go to Grant's Cove to help bring . . . no . . . no . . . that's not going to work. Why would we go to Grant's Cove to bring anything back? The only things Grant's Cove has that we don't have here is a motion picture palace and the library," Amber said.

"We need to think of something different. We need to get a grown-up to help us. Mr. Shaw isn't going to just hand over a letter that he won't let his own grandson read," Robyn said.

"A grown-up. Who?" Jessica asked.

"Mrs. Wilson could help us," Amber answered. Mrs. Wilson was a surrogate grandmother to the girls who frequently *saved* them from their parents.

"Why would she do that?" Robyn asked.

"Then *you* think of something. Everything *I* say you find something wrong with," Amber said, folding her arms across her chest. She kicked at a stick lying in the path.

"Look, isn't that Mr. Shaw?" Jessica asked, pointing in the direction of an old man dressed in a light brown linen suit walking toward the train depot. The girls looked up just in time to see Mr. Eli Shaw step inside the train station. The 11:05 whistle sounded as the train rounded the bend at the edge of town. It would be in the station in a few minutes.

"Let's follow him. Maybe we can find out about the letter once we're on the train," Amber said.

"ON the TRAIN!" Jessica and Robyn shouted in unison.

"I can't go on the train," Jessica said.

"I'm *not* going on the train," Robyn added. "Besides, in case you've forgotten, my father is the train master. He'd never let me get on the Sacramento train just to follow one of our neighbors. And what would your father say, Amber?"

Amber sighed. Her father was the mayor. "Okay. Then we'll ask your father where Mr. Shaw is going."

"I already *told* you, Sacramento. The 11:05 stops in Sacramento.

Sometimes Amber I don't think that you remember anything that I've taught you about the train schedule." Now it was Robyn's turn to kick at the stick.

"While the two of you were arguing, I've been thinking that we should just go over and tell Mr. Shaw that Three feels bad about whatever happened regarding the letter. Maybe he will tell us what's in the letter, and then we can ask to see it. That's what I think," Jessica said, as she began walking up Main Street toward the train station. While the girls were talking, the 11:05 pulled into Poplar Cove and passengers began getting off.

"Wherever Mr. Shaw is going it must be very fancy. He's wearing his Sunday-go-to-meeting clothes," Jessica added.

"You're right. I hadn't noticed that he's wearing his best clothes. Where's Mrs. Shaw?" Amber asked, as she and Robyn rushed to catch Jessica.

"Mrs. Shaw, oh my goodness. Mr. Shaw never comes to town without her," Robyn answered. The girls turned and looked back down Main Street, as if expecting Mrs. Shaw to step out of one of the businesses. When they turned back toward the train, Mr. Shaw was helping an older, pretty woman out of one of the Pullman cars.

"She sort of looks like my Aunt Beatrice," Amber said.

"She does wear the same type of beautiful dress, and her hat is just gorgeous," Robyn added, as she looked over at the woman. She appeared to be near Mr. Shaw's age of sixty. The girls watched as the woman kissed Mr. Shaw on his right cheek.

"Who is that?" Amber boomed. Four newly arriving passengers turned toward the girls. "Who is that?" she repeated a decibel lower.

"No wonder Mrs. Shaw wasn't with him. He's meeting another woman," Robyn said, he voice choking. She was the more sensitive of the girls, tending to throw up a lot and cry very easily. "I really *like* Mrs. Shaw and who *is* that woman?"

"We have to find out who she is," Jessica said, "Maybe she's his sister."

"Sister. Yes, maybe she's his sister," Robyn replied, sniffing back some tears and wiping others and her runny nose on her shirtsleeve.

While the Triplets were speaking, Mr. Shaw and his new friend put her suitcases in the back of Henry DuPree's car. Henry DuPree was the local blacksmith and gas station owner. He frequently drove neighbors and strangers to their destinations, if he was at the train station when the limited arrived. He also had two cars that he let people borrow while they were in town.

"Look, Mr. DuPree is driving Mr. Shaw and his friend toward Old Mill Road," Amber said. "The Shaw's farm is on Old Mill Road. He wouldn't be taking a stranger to his and Mrs. Shaw's home. She must be his sister. See, Robyn, you jump to the wrong conclusion all the time."

"Hi, Three, we saw your aunt when she got off the 11:05 this morning," Jessica said, as she swept leaves from the front of her mother's beauty shop.

Three stopped, frowned, and said, "Aunt? Oh, Mrs. Barton. She's not my aunt. She's the nurse who saved Grandpa's life when he returned from the War."

Three walked away, leaving Jessica staring openmouthed in his wake. *Wait until I tell the girls that the stranger is a nurse who saved Mr. Shaw's life. Isn't that romantic? Maybe someone will make a motion picture of their time in the War. I, of course, would portray Mrs. Barton.* Jessica dreamed of being a motion picture star. She loved acting, because when she concentrated on her lines in a school play, she didn't lisp. Amber and Robyn would often tease her that it didn't matter if she lisped or not, because in silent motion pictures, no one could hear her.

"We know who you are," Robyn said, when she and the other Triplets met Mrs. Barton, the next day. They were in the post office that was housed in the train station.

"And I know who you are," Mrs. Barton replied, smiling at the girls.

Homer Jones Senior, Robyn's father, had the flu and had just returned to the post office after a day and a half at home. The girls were helping stack and sort mail and packages that were beginning to pile up in a preholiday rush.

The Triplets smiled back.

"I've heard you're very good detectives. If I ever need a detective or three, I'll be sure to call on you." Mrs. Barton paid the postage for a package she was mailing to New York. The three girls had stopped talking long enough to eavesdrop on her conversation and find out the package's destination.

"Good-bye," Lana Sue said, as she walked outside and down the street toward the middle of town.

A few minutes later she returned to the post office. "How much longer are you girls going to be working here?" she asked.

"Oh, we're almost finished, about another half hour. We need to get the packages ready for the 11:05," Robyn answered.

"Meet me at the Jefferson Five and Dime and Ice Cream Parlor. You do enjoy ice cream, don't you?"

"Yes," the Triplets replied in unison.

"I understand that you're good at finding folks. I might need your help finding someone."

Anyone stopping by the Jefferson Five and Dime and Ice Cream Parlor a few minutes after noon would have found Lana Sue and the Triplets deep in conversation in the back booth by the rear door.

"Well, do you think that you can help me?" Lana Sue asked, then licked the last of her chocolate milkshake off a straw.

"I don't know. Mr. Phillips keeps to himself. He comes into town less than Mr. Shaw does," Jessica replied.

"We have to think of a way to get him to attend one of the Armistice Day functions. I guess I'm going to have to tell you girls a secret. This is a secret that you cannot tell anyone, not your parents or the sheriff. Do you want to hear it?" Lana Sue asked.

"We can keep a secret," Amber whispered. The other two nodded. No one else in the store was close enough to overhear the conversation.

"I was assigned to the boys in the 369th Infantry Battalion, because I was the only colored nurse with any combat exposure . . ." Lana Sue began.

"You were *in* the War?" Robyn interrupted, the girls almost dropped their shakes they were so excited.

"No, I meant I'd cared for severely wounded men in an old Union Veteran's hospital. I didn't cry or fall apart when someone had to have their arm or leg removed. Although it was very difficult with the 369th, because some of the men were younger than my twenty-year-old nephew," Lana Sue replied.

"Oh," the girls whispered in unison.

"Mr. Shaw was in the 369th. He spoke at the school and told us all about it. Remember, Amber, you were out with the measles?" Robyn said, after a few minutes of awkward silence.

"Yes, but you told me what he said," Amber replied.

"What did he say?" Lana Sue asked.

"I'm not sure that I remember it all. But I'll try. Mr. Shaw's favorite cousin . . . I can't remember his name, who lived in New York, was drafted and asked Mr. Shaw to join him in the fight for democracy abroad. Mr. Shaw's uncle was a member of the 15th Regiment before it was renamed the 369th, and he wanted to carry on the family tradition. Even though Mr. Shaw was much older than most men being called to serve, the army needed men who were able and willing to help in the War effort, so they accepted him. He was sent to the front, because he has an excellent ear for languages, and he was able to translate many of the French and German words for the company. Once, because everyone was surrounded, he fought alongside his cousin after they reached Belleau Wood in France. Mr. Shaw's cousin was wounded and returned home, but Mr. Shaw remained with the 369th and was with them when they reached the Rhine. He didn't talk much about the actual fighting. Mostly he described how beautiful the countryside of France and Germany was and how much of it reminded him of Poplar Cove, except that the trees were different. He didn't like discussing the War. Mr. Shaw told his story very quickly and didn't wait for too many questions. You know he gets quieter and quieter every year. I overheard Mother telling someone that most of his friends have died."

"Thank you, Robyn, that was a nice summary. Do you girls know that the 369th was the most highly decorated division in the War? The extraordinary valor of the 369th earned them fame in Europe and America. I'm

sure that your school informed you of the feats of Corporal Henry Johnson and Private Needham Roberts." Lana Sue paused for a breath.

"We were told that they were attacked by a German unit while on the
Western Front, and even though they were wounded, they refused to surrender," Jessica interrupted.

"Yes, they refused to surrender and fought with whatever they had.
They were the first Americans awarded the Croix de Guerre," Robyn volunteered.

"Very good. You're correct, but they weren't the only Harlem Hellfighters to win awards," Lana Sue added.

"Harlem Hellfighters? Is that what the French called them?" Robyn
asked.

"Yes, that was the division's nickname. A little more than 170 men
and officers received individual medals, and the unit itself received the
Croix de Guerre for taking Sechault," Lana Sue added.

"Gosh, and someone from our hometown was part of that. But what
does the 369th have to do with Mr. Phillips?" Jessica asked.

"I have to find Mr. David Joseph Phillips. You have to trust me. I think
that he would listen to me if I were to meet him with you girls. I've been
given some documents that he needs to receive at the Armistice Day celebration. I came here to see Eli Shaw and to give him David Joseph's documents. Then Eli . . . Mr. Shaw said that David Joseph lived on a farm near
Marshall Cove."

"Why doesn't Mr. Shaw get Mr. Phillips to come to the parade?" Amber asked.

"Or, why doesn't Mr. Shaw just give the documents to Mr. Phillips?"
Jessica suggested.

"It seems as if Mr. Shaw and Mr. Phillips haven't spoken to each other
in over five years," Lana Sue replied. "I found that out when I asked Eli
the same thing."

"Five years? Why? What happened?"

"Eli won't tell me. Before you ask, I don't think that he'll tell any of
you either. He can be a very stubborn man," Lana Sue smiled to soften her
words.

"Then we'll just have to bring them together without them knowing that the other one will be there," Jessica said.

"Okay girls, let's figure out how to bring these two old War buddies together."

"I just can't believe it that Mr. Phillips was *in* the War? He's never attended any of the celebrations that I can remember," Robyn said.

"I thought Mom said that he spent the war in a tuberculosis sanitarium in Weimar. Besides, Mr. Phillips is only about twenty-seven years old. Wouldn't he have been too young to be in the War?" Amber asked.

"I believe that he lied about his age so that he could fight. But that is something that we would have to ask him," Lana Sue replied.


Two days before Armistice Day dawned cool, with just a trace of the fog that would settle into Poplar Cove by Christmas. Mrs. Lana Sue Barton borrowed one of Henry Du Pree's cars and, accompanied by Robyn and Jessica, drove the fifteen miles from Poplar Cove to Marshall Cove.

"Nurse Barton? It is Nurse Barton. What are you doing here?" David Joseph Phillips asked, as he wiped dust from his tan face. He moved slowly, dragging his left leg and coughing from the dust the automobile had stirred up. He stopped by the morning glory–covered fence that separated his front yard from the dirt road that led to Marshall Cove and extended his hand to open the gate. "Who are your two little friends?" He frowned and walked to the parked car and opened the passenger side door to let the girls out.

"Hi, Mr. Phillips. It's us, Robyn Jones, Homer Jones's daughter—he's the postmaster. And this is Jessica, one of my best friends from Poplar Cove."

"Pleased to meet you, Robyn. Jessica."

"David Joseph. I heard that you lived near here, and I have a surprise for you," Lana Sue said, stepping out of the car and hugging the young man.

"You're all the surprise I can take in a day. Whatcha doing in Marshall Cove?" He asked, standing stiffly with his arms at his sides. He did not return her hug. He shifted his weight from one foot to the other and did not look directly at Mrs. Barton. He spoke to a point a little to the left and be-hind her shoulder.

"I told you. I came to see you because I have a surprise."

"What?"

"You'll have to come with me to Poplar Cove to receive it."

"Where? Poplar Cove? Oh, yeah. There ain't nothin' there that needs my attention." He said, bending over and absently rubbing his left knee. "I don't know no one there that's worth knowing." He began to sweat and wiped his face with a dusty handkerchief.

"You know Mr. Eli Shaw, Three's grandfather," Jessica interrupted.

"Eli Shaw. He ain't no friend of mine. If'n that's what you came here for, you can get back in that automobile and go home." He coughed, wiped his face again, and turned to his farmhouse, nearly tripping over the two geese that waddled past.


Meanwhile, Amber was walking up the steps of the Shaw's farmhouse. It was late afternoon, and Mr. Shaw was sitting on the porch drinking a glass of lemonade.

"Anna, one of them Triplets is here to see ya." He turned and yelled through the screen door to his wife, who was in the kitchen.

"Actually, Mr. Shaw, I came by to see you."

"Me? What for?"

"It's about your time with the 369th Infantry. I have to give a speech at the Armistice Day celebration, and I was ill when you spoke to our school, so I was wondering if you could tell me about your time in France." Amber crossed her fingers behind her back, sat down on the top step, and took out her school writing pad and pencil. The light from the kerosene lamp in the living room gave just enough light for her to write clearly.

"Uh . . . well. Maybe I have a few minutes. Would you like some lemonade? Anna bring . . . now which one of the Triplets are you?"

"Amber, sir."

"Bring Amber some lemonade. Let me see it was nearly ten years ago that we came back home. Some things I remember it as if it were yesterday, others I can hardly remember at all. Occasionally, late at night I can still smell the gun powder and smell the blood." He shook himself as if to rid his mind of the memory.

"I nearly lost Jamie at Belleau Wood. He was shot, but we got him home. He's fine now. There were some good men there. I got a chance to use my French. We heard a lot of it growing up in Louisiana. Sort of came back real easy when I heard it every day. I learned German too; can hardly speak them anymore. No one to talk to." Eli paused, remembering the time in Europe.

He told the same story that Robyn had relayed to Lana Sue and Jessica.

"Did Mr. David Joseph Phillips fight alongside you?" Amber asked.

"We don't speak his name in this house," Eli replied, harshly. "Anyone who thinks that I would betray a trust is not anyone I want anywhere around my friends and family. He'd better stay in Marshall Cove and mind his own business, and I'll mind mine here."

"I'm sorry, I didn't mean to bring his name up. I just wondered if . . ."

"If what?"

"If you were in the War together."

"Not everyone from California fought together. Do you have all the information you need for your report?" Eli Shaw got up from his rocker and walked into the house.

"Yes, thanks. Thanks, for the lemonade, Mrs. Shaw," Amber said, to the closed door as she got up and began the long walk home.

*I hope that Mrs. Barton and the girls had better luck than I did. I didn't learn anything about why Mr. Shaw and Mr. Phillips don't speak,* she thought.


"David Joseph, I'm not leaving until you hear what I have to say. I don't care about your feud with Eli Shaw or anyone else," Lana Sue said.

"We're not leaving either," Jessica added, as she and Robyn stepped on either side of Lana Sue. David Joseph smiled briefly for the first time since their arrival.

"Well, I guess I can't leave you standing in the front yard. Come in,"

David Joseph said, opening the front door of his immaculately clean home and stepping inside. He motioned to a brightly patterned overstuffed sofa and a matching chair. Lana Sue sat in the chair, the girls on the sofa. David Joseph sat in a Bentwood rocking chair.

"I want you to know why we came to see you and why it's so important for you to return to Poplar Cove with us." Lana Sue sat up straight in the chair and opened her purse.

"Looks like this might take a while. Let me get ya some lemonade. We Phillips's have manners, even if others don't," David Joseph said.

"Oh just show us where the kitchen is, we'll get it. That way you two grown-ups can talk," Robyn said, jumping up from the sofa. Jessica got up also.

"Okay, thanks, the kitchen's over there." He pointed to a closed door to the left of the sofa.

"Maybe we can learn why he and Mr. Shaw don't speak to each other if we're not in the room," Robyn whispered, as the girls walked out of the room.

"David Joseph," Lana Sue began.

"Most folks 'round here call me DJ. Why don't ya call me DJ?"

"Okay, DJ. I know that you believe that you deserted the army . . ."

"That's why ya came, you and them girls? What's Eli been sayin'?" DJ interrupted, his face flushed with anger.

"Eli doesn't know that we're here, and he hasn't said anything," Lana Sue continued.

"Well, he's wrong. I ain't deserted the army 'cuz I was never in the army. I have TB and was in Weimar during the War," DJ said, looking down at his trembling hands and coughing violently.

"You were not at Weimar. You were with the 369th in France. You were wounded, shot in the left leg—the very leg that you favor so much."

He stopped rubbing his left knee, which he had been unconsciously rubbing since he sat down.

The girls returned to the parlor with a pitcher and four glasses. They poured lemonade for everyone and sat back down on the sofa.

"Girls, maybe DJ and I need to talk a little longer . . . alone. Would you mind returning to the kitchen?"

"Okay." Jessica and Robyn picked up their glasses and went back to the kitchen, but stood close by the door—which they had left open a crack—and listened as Lana Sue continued. "You left Fort McClellan two days before the end of March in 1919 and returned to Weed because your mother was very ill. In fact you returned home just hours before she died of influenza. However, all of your paperwork was signed off. You are an official veteran of the Great War, and we want you to march in the Poplar Cove parade with Eli Shaw. Now, whatever problems there are between the two of you, you can ignore for a day."

"I . . . I'm a Veteran? I'm not in trouble?" DJ asked, then drained the lemonade from his glass. He sat back in the rocker, mumbling to himself.

"Yes, you're a Veteran, and no, you're not in trouble. Also, the army knows that you lied about your age to enlist. Eli lied about his age too. He was too old to go to the front, so you both have secrets that don't amount to anything at all. No one is going to hold anything against you, either," Lana Sue said.

"I'm . . . I'm okay?" DJ's eyes filled with tears. He blew his nose on his handkerchief.

Lana Sue walked outside to the porch to give him a chance to compose himself.

"Gosh, Mr. Phillips thought he was a deserter. That's why he never attended any of the Armistice Day events," Jessica said, as the girls walked out the back door and around the house to join Lana Sue on the porch.

A few minutes later DJ met them outside.

"Eli was the only one who knew my real age and where I really was in 1917 and 1918. We had a real blowup. I was afraid that he'd use it against me some time. That's why I live here. I don't know why I felt that way, he only been kind to me. It's just . . . it's just . . . well, no one in Marshall Cove bothers me. I heard him speak about you, Miss Barton. He showed me a picture of you and him in the hospital. I'd recognize you anywhere. He always talked about how well you treated the 369th boys. Eli kept saying that he'd invite you to the picnic and dance. I knew if you ever came West that you'd find out about me. Here all this time you knew." DJ sighed heavily, as if a great weight had been lifted from his chest.

"I'd be honored to march in the parade. That is if the folks of Poplar Cove will have me."

"Of course we want you to march," Robyn said.

"I don't know how far I can go with this bum leg. It never really healed properly."

"There are doctors in a hospital in San Francisco that can repair your leg," Lana Sue said. "The army can help. Meanwhile, let's sit down and discuss your involvement with the Armistice Day celebrations."

Armistice Day was clear, cool, and bright, with none of the fog from two days earlier. People from the TriCove area began lining up for the parade at nine in the morning. The bell in St. Charles A.M.E. church rang out, and Eli Shaw and David Joseph Phillips, dressed in their army uniforms, rounded the corner of Calhoun and Main Streets together. Eli carried the American flag, and David Joseph carried the California flag. Everyone gasped, because most of the TriCove residents knew about the bitter feud between the two. Only the passing of the flags stopped the conversations, as everyone asked those standing by them, "what happened to end the feud?" Ten Veterans of the Great War followed the flags, then three Union Veterans hobbled past, dressed in their dark blue wool uniforms, followed by two horse-drawn floats. The parade was over in five minutes, and everyone crossed over to Main Square for a picnic.

"I must say, I was surprised to see the two of you walking together," Sheriff Brown said, as he handed Eli and David Joseph each a glass of iced tea.

"I came back last night after a long talk with Mrs. Barton and the girls. I was so scared about what I thought people might say that I lashed out at the only person who knew my secret," David Joseph said, glancing over at Eli.

"Yes, I couldn't believe my eyes when I heard the dogs barking and there was DJ in my front yard. After tellin' the 369th story to the mayor's daughter, I'd made up my mind to go see David Joseph and patch things up. The quarrel was stupid," Eli said.

.   .   .

"Ladies and gentlemen. May I have your attention, please? As all of you know, we're here to celebrate the end of the War, November 11, 1918. Later today we'll go to Morton's End and place flowers on the graves of our fallen heroes. But right now, let me introduce an unsung hero who has been living among us for years. David Joseph (DJ) Phillips, please step to the stage," Mayor Walker said, standing behind a podium he'd borrowed from the Grant's Cove library. "You too, Eli," Mrs. Barton was seated on the stage to his right.

David Joseph walked slowly to the temporary stage set up in the middle of Main Square. He was followed by Eli Shaw.

"Mrs. Barton, would you and Eli do the honors?" Mayor Walker continued.

"Mr. Shaw. I think you should have the pleasure," Lana Sue said.

Eli nodded and picked up a wrapped box that was lying on the table behind the podium. He slowly unwrapped the box and took out a small wound chevron.

"David Joseph, it is with a great deal of pleasure that I present you with this wound chevron for your bravery in 1918," he said, pinning the Purple Wound Chevron on DJ's uniform.

"Don't forget these," Lana Sue said, handing Eli DJ's discharge papers.


The rest of the Armistice Day was filled with dancing, food, and friendship, as family after family stopped by the Shaw-Phillips picnic area to wish both of them well and to see DJ's wound chevron. Three and his grandfather laughed and hugged each other and took turns taking some of the out-of-town folks for hayrides around the square.


"Mrs. Barton is really good at keeping secrets. She never told *us* about the real reason she wanted to see Mr. Phillips. Nor did she say anything about the wound chevron," Jessica said, after the clapping and cheering from the crowd died down.

"Some detectives *we* are. We couldn't find out what the fight between Mr. Shaw and Mr. Phillips was about, and we didn't even *guess* that Mrs. Barton wouldn't have traveled all the way to California just to give someone papers that she could have mailed," Amber said.

"We're going to have to turn in our junior deputy badges if we don't do better," Robyn added.

"Our next adventure had better be very exciting. Soon it'll be Thanksgiving, and absolutely nothing happens in Poplar Cove at Thanksgiving," Amber said.

"Remember what happened last year when we said nothing ever happens in Poplar Cove? I bet our next excitement will be lots of fun," Robyn said.

Little did the Triplets know what would be in store for them six months later, when a circus wagon would break down outside of town.

# DOGGY STYLE

*Christopher Chambers*

Quarter to four A.M., the morning after Super Bowl Sunday. Feathery snowflakes were falling in silence: a hushed, false reprieve from the sleet bombardment earlier that night. Thousands of liquored-up revelers had spilled out of Buckhead bars and clubs for the dark trek home to the Atlanta suburbs, after watching the Patriots embarrass the Rams. DeKalb County Chief of Police Wofford "Dub" Miller Jr. was grimly surveying the result, as the coroner's "meat wagon" pulled onto the slushy soft shoulder of Hairston Road. "Stupid sumbitches," the chief whispered to himself. "This never woulda happened if—"

A howl bit through the frosty black air, severing Miller's thoughts.

"Damn, Chief," an officer gasped. "That a wolf?"

Dub Miller drew up the collar of his Gore-Tex anorak. "Ain't no wolves here, shit-fer-brains," the chief grumbled. He gulped from his brushed aluminum travel mug, and the hot coffee mixed with George Dickel burned going down. "Just some pitiable stray, is all. Cold, hungry . . . smells the dead." The chief and his officers had been putting down a lot of strays this winter. Especially as Atlanta's sprawl chomped its way toward Stone Mountain, bringing blight along with malls and Jaguars and

3,000-square-foot lakefront manses. But this howl was not one Dub Miller had ever heard before. Not the whine of a freezing, frightened mongrel. This was a canine song: voluptuous tonics and dominants, bridges and themes.

Police officers and EMTs—DeKalb, Georgia State Troopers, Pine Lake and Stone Mountain Municipal—stood transfixed by the sound, until the chief's handset beeped shrilly: a crisp human tenor followed, over the static and feedback.

"*Chief Miller,*" the voice called, "*Send my GBI evidence control team down to the creekside, you copy? And if the DEA regional administrator calls, you patch her through, straightaway. I'm heading up.*"

The chief answered, gruffly, "Ten-four."

Dub Miller had met Georgia Bureau of Investigation Inspector Calvin Beauchamp only an hour ago. Already, Miller hated him. Not solely because Miller's older brother and uncle were retired "Kleagles" in the DeKalb-Fulton-Gwinnett Knights of the Ku Klux Klan. No, the chief figured Beauchamp for a transplanted Northerner, like many of the "fancy spooks" who'd invaded his county with the help of greedy developers. The arrogant black doctors, lawyers, computer-info-tech-whatevers—oh, they were bad enough. But it was the scumbag rappers, their so-called producers and parasites, plus millionaire Falcons, Braves, and Hawks, who really put a long, scraggly dog hair across Dub Miller's ass. *Highbrow niggers out here don't have the good goddamn sense to keep these hip-hop pissants out,* Miller cursed inwardly as he watched Inspector Beauchamp trudge up a snowy embankment marked with yellow tape and lighted by sputtering orange flares.

Beauchamp was at least four inches taller than the slight, birdlike Miller. A little gray painted the black hair of his temples and moustache. He was wearing tortoise shell glasses that matched his skin color; the lenses were wet from falling snow. GBI Special Agent Rick Cooper flanked him. Cooper was carrying a shallow cardboard box, like the bottom of a beer case.

Miller aimed a Maglite beam into the box and inspected the contents: several glassine baggies of a white powder. A six-ounce Ziploc of little empty vials. Several teabag-sized foil packets. Some joints, and a few squat cigars sliced lengthwise and stuffed with ground, leafy matter. Miller sucked his teeth. "Didn't find any cash?"

Beauchamp raised an eyebrow. "No, Chief, we didn't. This contraband was secreted inside a nylon satchel. Strangely, it wasn't in the water, or the vehicle. It was hanging from a branch on a felled pine . . . big one bridging the creek ravine."

"That so?" Miller had put on his best nonplussed look. "Whachewawl's theory? I mean, we called GBI onacounta the Smitty .38, the outta state tags . . ."

Beauchamp answered, stonefaced. "We'll know more once we trace the Smith & Wesson and the SUV's winched out of the water. As for the stash, it looks like what the DEA calls a 'Hollywood Pu Pu Platter.' A Pu Pu's a mixed tray of appetizers at a Chinese restaurant. Hence the drug nomenclature. First menu item is 'El Diablito.' That's heroin, a deck or so—that's fifteen grams—mixed with cocaine and then rolled into joints with Mexican cannabis."

Agent Cooper spoke next. Miller was comforted by the young man's thick drawl. "Two types of coke here: powdered for the Diablitoes and the cheap cigars, and crack for basing with the heroin. The crack mixture's called 'P-funk,' or a 'Belushi Speedball,' while the cigar is called a 'Gangsta Torpedo.' "

Beauchamp added, "Interesting you mentioned cash, Chief, because one needs cash and connections to afford this kind of party. To buy, to transport. *Unhindered.*"

Miller laughed. "Somebody got 'emselves perished. I'd call that 'hindered!' "

Beauchamp ordered Cooper to take the box to a GBI Chevy Suburban, then ushered Miller toward three occupied black body bags lying on the icy pavement.

Miller asked, "Y'awl didn't see any dog tracks down by the creek didya?"

"Not unless they're in the ice under the snow layer. Why?"

"Nevermind. Um . . . you think they Yankee dealers? I mean, we got hip-hop folk, athletes out here, but they behave."

Ignoring Miller, Beauchamp knelt, unzipped the bag, and took the frozen hand of a young black woman, saying, "This girl had the fake driver's license, right?"

Miller nodded. "Yep. But her old high school ID say she from College Park. Real bad area, near Hartsfield Airport."

"This pink hospital wristband she's wearing is what the Panther-Six Mens' Club gives its girls for ID. She was a stripper, Chief."

"Ha! How you know about that place?"

Beauchamp moved to the next body. "White male, age twenty-six. These throat lacerations . . . blood loss, plus the cold, must've produced shock within seconds."

"Tore his neck up on the SUV's broken glass, likely," the chief surmised. "Others don't have no fatal crash trauma. Maybe they was thrown clear; only the females hit the water, drowned."

Beauchamp flipped the contorted, frozen body over to expose the buttocks and thighs. "Where was he found . . . in what position?"

"Across't that log you talked about. Facedown." Miller took another swig from his travel mug. "So?"

"Lividity's wrong for facedown. Purple marks on his rump, back. You certain no one came up on this site before the State Troopers, maybe moved him?"

"Hell no."

Beauchamp slid to the third body. The young black woman's eyes were still open. Glassy. Her gentle twisty-braids glistened with frost. "She's pretty," Beauchamp whispered. "Looks just like my niece. *God.*"

Miller suppressed a snicker. So *Sherlock Spade ain't so tough.*

Beauchamp stood up, icily composed. "So where's her brother, Sekou Toure Belleweather, age twenty-seven, according to the wallet you recovered?"

"Aside from the last names, how you know they siblings, not married?"

"No rings. Plus an expired Fordham University ID in the wallet had the same address as female subject number two."

Two gunshots pierced the night. A terrified female voice crackled over the police frequency: *"Ten-thirteen! Officer needs assistance!"*

A Stone Mountain patrolman yelled, "That's Lizzie! She was on the ridge taking accident scene photos!"

Glocks and Berettas drawn, cops charged up a snow-swept rocky hill, Miller and Beauchamp close behind. Flashlight beams crisscrossed on the officer, weapon aimed, but shaking violently. At her feet was a young black man's body, frozen in a seated position, facing a snow-blanketed mound.

"Dog tracks!" shouted a DeKalb officer. "Down there to the hollow!"

"Leave it be!" Dub Miller yelled, winded from the climb, pulse thumping.

The female officer lowered her weapon, panting, "Big . . . big pit bull."

Beauchamp turned his penlight on the frozen man's face. The eyes were splayed in horror, but there wasn't a mark on him, save for a few rips in what was a very expensive Marc Jacobs leather peacoat. Beauchamp clamped the penlight between his teeth and scooped away the snow around the body. The chief swallowed hard when, under Beauchamp's light, he saw drag marks in the crusty layer of sleet beneath the fresh snow.

"Somethin' . . . dragged this boy up against these here oak roots? Jesus Lord."

Beauchamp brushed off the mound. It wasn't a gnarled root. It was a dead dog. Miller backed away and bounded back to the road. And the howling began anew.


The big silver Lincoln Navigator skidded hard to the right. Adam Horowitz jerked the wheel into the skid, compensating. "Route 10 . . . connects to I-285, right?" he gasped. "Redan Road . . . that's too far south, right Sekou? *Sekou?*"

"I ain't feelin' this whining, cuz! You sound like those nouveau-riche down here who can't drive in a little snow! Can't *wait* to get back to New York!"

A young woman with twisty-braided locks and high cheekbones leaned up from the backseat. "This isn't a little 'snow,'" Sekou. It's a Georgia ice storm. These SUVs brake like cars, don't be fooled. Maybe you'd be more concerned if you weren't half-geeked on champagne and those Diablito blunts."

"Soje, hang back out my grill. You and white boy Adam here'll be hugged up and warm in the hotel by dawn."

Sojourner Sanaa Belleweather strained over to buss Adam's pale cheek, then tweaked Sekou's goatee, which she called his "soul patch." "Big brother, let's just stop at a Waffle House and wait the storm out. *Please.*"

With a deep sigh, Sekou said, "This's our last trip. Now we got working capital for our design company, Umoja. No bank was gonna give us a line of credit, and Mom and Dad are tapped out, or talking that we got-live-right-suffer-and-sacrifice mess. Like their hypocrite asses got a right to comment? This is the second Bush Era . . . we gotta bum-rush the doors slammed in our face." He squeezed his sister's slender hand; she settled back. Sekou wasn't done, though. "And Adam—he needs these gigs, too. Parents straight up kick him out for loving *you* and leaving med school."

"I can speak for m'damnself, Sekou," Adam said. "And Five-O be thick out here—you see that last accident we passed? Car flipped clean over. Say we go back, or pull over."

"Yo man, *drive*. First, no worries with Five-O. Trust me. Second, hell with our so-called customer in Lake Estate. Welshing niggah's probably too high to answer his doorbell. If he weren't a basehead, he'd've been playing in the Super Bowl and not watching on his wide-screen. Nothing but a gangsta with gangsta homies. And his trick-ass wife with her record label crew and bourgie sorors, sitting there complaining about *our* product, *our* service. Nah, I ain't havin' it."

Adam grumbled. "The wife paid us with a Def Sounds Productions corporate bank draft . . . and you accepted it? Makes us look like a bunch of *pishers,* Yo. As *farkatke* as you renting this Lincoln on your own credit card!" When a faint whimper came from the rear, Adam added, "And let's not forget this underage drunk twat they saddled us with. How many dicks did this bitch su—"

Sojourner snapped. "Watch your mouth, Adam—you were taught better! Lord . . . she's sick again . . . I don't want her throwing up back here. Adam pull over."

Sekou barked, "Both y'all shuddup! Yeah, pull over—put the damn blinkers on! *I'll drive.* And Soje, hang'er head outtha' window if you have to!"

Two dogs emerged through from a curtain of pelting sleet. One animal was stout, boxy. It turned to nuzzle and exhort the slower animal, whose shaggy red fur was encrusted with ice, toward the glow of a streetlight. The road was the last obstacle. Then up another wooded hill, and finally, refuge in a culvert hidden by stands of pines and bare live oaks. He'd scouted it that morning: a hot pipeline nearby for warmth, plenty of muskrats and rabbits to hunt and eat.

The younger dog could hear worn joints pop as the older companion slid to cold ground, panting. He licked the froth from his old friend's grizzled snout. Yes, one crushing bite to the throat could end his friend's misery. A bite like he'd delivered so many times to other dogs, to the gleeful howls of those hairless two-leggers. They'd thrown the green paper when he'd emerge from the pit, bloodied yet victorious. They named him "Goblin," and at night, he'd guard their den. He'd bark and snap whenever rival packs of two-leggers would invade. The fire and thunder would shoot from sticks in their naked paws. A rival two-legger would scream when the fire hit him, and Goblin'd finish him off, jaws locked around soft parts. But then came the morning when the fire skewered Goblin as he slept. While the two-leggers battled over the white powder, Goblin limped away. To den and hide. To die. Pup two-leggers found him. They heaved rocks at him. But they ran when they heard a snarl and cried when old yellow teeth bit their haunches. The pup two-leggers called Goblin's rescuer "Brokebottom," because he often dragged one hind leg. Brokebottom sniffed Goblin, head bowed as a friend. With the next sunrise, he brought Goblin meat, nudged him to drink from the gutter. Goblin healed and soon was strong enough to follow Brokebottom far from the dens of the cruel two-leggers. That was a season ago. Now, Goblin smelled the tumors inside Brokebottom's body. Now, he just wanted his savior to rest at ease.

Cropped tail erect, pointed ears up, Goblin scoured the air for the two-legger machines that prowled the roads. Sensing nothing, he nosed Brokebottom up on four shaky legs. The two-leggers would abuse and starve you, but they'd often die themselves to avoid hitting you with their machines. Goblin herded Brokebottom into the road. Sleet stung their eyes. Raw paws crunched down on the icy pavement.

Goblin heard a whosh, a hum to his right. Suddenly, another, to his left. Two machines, one closer, faster. He pushed his shoulder into Brokebottom's haunches. From around a bend—a roar, and lights flashed. The machine was bearing down on Goblin. This two-legger wasn't going to stop.

Giving his last measure of strength and love, Brokebottom wheeled around and slammed into Goblin's flank: Goblin fell away, sprayed by gravel, fumes, and wet windwash.

A dull thud. A yelp.

The silvery monster twisted around the curve, disappearing as suddenly as it appeared. Goblin heard a distant shriek of metal hitting metal, then silence. Slowly, he rose from the pavement, shook the ice from his coat. Yards away lay his old friend. Goblin approached, touched his nose to Brokebottom's. No breath, no whimper. Goblin whined and tracked in a circle, stopping once to nudge his lifeless friend. Then, a mournful howl left Goblin's throat. Those jaws could snap like a toothed clamp, but soon, they gently closed around Brokebottom's scruff and pulled the companion up the ridge. Goblin then stood motionless, ears raised as the sleet hissed around him. Inwardly, he begged Brokebottom's gentle spirit for absolution for what he was about to do. When he heard no reply, he trundled back down to the road anyway. To follow tire tracks.

Sojourner knew she should have driven. But she deferred to her brother. Her mother said never challenge manhood assertively. White people did that to our men from the day a boy emerges from our body, she'd say. "Oh God, Mommie," she muttered through bloodied, quivering lips. Not challenging Sekou found her wedged between the twisted edge of the Navigator's front passenger seat and a panel of the right rear door; shards from the shattered side window hung like icicles. A tree branch poked through; cold wind blew across her face like a razor. "Sekou!" she cried out.

"Soje? Soje honey?" It was Adam's voice, from outside, from above. "I'm gonna open the door, slowly, 'kay? Don't look down, just follow my voice."

The voice didn't calm her, for now she could smell gasoline, ozone. But the odor didn't terrify her as much as the noise: water, now swirling around her. The rear cargo hatch popped; Sojourner could see Adam's face. The girl, who called herself "Alize" crouched behind him, swaddled in his coat.

"Reach up, baby!" Adam exhorted, as Sojourner struggled to lift her arms. "Do you have pain . . . your shoulder, collarbone?"

"Nah-uh," she grunted as she reached for him. Adam pulled Sojourner free just as the SUV settled into the black water. Only then did Sojourner realize that Adam and the girl had been straddling a long pine log bridging a creek that was high and fast from days of rain, and then, a dam of ice.

Adam kissed Sojourner's cold cheek. "Sekou's on the road," he muttered. "He's pissed . . . I think he may have the .38 with him."

"Oh, God . . . no Adam!"

"It's okay, it's okay, honey. I zipped the leftover product in the bag. Safe."

Sojourner thrashed free, almost losing her balance and plunging into the freezing water. "*Asshole,* I meant my brother! You left him up in the middle of the road? He's high, Adam!" She broke down, sobbing, "High."

"I-I want . . . my mama," the girl whimpered.

"Wh-what's your name?" Sojourner asked. She reached across Adam's body and touched her, gently. "Your real name?"

"Myesha. And . . . uhhh . . ." her strained, high-pitch voice broke, ". . . I want my *mama.*"

Sternly, Adam said, "Honey, take her hand. Slide along the log, get right up on the slope and then up to the road. I know it's dark, slippery. Take it slow."

"You leave the package, ya hear, Adam? Forget the cops, I don't want you on this log . . . it's gonna fall, baby, and I smell the gas from the—"

"Soje please, I'll be all right. You guys go first."

In the muted red light, Sojourner could see him smile. She then took

Myesha's hand. "Hold on to the hem of my coat, all right?" They crawled along the log like inchworms in the dark, leaving Adam to shout encouragement.

Adam couldn't see them anymore after they'd crawled only a few feet. Now it was time to fetch the bag he'd rescued from the wreck. He shimmied toward the other end of the log; the bag, a North Face pack, hung from a branch. He reached into the blackness for the padded nylon strap.

It felt like his sweater sleeve had snagged on a branch. Before he could yank his arm free, something jerked him forward. For a second his brain mused that it was Sekou, playing, taunting.

But when he looked up, he saw two red eyes staring back at him and felt a hot musty breath on his face. Adam's mouth formed a scream, but his throat couldn't make the sound, because Goblin was tearing it out. Quietly.


"Unh-unh, I don't see your brother nowhere," Myesha said, stumbling barefoot through the ice and newly fallen snow. "There go his cap."

Sojourner stooped to pick up Sekou's Kangol driving cap. It was visible in the meager glow from a streetlight maybe a hundred feet down the road.

Both young women whipped around, shuddering when they heard a splash from behind and below. "Adam? *Adam!*"

"*I* ain't goin' back down there!" Myesha mewled, backing away.

Sojourner grit her teeth and tumbled back down the embankment to the fallen tree. It was more familiar now, by touch, and her eyes were adjusted to the dark. "Just look for my brother, Myesha!" Sojourner hollered over her shoulder. Then she called into dark enveloping the other end of this pine bridge. "Adam, damn you, I said leave the fucking bag!" She lurched forward. "Adam?"

His body flopped out of the blackness. It hung like a limp rag over the end of the log, blood drizzling into the swollen creek. Mute with horror, Sojourner backed up the log, crablike. Stopping only when she heard panting behind her. Then a snarl. Low, almost monotoned.

Myesha heard a woman's wail, followed by another splash. Then nothing. She stood petrified on toes she could no longer feel. Blurred vision caught the sight of something large and black, scampering up the embankment. Loping toward her, now. Accelerating. Leaping. Eyes red as hot coals. And she saw her Mama again, in an eternal dream.


"You all right, Chief Miller?" Calvin Beauchamp quizzed. He was leaning into the open passenger-side window of Miller's huge Ford F150 pickup. Miller was sucking shallow breaths; each exhale was laced with Dickel. "And I noticed . . . your right headlight's out. Dangerous in this weather."

"Then I'll write m'self a ticket an' pay the fine," Miller huffed. He'd been squeezing the steering wheel so hard that his knuckles turned from pink to white. He was sweating, despite the cold. "Listen now—this ain't no drug homicide. Ain't never been no drug homicide in this county. Not on my watch!"

Calmly, Beauchamp scanned the passenger compartment. A cell phone was on Miller's lap, still glowing green from a call. "Checking in with Animal Control over that dead dog?"

"Huh? Um, nah, m'wife . . . fifteen years, and she still frets. Look . . . *damn* . . . I'm tired, is all . . . an' it's cold as a brass monkey's nutsack out here."

Beauchamp said, "Chief, perhaps it's time for candor, now. It's no accident that I'm on this case. You see—"

Miller's two-way beeped. "This is Miller, g'head."

*"Dog looked like it was dragged, too. Coroner's investigator says the animal's pretty busted up. But the human . . . I dunno, the C.I.'s on her way down to get some equipment."*

"Say again?"

*"Well . . . uh . . . she says an autopsy might say different, but from what she sees this minute, this fellah here looks like he died of a coronary."*

"O.D.? Using them drugs GBI found?"

*"Naw sir. Like he up and died of fright."*

Miller's jaw tightened for an instant. "I'm headin' back up." He clicked off the handset, grabbed the cell phone, and slid out, leaving the key in the ignition and that sole headlight burning snowflakes as if they were moths. "You comin'?"

"Soon. The DEA's finally checked in. Cooper's speaking to them now."

Agent Cooper arrived as soon as Miller struggled up the rocky slope. "We all set, Cal," Cooper reported. "Give the word, and we'll go up and get 'im."

"No, too many uniforms around. They're as loyal as puppies. Plus this crime scene's . . . bizarre." Beauchamp was staring at that darkened, cracked headlight as he spoke. "Cooper . . . I'm about to do something utterly capricious."

"You, Cal? Naaaaw." But Cooper frowned when Beauchamp crouched and pulled out his penlight.

There was a red smudge along the headlight crack, as if someone gave the glass a hurried wipe. Beauchamp took off his leather glove and ran his finger in the silver pickup's wheel well. It came away caked in sticky, unoxidized blood. Beauchamp knew it by that coppery smell. Cooper dropped down beside his mentor as Beauchamp aimed the narrow penlight-beam at a six-inch stand of brown hair.

"He was wound up about dog tracks," Cooper whispered, "and that awful howling. And we got a dead dog up there laying next to a dead amateur dealer."

"Go get the State Troopers now," Beauchamp said. Softly.


Some officers had positioned their Maglites in the deepening snow as ersatz spotlights on Sekou Belleweather's frozen corpse.

"Don't nobody touch him till the C.I. gets back up here," the chief ordered. "Matter of fact, go down and see what's holding up the GBI folks."

"You be okay alone, Chief?" an officer asked. "That other dog might be—"

"Gw'on! I look helpless to you?"

Once the officers ambled down the hill, the chief rifled Sekou's jacket pockets. Nothing but lint, till he slipped his hands into an inside seam flap and pulled out a slip of blue paper. A check. Payor: Def Sounds Productions. $13,500. "Shit." He shoved it into his trouser pocket, then peeled away toward a grove of tall pines when the officers returned with the coroner's investigator.

The snowfall was intensifying, the darkness, palpable; Miller could hardly see even though the lights around the dog and Sekou were barely one hundred feet away now. He tugged out his cell phone; the lit keys made his face and the snow glow green. "Y'awl had problems before," Miller spoke. "Now y'awl got *trouble*. Cleaning this up gonna cost you extra!" The listener cursed, and Miller shot back, "Yeah and I did try to scare 'em, not kill 'em, so don't blame this clusterfuck on me! Road was icy! Hell anything coulda happened—and that's why you asked me to chase 'em down, huh? Blame it on the ice. Well, somethin' *else* got to 'em, and it weren't no ice."

Whomever Miller had called hung up. Miller spit angrily at the ground then took two steps toward the glow of his officers' flashlights. He halted when he heard the thud of feet in the snow. From behind. He whipped around, chest heaving. Nothing. He grinned, then turned back to the lights, squinting through the blowing flurries.

A shadow moved into his path. Miller stopped, dead.

"*Aw shit . . .*" he gasped.

Two eyes that belonged to Inspector Calvin Beauchamp bored him through the near-white-out. "Wofford Miller Jr., I have a material witness and detainment order issued for you on behalf of the Georgia Attorney General's Office . . ."

"Git the hell outta town!"

". . . in connection with conspiracy to obstruct justice, conspiracy to traffic in controlled substances, and acceptance of bribes by a public official." Beauchamp smiled for the first time that cold night. "Let's get in out of the snow, Chief."

"You crazy! You ghostin' me all this time—waitin' for this here stupid car accident to—"

"Clearly, Chief, this wasn't an accident. Though you seemed to have been in one very recently. Georgia weather's a killer in January, eh? Now, I don't want to cuff you, nor make a scene in front of your people. Agents and state police are on their way to the home of Darius and Solange Johnson, he of the Atlanta Falcons, and she, well, a 'pharmaceutical rep' for some of her husband's teammates, sycophants, and her 'music industry' acquaintances. You had a nice gig, Miller. Couldn't stem the tide of all us 'culud' folks moving out here, so you might as well augment your pension by making money off the *bad* apples among us. Poetic justice?"

Miller backed up. "*Fuck* you . . . y'awl think I'm stupid . . . I know what's goin' on here . . . you tryin' to kick out . . . the last white man in charge . . . in this county! Blame drug murders on me an'—"

Beauchamp's eyes suddenly widened behind his thick lenses. "Miller . . . hold up . . ." Scowling, Miller reached into his anorak's cargo pocket. Beauchamp yelled this time, "*Miller! Hold still!*"

"Shit, I ain't gonna drawn down on you—just grabbin' for my radio. Self-righteous, prick-ass . . ."

Miller felt his heart plummet to his knees. For now, he was hearing a low growl. He turned around, slowly. There . . . a boxy black shadow punctuated by red eyes. And fangs, gray, like the fallen snow in the darkness.

"Aw fuck me . . ." Miller shuddered. "Beauchamp . . . Beauchamp . . . you armed?"

"Never carry, Chief," Beauchamp answered with quivering lips.

The dog—a huge black pit bull terrier—didn't attack. "Why don't he bark?" Miller called.

"Miller . . . keep quiet . . . just back up, slowly."

"Hell widdat. I'm getting my boys ta . . ." Miller's jaw dropped as the animal sat down in front of him, just three feet away. But its snout remained curled in a snarl. "What's this sumbitch want with me?"

The dog didn't even look at Beauchamp when he replied, "You picked up on that, too, eh? Maybe it's blood, the hair, on your F150 . . . you hit that dog up there, didn't you? What—did you booze up, take your eye off the road, while you were chasing this Belleweather and his companions . . . chase them down for your cut?"

"Are you . . . you fucking looney?"

"I guess your friend here is the only witness."

"Huh . . . you hear yourself talkin'?" Miller took a step back; the dog rose up. It drew closer, then sat again. "*Shit!* You listen here, Beauchamp—that was an accident. I was just scarin' 'em . . . just flash my lights, nudge 'em. The Johnsons were pissed off . . . didn't like the product these kids brought . . . kids knew we wouldn't interfere, just stay clear of the state troopers . . . safe for Super Bowl . . . bring down their little Pu-Pu, and Lord knows what from up North . . . let these fancy niggers party . . . jus' long as there's no sales . . . private use . . . no sales . . . no violence. That's my rule. But I didn't kill them kids . . . I swear."

The dog's cropped ears turned like radar: DeKalb and Stone Mountain officers were shouting for the chief. The dog locked eyes with Beauchamp, and instantly, Beauchamp remembered the looks of terror on Sekou, Sojourner, Myesha. Sekou's jacket, ripped. Adam's throat, ripped. Drag marks, laid in the ice hours ago.

"*Oh my God,*" Beauchamp muttered. Disbelief washed over him for what he was about to say to an animal. "You . . . it was you. But why hurt those kids?" It was as if Beauchamp expected a human reply.

And he got one. The dog's ears dropped. Its massive head hung, and Beauchamp heard a solitary whine.

The voices of officers and the sweep of flashlight beams drew nearer. Miller saw his opportunity; he spun around and tried to sprint through the calf-deep snow. He'd run only a few feet before the dog was on his back, tearing out the tendons and muscles at the base of his skull. The officers seemed entranced by the surreal sight, if only for an instant. But they recovered and aimed their weapons. They feared hitting the flaying, screaming Miller, until the dog raised its red-frothed maw. And gave a single bark. An exhortation.

Nine millimeter rounds popped as the dog fell backward with a yelp. Beauchamp rushed forward—to the dog, not Dub Miller. The dog licked Beauchamp's bare wrist, then its tongue didn't move. While one officer called for an EMT, the others stood in shock as Beauchamp strained to lift the heavy animal, blood streaming.

Beauchamp said, voice soft, "Chief Miller's to be cuffed in the ambulance . . . if he's alive."

Dumbfounded cops cursed after Beauchamp as he struggled back to the now taped-off area, where an old shepherd-Irish setter mongrel named Brokebottom lay next to a human named Sekou. Both dead because of greed, rage, lust, apathy, fear, hubris, loss. Beauchamp laid the born killer named Goblin between them.

Agent Cooper jogged up, flanked by two state troopers with their Berettas drawn. He halted by Beauchamp. "Christ Cal . . . wh-what's this all about?"

"Penance," Beauchamp answered. "Doggy style."

# FOR SERVICES RENDERED

*Tracy P. Clark*

Life is funny. Not funny ha-ha, but funny weird. Funny strange. I was itching for work and made the mistake of appealing to the patron saint of private detectives to send me a case. Had I known the petition would send me the one I got, I'd have stayed in bed with the covers pulled over my head.

My undoing was the part of the appeal that went, "It doesn't have to be the crime of the century, just something to get me out of the office." Three hours later, I was locked in to finding old Mavis Conroy's half-blind dog that'd gone missing.

Yep, life was one big yuck-a-rama.

I'm Eve DeHaas. Private detective. I earn my living, such as it is, sticking my nose into other people's business . . . for money. I'm thirty-three years old, black, five years off the police force, and, with one eye closed, I can shoot a rusty penny off a baboon's backside. That last bit's not something I advertise—if I did, some idiot would ask me to prove it—and, well, that just wouldn't be fair to the baboon.

It was a hot Tuesday in July, the clock hands inching their way toward high noon, when Conroy and my grandfather, Edwin Priester, dropped by my office, unannounced, to see me. I was leaning back in my swivel chair, an iced coffee within reach, the morning's paper laid out across my lap—

chillin'—when they walked in just as bold as you please. To my grandfather, the case of the missing pooch was "business" that he was more than happy to toss my way—us being family and all. This alone told me two things. One, my grandfather had way too much time on his hands, and two, he had absolutely no idea what the hell I really did for a living.

I folded the paper, tossed it on my desk, and eased my reading glasses off the bridge of my nose. "You want me to look for a *what*?" I asked, as he sat completely guileless across from me in one of my client chairs. He'd just turned seventy-six, but was as active and as in control of his faculties as he'd ever been. Or so I'd thought. He fixed me with eyes the color of strong coffee.

"Don't tell me you're turning down business," he said.

I looked at him, flabbergasted. "This is what you call business?"

"It's legitimate work," he said. "Looks like you can squeeze it in." He eyed the folded newspaper in front of me. "It's a *case*."

I looked from him to Mavis Conroy. She was all of four feet, thin as a rail, but sourpussed and flinty eyed, which more than compensated for her lack of height. The shortness on top of the flintiness made for a disarming combination. I might have been able to muster up at least some enthusiasm for the whole thing if Mavis Conroy hadn't been the neighborhood curmudgeon who, when I was a child, tottered around the block on a thin wooden cane spearing minute pieces of trash off the sidewalk and butting her stout nose into the affairs of others. The self-professed arbiter of the community's morals, she was the tallyman who measured with great alacrity and diligence the comings and goings, the ebb and flow, and the how much and how oftens of total strangers' lives. She hated kids, wasn't all that wild about adults, and had no qualms about saying so. Playing anywhere near her property line was putting your life at risk. And a ball tossed, batted, thrown, or rolled across her grass was a lost ball, and that was all there was to it.

Caldonia, her canine life partner, a stocky little thing—all blue gums and firecrackers, loyally pitter-pattered behind her mistress, straying away only long enough to terrorize squirrels, nail a mailman new to the route, or poop on somebody's roses. The pair was as popular as urban blight and falling property values.

"Not yet it isn't," I said, taking a sip of coffee before all the ice melted and ruined it.

Old lady Conroy, clutching a faux rhinestone leash and a rubber squeaky toy in the shape of a milkbone, sat quietly, appraising me, making me nervous. Apparently, she'd agreed to let my grandfather turn the screws without any help from her. I smelled a trap. But I was no fool. I ate traps for breakfast.

"Mavis here is the victim of a crime," my grandfather said.

I glowered at Conroy. She glowered back. She'd chased me out of one of her backyard apple trees when I was eleven, and none too gently. I'd climbed up there on a dare, but I doubted she'd remember. I reached for my Rolodex. "I'll give you the number for the police. They'll come out sometime between now . . . and next Christmas. You can fill out a report. You might also want to contact the Animal Control people. I've got that number here, too . . ."

My grandfather cleared his throat and leveled his eyes at me. "Eve, can I see you outside in the hall for half a minute? Excuse us won't you, Mavis?"

I sighed and followed him out into the hall, closing the door behind us.

"Don't you find things?" he asked, crossing his arms across his chest.

The hall was empty except for him and me, but someone was strangling a clarinet down the hall at the music school, and it didn't sound like the instrument was going quietly.

"Sometimes I find *people*," I said, my voice lowered.

"Well, to poor old Mavis in there, Caldonia *is* people."

"Well to poor old me out here in the hall, Caldonia is a *dog*. Grandy, I am not taking this."

"You're too busy?" He asked.

I was not too busy. In fact, I wasn't busy at all. Hence my morning's petition and the iced coffee. But . . .

"I could be busy any time," I said. "And then what would happen? I'd be out looking for a forty-year-old dog with a hearing problem."

"Probably wouldn't take you but half a day," Grandy said. "How many other detectives made the honor roll three years straight?"

I buried my face in my hands.

"*I'll* pay for your time," Grandy said calmly.

I dropped my hands. "Oh, no you won't," I said, shaking my head adamantly. "No sir. I am not taking money from you."

"Then do it as a *favor* to me."

We locked eyes for a time. I was trapped, good and thoroughly. I clinched my eyes shut and grimaced, listening as the valiant clarinet breathed its last.

"If anybody I know finds out about this I'm going to have to move, you know that, right?"

Grandy draped a long arm over my shoulder and squeezed affectionately. "And you know me and my Priester gumbo'll be right along with you so you don't get lonely."

Back inside I faced Conroy again. "I'll see what I can do," I told her. I hoped I sounded pleasant.

"Sounds kind of some-timey to me," Conroy said. "Just so you know, I'm only paying if I get Caldonia back." She stuck her bony chin out defiantly. "Money doesn't grow on the backyard bush."

I looked at Grandy, wanting to scream.

"Now, Mavis," he said, patting her hand. "No granddaughter of mine is gonna do a shoddy job. She'll find Caldonia for you. Don't you worry about *that*."

Conroy didn't look convinced. "Seems to me this is the same Missy I found picking crabapples off my back tree one summer Sunday." She narrowed her eyes at me. "Remember Edwin? I'd like to think a certain somebody has learned a little discipline since then. I'm payin' detective fees, I want one knows a little something and won't be distracted by the first crabapple comes along."

My grandfather grinned and avoided eye contact with me. Good thing too, because I was staring daggers at him. "Now that was more than twenty years ago, Mavis," he said, clearing the chuckle out of his throat. "Don't think Eve's partial to crabapples anymore."

"All right then," she said, "just as long as we agree. I won't be paying for nothin'."

That wasn't exactly how the whole PI thing worked, but I let it go. Explaining things would only keep Conroy in my office longer. I also dispensed with the standard contract. Mavis Conroy's "case" wasn't going on any record I held sway over. I bit back a tantrum and smiled. Then spoke. "Sounds reasonable."

And then she was gone as quickly as a gust of ill wind. I grabbed for the phone and called Animal Control. The sooner I found the dog, the sooner I could give Conroy the big adios. Expedience was all.

"What breed is the dog?" the guy on the phone wanted to know.

I made a contemplative face. "Is mutt a breed?"

"*No,*" he said.

"Well, look, you can't have that many dogs down there that answer to Caldonia," I said. "She's old. She's brownish. She's got beady eyes, and she looks like somebody just ran over her with a pickup truck."

"Where'd you lose her?"

"She disappeared from a yard at 89th and Indiana."

I could hear the sound of paper flipping on the other end. "Nope, no pickups in that area since last week. Does she have a license?"

I narrowed my eyes. "I wouldn't think so."

"We got tons of dogs," he said. "I just can't walk up and down the cages yelling, 'Caldonia' at the top of my lungs. I'll have to have somebody check when they can and maybe get back to you."

"*Maybe* get back to me?"

"Best I can do, lady," he said.

"Yeah, yeah," I said, hanging up. "Put it to music."


Mavis and Grandy were waiting on Mavis's front porch when I drove up around one. Her front lawn, as always, was a thing of beauty. The lush grass, the pampered tulip beds and rose bushes rivaled those found in castle gardens. Here was where the grass grew greener. There were no weeds anywhere, no crabgrass, no nothing that had not been clipped, mowed, sprayed, or sculpted into submission. Even the birds appeared to fly in formation when they passed over Mavis's little plot of Shangri-La.

I climbed the porch stairs and right away Mavis thrust an eight-by-ten glossy of Caldonia at me. The dog stared back at me glassy eyed, a Santa's hat on her nearly bald head and a ring of shiny sleigh bells gripped in her blue gums.

"That was taken two Christmases ago," Mavis informed me. "But she looks just the same . . . she won't be wearing the hat, of course. That's upstairs in my top drawer."

My grandfather, dark and lean, his hair snow white, stood protectively beside Mavis.

"See? You got a visual aid. This won't take you no time at all."

"From your lips to God's ears," I muttered under my breath. I was sure Grandy heard me. There wasn't a thing wrong with his hearing.

"Let me know the minute you find somethin'," Mavis yelled, as I trudged off down the street with the dog's picture rolled up—a little too tightly—in my fist. I eased my sunglasses on to mask my identity and then set off to canvass the neighborhood.

Caldonia and Conroy had lived on this block for more than forty years. I wouldn't think any of the neighbors would take Caldonia even if she were the last canine on a planet where dogs were legal tender. But one can never *assume*.

"We'll be right here waiting if you need some backup," added Grandy.

*God forbid.* I pulled a face and wondered just when my life had shifted so completely from the sublime to the all-out ridiculous.

"Do it as a favor to me, he says," I muttered as I walked. "Looking at me all innocently. Blackmail that's what it is. *Emotional* blackmail. We're going to have a little talk when I get back. Set some ground rules. Some limits. Lost dog. I don't *think* so. Am I not grown? This is it. *This* is the last time he gets me."

I turned back to see Grandy and Mavis Conroy lazily swinging back and forth on the porch swing, enjoying the breeze, waiting for results.

"Just swinging there. Not a care in the world," I muttered. "Why not? I'm the one running around like a fool. Oh, yeah, *serious* ground rules will be set."

To say that Mavis's neighbors did not share her concern for her pet was to overstate the obvious. A couple of folks actually laughed in my face before slamming their doors on it. Still others greeted the news of Caldonia's loss as a cause for national celebration. One man even offered me ten bucks *not* to find her. And by the time I'd made it to his house, I was more than tempted to take the sawbuck.

"I'm sorry to bother you," I began at a house three blocks over. "I'm looking for a dog." I smiled, hoping I looked friendly.

The elderly woman on the other side of the screen door blinked at the photo, then at me, her rheumy eyes taking in every inch of my 5'8" frame. She looked at me hard, as if trying to memorize my face for the police artist. Hanging off her frail frame was a bulky yellow cardigan pulled over a formless blue housedress. Knee-high support hose rolled down just below her baggy knees, which looked like pockets. Her swollen feet were wedged into a pair of overrun slippers.

"Lost your dog, eh?" She cackled, revealing a toothless cavern.

"Sort of. I'm looking as a favor." *A BIG favor.* "Have you seen it?"

"Can't say that I have. That's a real good picture, though. I love Christmastime. Not too many dogs on this block, though, so I'd notice that one right off. Let's see, there's my Buster Lee, Luke Jarrett's Delta, and I heard something barking from the Lockes's yard last couple nights, but I haven't made its acquaintance yet. Nothing at all like that little scrawny thing running around loose, though."

"Where do Mr. Jarrett and the Lockes live?" I asked.

She studied me some more, perhaps trying to make up her mind whether or not I looked like a dog killer with recklessness on my mind. Then she pointed a crooked finger toward a house across the street and one two doors down from hers.

"And if you're planning on stopping by the Lockes, tell them to keep that dog quiet. Folks need sleep."

"Thanks, you've been a big help," I said. I dug into my back pocket and took out one of my business cards and gave it to her. The card had my office number on the front and Mavis's number written on the back. "Please, if you see the dog, you can call either number."

"I sure will," she said. She shot me a warm smile and then closed the door gently behind her. The polite good-bye was a nice change of pace.

I rang the doorbell at the Jarrett house, but got no answer. I pressed my ear to the door but didn't hear anyone stirring inside. I tucked one of my cards into the corner of the mailbox. I'd hit the house again on my way back, if I didn't turn up anything else.

On the Locke's front porch, I stumbled over an oily lawnmower. I'd noticed the thing from the sidewalk, and after I'd wondered why it was sitting there, I'd made a mental note to maneuver around it. Even still I misjudged the machine's width and tumbled off balance into a crummy shovel that smelled like the unpleasant end of a pack mule. Feeling stupid, I self-consciously scanned the street to see if anyone had seen the stumble and then checked the back of my pant leg. I didn't have to be a detective to know that the smear across the back of my right calf was not potting soil—all I needed was a nose.

"Great," I muttered. "Just . . . great."

I hunted around the porch for something to wipe my pants with. A neon orange flyer taped to the back of the mower's mulch bag caught my eye, and I ripped it off and used it. I discarded the soiled flyer advertising B&B Landscaping Services into an empty flowerpot near the door. Feeling quite the martyr, I jabbed the doorbell with a lot more force than needed and sighed long and deep, as if the entire weight of the world was on my put-upon shoulders.

A gangly preteen with heavily lidded eyes that gave him the look of an old hound dog answered the third ring. His nose, short, smooshed, and turned up impishly at the end, resembled that of a Pekinese. His nose and eyes seemed to battle for dominance on his pimply face, and they were offset by a neat little Afro covering his square head. Dressed in baggy jeans, worn low on his hips, and a blue T-shirt that looked three sizes too big for him, the boy posed his lanky arms akimbo and glared at me.

"Yeah?"

I'm looking for Mr. or Mrs. Locke," I said. "Are either one of them at home?"

"Nope," he said, impatiently shifting his weight from one Nike to the other.

"You live here?" I asked.

"Yep."

"Left your lawnmower out," I said.

The boy glanced over my shoulder at the mower. "Yep."

I peeked into the house from the doorway. No dog. A bowl of fruit sat artfully on the coffee table in the living room, which I could see from the screen door—a cornucopia of apples, grapes, oranges, and pears. The place smelled faintly of lemon wax and . . . nut bread? My stomach grumbled, and I was suddenly hungry.

"I'm looking for a dog. Her name's Caldonia. Have you seen a stray wandering around? . . . Maybe while you were walking your dog?"

The boy blinked. "I don't have a dog."

"Your neighbor heard barking. It sounded like it came from your yard."

The boy shook his head no. "Dogs wander around here all the time. Some of 'em bark."

I held up Caldonia's picture. "This dog look familiar?"

The boy flicked a look at the photo with an air of disinterest. "Nope."

"You sure? Take a closer look," I said, testily. I'd just stumbled over a smelly lawnmower. I was in no mood to play.

He glanced insolently at the eight-by-ten. His answer didn't change. Nope is what he said; nope is what he meant.

"Do you know a Mavis Conroy?" I asked. "She lives a few blocks over."

"Nope."

"What's your name?" I asked.

"Why? You the police or something?"

Finally, something with more than one syllable in it. "It'd be nice to know who I'm talking to," I said, patiently.

"I don't know who *I'm* talking to."

The kid had me there. I handed him one of my cards.

"How old are you?" I asked.

"How old are *you*?"

We stared at each other for a time.

"It's been real," I said.

The boy pushed the door shut in my face.

"Aren't kids precious?" I muttered, hitting the Lockes' front walk. "Makes me want to run right out and have one or two of my own. The little dears."

No one else on the block had seen Caldonia, which forced me to repeat the indignity one block north. Time lagged, seeming to pack several years' worth of agony into every sixty seconds. When two preschoolers whizzed past me on Big Wheels and called me "The Doggie Lady," I called it quits. Not for the day, but for good. Grandy would just have to get over it. I stepped up my pace and headed back to Conroy's, stopping abruptly when I heard my name being called from behind.

"Eve!?"

I turned, scanned the sidewalk, and watched as Grandy trotted toward me waving excitedly.

"Good news," he said when he reached me. "Mavis got a call about the dog. Some man found her wandering around. Says he'll bring her back if there's a reward."

"*If* there's a reward? That's extortion!"

"Well, extortion or no extortion," he said. "The woman wants her dog back. I thought you'd appreciate the news."

"What? He just called up and said, 'Hey, I have your dog. How much is she worth to you?'"

"Pretty much. He said for you to come alone to pick her up."

I held up my hands. "Whoa, you *who*?"

"*You you*. And don't get an attitude. Let's walk."

Grandy pulled me gently by the arm toward Conroy's. I had the good sense not to dig my heels in, but it took everything I had not to.

"Grandy," I said. "We need to talk."

"What about?"

"What *about*?"

We stopped in the middle of the sidewalk, and he turned to me. "One little dog to you," he said, loosening his grip. "Mavis Conroy doesn't have much. Caldonia means the world to her."

I stood motionless for a time, then walked off without another word, thoroughly chastened. Grandy following behind.

"Where you headed?" he asked.

"To see a man about a dog."

.  .  .

When we got back to Mavis's she had five crisp ten-dollar bills rolled up in a rubber band waiting for me. My warnings about crackpots and opportunists fell on deaf ears, and I was quickly sent packing, money in my pocket, to bring Caldonia home—my rendezvous with absurdity to take place in front of the toddler swings in Carver Playlot two blocks up.

The tiny lot was deserted when I got there, except for a couple of little girls in braids half absorbed in burying naked Barbie dolls in the sandbox. I smiled benevolently. They stuck their tongues out at me. I blew them both raspberries and thanked God I had no children. I checked my watch and then looked up and down the street for my dog blackmailer. The street was clear. I leaned against the jungle gym to wait. After about five minutes, the little gravediggers exhumed their property and left. About thirty seconds after that, a man, fortyish, wiry and average in height, dressed in a white undershirt and wrinkled chinos entered the playlot schlepping a big television box. He approached me, nervously, checking behind him as he came.

"Here's your dog, lady," he said, plopping the box onto the soft sand in front of me. "There's a reward, right?"

"The dog's owner is offering something for your trouble," I said. "You mind opening that?" I asked pointing to the box. "I'd like to make sure the dog you have is the dog she wants. After that, the money's all yours."

The man didn't move.

"I don't like dogs," he said.

"I don't much care for them either," I said. "But we all gotta do what we all gotta do."

"Me not likin' dogs is why the thing is in the box and not on a leash," he said. "You just give me the money and I'm on my way, then you and the box can have a good time."

Inwardly I groaned, knowing that I'd been jerked around . . . a second time. I glowered at the man as he babbled on defensively. I watched his lips move a mile a minute, having tuned out his actual words. Didn't matter. He was weaving a tall tale I had no time for. The more his lips moved, the angrier I got.

"Eh, you see? My brother is really the one who found the dog," I heard him say when I tuned back in. "But he had to go to work. He asked me to bring it back. Which I didn't mind doing, as long as I didn't have to touch it or have it jump all over me. You know how dogs are." His smile was weak.

"Where'd your brother find him?" I asked, forcing the man to lie to me some more.

"Around . . . the neighborhood," he said.

"Uh-huh. Where *exactly?*"

"You know, around the neighborhood. It's a dog. They wander. So, you know, the money now . . . then the dog when I'm out of here."

I kicked the box hard, nearly toppling it on its side. Nothing moved inside or yelped in protest. I sneered at the man. He began to sweat on his top lip.

"It's asleep," he said. "It nodded off."

I crossed my arms in front of me.

"OK, forget it!" He snapped, snatching up the box, turning and stomping off in a cloud of indignation. I watched him go. Five feet out, he turned on angry heels and walked back, dropping the box down in front of me again.

"Do you want this dog or not?"

"Where'd you get my name?" I asked.

"What difference does that make? Do you want this mangy mutt?"

I walked away without answering.

"Unbelievable," I muttered as I trudged away. "Absolutely *un-be-liev-able.*"

"Hey," he shouted after me. "HEY!"

I kept walking, ignoring him.

"Nutcase," I muttered, shaking my head. "With nothing *but* time . . ."

Suddenly, I heard the fast approach of running feet and stopped, then turned just as the man threw himself at me, his arms outstretched in a frantic grab. Down we went in a hard tackle, scrambling around in the dirt like a couple of rough-housers at recess. He had me pinned on my stomach, his clumsy fingers groping around my pockets for Conroy's reward money.

"That's it," I grunted, gritting my teeth and bucking like a wild horse. "Don't make me hurt you!"

The guy kept groping, "WHERE'S THE MONEY!?"

"Hey, HEY, watch the hands, fool!"

I managed to wiggle my left arm free and shot him a sharp elbow to the Adam's apple, which sent him tumbling back in agony. Dazed, but just for a moment, his discomfort gave me enough time to twist over on my butt and reel off a kick to his midsection. He doubled over, grasping his stomach, but he didn't stay down long. He lunged for me again, this time his hands grabbing for my throat. I clambered out of striking range, crawling away on hands and knees, but he caught me by the ankles and flipped me over like a pancake. He pounced, but missed. As he flew toward me, I kicked up violently, landing a solid kidney punch to his right side. I scampered to my feet, just as his body smacked the ground.

"Now you're going to get it," he threatened, rising up and charging at me like a mad bull. I quickly pulled the money out of my pocket and waved it at him, enticing him.

"This what you want?" I asked. He stopped mid-charge, his greed obviously superseding basic instincts.

"It's yours," I said, tossing the wad to the dirt halfway between us. He went for it, bending over with great effort to pick it up. When he grabbed the bills, I hammered down with both forearms onto the back of his neck and he crumbled over in a sweaty heap. Lights out.

I pried the money wad from his unconscious hand, brushed it clean, and put it back in my pocket. Leaning down, I pulled the man's wallet from his back pocket and took out his driver's license, reading it.

"Leon Pettis?"

I didn't recognize the name, but his address sure registered. I put his license back into its plastic sheath and tossed his wallet down next to him. Pettis began to stir and groan. Just to satisfy my curiosity, I walked over to the box and opened the lid. Inside, there were three thick telephone books and a lot of wadded up newspaper. I sighed and fought back an impulse to give Pettis another good kick to remember me by.

"Keep the money, then," Pettis said when he'd regained his composure. He sat up, holding his side, staring hard at me.

"Shut up," I said.

"I could press charges," he blustered.

"You're missing the big picture here, Leon."

He looked startled that I knew his name.

"For *you* the charge would be assault. I was just defending myself. Tack on the attempted extortion charge and . . . well, I don't think I have to say anymore, do I?"

Leon Pettis blanched and then began to talk a blue streak even without me asking any questions. Pettis had never laid eyes on Caldonia. The son of the old lady I'd spoken to earlier, he had gotten my card from her and had half-baked a pathetic scam for pocket money.

I moseyed back to Mavis's house, feeling truly put out. As I rounded her corner, I caught sight of my grandfather and her still sitting quietly on the porch, this time a pitcher of frosted lemonade on a café table between them. Mavis fanned her face with a wrinkled magazine insert from the morning's paper.

"No need to ask how it went, since you're not towing a dog along behind you," my grandfather said as I pushed open the gate. I told them about Pettis and my roll on the wild side in between sips of lemonade.

"Caldonia will be missing her treat," Conroy said, her face creased with worry. "Banana Surprise. I feed it to her every night. She's probably fretting her poor self to death."

"What's that, Mavis?" Grandy asked. "Banana Surprise?"

I only half listened. I thought I heard the word bananas and something niggled a spark of remembrance in my head, but I quickly lost the recollection.

"It's bananas and anything else sweet I can come up with out of the refrigerator. That's the surprise," she said. "Caldonia swears by it."

I looked out over Mavis's front yard, at the well-tended flowers and the pretty grass. Then turned to watch Mavis as she sat in her chair, her cane propped against its arm.

"Who cuts your grass, Mrs. Conroy?"

"What's that?" she asked.

"Your grass. Who cuts it?"

"A couple of boys from the neighborhood come by every week. Or used to. I have not been at all satisfied with the work they've been doing. I like my grass exactly three-quarter inches. But young people today . . . so little pride in their work." The last remark was addressed to my grandfather, who nodded, apparently agreeing with her.

"What do you mean 'or did'?" I asked.

"I fired them Saturday, I guess it was. I came flat out and told both of them I was not at all satisfied. One of them got downright uppity, too. That's when I fired them. And I refused to pay for the half job they did do."

"What were their names?"

Conroy shook her head. "I don't know. They were tall and skinny with big shoes that clunked when they walked. They came around the beginning of the summer passing out flashy flyers."

I pulled my car up in front of the Lockes' house, got out, walked up to the front door, and rang the bell. The dirty lawnmower was gone, but, this time no one answered the bell. Undeterred, I knocked hard against the front door and waited a polite length of time before peeking, impolitely, through the front picture window. I didn't see anyone milling around beyond the gauzy drapes. I glanced at my watch. It was almost 4:30. I'd have to wait.

"I hate waiting," I muttered. "Really, really hate it."

I headed for the Lockes' backyard, which was hemmed in by a worn chain-link fence. The gate was closed, but not locked.

"That's an invitation if ever I saw one. People really ought to be more careful."

I tipped into the yard, easing the gate closed behind me. The backyard was neat and tidy, the lawn recently mowed and edged. I didn't care what Mavis said, the kid did good work. Someone was growing vegetables in a thin plot of land that ran the length of the yard—green peppers, cauliflower, cabbage. I made a face at the cauliflower.

A huge shade tree with long, expansive branches, towered over a small aluminum tool shed that sat against the back fence. A greasy Weber grill and a tiny redwood picnic table sat on the Lockes' deck, perfect for outdoor cookouts. I did not see Caldonia. I craned an ear, but did not hear any whimpering or scratching, either.

I walked over to the shed. It was padlocked. I doubted the dog would be in there. It was too hot a day and too small a space. But I rapped on it anyway, for thoroughness's sake. Nothing barked back at me. Good news for Caldonia, disappointing news for me. There was nothing to do but wait out front for the Lockes to come home. They surely could get more information from Junior than I could without having to throttle the little rug rat.

I waited it out in my car, head pressed against the headrest, windows rolled down to allow for breezes, scanning the quiet street from behind the anonymity of my sunglasses. Anita Baker sang on the radio. If I'd had a book, a tall iced tea and a fresh Cobb salad, it would have been an OK time.

"Caldonia. Cal-do-nia," I muttered lazily. "Who names a dog Caldonia anyway?" I pictured the dog in my head as I remembered her—spindly legged, practically toothless, hairy in spots, bald in others, antisocial. And then I took stabs at naming her more appropriately as a means of passing the time. "Ugly . . . Homely . . . Surly Sue . . . Gummy Knobs."

The name game ended when a tan LeBaron coasted into the spot in front of the Lockes' bungalow and a petite woman who looked to be in her late forties, hauling a briefcase, tote bag, and shopping sack scrambled out and headed for the front door. I gave her enough time to get in, lock the door behind her, put her bags down, and turn the lights on before I made my way to the doorbell. In this neighborhood, running up on some-one from behind was an invitation to be maced, and I had already had all the excitement I needed for one day.

Mrs. Locke answered the door on the second ring, peering cautiously through the thin crack.

"Yes?" she asked, tentatively.

"Mrs. Locke, my name's Eve DeHaas. I was by earlier. I spoke with your son about a missing dog. He was a big help, and I'd like to ask him a couple more questions, if I could. Would you know where I could find him?"

"Bernard? No I'm afraid not. What did you say your name was?" I held up one of my cards.

"You're a private detective looking for a missing dog?" she asked quizzically.

*Sad but true.* "Family situation," I said. "Do you expect Bernard soon?"

The door opened wider. "He should be here any time. Would you like to come in and wait?"

"Thanks."

"Please, have a seat in the living room. I'll be right with you."

Mrs. Locke looked to be about 5'4", a good four inches shorter than I and pleasantly plump in a motherly kind of way. She smelled faintly of lavender and, in contrast to her son, bore no resemblance to man's best friend. Her warm, brown eyes were keen but kind, and everything about her was precise. From the top of her head to the soles of her feet there was symmetry. She offered me a seat on the sofa and something cool to drink. I politely declined the drink. She placed her bags on the dining room table. Several bunches of bananas stuck out of the top of the one from the grocery.

"Someone sure likes bananas," I said, when Mrs. Locke joined me in the living room.

"My husband," she said. "But I haven't been able to keep them in the house lately. He's eating them almost as fast as I can buy them."

"Mrs. Locke, do you own a dog?"

She blinked. "A dog? No, we've never owned a dog. Why do you ask?"

"Someone mentioned hearing a dog barking from your yard."

"Oh, that. Bernard *was* dog-sitting for someone recently, but the little thing barked too much. I told him he'd have to make other arrangements. Nothing worse than trying to sleep with a dog barking in the night."

I showed Mrs. Locke Caldonia's picture. "Is this the dog?" I asked.

She took the picture in her hands and studied it. "That sure looks like it. She was a real unusual looking dog. This the one you're looking for?"

I nodded yes. "How long has Bernard been in the landscaping business?"

Mrs. Locke was still on Caldonia and answered distractedly. "Oh, three years, I guess. He's doing real well with it, too. What would Bernard be doing with somebody's missing dog?"

I started to answer, but the sound of a key turning in the front lock stopped me. Mrs. Locke and I watched the door as it opened slowly. It was Bernard. He looked much the same as he had earlier in the day, except for the startled look on his face.

I got up from the couch slowly, watching him, hoping he wouldn't run, but knowing he probably would.

"Bernard, where'd you say you got that dog you've been . . . ?"

That's as far as Mrs. Locke got. Bernard bolted out the front door, slamming the screen door shut behind him. I sighed and took off after him.

"Why do they *always* run?"

I hit the front porch just in time to see Bernard bolt across the street. He took off down the block, cutting across lawns and weaving between parked cars. I was a good distance behind him, skirting bonsai bushes, and stumbling over those damned decorative wood chips homeowners have such an affection for, but I managed to keep him in sight. Mrs. Locke's voice shattered the early evening's silence. "BERNARD MORRIS LOCKE, COME BACK HERE!" Such a big voice for a small woman.

Bernard Morris Locke did not come back. He didn't even slow down. All I saw of him were the soles of his shoes, and the back of his T-shirt and baggy jeans as he swerved from parked car to front lawn in a mad dash to who knew where. Surely the heavy shoes he was wearing sooner or later would slow him down?

*Yeah, right.*

I could let him go. He was a kid after all. He'd have to come home eventually. As I ran through alleys after the sprinter from hell, I thought that that probably would be the wisest thing to do, the adult thing. But something in me wanted to run the little dog thief down and stuff his Nikes, laces and all, down his lying little throat. This impulse won out.

Bernard's blue shirt ducked into a narrow gangway that separated two multi-unit apartment buildings just ahead of us. I slowed some and then ran in after him. The gangway was deserted except for a half dozen smelly garbage carts lined up alongside the brick walls and a dirty tabby cat cleaning itself on a first-floor windowsill. I didn't hear the clunky shoes thudding on the asphalt; I didn't see the blue shirt. But I did smell liver and onions cooking somewhere inside.

"Ah, hell!" I spat out, breathing heavily. I'd lost him. "But I couldn't have." I scanned the passageway for stairways leading to basements, or fire escapes leading to accessible rooftops. Just as my eyes followed the line of a fire escape to my right, a flurry of blue pounced down toward me. It was Bernard trying to jump me. He missed, just clipping my left shoulder on his way to the concrete. When he hit, he lay there on the ground for a time, clutching his side, heaving in and out like a steam engine, a sweaty ball of exhausted protoplasm.

"Where's the dog, Bernard?" I asked.

He was breathing so heavily that nothing but wheezy air was coming out. This kid was in terrible shape. I made a mental note to mention it to his mother. I leaned against the side of the building and waited for Bernard's breathing to even out. It took longer than it should have. While I waited, I took a few well-deserved breaths of my own. I was thirty-three, after all. When Bernard was able to stand, I marched him back to his house, keeping a tight grip on his shirt collar, just in case he got his second wind.


I found Caldonia enjoying yet another bowl of Banana Surprise in the basement of one Terrell "Bird" Williams—the other half of B&B Landscaping. Bernard and Bird, apparently, snatched the dog, planning to hold her for ransom. Banana Surprise, a delicacy that Mrs. Conroy had talked about to all and sundry, was the only thing that would keep her quiet, so they ended up feeding it to her all day long, which was why Mrs. Locke was always out of bananas. Bernard and Bird were asking for $5,050—the fifty dollars was what Mavis owed them for services rendered—I'm still trying to figure out what the $5,000 was for.

Bird's mother found a crudely written ransom note in Bird's underwear drawer; he'd misspelled the word *kidnapped*. The note had been waiting for one of the boys to work up enough courage to deliver it to Conroy. Scrawled at the bottom of the note was a postscript warning Conroy not to use exploding money. I blame television.

I returned Caldonia, washed my hands of her and Conroy, and left the fate of the kidnappers in the hands of their respective mothers. The last I'd heard, both were performing lawn maintenance for Mavis free of charge, and they were required not only to bring a lawnmower and clippers, but also a ruler.

Both, I'm told, have become quite expert at preparing Banana Surprise.

# THE PRIDE OF A WOMAN

*Evelyn Coleman*

It's not every day I kill someone. I am a nonviolent being. I walk the path of peace unless, of course, you fuck with me. I tried to explain this to the guy who threw me up against the wall. I said, no, actually I pleaded, "Look, you don't want to jack me up, I don't have any money. I never carry a purse."

He laughed, the ring of ignorance chiming in the air. "Bitch. I don't care if you've got money. It ain't money I'm after."

I squinted in the moonlight. He had a scarf over his mouth like I couldn't recognize those murderous crystal-glass looking eyes again. He held his hand over my mouth, struggling with his belt. I knew he wasn't going to rape me—and live.

He didn't know it though. I could see he thought he was going to kill me when his scarf slid off. His mind focused on the task at hand, as spittle curdled in the corners of his mouth. He thought he was going to get some too. It hadn't entered his pin-sized mind the possibility I wouldn't let him. He snatched my skirt up. Fumbled around like a seeing man searching for his glasses on a bedside table at night. I squeezed my thighs tighter. He stopped fumbling. Switched out a glinting blade with his left hand, held it to my neck, the elbow of his right arm cutting off my wind.

"Move an inch, Bitch, and I will slit your throat."

I did not move. I smiled.

"What the fuck?" He backed up. Moved his elbow to swiftly grab my neck.


Two A.M. is not an unusual time for my phone to ring. And it isn't odd that I answer it either. I'm a detective. Old school, flat-footed from walking a beat, suits that don't fit worth a damn, and a hard-on when I wake up 'cause ain't nobody sleeping with me.

"Detective Medearis here," I said. "What? Who? Yeah, I'm on it. Give me ten."

I rolled out of bed. My Glock dropped to the floor, hit my toe. "Shit." I'm hopping now. Washing the toilet seat in the dark. Throwing water on my face; that's so I can wake up enough to not scald myself in the defective shower. For some reason I cannot remember, right is hot, left is cold.

When I arrive at the scene, the police lights got the joint looking like daylight, yellow tape flapping in the wind. This is a warehouse district. Not much to see or do. I drop down at the spot, since the FOS has told me he ain't seen nothing like it. This guy's been a cop in New fucking York. He's right. This is a new one for me too. Somebody has cut this guy a vagina. Whew, it stinks to high holy heaven.

I stood up, "Got this on tape folks?"

Spenser, the guy I'm grooming to take over the world, said, "Yep, right here, video live."

He's young, new to the force. Doing pretty good, so far haven't seen him lose his lunch once.

Joey, a homophobic idiot, said, "I think he's a heshe?"

"There's no such thing as a heshe, dumbass. They don't like being called that. Damn," Spenser said. "Besides I got his rap here. Last I knew he was your average pervert. Too many prior rapes to count."

"Any witnesses, Cowboy?" I called Spenser Cowboy because he insists on wearing alligator boots with metal tips on the end. We're in Atlanta not Texas.

"Yes, over there, leaning against the fancy ride."

I turned around. Stunning. Absolutely stunning. Long hair, shapely breasts, legs that even a brick house couldn't do justice. A package alright. But what was she doing out here?

"Hello, Miss."

"Hello. I'm sort of in a hurry. So could we rush this?"

I stared at her. She had hardly any makeup on. I should know since both my sisters drove pink cars for years. One year they had a Mary Kay Christmas tree. You don't see this kind of looker every day.

"Miss, Miss . . . what is your name?"

"Dr. H. Winston," she said, holding out her hand.

I shook it. Not half as soft as I'd expect them to be. A little weird feeling. Maybe she's sweating.

"Dr. Winston, could you tell me what you saw? First, though, what were you doing out here?" Cold though, as a chunk of ice.

"I own these buildings. I stopped by to pick up something in that building over there. I came out because I heard someone screaming. I saw a woman running that way." She pointed toward the street lamp at the corner. "I spotted something over there on the ground. I wasn't sure what it was, but I called 911." She shrugged.

I watched her. Not shaken, no trembling fingers, nail polish bright red to match lipstick. Neat as a freaking Five Star General. And something about her looked familiar.

"Have we met before?" I asked her.

"I don't think so," she said, smiling. "I haven't been here that long."

"Did you see what the woman looked like? What she was wearing? Anything?"

"No. It's dark."

"Then how did you know it was a woman? Maybe it was just a man dressed up like a woman to disguise himself?"

"I assumed it was a woman because of the screams. It sounded like a woman, that's all. When I saw her, it looked like a woman too."

"What was she wearing?"

"A dress, skirt and top, not sure which, high heeled shoes, long hair, flowing down her back."

"That sort of fits your description."

"I suppose so."

"Were her heels as tall as yours? They're pretty steep." She had on what my grandmother called hooker shoes, thin tall heels, gravel stuck to the bottom, with ankle straps wrapped around two or three times. Hookers wore them, but so did other women. Today women and hookers are hard to tell apart if you're going just by clothes. Makes it hard on the vice boys. "Are you alright?" I asked, just to see what she'd say.

"Yes, is the man alright?" she asked.

"What makes you think it's a man? Did you walk over there?"

"No, the officer who questioned me told me that it was a man. Is he alright?"

"No. He's dead," I said, watching her face for reaction. None. Nada. I couldn't explain why I didn't like her. She was the most beautiful woman I'd remembered seeing since Pam Grier. It was something about her. I checked her shoes and panty hose for rips or stains. The heels looked worn, but even perfect people can't control poor shoe manufacturers. Spotless, flawless, too perfect, everything in order. Maybe somebody shanked this guy for her. Maybe she paid. Then why stick around and call? Maybe I just know she's out of my league and I don't stand a chance sleeping with her. Uh-huh.

"You come here often this late at night?" I could hear the suspicious quiver in my voice. Damn, she unnerved me.

"No. I'm leaving for a business trip tomorrow. I had important papers I needed to pick up."

"May I see them?"

"Sure," she said, a slight smile on her lips. "If you must." She reached inside the Mercedes, pulled papers from an open briefcase. "I'm not sure what this has to do with what I saw. But why not."

I recognized rows in the briefcase under the thin sheets that covered them. Rows of cards? What makes that indentation? What the hell. I checked the papers. I had no clue what they were, some kind of graphs. "What is this?" I asked her.

"Science. I'm a scientist."

"Oh," I handed them back to her. Didn't bother explaining. I flunked science, and I mean general science. "Do you have a card or something so we can get in touch with you?" Smooth. Real smooth. I grimaced at my own awkwardness.

"I gave the other officer all the information," she said. "May I go now?"

I took a deep breath. Truth was I didn't want her to go. Strong women I couldn't trust intrigued me. "Here's my card. If you think of anything, give me a call."

She turned the card over in her fingers like a practiced magician. I expected my card to disappear.

"I will do that. By the way," she said, opening her car door and climbing in. "Did that woman kill that man in self-defense?"

By the way? Cool, too cool. "That's what we've got to find out."

She caressed the steering wheel, her car door slightly open. Card still balanced expertly between her delicate fingers. She glanced at the card, looked up at me. "Detective Medearis? Are you Hispanic?"

My knees quivered. Her eyes were like black pearls. Her skin Tootsie-Roll dark. My favorite candy—had two in my pocket. "Nope. African-American, Black, Negro, Colored are only a few of the names I've been called." You forgot a name—asshole.

"Good. I like my own kind," she said smiling. She turned the key in the ignition. "Call me," she said in a seductive whisper.

I might as well have screwed her right there. That's how hard I was, sweat dripping, knees weak, felt like I might have actually wet my underwear too. Damn, I wouldn't call her. She was trouble. I was single now and liked it that way. Maybe not the waking up alone part, but everything else worked in my favor. Women, can't live with 'em; catch hell if you marry 'em.

"Detective Medearis, did you hear me?"

"Sorry. No, Spenser, what did you say?" I kept looking at the fumes from the Mercedes pipes. A diesel. You hardly saw a woman driving a Mercedes diesel anymore.

"We have a problem."

"Other than a dead man with a hole cut in his body shaped like a vagina?"

"Yep. There's another dead man in the Dumpster."

"What? You got to be kidding me."

"Nope. Come see."

I followed him to the Dumpster. The guys had left the top open. Everybody was working the scene by now. ID folk snapping photos the old-fashioned way. I stared into the Dumpster. I could see the drug paraphernalia. This was bad. Real bad. I knew the body. Or, let's say I knew who the man was, and I also knew heat would be on this like an iron poke at a cow branding. Shit, shit, shit. And I thought I was going on vacation.

"Get me the TOD on both these guys. Make sure nobody fucks up the evidence either. This will be tight." I shook my head. When somebody whacks the son of a prominent doctor in town, even if he is low-life-scum-of-the-earth-drug dealer, everybody is under the gun.

I walked back to my snazzy new sports car. Yeah, in my dreams, for now the Green Hawk would do, a 1999 Chevy issue. I hated this chubby car. I was just happy I didn't have to hop in it when Miss Sleek Mercedes Benz pulled off. I still needed to check out her story. Or, did I just want to find a reason to give her a call?

The next day I had to call. It seems that the two guys died within minutes of each other. And according to the ME some time lapsed maybe between the time Dr. Winston should have seen at least one of them and the time she phoned the police.

Maybe she also saw something she forgot. Like how handsome I was. Funny. *Handsome* wasn't one of the names I'd been called lately. Women said I was cute. You have to work hard to get the pussy if you're just cute. Handsome though, legs pop wide open for you. Check out men who have sexual harassment suits against them. Guaranteed, ugly ass men mostly.

Look at Spenser, young hotshot cop, hair thick as a Persian rug. Women at the precinct got drool coming out of their mouths and maybe other places when he walks by. It's never been like that for me. When it came to women, I didn't have it. You know that lockbox Gore was talking about. Well the women I know use that box. All except my ex-wife—for a hot minute, she let me have a key. Then just ripped it back out of my hands.

The captain yelled, "Detective Medearis, I need to see you in my office."

I looked around. Hell, I am not even five steps away from her office. I walked inside. "Do you have to scream at me like that? Damn, I thought that was over two years ago."

"Funny. Did you read this?"

I picked up the newspaper. Freddie Lowenstein Jr. was a yada, yada, MIT graduate. Yada, yada, yada. "Okay, so they forgot he graduated from three DWI schools, a drug program, and still he was smart enough to make drug salesman of the year."

"You should go on TV. Get your own comedy show like that Bernie Mac or Cedric the Entertainer. Now what do you have on Freddie Lowenstein's case? Get something before I got folk downtown on my butt."

"I used to be on it," I said, smiling.

"Can you get serious and stay focused? Oh wait; you can't do that. That's why you're *not* on my butt anymore. Now cut it out."

Carol Jordan was my wife, before she became my captain. She was way too bossy even then. I loved her though. I mean I dug this woman. But she dropped me like a pot of hot grits the minute somebody told her I was sleeping around. You would think a smart detective would have at least gotten the evidence before firing my ass. But she "couldn't handle the uncertainty of my life." What uncertainty. Hell, we did the same exact job. I have no idea why women always think they are more trustworthy than men. All you have to do is check the record, and you see it ain't so.

"Are you going to say something, or stand their gawking at me Medearis?"

I sighed; the kind of sigh only a man who knows he's lost the best thing he's ever had can sigh. "Okay. Somebody did Lowenstein and this Vagina guy. Did he make the paper too? Never mind. The ME isn't finished, but it looks like they were done around the same time, maybe not together but one shortly after the other. The dude with the vagina was killed last. We have a witness who heard a woman screaming; then saw the woman running away from the scene. Looks like he pissed the killer off."

"According to your report, your witness didn't really see much. What'd she say about the woman running away?"

"It's there."

"Come on. That's it? How does she even know it was a woman if she didn't see any more than you wrote?"

"Hey, I can question her again if you want me to?"

"It's okay. I sent Spenser over, he seems to have a way with women."

I took a deep breath. Radar. Nobody can convince me women don't have some kind of radar shit working for them. How does she know I had eyed this woman? Now I don't stand a chance. Spenser. Shit.

At the end of the day I had nothing. The Vagina was out of jail on bond for raping some young girl, twelve freaking years old. Nobody gave a shit that he was dead. At least, I sure didn't. I wanted to beat the dog crap out of any fool who messed with a young girl. Man, that freaked me. Somebody should have cut that dick off long ago. As for the big shot, somehow he died of natural causes. I suppose he climbed his ass in the Dumpster to die. Yeah right. That's what I had.

"Hey, yo, Detective Medearis, I got something for you."

I stared at him. "You've got lipstick on your cheek. Where've you been Cowboy?"

"I went to see Hannah. She remembered something else."

"Who the hell is Hannah, Spenser?"

"Our witness from Vagina."

"On a first-name basis? Is that Hannah's lipstick too?" I asked. If a Black man could turn green I'd have been the Incredible Hulk about then.

"What can I say, I got the moves with the ladies," he said, dusting his lapel.

"You know you can get your ass moved out of the department fooling with a witness, Spenser."

"I'm kidding, Detective, chill out. That girl, Marci at the reception desk asked me for a birthday kiss. It's her birthday," he said raising his eyes.

"You've got a lot to learn, son," I said. I knew for a fact it wasn't Marci's birthday unless it came twice a year. "Get on with it. What did Hannah tell you?"

"She said she saw the woman stop under the street lamp and look back. She thinks the woman might have seen her, and now she's a little scared if we name her as a witness."

I couldn't believe this shit. That woman scared. Please. "That's it? That's what you got?"

"That's not it, but she made me promise that I would tell you this before I told you what she saw. And that you'd promise you won't leak her name to the press."

"And you agreed? What? You think we're a PR firm?"

"No sir. I just think we should protect our witnesses. Specially the beautiful ones."

"Oh, I get it. Let the ugly women die, just save the pretty ones." I shook my head. "What did she see?"

"She said she saw the woman stick something in her purse while she was standing under the light."

"Something like what?"

"She doesn't know."

"Okay, your news is that she saw the woman stop under the light and put something in a purse, and you think that will help us. What about why she waited before calling the police? You ask her that?"

He stood there for a minute biting his lower lip.

"Did you even check out Hannah's story?" I asked. "Does she own the buildings? Did anybody see her there before?"

"I checked that this morning before I left. She owns six warehouses in that area. One of them she visits frequently. She's stinking rich. She went to MIT. She used to be a professor. Moved here a while back, then left, then came back. She's been working at the CDC for two years. She owns a bunch of other property throughout the city. She's never been married. Has no boyfriends that I could find. She's beautiful, sexy, and smart, and when this is over I think I'm going to marry her."

He said this with a shit grin on his face. "You're joking right?" I said, praying he was. What if I decided to marry her? She would be on my Halle Berry, J'Lo list of women I would marry if they would give me the time, day or night.

"Of course I'm kidding. I have a girlfriend. I love her."

Was he for real? The phone rang. I answered it. "Detective Medearis here."

"Detective, could you come over here please, quickly. I think someone is following me."

Like a schoolboy I wanted to say, so Hannah, why don't you call Spenser? Instead I answered like the Mr. Cool I know I can be if I try, "I'll get a black and white over right away."

"No, please. I'd rather it was you."

"I'm off duty, Dr. Winston," and playing hard to get.

"I need to talk to you. Honest," she said.

I could hear a new element in her voice. One that I hadn't heard before. She was trying to seduce me. Soften me up. But I couldn't shake the feeling I'd seen her before. Cops don't forget faces. It can be a matter of life and death. I had to be wrong though. I couldn't imagine I could forget where I saw a woman who looked like that. I tried to relax my shoulders. Think. Did I arrest her before?

"Give me thirty minutes to an hour," I said. "If you get too spooked before I get there, just call 911, okay."

"Make sure she doesn't have any priors," I said to Spenser. "I know this woman from somewhere. And there had to be a reason she didn't call the police right away."

"Maybe she didn't come out when she first heard the screams? Maybe the woman she saw screaming just happened along, saw the body, freaked, and ran away."

"Yeah, and maybe someday the tooth fairy is going to pay me all the damn money he owes me. Something isn't right about this story. Think about it. She described a woman who fits her own description. Why? If someone else happened to have seen her they would be giving us her description, but we couldn't tell it from the running away woman. I know I'm missing something here. I just don't know what it is."

I called the ME's office. "You got anything more on Vagina or Lowenstein?"

I repeated what he'd said as I wrote it on a pad. That way if I said it wrong he'd correct me. "He ejaculated before it was cut off, probably on his body. Hmm. And he was alive when it was removed. Now that's interesting too. What about the Dumpster? Drugs. What type drugs? Okay, he shot up heroin. Fresh needle mark. Is that what killed him? No, no heroin overdose. Just must have had it with him. Getting ready to shoot up. The fool gets in the Dumpster to shoot up and just dies? Traces of something on his clothes, but you don't know what it is. Sending it away. Hmm. But you think the blade belonged to Vagina? Okay. Thanks."

"No priors," Spenser said. "She's clean as a whistle. Not even a traffic ticket."

"Spenser, when you went to see Hannah, did you notice anything unusual about her?"

"That she is beautiful."

"Acknowledged. Anything else? She make you uneasy at all?"

"Me and a million other guys probably."

"I don't mean that. I mean something else."

"Nope."

"What about her house?"

"Nothing."

"What kind of scientist is she at the CDC?"

"Not sure. Something about nuclear medicine."

"Nuclear medicine. I pictured her in my mind. Man was that easy. I could see every detail, her long hair, her red lipstick, red nail polish, ankle shoes—ankle shoes. And, something about her so familiar.

I picked up the phone, dialed the ME again. "Listen, can you check the body one more time for me, check the ding-a-ling too."

I hung up. Dialed again. "CDC, may I speak to somebody in personnel?" I talked to them. Two years, she'd been working there two years. She came from MIT there. MIT. Interesting. I remember arresting an MIT professor before. Nah. Couldn't be.

I called Dr. Lowenstein's office. No one answered. "What kind of doctor is Lowenstein?" I asked Spenser. "You know?"

"No, just that he's some big shot."

I looked up Lowenstein in the yellow pages. Just as I thought.

"Come with me, Spenser," I said. "I'll teach you what a real detective does." I drove to the warehouses. Walked from where Dr. Hannah Winston said she stood after running out of the warehouse. I had Spenser walk to the street lamp and pretend to have a purse. I couldn't make out what he was doing one way or the other.


We drove over to see Dr. Hannah Winston.

"Hello Dr. Winston," I said.

"Thank God, you're here," she said. "I think a man followed me today."

"A man this time? Not a woman?" I said, scanning her house.

"No. But I'm sure whoever it was followed me."

"Is that the briefcase you had at the warehouse that night?" I asked.

She looked over at a large inlaid oriental desk. The soft Italian leather briefcase was closed. I could see you needed a key to open it.

"Weird how you had your briefcase open in the car that night." I said.

"What do you mean?" she asked.

"I've been trying to figure out why would a woman come out in the middle of the night to get papers for a business meeting she had to leave for and yet she doesn't leave? Women plan things better than that. Don't they, Dr. Winston?"

"What are you getting at? I was going out of town, but my plans changed. Women can also change their minds."

"You had money in your briefcase that night. Didn't you?"

She stuttered. For the first time I spotted sweat on her upper lip. "No, I didn't. I told you I came to pick up papers."

"I saw the money. It didn't register immediately. I couldn't remember what made those kinds of impressions. Then I remembered you flicking my business card between your fingers. I've only seen two kinds of people handle cards that way, magicians and you know who else, don't you, Dr. Winston? And that's how it all came together."

My cell phone rang. "Uh-huh. Yep. Just like I thought. Thanks. You're sure about that?"

"Dr. Winston, could I see your shoes from the other night?"

"My shoes?"

"Yes, your shoes. Am I not speaking clearly?"

"I don't have them."

I shook my head. "You don't have them. Why is that?"

"I messed up my heels running in that gravel that night, so I threw them away."

"Granted you messed them up alright. Let me guess, skin and bone fragments right?"

She didn't move, just stared at Spenser, as if her doe eyes could get him to rescue her.

"You know what gave you away? You don't really think like a woman. First off, a woman would have tried to put some clarity on what she'd seen. Women observe so much in the dark. Leave a pair of earrings in someone's car, and a woman will find them in no time flat. They can look at pieces and put the puzzle together. Men." I shook my head. "Somehow we need more pieces, and they need to be in some order before we can really get the picture. Take my wife, the police captain, okay, ex-wife, beautiful Black, sexy woman, but power and brains to knock your joans off. She could have solved this the first night.

"Me, it took me a few days. First off, she would have remembered where she'd seen you before. 1991. Right? Card sharking at a poker game in what—a warehouse. I busted you. Right. You sailed out of that on probation, first offense. Even then I couldn't figure out what a smart person like you, a college professor, was doing sharking cards. Money. You needed big money. For the operation. Am I hot?

"The way I figure it, Lowenstein's druggy son, who was in your class at MIT, figured out who you were—his old school buddy—and was blackmailing you since the CDC hired you as a gorgeous woman. Right. You killed the sucker, nuclear medicine-wise. And since it could only be proven he died of natural causes, who would care if he climbed his ass into a Dumpster to take a hit. You had on gloves. They left a powdered residue. When I shook your hand that night they felt chalky. I suspect latex, the kind that have powder to keep bad skin reactions down, huh. Am I right so far?

"The Vagina. That's where you really fucked up, so to speak. I think he caught you dumping the body. And being the low-life ignorant rapist he was, he thought he'd snatch a little tang from a beautiful woman. Cold? Hot? Hot I bet.

"One problem. Lowenstein is a plastic surgeon, so you still got your man thing on. When homeboy realized that, he probably wanted to beat the living shit out of you. But you were too fast. You beat his dick off with your spiked shoes, then cut him the Vagina you wished you had, and watched him die. You left the razor behind since it was his anyway. No fingerprints, thanks to your latex gloves. You cleaned your shoes off, knowing we'd have no reason to test them, since you were the witness and not the woman anyone could have spotted over the body. Pretty smart. Explains the time element we've been struggling with. See we know you didn't call the police right away. Hot?

"To cover it all up and send us on another path, you saw the fictitious woman. Then you realized somebody might try to identify the marks on the withered old thing and try to figure out what did it. So you invented the woman-putting-something-in-her-purse sighting. Nice touch; to throw us off further, by the way, you were being followed by the unknown murderer. Am I right so far?"

Hannah was crying. "Give her a kiss and take her away—in handcuffs, Cowboy."

"I'm not kissing nobody but my girlfriend ever again," Spenser said.


Later Spenser asked me, "I don't get it. How did you know because of the cut out Vagina?"

"You've got to think like a woman. If a man tries to rape you, what's he using? His hard-ass dick. Once you beat the shit out of that, you're pretty much done if you're a woman. See, it's the Vagina you want to protect; you ain't about to give this same low-life piece of shit the most sacred part of your body—the Vagina. No way. You save that for the man who deserves it."

"Captain, can I see you?" I asked, pushing my bouquet of roses ahead of me in the door. God knows I want this woman back.

# THE BLIND ALLEY

*Grace F. Edwards*

## PROLOGUE

*Harlem—1954*

The mist had already emptied the streets when Rhino stepped off the bus, and he was alone on the corner of 8th Avenue and 148th Street. He narrowed his eyes behind his thick lenses and strained to see how long it took before the outline of the vehicle dissolved, not so much into the hot August darkness as into the well of his own defective vision.

The bus lumbered uptown and out of sight, yet he lingered, caught now by the on-off neon flash from the Peacock Bar and Grill. He stared at the brightly lit bird above the entrance and watched the huge neon plume shower a brilliant array of light across the sidewalk. Except now, one of the tail feathers in the bird's plume lit out of sequence, stayed brighter longer, and seemed to turn off when it felt like it.

The bar appeared to be crowded, full of weekend noise, but he wanted to rush in anyway and demand to know what was happening with the bird's feathers. He did not move. Instead, he stared harder, expecting at any minute to see a familiar name flash on the sign and light up the corner in some strange orange-and-yellow warning.

He spun around and glanced quickly over his shoulder. Still alone. Sound had come only from the wet tires of a bus headed downtown, its high beams pushing aside the wavery shadows as it passed.

Finally, he moved across the slick pavement and made his way into number 1048, a small, nondescript four-story tenement that seven families called home. He paused in the faded marble lobby and looked around. Finally, he was also home.

The door leading to the rear courtyard was ajar, and familiar sounds drifted toward him, muted by the rainwater trickling through the drainpipe. They were blues notes, deliberate and disjointed, as if someone were practicing. The pause between the beat was filled with echoes of laughter.

*. . . So. The Alley's still goin' strong. How 'bout that . . .*

He sat on the steps, listening, with his small suitcase resting on his knees.

*Maybe. Maybe she's there . . .*

In one motion, he rose to his feet, unfolding his gaunt frame and pushing the shabby suitcase into the recess under the stairs.

*. . . Fuckin' bitch. If it wasn't for her, none a this wouldna happened. None a this . . .*

He moved from habit, like a cat, down the narrow steps and into the surrounding darkness toward the music, his pink fingers fanning against the rain-slick walls. In the courtyard, the rain hung like a dark curtain, obscuring the passageway leading to the Alley, but he did not pause.

*Two years is damn long to be away, but I'm back now, not stayin' but gotta let these sombitches know what they done was wrong. And somebody—Matthew, Cryus, and specially that bitch, Rose—somebody gonna make it right.*

# APARTMENT TWO

*Matthew Paige*

Matthew Paige, sax player and lead man in the tight combo that kept the Blind Alley jammed on the weekends, hadn't intended to fall asleep on the sofa, but the heat had drawn away what little energy he had. The curtains hung limp in the living room window, and what breeze there was, wafted in hot and steamy. He had closed his eyes, intending to just take five, then rise again refreshed enough to do something useful around the apartment.

Instead, he had fallen asleep and dreamed he was being stabbed in the throat. He saw the knife, gripped in a disembodied hand. It descended and severed his windpipe and his cords and splattered blood over the sofa where he lay. He wanted to scream out to his wife, but sound was frozen somewhere in his chest. He was going to die.

"Matt!" Sandra leaned over the sofa, shaking him. "Matt. Wake up. What in the world is on your mind to make you grunt and groan like that?"

He woke, bathed in the sweat of fright and August heat. The television was still on, just as he had left it, still tuned to the McCarthy hearings. Sandra clicked the set off. "Why were you looking at television anyway, with your head hurting the way it is?"

Matthew rubbed his eyes, trying to remember. The room was so hot he could barely breathe. Earlier, he had taken off his shirt and pants. Now he looked at his arms and legs, red brown, tight muscled, and damp with sweat. He brushed his hands to his forehead.

"I don't know, I—"

Sandra handed him a B.C. headache powder and a glass of lemonade. "McCarthy." She was careful to speak low. "Who needs to watch all that noise on TV? That communism stuff ain't none of black folks' business."

Matthew frowned. "Try tellin' that to Paul Robeson when he was ambushed at that rally upstate. Even the cops joined in."

He could have gone on, but it was too hot to argue. How long had he slept? Better to drain the glass before the ice melted. The tart sweet taste on his tongue nearly loosened the constriction in his temples, but he knew that his pain, part heat but mostly champagne hangover, would take its time before subsiding, B.C. or no B.C.

And the nightmare didn't help.

He concentrated on the beat in his head, brought on by the all-night birthday party for Big Buster, the number banker, that had had the Blind Alley Social Club in the basement jammed and the drinks flowing like the Hudson.

Matthew dimly remembered playing the closing number, notes coming so cool and loose that the crowd stayed on its feet and the walls vibrated until 7 A.M. Now, after too little sleep, his head felt hollow and like someone was tapping a large brick against it.

He remembered turning off the window fan in order to hear the television, but found that the whir of the fan held more substance than the droning of the pinched-faced politicians on the screen. Then he must have fallen asleep. And dreamt the dream, which he could not now recall.

"I must be gettin' old, Sandy. How come I can't even remember a dream, a bad dream. I hope it didn't have any good digits in it. We could use some extra change."

"Forget the numbers, Matthew. How are you gonna play again tonight? You're in terrible shape."

Matthew placed the glass on the table and looked at her. "Sandy, I haven't missed a weekend since the Alley opened, and I don't intend to miss tonight. Blue hired me to entertain, and that's just what I'm gonna do. Maybe I'll sit back and let Maxie or Gee take the lead, but I'll definitely be there."

He was looking at the saxophone on the stand near the piano as if it were one more person in the room.

Sandra followed his gaze and decided that death was the only thing that would stop him and even after, he would probably ease back and sit in just to keep the boys on key.

"Have it your way," she sighed, "but this burnin' the candle at both ends has got to stop sometime. You're thirty-five years old. You have a day job. You have a wife and son to think about." She picked up the empty pitcher and left him to wrestle with his hangover.

The room was mercifully quiet, and Matthew lay on his back, this time intending to study the cracks in the ceiling.

When he woke again, the bright sunlight had given way to purpling shadows, and a cooler breeze blew though the open window.

In the kitchen, he read the note propped against the covered dinner plate.

"Theo needs new sneakers. We'll be back by 8."

Matthew crumpled the paper. He had promised to take his son shopping and cursed himself for allowing a Saturday afternoon to slip by the way it had.

He moved through the empty rooms toward the bathroom, followed by the thread of dream he tried hard to remember.

Even the icy shower was not enough to recall the wraith-like image that floated just on the other side of memory.

. . . *Dream probably didn't mean nuthin' except to tell me that champagne is too rich for my blood. Need to stick to my scotch, tasty, tried, and true.*

He turned up the tiny radio on the bathroom hamper and caught the tail end of an Illinois Jacquet solo. The notes, smooth and mellow, managed to dislodge some of the hard knots inside his head.

Later, though Sandra and Theo had not yet returned, he dressed, picked up his horn, and headed downstairs. He knew that most of his guys were already in the Alley rehearsing, getting a jump on the evening.

But he needed to walk around the block, get some fresh air in his lungs before heading there.

The Blind Alley Social and Athletic Club, situated at the end of a dark corridor in the basement of Matthew's building, usually opened around nine, was crowded by midnight, and jammed to the walls around 3 A.M. when the regular bars closed.

As long as Matthew had been playing there, the only athletics he had witnessed occurred when Big Blue, the owner, had to bounce an occasional troublemaker, the "athletic" part was dropped when Blue acquired his .38 special and erected a sign that advised:

WELCOME TO THE BLIND ALLEY CHECK ALL HATS, COATS ARTILLERY AND ATTITUDES AT THE DOOR

And since that time, had maintained order on his reputation alone.

Most folks were regulars who drifted in after the Peacock Bar across 8th Avenue closed for the night. Matthew wondered what would happen if the Alley were ever raided. There was, as far as he knew, only one entrance and the thought made him nervous when he allowed himself to think about it, which was not too often.

He stood on the corner watching the strollers. The air was heavy, and he felt a small scatter of raindrops, yet 8th Avenue was a parade of Saturday night movie, dance, and flashing party colors. People were going places. Others were rushing home from hairdressers, cleaners, and barbershops to prepare to join them.

He watched the crowd in the bar and knew that in a few hours, the Alley would be jammed also, despite the rain. He returned to the building, moved through the lobby, and paused at the rear door. As usual, there was no light leading down the stairs to the courtyard, and, as usual, he counted the steps in the dark.

Midway through the corridor, a quick brush of movement behind him—too loud for a cat or the dry scratching of a rat—stopped him in his tracks. *Who's that?*

He turned his back toward the mouth of the corridor, moving fast, not wanting to be caught where he had no room to maneuver. And not wanting to think of Sandra's warnings! Matthew, you make good money at the Post Office. Nine to five. Five days a week. Why hang out in an after-hours spot?

And he: assuring her that the Blind Alley was safe (compared to some of those joints where folks had to cut a way in and shoot a way out, but he never mentioned those clubs). Now here he was, moving down a dark corridor with neither a gun nor knife. Just his saxophone, for which he would rather die than use to defend himself.

He held the case under his arm and peered out, scanning the dark courtyard. The rain was hard now, drumming a staccato beat atop the garbage cans.

Nuthin' . . . Just this hangover still hangin' on. Got me jumpin' at nuthin'.

He tuned again and moved toward the club.

The place was large and dark, and the essence of last night's cigarette smoke and whisky clotted the air, but Jimmy was there, leaning over the piano, concentrating hard, and Maxie stood to the side, picking up Jimmy's rhythm on the bass. The tables circling the dance area reflected the shimmer of small candles set in tin saucers. And when Blue called out from behind the bar "Man, everybody's here. Why you took so long?" Matthew smiled, ready for the night, ready to believe that the sound in the corridor had been a figment of his imagination, just like the dream that had earlier wakened him in a cold sweat.

At midnight, the Alley was jammed.

From the stage, Matthew peered out onto the crowd, waved to the dancers on the floor nearest him, then focused on the band again.

Jimmy, still hunched over the piano, ended his solo, and Maxie eased in. Matthew listened to the descending chromatic bassline and raised his horn, waiting to pick up the cue. He was feeling good, and the horn would deliver the feeling to the crowd.

But in the split-second pause between Maxie's note and his own, he heard a sudden slam that carried above the shading of the music and low buzz of the patrons. Someone had fallen over or knocked over a chair and did not bother to pick it up.

Several persons turned to look. The dancers stopped dancing. Small talk spun away into flat silence.

Blue, pouring a drink at the bar, paused and squinted toward the door. "Well ain't this some shit."

On the bandstand, Matthew tried to look beyond the narrow glare of the spotlight but caught only a vague movement. Then the figure came into focus as it approached the bar. "Well, I'll be damned," Matthew whispered.

He signaled the bassist to keep the beat, although the dancers appeared frozen in position. Then he stepped off the small stage.

"Well, well. Didn't expect to see you back so soon, Rhino."

The man turned to scrutinize Matthew, then stared out at the crowded floor, his thick glasses already fogged with sweat.

"Things happen, Matthew. Things happen, and I'm out. I guess they figured no point holdin' me for getting rid of a cat like Tommy. I probably did 'em a favor."

Matthew felt his throat tighten and remnants of the dream came back. "Tommy was my friend, Rhino."

Rhino shrugged, his face pale and expressionless in the dim light. He fumbled in his pocket and threw a dirty, crumpled bill on the counter. "Gordon's, straight up."

Blue moved to the center of the bar, leaned against the back wall, and folded his arms across his chest. "Not in here. Not tonight. Not never . . ."

The music had stopped completely now, and Blue's voice, hoarse with anger, carried through the crowded room. "Not never, motha-fucka. Tommy was my ace."

A scatter of murmurs rose from the dancers. "You tell 'im, Blue."

"That's right. How he blow Tommy away and come back actin' like nuthin' happened."

Rhino turned from the bar and faced into the darkness of the dance floor, his eyes darting like pinpoints behind his thick lenses. Then he turned again and placed his hands on the bar. Matthew stared at the thin, colorless fingers and the lost dream came into focus. He saw the knife coming down again.

"So that's the way it's gonna be?" Rhino asked no one in particular, scanning the crowd and the bandstand.

"That's the way it's gonna be 'cause that's the way it is," Blue said. He stepped forward to lean on the bar and cross his arms. The overhead light accented the frown on his dark face.

Rhino picked up the bill from the counter and balled it in his fist. "Well. We gonna see about that. Tommy got what was comin', and I still got some shit to finish."

"Well you ain't hardly finishin' it in here," Blue said, reaching under the counter. "Git the fuck on out."

Matthew stepped back out of range, as Blue came up with his .38 and took aim.

The dancers came to life and scattered, piling into the tiny rest room and the coat check room. The musicians stashed their instruments and ran for the narrow kitchen, nearly trampling the cook.

"See what I mean, Rhino. Your pasty pink ass ain't back on the scene a hot second and already your shit done hit the fan." Blue then rested the gun loosely in the crook of his arm and motioned toward the door again. "So like I said, take your fuckin' face on out the place."

Rhino backed away from the bar, his ears ringing from the nervous laughter. The crowd had emerged again now that Blue had everything under control.

At the door, Rhino turned and stared hard, causing a few of the patrons to shift uneasily and melt back into the shadows. Would he recognize them another day? Catch them unawares?

Matthew, against his will, had edged through the crowd, drawn by the expression on Rhino's face. Behind the thick lenses, Matthew read the history, and for a moment, something inside him paused. He remembered the day the boy's fifteen-year-old mother had stared at the colorless infant and then walked away. Didn't linger long enough to even give him a name. Devil, was all she had said. And the Sunday when Sister Marthie had baptised him in her storefront Temple of the Heavenly Light, because the priest had not seen a father's name on the birth certificate and had refused.

*So we all chipped in for the baptism and for the party afterward. We even bought his outfit. But after that, it was one thing, then another. School lasted just long enough for him to find his way out the door and outrun the other names. Grandma's face stayed in a puff. Lids half-mast from all the cryin'. One thing after another. Damn!*

Matthew was never quite certain when the rage crawled inside the boy, but he and everyone else knew when it began to creep out.

He remained silent now as Rhino opened his hand and let the crumpled bill fall to the floor. "Here you go, Blue. You gonna need this before I do . . ."

Then he turned in the silence and disappeared through the door held open for him.

Matthew followed through the corridor to overtake him, to ask just what he intended by the remark.

*If he plannin' to toast the joint, least be man enough to say so. So we could be on the lookout and—*

But Rhino had already approached the stairs and, as Matthew watched, seemed to float through the dark, like a wraith, as if the steps did not exist for him.

Matthew reacted as if a sudden cold front had moved in, displacing the weight of the August heat. He returned to the bar where Blue had a double Cutty Sark waiting.

"What you think, Matt?" Blue said. He filled another glass for himself. He had not had to pull the piece in quite a while, and Rhino's sudden appearance had caused his hands to shake, bad news for a bartender.

Matthew sipped his drink through a thin straw to avoid aggravating his sore chops. He listened to the pianist glide through an Errol Garner riff, trying to recapture the mood, but the feeling had been lost, replaced now by a fine tension that held everyone's eyes toward the door.

Matthew drank quickly and signaled for a refill.

"Can't figure how he's out so soon," Blue said. "Zip to twenty and out in two don't make no sense unless he cut a deal, ratted out somebody in the joint. Yeah, that's it. Maybe—"

"It don't matter how or why," Matthew said. "Point is, he's back and a lot madder than when he left . . ."

He glanced at his watch. "Hell, it's 1 A.M. If it wasn't so late, I'd wake up every damn body in the building, just to pull their coat."

Blue wiped the counter and glanced at the thinning crowd. Most people were heading toward the door.

"Don't think about the clock, man. Folks already got the wire. We been in 1048 long enough to know how the news seeps in though the bricks and plaster. Come in up the radiators if it's extra bad."

Matthew nodded and placed his glass on the counter. *Blue's right. I woke up in that sweat, shoulda known bad news was 'round the corner. Old folks say "fish fry, birds fly, and one thing, baby, is dreams don't lie." Tell you everything you need to know. Especially if you don't want to know it. Shoulda been on my P's and Q's from the jump.*

The musicians had packed and now drew a faded quilt over the piano. "What's happenin' tomorrow?" the bassist asked, glancing at the chair Rhino had kicked over.

"Same time, same station," Matthew said, before Blue could answer.

"Yeah, see y'all tomorrow," Blue said absently.

Matthew looked around. *Hell with it. Why let Rhino upset things. The joint is cool, and not far to go if anybody got himself too drunk to navigate, which hardly happens.*

Matthew removed the mouthpiece from his sax and placed the instrument in its case.

Blue watched him the whole time. "So what you think?" he asked again.

Matthew moved his shoulders slightly. "I don't know. Maybe he's just talkin' trash." But as he snapped the case shut, his mind was racing. *What shit did Rhino have to finish? He was always strange, actin' like he only ate nails for breakfast, but no one figured he would actually ice somebody. And least of all, Tommy. Who is he after now? Could be anybody in the house. Maybe it's Rose. He was always starin' at her and breathin' hard. Could be Cyrus. Or Effie. Shit. In the dream, it was me!*

He paused at the door to watch Blue sweep the paper cups from the table into a large carton. Next Blue would put up the chairs, clean the floor, then tally up for the night.

"Want me to hang around?"

"Naw, man. I got it covered. Betsy's here. On my hip with a full clip. She'll see me up two flights. If anything go down, we ready."

Matthew opened the door and gazed into the corridor. He could see nothing. It was as if night had squeezed away all dimension. He could not tell if the passageway was long, short, narrow, or wide.

More than once, he had listened to some of the regulars, after a few drinks, debate whether the alley existed at all. They just seemed to float through it, they said, not feeling walls, ceiling, or floor.

*But those were the hooch hounds, the wide-mouthed, two-drinks-a-minute boys, elbows up and heads to the side, throwin' down gin like they heard prohibition was comin' back.*

And Matthew was usually sober when he stepped into the corridor leading to the alley. He moved blind, with faith tapping like a walking stick.

Once, he had asked Blue why he didn't put a light in the corridor, and Blue had looked at him impatiently.

"I'd have to change the name, man. Alley wouldn't be Blind no more.

Besides, people just kinda follow the music, you know. The sounds is they guide."

Matthew glanced back into the club. There was no sound now. Only a thin crackling noise from the cellophane-covered ceiling globe, which was still revolving, scattering star-like chips of light across the empty dance floor and across Blue's face as he moved with the broom.

Matthew finally closed the door and tried to imagine this scene through Rhino's defective vision and his all-encompassing anger.

*Hell with this. Gotta have a serious converse with everybody in the house. Sooner, the better.*

He moved carefully, holding the horn in its case against his chest. The alley closed in. He heard the scratching sound and knew someone was waiting.

# A MATTER OF POLICY

*Robert Greer*

*For Phyllis*

Cordell Hopsen was in a shitpot of trouble again. Not bad debt trouble this time, or woman trouble, or gambling trouble, or even trouble with the law. This time the trouble was more serious. This time he had beaten flashy-dressing, slow-thinking Billy Pinkey at five straight games of eight ball, taken him for a thousand dollars, and then, gloating, squeezing his testicles in typical 1971, in-your-face, baddest-brother-in-the-'hood fashion, he'd called Pinkey a jelly-headed, sissified, tit-sucking mamma's boy. Cordell was in trouble, all right. Trouble enough to threaten his life.

As Cordell stuffed the final game's winnings, two crumpled, damp, hundred-dollar bills, into his shirt pocket, Pinkey let out a deep-voiced rumble: "Don't cup your nuts at me, you slimy throwback. I'll give you a real reason to hug your jewels." Pinkey cocked his arm and raised the fat end of his pool cue above his head, as his girlfriend, Retha Ann Stitt, and his half-sister, Coletta Burns, rushed toward him across the width of the stale-smelling barroom, pool hall, and eatery.

"Drop the cue, Billy," Retha Ann shouted, grabbing for the pool cue. But the well-worn hardwood stick slammed down against the edge of the pool table with a loud snap, sending half the cue skittering across the floor and a crowd of twelve onlookers, who'd been waiting to see Billy and Cordell tangle, scrambling.

Trapped between the pool table and a greasy cinder-block wall, Cordell, who was just under five foot seven, crouched down, ready to spring at the much larger Billy. When Billy cocked the broken half of the pool cue for a second swing, Retha Ann and Coletta screamed in unison. The head of the pool cue came to a dead halt with a loud midair thud, as it slammed into its outstretched lower half, which C.J. Floyd had retrieved from the floor. "You heard the lady, Billy. Drop the cue." C.J.'s eyes darted back and forth between Billy and Cordell, men he'd known since kindergarten. Watching Billy recock his arm, C.J. shook his head in protest. "I wouldn't do it." The words were delivered with a deadly earnestness. C.J. had been back home in Denver for only a month after spending two one-year tours as a machine-gunner aboard a 125-foot navy swift boat that had patrolled the twisted creeks, dense jungles, and humid swamps of Vietnam's Mekong River Delta.

"Ain't your fight, C.J.," said Billy, contemplating whether or not to take on the six-foot-three, two-hundred-thirty-five-pound Floyd.

"Better listen to C.J.," hollered Coletta, her voice escalating in terror.

Billy thought for a moment, pondering his next move. He'd won $18,000 three days earlier playing Policy, the numbers lottery game of chance that old black folks and all white people called "the numbers." It was the most he'd ever won playing Policy, and the way he saw it, Cordell had just stolen a thousand dollars of his winnings. War hero or not, C.J. Floyd had no right to interfere.

Ignoring C.J.'s plea, he took another powerful cut at Cordell's head. In the seconds it took Cordell to dodge the blow and Billy to take aim again, C.J. tackled Billy at the knees, sending him crashing headfirst into the floor. Seconds later C.J. and Nobby Pittman, the bar and pool hall's owner, were on top of Billy.

"You ain't gonna get my liquor license lifted for killing nobody in my place," barked Pittman, a fifty-five-year-old onetime semipro football player, with skin so dark that it seemed to have a sheen. "Hell, no!" he added as they pinned Billy, thrashing and cursing, to the floor.

"That little weasel was cheatin'," Billy coughed out.

"You lost!" Pittman shouted. "Be glad you didn't lose your whole damn wad."

"I'll kill that little rodent," mumbled Billy, arching his head skyward. "Where the shit did he go?"

"He's gone," said Retha Ann, who was down on one knee, stroking Billy's head. "As soon as you hit the floor, he ran out the door."

"Gone with my money," said Billy, spent from struggling with Nobby and C.J.

"There's more where that came from, baby. You're still fat in the wallet," Retha Ann said with a grin.

Billy gasped for air. "I'll kill the mother."

"Let him up, mister, please," said Retha Ann, looking pleadingly at C.J.

"Yeah, let him up," Coletta chimed in.

"You gonna behave?" asked C.J.

When Billy didn't answer, Nobby kneed him in the ribs.

"Yeah," said Billy with a painful grunt as both men shifted their weight off him and stood.

Billy lay motionless for a moment, with Retha Ann still stroking his head and Coletta hovering over him, shaking hers. Struggling to his knees, rubbing his back, and dusting himself off, Billy shot Nobby and C.J. a look of defiance. "All that goes around, comes around," he said, glancing toward the exit. "I'll get even with that little rodent sooner or later, in spite of the two of you. Come on, Retha Ann, let's get the hell out of here." He locked his arm in hers and lumbered through the door and out into the star-filled night, with Coletta bringing up the rear.


The next morning C.J. was in the basement of the Victorian building across from the Denver city jail that housed his uncle's bail-bonding business, carefully sifting through a coffee tin filled with cat's-eye marbles, looking for an eighty-year-old steely he had mistakenly dropped in two years earlier, just before leaving for Vietnam. Surrounded by earthen walls dotted with creeping mold and struggling to see in the dimly lit cellar, he methodically extracted several marbles from their dimpled cardboard notches inside the tin and stared at them.

You could tell a lot about twenty-two-year-old former first army sergeant C.J. Floyd by taking inventory of the things he discarded and the things he saved. C.J. saved ticket stubs from movies and every manner of game. He had section 34, row 8, seats 11 and 12 ticket stubs from the Broncos' inaugural 1977 Super Bowl appearance in the New Orleans Superdome. He had two ticket stubs each from the Denver openings of *Bullet, Goldfinger,* and *Lady Sings the Blues.* His tiny apartment above his uncle's bail-bonding offices was cluttered with coffee cans full of cat's-eye marbles and hundreds of rare jumbos too. Over the years he'd amassed tomato crates full of mint-condition records, 78s and 45s, crates that filled one corner of the basement and sat blanketed in dust. During his youthful years of collecting, he had accumulated scores of tobacco tins and dozens of ink wells from all around the world. But C.J. Floyd was no hoarder of trinkets or warehouser of superfluous, gaudy, late-twentieth-century junk. He collected because he liked to, and because collecting things connected him to his past.

Conspicuously missing from C.J.'s collectibles were report cards and family-oriented board games that meant interacting with other people instead of going it alone. There were no albums filled with Little League pictures or photographs of grade-school field trips to the zoo. No yearbooks or kindergarten finger paintings. No team sports letter jackets or souvenirs from the prom. C.J.'s collectibles were the treasures of a loner, artifacts assembled by someone who had raised himself.

C.J.'s collection of antique license plates represented a collector's equivalent of the Nobel Prize. The license plates said more about him than any of his other collections. He had started the collection during his teenage years, when his uncle's drinking had reached its peak and street rods and low riders had taken the place of family in his life. The pride of his collection were a 1916 Alaska plate and his prized 1915 Denver municipal tag. Both had been fabricated using the long-abandoned process of overlaying porcelain onto iron. Although the collection was impressive, it remained incomplete, and his uncle, one of the few people who had ever seen the entire collection, suspected that, like C.J., it would never be whole.

C.J. looked up from what he was doing toward the sound of footsteps on the cellar's creaky wooden stairs. "You down there, C.J.?" a voice echoed.

"Yeah," C.J. called out, responding to the familiar tone of his uncle, Ike Johnson, a tough-as-nails former marine whom every Denver cop, street thug, dope dealer, prostitute, and politician knew simply as "Ike."

"Figured it," said the arthritis-ravaged Johnson as he waddled toward C.J. across the uneven dirt floor. "Got some news for you. It ain't pleasant, but I thought you'd wanta know."

"Shoot," said C.J., looking up into his uncle's face. At sixty-three, Unc, who'd once towered over C.J., was losing his battle with arthritis, diabetes, and alcohol. Stoop-shouldered and shrunken, he was a shell of the man he'd been just two years earlier when C.J. had left for Vietnam. "No need to hold back."

"Guess not. Sure won't bring the man back." Unc looked C.J. squarely in the eye. "Couple of hours ago the cops found Billy Pinkey sprawled out dead as a dewdrop in the middle of a Five Points alley. His head had been split open like a ripe summer melon. Cops told his mamma and that half-sister of his, Coletta, that it was probably a meat cleaver that brought Billy to his end. His mamma's upstairs cryin' her eyes out right this minute. Looks like Five Points's got another killin' on its hands."

"Damn," said C.J., thinking about Billy and pondering what was happening to the black community that had been his home away from home as a child. He methodically replaced the marbles he'd been holding in their slots and wrapped an arm around his uncle's shoulders, aware that Billy Pinkey's mother, Marguerite, and Unc had enjoyed an on-again off-again romance that spanned more than twenty years. "Anything I can do to help?"

"Find out who killed Billy," said Unc, patting C.J.'s hand.

"What?"

"You heard me. Find out who killed the boy. I've gotten too old and too slow to handle that kinda work. Besides, Marguerite would never forgive me if I tried and failed."

C.J. eyed his uncle with dismay. "I wouldn't know where to start.

Finding folks has always been your thing, Unc," said C.J., acknowledging the fact that Ike Johnson had spent a lifetime being not simply a bail bondsman but a bounty hunter as well.

Ikeen eyed C.J. with an earnestness his nephew hadn't seen in years. "You just finished two years trackin' down them Vietcongs, and they was shootin' at you. Think of this as the same thing without the shootin'. It'll be a piece of cake."

C.J. set his tin aside and stared at his uncle. C.J. had never once disappointed the man who had raised him; not since the day Ike's rolling stone of a brother and C.J.'s mentally unstable mother had dropped C.J. on Ike's doorstep at the age of four. Even during his tumultuous teenage years, when his uncle's drinking had been at its zenith, C.J. had never been able to say no to the old man. C.J. suddenly found himself thinking about how over the years, and against all odds, Unc, the only black bail bondsman on Denver's otherwise all-white Bail Bondsman's Row, had carved out a name and reputation for himself.

"I'll help you," said Unc, noting C.J.'s look of confusion. "I may not be able to wrestle with your new-age roughnecks, but when it comes to logistics, sortin' things through, and finessin' the cops, I can still hold my own."

C.J. rolled his tongue nervously around his mouth, recalling how his uncle had once chased bond skippers across most of the West, sometimes hog-tying the worst of them for delivery to city and county jails in ropes, barbed wire, and chains. "Why don't you let the cops handle it, Unc?"

Ike Johnson glanced up toward the first floor, where Marguerite Pinkey was waiting, and shook his head. "First off, there's Billy's mamma. Got a duty to find out what happened to her child. Second, in case you forgot, this here's still America. Ain't no white man with a badge really gonna care much about findin' out who split another black Five Points gangster's head in half. 'Case you missed it, C.J., this ain't Vietnam. You back home now."

C.J. thought about the friends he'd left on the battlefields of Vietnam: country white boys from Iowa, brothers out of Harlem, San Antonio Latinos, and South Florida Jews. Gritting his teeth, he stepped over to a tobacco tin sitting on a dusty end tale, opened the tin, and eyed the cellophane-wrapped Purple Heart and Bronze Star that rested on the bed of cotton inside. He stared at the medals for more than a minute before snapping the lid shut. Looking up at his uncle, he said, "Where do I start?"

Marguerite Pinkey was an aging, fair-skinned, large-boned, onetime knock-out of a black woman with thinning, too-often-dyed reddish-brown hair. Her face was puffy, and her eyes were bloodshot from a night and morning of crying. The coffee she was nursing had turned cold by the time she'd repeated the story of how the police had found Billy. How she'd thrown up when she'd be forced to identify Billy's body, and how she had wandered Five Points aimlessly for more than an hour afterward until Coletta Burns had found her sitting at the bus stop across from Mae's Louisiana Kitchen and taken her home.

"Cordell Hopsen's the one who killed my Billy," said Marguerite, staring zombie-like at C.J. "Coletta's sure of it," she added, spinning her coffee cup around in circles. "She said Cordell and Billy had a fight over at Nobby's place last evenin'. After the fight, Cordell came after my Billy and killed him. That's what happened. I know it."

"Maybe not," said C.J. "I was there at Nobby's," he added, watching his uncle struggle to separate a stack of coffee filters from one another with aging, arthritic fingers. "There really wasn't a fight. What happened was Billy almost beaned Cordell with a pool cue after losing a thousand dollars to him at eight ball. He claimed Cordell was cheating."

"Then he probably was," Marguerite said indignantly.

Winning his battle with the filter paper, Unc slipped a new filter into the brew bin of his coffeemaker before glancing up. "A thousand dollars! Where'd Billy get that kinda money?"

Marguerite looked surprised. "I thought you knew, Ike. Last week Billy got lucky at Policy. He hit the numbers for eighteen thousand. It was all over Five Points."

"Did the cops find any of the money on him?" asked C.J.

"No," said Marguerite. "His wallet was missin', and according to Coletta, so were his watch and glasses. Don't matter. I still say it was Cordell lookin' for revenge."

"Was Coletta the first person the cops called after they found Billy?" asked C.J.

"Yes."

"Why'd they call her?"

"'Cause they couldn't get in touch with me, I guess. And she is kin. She and Jeffrey Watkins are the ones who identified Billy's body."

"I see," said C.J., trying to picture Jeffrey Watkins, Coletta's itinerant saxophone-playing boyfriend, a man he hadn't seen in three years. "What about that girlfriend of Billy's, Retha Ann? Has she talked to the cops?"

"I don't know. But I do know this. She's a real sweetie. She and Billy were plannin' on gettin' married next year." Marguerite broke into a series of false starts and began to cry. Choking back tears, she said, "She's the best thing that ever happened to Billy. She's got money and class. And she's been in newspapers, you know."

Ike Johnson shot C.J. a look that said, *check the girlfriend out,* just as the coffee began loudly gurgling its way into the coffeepot behind him. When the coffee finished brewing, Unc squeezed Marguerite's shoulders reassuringly and said, "How about a refill to warm you up, and then I'll take you back home."

"And you'll find out who killed my Billy," said Marguerite, choking back a new rush of tears.

"Guarantee it," said Unc as a final orphaned gurgle erupted from the coffeemaker.


Rosie's Garage was a Five Points enterprise zone business success and automotive-repair-shop jewel. Once a rundown eyesore of a gas station, Rosie's now sported a spotless concrete drive, three service islands with six late-1940s-style pumps, and a garage with three service bays. The tall, stately antique pumps with their crowning white enamel globes had become late-1960s Denver landmarks, and whenever Denver politicians wanted to showcase black community business successes, they never failed to single out Rosie's, the place where most Five Points gossip got its legs.

Roosevelt Weaks, the garage's six-foot-five behemoth of an owner, was counting out change from a twenty to a customer at the front-office cash register when C.J. walked in. After he finished, he said the same thing he did after every business transaction: "Come see us again, now, hear?" When he looked up and saw C.J., a smile that mirrored their long-term friendship spread across his face. "C.J., my man, hear you've been playin' referee," he said, sliding the twenty under the till.

"Where'd you hear that?" said C.J., giving Rosie a quick high five before pulling up a nearby stool.

"Coletta Burns. She stopped in here 'bout an hour ago and filled up that little MG of hers. Said you kept Cordell Hopsen from gettin' brained by her stepbrother over at Nobby's last night."

Looking chagrined, C.J. said, "I did, but Billy got himself killed a few hours later."

"Heard that too. Terrible thing."

"Any rumors about who might have punched Billy's ticket?"

Surprised by the question, Rosie said, "Hell, C.J., if I didn't know better, I'd swear you was a cop."

"Just wondering. Unc asked me to nose around a little, you know, on account of his connection to Billy's mamma, Marguerite."

"Oh," said Rosie, nodding understandingly. "Ain't heard much, but I can pretty much tell you why Billy bought the farm."

C.J. snapped a bag of corn nuts off a half-empty display rack on the counter. "Go ahead."

"The blockhead had been flashin' the money he won at Policy around the Points for damn near a week. Even gave me a little taste of it. Paid me forty-five bucks the other day to wash, wax, and tune up that junker Plymouth of his."

"Sounds to me like Billy was itching for a visit from Bonnie and Clyde."

"Better than takin' another hit from Coletta. The girl was into him for ten grand, easy. I know for a fact that Billy put up a good slice of the money it took to set her up in that dance studio of hers that went south." Noticing a look of confusion spreading across C.J.'s face, Rosie added, "Billy fronted her the money to start a dance studio down here on the Points while you was in Vietnam. It lasted a year or so. Folded four or five months before you come home. Word is Billy was real mad about losin' his money, and folks say he was thinkin' about takin' Coletta to court. Don't know why, though. Wasn't no way in the world she could've paid him back. Every dime she makes sale clerkin' at the May D&F goes to keepin' that connivin' leech of a saxophone-playin' live-in of hers in whiskey and silks."

"Jeffrey Watkins?"

Rosie nodded.

"That's the second time today his name's come up."

"Here's a third. When Coletta stopped in here for gas, the whole front seat of her car was jammed packfull of Billy's clothes. I recognized 'em right off. Them flashy Hawaiian shirts and straw hats he was fond of wearin'. I think she was takin' the stuff to Watkins. You ask me, it's sorta sick."

C.J. nodded, mulling over the information. "Anybody else who might've had it in for Billy?"

"Nobody I can think of 'sides Cordell. Ain't no one seen him, though, since he and Billy locked horns. Word on the street is the cops are dyin' to hear his story."

C.J. stroked his chin. "Cordell's wired a little strange, but I'm not sure about him being a killer."

Rosie eyed C.J. sternly. "Things around here have changed a lot since you went to Vietnam, C.J. Ain't no way of tellin' what folks is capable of no more. People been at each other's throats over that war. Choosin' up sides and pointin' fingers, if you get my drift. And not just white folks—black folks too. There's a bucketful of tension over that war, C.J., and tension makes for strange bedfellows, as they say."

"What's that got to do with Cordell?" asked C.J., eyeing the foot-long keloid running down his left forearm, a scar left behind from a battlefield encounter with a flying piece of shrapnel.

Rosie looked around the room to make certain no one was listening. Lowering his voice, he said, "Cordell's got connections downtown. The high-rankin' political kind, if you know what I mean. Word makin' the rounds is he's an informant for the cops, fingerin' everything from war protesters to dope dealers down here on the Points."

C.J. laughed. "There's no way in hell that little worm would have the kind of information worth killing for."

"Maybe not. But I know for certain he's one of the reasons the cops been able to pretty much wipe out the dope traffic around here. Maybe the cops and the politicians were through usin' Cordell. Could be it was time to wipe the slate clean."

"You've been watching too much television, Rosie, but I'll be sure to ask Cordell about his snitchin' ways when I see him."

"Good luck findin' him. He's as slippery as an eel."

"I'll find him," C.J. said emphatically. "I know where eels like him hang out. One last question before I hit the bricks. What's with Billy's girl-friend, Retha Ann? Never saw her in my life before the other night."

Rosie smiled. "Girl's slummin', my man. She lives in Cherry Hills with the white rights, and her father's a judge. Hear tell her daddy don't like her hangin' around us unwashed types down here in Five Points."

"Things *are* changing," said C.J. with a start. "Black folks in Cherry Hills! And without so much as a mop, an apron, or a broom."

"Think she might've had reason to do Billy in?"

"No, but her father might've."

"Yeah," said Rosie, nodding and stoking his chin.

"Gotta go. Time's money," said C.J., rising from the stool.

"Speakin' of money, you owe me fifteen cents for the corn nuts."

C.J. reached into his pocket and flipped Rosie a quarter.

"Where you gonna start?"

"With the obvious, a bucketful of eels," said C.J., heading toward the door and leaving Rosie looking dumbfounded.

C.J. slipped on his Stetson, buttoned his vest, and lit up a cheroot as he headed for his two-tone red-and-white 1957 drop-top Chevy Bel Air, a car Rosie had helped him restore before he left for Vietnam. As he slipped behind the wheel, he began mapping out a preliminary strategy for finding Billy Pinkey's killer. First he'd find Cordell; then he'd talk with Coletta and Retha Ann. That evening he'd do a little snooping, maybe scope out Billy's Five Points apartment. He was glad Unc had asked him to help find Billy's killer. Playing detective was turning out to be the adrenaline jolt he needed, he told himself as he nosed the Bel Air down Speer Boulevard toward the hobo jungles of Denver's Platte River valley to look for Cordell. And on top of that, it was a hell of a lot safer than Vietnam.

"The cops say the motive for Billy's murder was robbery all right," said Unc, looking up from the basket of fried chicken wings on his desktop and tossing the last of the bones onto a nearby paper plate. "Sure you don't want nothin' to eat? I can order more." When C.J. didn't answer, Unc said, "Cops only found forty cents in change in Billy's pockets. And would you believe it," Unc said with a chuckle, "when I pressed 'em for more information, SOBs told me to keep my nose and my crippled black ass outa police business." Realizing that C.J., who'd been jotting notes on a legal pad, was only half listening, Unc picked up a chicken bone and tossed it at C.J.'s head. "You listenin', boy?"

C.J. nodded.

"Now that we're on the same wavelength, mind tellin' me what the hell you doin'?"

"Trying to figure out who killed Billy."

Forcing back the urge to laugh, Unc said, "You spent the whole damn afternoon and a good part of the evenin' lookin', and you couldn't even find Cordell. Then you tried callin' the daughter of the only black district court judge in the state, hopin' she'd incriminate herself in a murder." Unc shook his head. "You got a lot to learn, C.J. A hell of a lot."

C.J. stopped writing, set his tablet aside, and looked up at his uncle sheepishly.

Unc patted C.J. on the shoulder reassuringly. "Don't take it so hard, C.J. Everybody gotta learn. Here's a few hints for you before you spring yourself on Coletta and go breakin' into Billy's apartment, like you said you gonna. Whoever killed Billy killed him over money, to get revenge, or outa spite. Eighteen grand's a powerful incentive, but revenge and spite are powerful motives for killin' too. When you go talk to Coletta, keep her on the defensive. That'll make her nervous. See if she sweats. People with nothin' to hide usually don't."

C.J. nodded, taking his uncle's instructions to heart as he glanced out the window toward the fading light. "Got any other tips?"

"Take these with you," said Unc, sliding a .38 and a slim jim door jimmy he'd taken out of his top drawer across the desk toward C.J. "The gun's registered. The slim jim's on me," said Unc, watching C.J. eye the two objects tentatively. "Just remember when you jimmy the door latch, wait for a click before you push the door open."

C.J. nodded and slipped the slim jim into his shirt pocket without touching the .38.

"What about the pistol?"

"Think I'll need it?"

"Maybe, maybe not. But let me ask you this. When you was in Vietnam, did that boat you was on ever go out on night patrol without its machine gun?"

C.J. thought for a second before reaching for the .38 and slipping it into the back pocket of his loose-fitting pants.

"Call me if you need me," said Unc, picking up the remote and snapping on the TV. "I'll be watchin' the fights."

C.J. nodded, stood, and headed for the front door, leaving Unc listening to a gravel-voiced TV announcer belt out the Friday night fight ticket.


C.J. didn't like spying on people. It made him feel guilty, but he'd spent the last five minutes peering through the first-floor window of Coletta Burns's small Five Points bungalow, watching as Coletta and a bare-chested Jeffrey Watkins played kissy-face on a red velvet couch in front of a flickering black-and-white TV. Running down the list of questions he planned to ask Coletta, he rose from behind a large mugho pine, strolled up the steps to the front door, and rang the doorbell.

"Whatta you want?" asked Jeffrey Watkins, swinging the door open in response to Coletta's broken, badly out-of-tune, three-note door chime. Watkins, a stubby, balding, forty-year-old black man, seemed to enjoy the fact that he was standing a full step above C.J.

"I'm C.J. Floyd, and I'd like to speak to Coletta."

"I know who you are." Watkins screamed back into the house, "Coletta, there's somebody here at the door wants to talk to you."

Puffing up her hair and adjusting her clothes, Coletta shouted, "Let 'em in."

Watkins grunted out an unpleasant, "Come in," and led C.J. back into a room that had the overpowering smell of burned cabbage.

"C.J.," said Coletta, rising from the couch to shake hands. "What brings you out?"

"I'm trying to find out what happened to Billy." Noticing Coletta's surprised look, he added, "as a favor to my uncle and Billy's mother." He was well aware that Coletta and Billy had shared fathers, not mothers, and that Coletta's relationship with her stepmother, Marguerite Pinkey, had always been a lot colder than lukewarm.

Coletta forced back a frown. "I bet you that old redbone witch told you I had somethin' to do with what happened to Billy."

"No."

Coletta glanced at Jeffrey Watkins, who was now standing next to the room's soot-stained fireplace with his right hand resting on the tarnished bonze head of a cast-iron poker. "Well, if it's information you want, chew on this. That eighteen thousand Billy claimed he won at Policy wasn't all his. I know for a fact that he had a partner."

"Any idea who it was?"

"I'd put my money on that new girlfriend of his, or his mamma."

"And you think one of them might have killed him for their share of the winnings?" C.J. eyed Watkins, whose hand was now cupped tightly over the head of the poker.

"Woulda and coulda," said Coletta. "Shit, everybody knows that mamma of his used to be a madam. Anybody capable of sellin' their body is capable of sellin' out their son."

"Food for thought," said C.J., shooting another glance at Watkins. "What's the story on Billy's girlfriend, Retha Ann?"

"She'd been hugged up to Billy since the beginnin' of the summer. Latched on to him like a magnet. She coulda killed him, I guess. She knew where he kept everything in his apartment, includin' his money. Could be she decided, rich girl or not, she needed the Benjamins."

"Could be," said C.J., remembering his uncle's directives. *Put her on the defensive, make her nervous.* "Any truth to the rumor that you owed Billy money or that he was planning to take you to court over the fact?"

"I didn't owe Billy nothin'!" Coletta's bellow forced Jeffrey Watkins's hand, causing him to move the poker he'd been fingering forward in its stand.

C.J. considered pulling the .38 as his thoughts turned to the 50 caliber machine he'd manned during Vietnam. A gun he'd named Fat Annie, and eaten with, slept with, prayed with, and killed with for two long years. In his book, guns were meant for only one thing, and he knew that if he pulled the .38 he'd more than likely kill Jeffrey Watkins. "Don't be stupid, friend," he said, locking eyes with Watkins. "Slip that poker out of its holster and trust me, you'll never see another day."

Recognizing that C.J. meant what he said, Coletta shouted, "Get out of here, C.J. Get out of here now!"

"I'm gone," said C.J., stepping his way backward toward the front door as Watkins, poker in hand, tracked him step for step. "Nice seein' you," he added, holding the front door open with his butt and letting it slam in Jeffrey Watkins's face before he turned to trot back to the Bel Air.


Billy Pinkey had lived on the fourth floor of a low-rent Five Points apartment building that looked as if it had been intentionally constructed to appear rundown. As C.J. made his way up the creaking wooden spiraling center-atrium staircase, he kept asking himself what Coletta Burns could possibly be hiding. She hadn't seemed too upset about her half brother's death, and the only thing that had set her off was his accusation that she owed Billy money. He suspected that she probably didn't have the nerve to kill Billy herself, but he wouldn't put it past Jeffrey Watkins. On the drive over to Billy's he'd had the feeling that he was being followed, but after parking the Bel Air he'd scouted a two-block perimeter, looking for a tailer, and turned up nothing.

The building's five-story atrium echoed with the noises of crying children and blaring TVs. Billy Pinkey's apartment was at the end of a dark hallway. C.J. approached the door casually, looked around, slipped his slim jim out of his pocket, and popped the door open in a matter of seconds. Stepping inside, he flipped on a light. The first thing he noticed was that the room looked orderly. To his right, a World War II-vintage army footlocker, a rickety porch rocker, and a couch marred with cigarette burns filled a tiny living room. Scraps of paper, a week's worth of the *Denver Post* sports pages, and a pocket-sized calculator rested on top of the footlocker. Suddenly C.J. thought he heard a noise from the kitchen, and he hit the floor spread-eagled, fumbling for his gun. Quickly realizing that the sound was a Venetian blind banging against a half-open window, he hopped up and searched the apartment's kitchen. Finding nothing of interest there, he next searched Billy's bedroom. Nothing seemed out of place, and except for a few of Billy's flashy clothes that Coletta had evidently left behind and a .32 stashed in the top drawer of a dresser, the bedroom could have been his own.

The apartment's neatness told C.J. that the cops hadn't yet made it to Billy's. Billy Pinkey had been dead for close to twenty-four hours, the victim of a violent street attack, and his death wasn't important enough to warrant a simple visit from Denver's finest. Shaking his head as he walked back to the living room, C.J. considered the fact that when it came to black folks, some things never changed. He sat down on the lumpy couch, pushed the sports sections aside disappointedly, and picked up a torn half-sheet of paper from the top of the footlocker. One side of the paper was filled with six columns of penciled numbers. The words *good bet, possible winner,* and *lucky set* had been scribbled near the lower right edge of the paper. *Lay down $50.00* jumped out from beneath the scribbling. The two zeros after 50 had been boldly double-underlined. C.J. picked up a second half-sheet of paper with a similar set of columns, numbers, and notes. Certain that the two half-sheets probably listed the numbers Billy had used to come up with the winning combination for his $18,000 Policy hit, C.J. was about to stuff them in his pocket for Unc to have a look at. It wasn't until he placed the torn sheets together that he realized that the handwriting on the two pages was different. On one sheet the numbers and notes had been written in large, looping, bold black script. On the other sheet of paper the writing resembled chicken scratch, and the numbers were tiny and much lighter.

C.J. spent the next several minutes scrutinizing the writing styles on both half-sheets, concluding in the end that two people had done the writing and that one of them was very likely Billy's Policy partner and killer. There was something about the bolder of the two handwriting styles that C.J. even thought he recognized. He couldn't put his finger on it, but he swore he'd seen the handwriting before.

Satisfied that he had gleaned everything he could from his search, C.J. slipped the papers into his pocket and checked his watch. It was eleven-thirty. He hadn't eaten all day and kicked himself for not sharing in his uncle's fight night chicken-wing feast. At least he'd made a dent in things, he told himself, as his stomach began growling. The next day he'd run the handwriting issue past Unc, track down Cordell, and have a face-to-face meeting with Billy's girlfriend, Rhetha Ann. But for now he needed to feed his face, and luckily he still had an hour and a half before Nobby's place closed. With his stomach still rumbling, C.J. slipped out of Billy's apartment, down the staircase, and out into the night.

Halfway into the eight-block drive to Nobby's, the driver of the car that had been tailing C.J. ever since he'd left Coletta's turned on its lights.


For a Thursday night, Nobby's was jumping. People were lined up two-deep around the bar, ordering drinks as if the evening had just started, and the jukebox was blaring "Standing in the Shadows of Love," a cut from a Four Tops tape that C.J. had worn out during his first tour of Vietnam.

C.J. negotiated his way across the crowded barroom and past the pool-table area toward what Nobby called a restaurant, stopping briefly to shake hands and acknowledge friends. A small, apartment-sized kitchen with a painted concrete floor and a table with six rickety chairs made up the restaurant. An order window poking through one of the room's grease-stained walls led to a kitchen where one of Nobby's part-time cooks was preparing food.

C.J. had his heart set on one of Nobby's juicy, three-quarter-pound cheeseburgers and fries. Fare that had probably pushed his cholesterol to unprecedented limits while he was a teenager.

Nobby spotted C.J. the instant he entered the room. Wiping his brow, he rushed over, and pumped C.J.'s hand. "Must be a full moon. Been swamped all night."

"Money, money, money," said C.J., shouting above the noise.

Nobby smiled. "Too bad it ain't like this every night. Then maybe I'd be able to afford a set of new shocks for my ride. What can I get for you, C.J.?"

"Cheeseburger, medium rare, fries, and a Coke. And an order of cole-slaw," C.J. said as an afterthought.

"Got ya!" Nobby jotted down the order, turned, and walked over to the order window, where a skinny, long-faced cook wearing a nylon stocking cap took the ticket. "Ten minutes and you'll be singin' my praises," Nobby called back to C.J. "Just like when you was a kid. Now, aside from my cookin', what brings you out tonight?"

"I've been looking into what happened to Billy."

Nobby's eyes widened.

"As a favor to Unc and Billy's mamma."

"Oh."

"Got any ideas?"

"Have you talked to that girlfriend of Billy's, Retha Ann?"

"I tried."

"You ask me, she's the one who put it to Billy. Prissy siddity bitch. Down here stickin' her nose in where it don't belong. I'd say you need to be tryin' to contact her a little harder."

C.J. made a mental note to try again to contact Retha Ann Stitt the first thing the next morning. He was about to ask Nobby how long Billy had known Retha Ann when one of the bartenders walked up.

"The high rollers' boat must've sailed in today, Nobby," said the bartender. "Need change for a couple of hundreds." He shoved two hundred-dollar bills at Nobby and nodded at C.J.

Nobby patted down his pockets. Realizing he didn't have that kind of change, he said, "I'll have to go get it from the back."

"Ain't no rush," said the bartender. "The way the two fish who gave me them hundreds are drinkin', I won't owe 'em nothin' more than a ten spot by the time you get back."

Nobby looked at C.J. and shrugged. "Gotta run." Giving C.J. a wink, he added, "And don't wolf down your food. Remember, you ain't a kid no more, C.J."

C.J. smiled, sat back in his chair, and watched a smoky haze waft up from the order window to the kitchen. A steaming burger and fries arrived a few minutes later, courtesy of the harried-looking cook. "I had an order of coleslaw too," C.J. said, pinching off a couple of fries.

"Wasn't none that I seen," said the cook. "Check your order ticket."

C.J. glanced down at the grease-stained check next to his plate. The order read: *burger, medium rare—$1.75, fries—50 cents, Coke—45 cents; total $2.70.*

"Guess Nobby missed it," said C.J.

"Guess so," said the cook, shrugging and walking off.

C.J. was two bites into his cheeseburger and still eyeing the order ticket when something began to gnaw at him. At first he thought it was the fact that in addition to dropping his coleslaw order, Nobby had raised his prices. Setting his burger aside, he picked up the ticket and examined it closely. It wasn't until he had read through the order a couple more times that he realized it was the handwriting that was holding his attention. Suddenly his stomach began to quiver the same way it had whenever his patrol boat had set out on a night mission in Vietnam.

Reaching into his pocket, he slipped out the two half-sheets of paper he'd taken from Billy's apartment and spread them on the table. As he silently read off the numbers on the greasy order slip, he realized that the 5s and 7s were dead ringers for the 5s and 7s on one of the torn half-sheets. He swallowed hard as he realized the looping e's and undotted i's in *possible winner, lucky set,* and *good bet* were nearly identical to the e's and i's in the words *burger, fries,* and *medium rare.* But the clincher was the identical set of double underlines beneath the seventy after the $2.70 total on the order ticket, and the zeros after the $50.00 at the bottom of the half-sheet of paper in front of him.

Coletta had been right about Billy having a partner, and the partnership had probably cost him his life. But the question C.J. needed answered more than anything was why. Shoving his half-eaten burger aside and holding the order ticket and the papers from Billy's apartment out in front of him as if they were contaminated, he rose from his chair.

"You can pay at the bar," the cook called out through a rising pocket of smoke. "Just show 'em your order ticket up front."

C.J. didn't answer. He knew the drill. Instead of heading for the bar, he turned and headed for Nobby's office.

A two-inch-tall stack of five-dollar bills, a short stack of tens, and a fifth of Jack Daniels occupied the middle of Nobby Pittman's desk. Nobby looked up, surprised, and his eyes shot toward the top desk drawer to his right when C.J. pushed the door open and walked in. When he realized who it was, he let out a sigh. "Shit, C.J., you scared the hell out of me. Thought you might be a damn robber."

"No," said C.J., his tone noticeably somber.

"Drink?" asked Nobby, shoving the Jack Daniels across the desktop.

"Nope."

"Suit yourself. Whatta ya need?"

"A few answers, Nobby. That's all."

"'Bout what?"

"About Billy Pinkey's murder."

"Can't help you there."

"I think you can." C.J. stepped up to the desk and laid down his dinner order ticket and the two half-sheets of paper he'd taken from Billy's. "Recognize any of these?"

"Yeah. The one on the left is the order I took for your dinner. Never seen the others."

"I think you have."

"You callin' me a liar?" Nobby sat up straight in his chair.

"No. Just hoping to jog your memory."

"I said I never seen 'em."

"Strange. The handwriting on the sheet to your far right matches the writing on my dinner ticket."

Nobby eyed his top desk drawer once again. "Damn, C.J. Bein' a war hero ain't enough? Now you a handwritin' expert too?"

"Don't claim to be either, Nobby. But I'm betting a real handwriting expert will say that the writing on that one piece of paper and my dinner ticket are a match. Why'd you kill Billy, Nobby?" asked C.J., remembering what his uncle had said about ratcheting up the pressure on a suspect.

Nobby scratched his head, eyed the desk drawer once again, and smiled. "Let's say we keep what's on them papers 'tween me and you. You stand to make yourself two grand richer if we do."

"Can't."

"Four grand, then."

C.J. shook his head.

Nobby shrugged. "Suit yourself." With a flick of the wrist, he opened the desk drawer, pulled out a snub-nosed .38, and aimed it squarely at C.J.'s chest. "You just spent two years seein' what bullets can do to a man, C.J. Take the four thousand."

When C.J. didn't answer, Nobby shook his head. "Billy tried to stiff me. Keep all that money for hisself. You believe that? With me bein' the one who picked them numbers, and me layin' down half the cash. Never should've let the Policy runner give Billy all that money. But I trusted Billy, C.J. Like I always trusted you kids. See what you get for puttin' your trust in someone? Guess eighteen grand was just too much of a burden for Billy to handle. Especially with that new high-yellow woman of his. When I come for my money, Billy said he wasn't gonna give me squat. Said his woman told him possession was nine-tenths of the law. I pleaded with him for my money for the better part of a week, but he wouldn't budge. In the end I had to get what was mine, C.J. You understand."

"Not really." C.J.'s response changed the pleading stare on Nobby's face into a look of rage. Nodding toward a darkened corner of the room, Nobby said, "I want you to walk over there and park your ass in that chair in the corner while I think this out."

"You think long, you think wrong," said C.J.

"Don't play funny man with me, C.J. Sit!"

C.J. eased down into the lumpy overstuffed chair, his eyes locked on the .38. After a half-minute of silence, Nobby said, "Gonna have to kill you, C.J. Ain't no other way."

"You need to be smarter than that, Nobby. One killing, and you might be able to plea-bargain your way down to life. Two killings, and you'll get the gas chamber for sure."

"If I get caught. Get up. We're headin' out the back." Nobby motioned C.J. toward a doorway in the opposite corner of the room that led out into the alley. "Go ahead. Move."

C.J. headed for the door, looking for the right moment to pull his own .38. As he thought about making his move, the smells and sounds of the Mekong River Delta filled his head, and as he slipped through the doorway and out into the moonlit night he swore he could hear the sounds of F-100s and machine-gun fire in the distance.

"We gonna walk down two blocks and around the corner down to where they found Billy. Sorry to say, C.J., it's the same place they'll be findin' you. I'm figurin' that when the cops start to scratch their heads, they gonna think we got us a serial killer down here on the Points. And don't think about runnin', C.J., 'cause if you do, I'll just plug you in the back."

C.J. spotted a Dumpster jutting out in the alley ten yards ahead, and he felt a sudden rush of hope. He'd leap behind the Dumpster and pull his .38, and then it would be Nobby dropping in the alley instead of him. A few feet from the Dumpster, C.J. heard a familiar voice behind them shout, "Hold your horses right there, Nobby!"

The two men turned in unison to see Ike Johnson standing a few feet behind them, his shrunken silhouette awash in the glare from an overhead streetlight. Unc was aiming the .45 he'd carried as a member of the elite all-black World War II transportation unit known as the Cannonball Express directly at Nobby's midsection.

"Had my eyes on you ever since you stepped out your back door, Nobby. I don't know what the hell's goin' on here or why you're holdin' that pea shooter of yours on C.J., but I know you better drop the damn gun."

Nobby squeezed off an errant shot as Ike took a knee. Steadying the .45 with both hands, Ike returned fire. His second shot slammed into Nobby's right thigh, sending Nobby sprawling face first onto the ground.

C.J. was on top of Nobby, knee to the back of his neck, in seconds. Looking up at his uncle, who still had his .45 trained on the moaning man, C.J. said, "Nobby killed Billy. It was all over money."

"Figures," said Ike, looking back toward the half-dozen heads that were now poking out Nobby's back door. "Best get our story together for the law. You can be sure one of those folks back there'll be callin' the cops."

"When did you get here?" asked C.J., watching blood stream from the wound in Nobby's leg.

Ike smiled. "Been trailin' you all day. Checkin' out how you was doin' with your assignment."

"What?"

"You may have been a big dog in Vietnam, C.J., but when it comes to bail bondin', bounty huntin', and dealin' with the Five Points bottom feeders, 'round here, you just an unschooled pup."

"So you decided to glue yourself to my tail?"

"Watched you make your phone calls, followed you to Coletta's, Billy's apartment, and finally to Nobby's," Ike said with a smile.

"Why?"

The look on Unc's face turned icy serious. He looked at Nobby Pittman, writhing in pain, and then back at C.J. " 'Cause C.J. You the only kin I got in the whole wide world, and on top of that, when it comes to breakin' in new hires, it's a matter of policy."

# SMALL COLORED WORLD

*Terris McMahan Grimes*

For all the dubious skills I've mastered over the years—the ability to talk grown-up to my babies and baby talk to their daddy, the ability to steer with my knees while reaching to the backseat to pop the kid who's acting up, or the ability to speak several dialects of Caucasian, including both North and South Valley Girl, Berkeley Breathless, and Bureaucratus—the one that I regret not mastering is the ability to projectile vomit at will. Forget super powers, if I could have had just one power that Wednesday afternoon that Ada Perkins, my newly appointed slash anointed supervisor chose to reprimand me, it would have been the ability to drench her in bile of my own manufacture. I sat in the deliberately undersized chair in front of her desk, imaging the partially digested contents of my stomach glomming on to that wig of hers that only fooled white folks. I could just see it eating through the St. Johns knit she wore a little too well, tarnishing those gold buttons, dripping onto her shoes, and making sizzling sounds as it ate through the leather.

Ada Perkins clutched a heart-shaped rubber stress ball. She gave it a few squeezes. She took a deep breath, closed her eyes, and kept them like that for a count of ten, opened them again, and fixed them on me. She said, "Don't you ever speak to the secretary without my permission." Because

English was her second language, she tended to overenunciate. She'd grown up in the Mississippi Delta speaking Anglish, a kind of Afro-English dialect, and worked hard to keep it from tripping her up. She went on, "I am the under-deputy assistant secretary of this agency, not you. I am the governor's surrogate, not you. Do you hear me?"

I heard her. I relinquished my vomit reverie and stood up. I didn't have any epaulets to rip off, no sword to break over my knee, so I ripped the page out of my notebook and slammed them down on her desk. 'Fuck you! I quit!' I said. And I walked out. It felt so good. My endorphins were kicking. Unfortunately, endorphins fade fast.

I'm a grown woman, a professional, with an MBA from one of the finest institutions in the nation, CSU Sacramento. I'm married with two children and a house in the suburbs. Growing up, I was a daddy's girl, but no matter how hard I try, I'll never outgrow being my mother's child. That's why by the time I got back to my cubicle—cubicle-dwelling being another indignity I've had to suffer since getting this so-called promotion—my mother tapes had clicked on and were blasting full volume. "What in the world have you gone and done, child? Did you even stop to think it through? Now you got no job now, no income, and you got a house note, a car note, and anything else you can get a note on note. And the language you using these days; Lord have mercy." The tapes played over and over and over, beating my brain to mush. So when Mother's phone call came through I was ripe for the plucking. I was vulnerable. That's all you need to know to understand how I got mired in another of Mother's messes, how I got stuck overnight in a little tar paper shack outside Pixley, California, with an eighty-seven-year-old would-be suitor, how I had to answer nature's call at three in the morning in a Brer Rabbit molasses bucket, and how I learned a lesson about murder that cut both ways.


I picked up the phone. "You ready?" It was Mother, her inquiry ricocheting off my hello. She wasn't on my calendar, but that's never stopped her. Pinning Mother to a little square on a piece of paper accomplishes little.

"What am I supposed to be ready for?"

"We going to go get Sister Venable from the jailhouse."

"What's she there for?"

"Assault and battery."

"That little ole lady?"

"We don't have time for all this chit chat, child. You better come on before I change my mind and take this girdle off."

This was serious indeed if Mother was fully girded, long line bra fortified, and clean handkerchief endowed. I told her I was on my way. Then I signed out—twenty years of state service is a hard habit to shake—and left.


"All Venable has to do," Mother explained, "is take her medicine and collect that little nut check every month, and she won't even do that."

"What's the medicine for?"

"To keep her from acting all crazy."

"I meant what disease is it for?"

"She doesn't have no disease, 'cept sugar. Venable is just crazy."

"Doesn't somebody look after her?"

"Remember Quintelle, Quintelle Jackson?"

"No."

"Yes, you do. She's Nay Nay's cousin's girl."

"Mother, I do not know Quintelle. I do not know Nay Nay. I do not know Nay Nay's cousin, and I most decidedly do not . . ."

Mother cut me off, "I think you're getting a little besides yourself, Miss Lady."

"Maybe I am, I've had a rough day. But it's a stereotype to assume that all black people know each other, even if the one doing the assuming is black."

I'm not sure what a jaundiced eye is, but I think Mother looked at me with one. She said, "Just live on, child. One day you'll realize it's a small colored world." Then she went right on telling me about Quintelle. "The county pays her to do some cleaning and a little cooking, but she's only there a few hours a week. Toni from across the street looks after Venable the rest of the time. She's the one went over there this morning and found out Sister Venable wasn't there, so she called me."

"Why'd she call you?"

"She knows I care about people," Mother said. That wasn't exactly how I would have described her. Overly involved with her neighbor's affairs would do if I were feeling particularly generous, plain old-fashioned nosey would suffice if I weren't.

I said, "I don't see why Toni would think something was wrong just because Sister Venable wasn't home."

"Venable doesn't get out much since that doctor she used to see called down to DMV and had them snatch her license, and Toni had to hide the keys to that big old Chrysler of hers. Besides, lately she's been acting a little more touched than usual. The other day, Quintelle took her down to that farmers market on K Street Mall, and there was a preacher holding service on one of the corners. Quintelle said something came over Venable when she saw him." Mother chuckled. "Do you know she ran off and left her walker?"

We arrived at the jail and parked. That was the easy part. Getting Mother though the metal detector with five thousand metal stays in her long-line bra was the hard part. The metal detector kept beeping and spitting her back out. I'd read about a female attorney who'd been forced to remove her underwire bra rather than miss an important pretrial conference. The officers staffing the metal detector gathered in an uneasy huddle. It was obvious they didn't want to ask Mother to unharness herself. A 42 triple D is a terrible thing to set free in a public place, and I think they knew it. Finally, they settled on giving Mother one more going over with the handheld wand and let us in.

"Mrs. Venable confessed to the 'Rag Doll Murders,' " the release officer informed us.

Mother chuckled uneasily. "You don't believe her, do you?"

The officer took a moment to examine Mother before responding. "Ma'am, the Rag Doll Murderer killed a woman with his bare hands, lifted her body over an eight-foot chain-link fence, and hid it in a Dumpster. Mrs. Venable uses a walker to get around." Relief flooded Mother's face. She let out the breath she'd been holding and fanned herself with her hand.

They rolled Sister Venable out in a wheel chair. She sat with her head down, her lower lip quivering. Mother turned to the officer with an accusing look. "Just a precaution," he said. "We didn't want her to hurt herself. She's been somewhat combative." Mother bent over and asked Sister Venable if she was all right. She didn't respond.

We were on the freeway when Mother tried again. Turning to the backseat where we'd strapped Sister Venable, Mother said, "What in the world were you thinking, child? Don't you know better'n to play with the police like that? Didn't you see what they did to that Rodney King boy?"

"I want them to lock me up and throw away the key."

"Why, Venable?"

"That's what I deserve."

"Venable, you taking your medicine?"

Venable pursed her lips and made a rude noise. Mother sighed and turned back around. "They can put you under the jail for all I care. See if I come down to bail your old behind out again."

Toni was waiting for us at Sister Venable's Second Avenue cottage. A small, heavy-chested woman about my age, she clucked over Sister Venable the way you'd expect a much older woman to, admonishing her for running away. "What you trying to do, Auntie Honey," she teased, "make us all have a heart attack?"

We settled Sister Venable in her recliner in front of the TV. She brightened in familiar surroundings. Pointing to a small table next to her chair weighted down with unguents, powders, and pills, she said, "I use fungi nail, now."

I didn't know what to say, so I told her that was nice. She nodded, pleased.

I squatted next to her chair for a little girl-to-girl chat. "Sister Venable, did you really want to go to jail?"

She gave me a solemn nod.

"Why?" I said.

"That's the only place I'd be safe."

"Safe from what?"

Her lower lip started to quiver again. She clinched it between her teeth and patted the top of my hand, shaking her head the way women do at church when the spirit overcomes them. Quintelle appeared at the door just then, and Sister Venable never did get to tell me what she needed protection from.

Quintelle didn't seem surprised to see us. Notwithstanding her as-shiny-as-patent-leather finger waves, and lavender scrubs, she was all business. Pausing only long enough to broadcast a greeting, she moved from the door to Sister Venable, picking up and straightening out as she went. She continued to work as Mother and Toni recounted Sister Venable's bid to get locked up for the Rag Doll Murders. When they finished, Quintelle went to the kitchen and returned with a beer. She placed it in Sister Venable's hand and continued with her chores. Mother raised her brows, but Toni held up both palms, the international sign for "please don't start nothing." Oblivious, Quintelle grabbed a broom and started to sweep the old, nearly theadbare carpet. Mother and Toni scrambled for the door, neither willing to risk losing a relative simply because she wasn't agile enough to avoid having a sweeping broom touch her feet. I followed, but at a less frantic pace. Quintelle swept us out the front porch down the steps to the walkway. She stopped and stood on the porch looking down at us. "Don't y'all worry, she said, "We gon' take care'a Miss Venable."

Mother wasn't so sure. "I don't think she should be drinking in her condition," she said.

Quintelle laughed. "Hell, she ain't pregnant, Miss Lorraine."

Mother's mouth snapped shut with such force I feared for her tongue. If there's one thing she can't stand, it's a smart mouth child. Mother lives by that old adage, "Spare the rod and spoil the child." It mattered little to her that the child, in this case, was forty-seven years old and not even hers. Quintelle is saved. She shouts in church every Sunday. She's gainfully employed as a certified nursing assistant, helping old folks like Sister Venable. She's also a recovering drug addict with self-control issues. And at six feet and a good 240 pounds, she's a big slab of muscle with titties. I didn't want any trouble, especially the kind that might involve me having to put up my dukes. Hooking my arm through Mother's, I commenced dragging her down the walkway toward our car, but she dug her Rockports in and assumed her combat position with her hands on her hips and her head cocked to the side.

Quintelle realized her mistake. I could see her consciously shifting, morphing into something oily and sweet. "Pardon my tongue, Miss Lorraine," she said. "The devil is busy today, ain't he? Dr. Houghton, he the one say it's alright to give her a beer now and then when she gets too riled up. It helps her calm down."

Mother stared at her a good fifteen seconds. Quintelle, a better woman than I, didn't even squirm. Finally Mother said, "What about all those medicines she takes? Won't that alcohol react with them?"

Quintelle raised her shoulders to show she was just as perplexed as Mother. "I don't know, Miss Lorraine, Dr. Houghton said it was all right."

"How long she been talking this mess about wanting to get locked up?"

"That's a new one, Miss Lorraine. That's certainly a new one on me."

Quintelle closed the door. Toni shook her head and turned to Mother, "That Quintelle is something else."

Mother didn't respond. Toni walked with us to the car. Mother was quiet, which is unusual for her. I, on the other hand, was bubbling over, having discovered the joy of minding other people's business. Funny how that works, now that I had troubles crowding 'round my door with the job or lack of one, someone else's problems—anyone else's problems—seemed so much more appealing. And to think, I'd criticized Mother for the same thing all these years. But this was different, I told myself. My interest was purely anthropological. Mother was plain old nosey, but I was a social scientist studying the culture and mores of crazy old people in the suburban community of Oak Park.

"Has Sister Venable always been like this?" I asked.

Toni chuckled. "Yeah, at least for the six months, or so, we've known her."

I wondered about Quintelle and Toni's penchant for using the royal "we" but let it pass. "Where're you from?" I asked more out of politeness than anything.

Toni cleared her throat and said, "Southern California."

"What part?"

"Oh, you know, LA?" she said, making it sound like a guess rather than a definite answer. But I knew, all right. The child was perpetrating. I could almost see the dust of San Joaquin Valley stamped in her pores. But who was I to judge.

The weather was trying to make up its mind whether to rain. A fat, lazy drop hit the top of my head; another plopped on the toe of my shoe. Mother was in deep thought, so deep that when she got to the curb, she kept walking right over the edge. I caught her before she could fall, and if Toni hadn't been there to catch me, both of us might have ended up in a heap in the gutter. We helped Mother right herself. She smoothed her skirt down muttering, "Something ain't right." I agreed, but I don't think we were talking about the same thing. After she'd gotten settled in the car, Mother reached out for the window and took Toni's hand in hers.

"I want to thank you for looking after Sister Venable the way you do. Not many people show such Christian caring now'a days."

Toni looked embarrassed. She stammered out a couple of "aw, it's nothing" and said, "I know how it is not to have anybody when you need help."

I pulled onto the street. Toni stood in the gutter where we left her. She was still standing there, her arm extended in an absentminded little wave, when I turned the corner.


I sat at the head of the conference table waiting for my staff to trickle in for the unit's bimonthly meeting. Melissa Bowers and Tracee Witherspoon huddled over a stack of photos. I couldn't tell what they were, but I hoped they weren't more of those "birthing process" pictures Melissa had been foisting on unsuspecting coworkers. Her wide behind as pallid as a hunk of haddock, splayed like road kill, angry red private parts stretched every which way—those photos had made poor Cedric Simmons so sick they'd had to rush him away on a stretcher, and had forced the folks in Labor Relations to work overtime scrambling to redefine sexual harassment in the workplace. Arietta Dunn swished in on her electric chair. Deftly working the chair's controls, she slipped into a spot on the other end of the table. Mick Johnston cracked his knuckles. He was wearing his trademark camouflage fatigues, the same thing he wore every single day, even Hawaiian shirt Fridays. I had just called the meeting to order when Ada Perkins stormed in, clutching my purse, my brief case with papers sticking out of it, and dragging my raincoat. She dumped them on the table in front of me.

"You quit, remember? You can just take your stuff and get out."

The others froze, not out of fear, but in joyful anticipation of a juicy confrontation, something with which they could regale more junior staff for many coffee breaks to come.

I said, "Did I ever tell you that before coming to agency I worked in personnel?"

"What's that suppose to mean?" Caution stiffened her.

"Did I sign anything? Do you recall my stating in writing that I quit?"

Ada Perkins froze the way a person might if she came upon a horrible auto accident moments after it happened. Her face grayed over. She started working her stress ball. Then she wound up like Satchel Paige and hurled it against the wall over Mick's head, turned, and stalked out. The ball clung to the wall a second or two before falling to the floor with a dull plop. The room was quiet. Then Tracee said, "Bless her poor, little, 'I come from private industry' heart." The others laughed, but I didn't. I was thinking of Brenda Delacore at the moment. Brenda Delacore, my putative subordinate when I labored as personnel officer in my old job, and she as my Iago. Good ole Brenda, my former assistant and nemesis, my friend and sometimes not, the assistant personnel officer, but rank and file's agent provocateur—Brenda would have been proud of the way I'd handled Ada Perkins.

I didn't get to enjoy my small triumph for very long. Both my beeper and cell phone sounded, almost simultaneously. I checked the numbers. They were the same. The agency secretary stuck his head in the door just then and asked if he could see me. He's a soft-spoken, scholarly, brown-skinned man, but his question wasn't really a question, so I stood, the cell phone in one hand and the beeper in the other, and followed him to his office. He took a seat in his leather wing-backed chair, and I found a place on the divan across from him.

"Ada Perkins tells me that your style of interaction is causing her a great deal of distress. She tells me that," he looked down and read from the paper in his hand, "you are discourteous to her, other staff, and the public. You foment discord, and you bring discredit to the agency." He looked up when he finished and stared at me through his rimless glasses. "Now, what do you say to that?"

"It reads word-for-word like that petition support staff signed against her," I said.

He didn't smile, but I thought I saw some movement around the corners of his mouth. He adjusted his glasses and said, "Ada has built up quite a bit of vacation time, and I'm suggesting she take a couple of weeks of it. Her vacation starts in a couple of days. Why don't you work from home until then?" My pager and cell phone went off again, as I was leaving the secretary's office. I answered the phone.

"Yes, Mother."

"Is that the way they have you answering the phone for the state?"

"Mother, this is my personal cell phone."

"Your daddy and I spent all that money sending you to all those colleges, and you can't answer the phone no better than that?"

"Mother, what do you want?"

"I want," said Mother, "for you to get your behind down off your shoulders. Then we need to check with Sister Venable's cousin to see if she's there."

Then she told me the rest. The street preacher was dead. A street sweeper found him in a downtown doorway cut every which way by somebody with a strong work ethic when it came to murder. Sister Venable was missing, and this time so was her 1964 Chrysler LeBaron. Quintelle had delivered the bad news. She'd answered the phone when Mother placed her early morning call to check on Sister Venable, and according to her Venable's door was standing open when she got there.

Sister Venable's house was locked up tight, thanks to Quintelle. Toni's shades were drawn, and the morning paper was still on the walk. It was obvious no one was home; at least someone wanted it to look that way. We rang the bell and knocked anyway.

An old man in a red flannel shirt came to the porch next door. "How you ladies doing this fine morning?" he said with a slight bow.

Mother broke into a wide grin. I promised myself that if she curtsied I would elbow her to death right there on Toni's porch. Mother patted her hair, leaned toward me, and whispered form the corner of her mouth, "A gentleman."

I stepped in front of her and said, "We're looking for Toni."

He said, "They moved. Truck came this morning just before day, loaded up the whole kit and caboodle and drove off."

I thanked the man and dragged Mother back to the car.

"We should have asked him some more questions," Mother protested.

"He told us everything we needed to know."

"Now what do we do?"

"There's nothing else we can do except maybe file a report with the police."

"I already called the police, and all the hospitals too."

"Mother, before we go any further, maybe you should tell me what the deal is with Sister Venable."

"She's missing, that what the deal."

"No Mother, the real deal, the one that began way back when in the Depression, or World War II, or something like that."

All of Mother's friends have pasts. One old sister, who's gaining on eighty, did a stint as a hooch dancer during the '40s in some of the less reputable clubs on LA's Central Avenue. One is rumored to have killed a man. Another, in her irrepressible youth, ran an elaborate ponzi scheme fronted by a white man, cheating well-to-do white folks out of a little of their discretionary cash. All are now God-fearing churchwomen, pillars of their communities, grandmothers and great-aunts, some lovingly raising the children of their children.

"She has a cousin she's close to down in the valley, in Pit Pat, I believe his name is Rollie . . ."

"Mother."

"Okay, okay. I don't know that much about her. I didn't meet her until she joined church a few years back, but she's always been a little peculiar. Annie Mae Williams, she the one we should be talking to. I hear tell, she grew up with her."

Annie Mae Williams ran a board and care facility for developmentally disabled adults out of her South Land Park home. She was a big, affable woman, in a spectacularly bad wig. It was impossible to tell her age, she could have been a hard-lived fifty, or a genetically blessed ninety.

"Back in Pit Pat, Venable sent a man to prison for murder," Annie Mae Williams informed us. "Testified against him. Said she saw him stab a man."

"Well, did he?"

"Some folks said he did, other folks swore he didn't. Venable the only one said she saw what happened. I'm telling you, people fell out over it, divided the whole town. You go down to Pit Pat and people still arguing about it to this very day."

"I never heard of Pit Pat. Is it in California?"

Mother and Annie Mae Williams indulged me with a "kids say the darnest things" kind of chuckle.

Miss Annie Mae said, "Pit Pat's in the Valley down near Pixley."

"Between Pixley and Corcoran," Mother added.

"Black Okies and Arkies like me, trying to get away from hard times settled Pit Pat—Pixley too—back in the '30s."

"When did all the killing and lying take place?" Mother asked.

"Nineteen sixty-four, April nineteen sixty-four."

"Who was the man?"

"Clay. His name was Clay, John Henry Clay. So sad. He had a school-age child, and another one on the way."

"Which side were you on?"

"Child, I could'a cared less. Those Negroes were always shooting and cutting on one another just so they'd have something to talk about. I stayed clear of all that mess, minded my own business, got my diploma, and left on the first thing smoking. But I tell you one thing, the wrong man went to prison."

"Why do you say that?"

"Guts," said Annie Mae. "My guts tell me he didn't do it."

Annie Mae Williams had to prepare an asthma treatment for one of her residents, so we thanked her and left.

"What do you think?" I said to Mother. We were back in the car heading no place in particular. "You think that nineteen sixty-four killing had anything to do with Sister Venable wanting to go to jail herself?"

"How could it? You're forgetting one thing," Mother said.

"And that is?"

"Venable is crazy."

"Well, what about the preacher, you think she had anything to do with his death? You think she killed him and then went on the lam?"

"Don't be funny. What reason would she have for doing something like that?"

"Maybe she didn't need a reason," I said. "Aren't you forgetting one thing—Sister Venable is crazy."

"You can play if you want, but I'm telling you Venable wasn't scared for nothing. Ask yourself this, just why was she so scared she thought the only place she'd be safe was under lock and key? And when you get finished with that, ask yourself why is she missing."

"You're the one said she was crazy."

"I said she was crazy, I didn't say the child was stupid. She didn't go 'round sticking her hand on hot stoves. She didn't put her clothes on backwards. She knew when to come in out of the rain. And she knew when to be scared."

I was suffering whiplash trying to keep up with Mother's wildly shifting theories. I was also beginning to understand what I'd heard in her voice earlier when she'd told me about the preacher's death and Sister Venable going missing—fear. She was plain, old-fashioned scared, the kind of scared that was likely to make her weekly dose of Black Draught unnecessary.

"Mother, do you know something you're not telling me?"

She bestowed upon me a look straight from the repertoire of Aisha, my seventeen-year-old, one of those "Duh!" looks. I pulled over and dropped my head to the steering wheel. I struggled against the urge to bump it until I lost consciousness.

"Why do you do this to me, Mother?"

"Do what?"

"Drag me into these messes only giving me part of the truth."

"I didn't drag you into anything."

"Okay, let's start from the beginning. What's going on? Why are you so scared?"

"You'd be scared too, if you used some of that education you got. Think about it, baby. Somebody killed that preacher. From what you told me, whoever it was did everything but nail him to a tree. I don't know about you, but somebody that evil scares me to death."

There were three of them, a short, portly Latino, a burly white man with a shaved head and tattooed neck, and a gangly black man with a biblical beard in a well-worn three-piece suit. They had set up church on the K Street Mall at the busy intersection of 10th Street, in sight of the golden glow of the capitol's dome. The white man was preaching a surprisingly gentle sermon on love, as the Latino man handed out religious tracts to passersby. Most refused them. The black man paced the sidewalk, his Bible open and his head down, softly mouthing a passage. I stopped in front of a floral shop to listen. A middle-aged black woman dropped a dollar into the collection basket at the feet of the Latino preacher.

"I wish they wouldn't give them money. That only encourages them."

I turned to see the florist standing in her doorway. I said, "I don't know, I kind of like street preachers." Although Daddy was more partial to street musicians, both he and Mother taught us kids to respect street preachers. "You never know," they'd admonish us, "how the Lord might return." We were encouraged, forced in my case, to make an offering, to drop our hard-earned and tightly clutched nickels and dimes into the baskets or old hats at their feet.

"They keep customers away with all that shouting and screaming."

I said, "One of them was killed yesterday."

"I know. That was unfortunate. I didn't mean to imply that I wanted to see them harmed or anything. It's just that they don't need to be on the streets. When it comes to violence, they're just as vulnerable as the homeless. Finding bodies in downtown doorways doesn't help business either."

The black man had switched to handing out the religious tracts. He headed toward us, and the florist retreated to her shop. He handed me a tract. I thanked him, introduced myself, and asked if I could talk to him. His name was Rev. Royal McFall, and he pastored a small church and soup kitchen in Del Paso Heights, but his true passion was his street-preaching ministry. I asked him about the preacher who had been murdered.

"I knew him," he said. "Lord rest his soul. He hadn't been preaching 'round here long, but I can say he truly was a man of God."

"Did he pastor a church locally?"

"No, as I said, I believe he was new to town."

"Did you know where he was from?"

"No, can't say that I did."

"Did he know anybody here? Were there people who came to hear him preach, people who seemed to know him?"

"Not that I can say. It's a hard fought battle out here for every soul won. Most people go out of their way not to hear us. Look around you, what do you see? People all but putting their hands over their ears, trying not to hear the word."

"What about hecklers?"

"We welcome them. When they start heckling, it means we're getting through, touching them in their secret places, making them uncomfortable with the knowledge of their own sinfulness. A heckler's merely a sinner crying out to be saved."

"Some of the merchants aren't too happy about you being out here."

"The money changers? I fear them not. Na'er one of them has the heart to do what I saw done to him."

"You saw the body?"

"I'm the one found him." He pointed to the bank on the corner. "Right over there in the doorway. He was cut so bad, the only way I could tell it was him was by his shoes." He paused and swallowed. There was something sad about the way his Adam's apple bobbed on his thin neck above his frayed collar. "You see, he had bad feet and he cut holes in his shoes for his corns." He dropped his head and prayed. I bowed mine too, and said amen when he finished. I thanked him and promised to visit his church some Sunday.

I was about to leave when I thought of something else. "What did he preach about? Did he have a theme?"

"Redemption."

Rain had started to fall. The Latino man was preaching. He stood unprotected, his arms outstretched, his face upturned, singing praise in a crystalline tenor so sweet it made my throat ache.


According to Miss Annie Mae the drive down Highway 99 to Pit Pat should take only a couple of hours, and maybe it would have if it hadn't been for the rain. It came down in wild, slashing, sheets, effectively disabling the Beemer's windshield wipers, and limiting my vision to a car length or two ahead. I'd driven back and forth for an hour on the stretch of highway between Corcoran and Wasco before I saw the turn-off for Pit Pat.

The town's single street was appropriately named Main. I pulled into its only business, a two-pump gas station slash convenience store that proudly proclaimed itself a purveyor of Royal Crown Cola and "fried fish plates." A shiny, black SUV of some improbable make, perhaps a Lincoln or Cadillac, and an old workhorse of a pickup were parked in the gravel close to the door. I parked as close to them as I could and got out, cursing myself for forgetting my umbrella.

Three men leaned over the counter. My entrance froze them in a kind of gangster modern tableau. The hefty one on the business side, in the burgundy velveteen jogging suit accessorized with gold chains, bore a fleeting resemblance to Barry White—if you squinted. The two on the customer side were younger, thinner, and more hip-hop inclined, sporting baggy pants, oversized jackets, and fanciful headgear.

The Barry White said, "Can I help you, ma'am?" He seemed annoyed by my presence, I a potential customer. I was annoyed he called me ma'am.

"Can you direct me to the home of Mr. Rollie Meeks?" I said.

"You know where the graveyard is?"

"I'm from out of town."

"JC go show her," he said to the young man wearing the Peruvian shepherd's cap. JC walked past me and out the door without a word. I followed. He climbed into the SUV, and I scrambled to get in my car and to get buckled up so he could lead me out into the darkness.

It would be overly generous to call Mr. Rollie's house a shack, and a little too harsh to call it a lean-to. It was his home, and Mr. Rollie welcomed me to the listing, tin roofed, one-room structure with the courtly grace of a country gentleman. "I don't get too much company," he said. "Least not none as pretty as you is." We sat warming our feet in front of his kerosene stove. I had the seat of honor, an old vinyl recliner that only reclined; he had an old chintz armchair. He smiled, and I smiled. I had more teeth than he had, but I didn't hold that against him. I sipped my Lipton's tea sweetened with a little molasses, and he sipped his. Outside the storm went virtuoso, tap-dancing on the tin roof and whistling through the cracks of walls papered with newspapers and old *Look* magazines.

I explained why I was there. Mr. Rollie shook his head and said, "Everywhere she go, she stirring up mess." He said he didn't know where his cousin was, but he chuckled and added, "She ain't gone far, that I know for sure. Honey always been funny like that, she likes to hide close in. When we was kids playing hide-n-go seek, she the one hide close to home base. You be counting, and turn around to go looking for folks, and she right there behind you. You didn't expect it. She ain't never got tagged out neither."

"Have you heard from her lately?"

"I ain't seen hide nor hair of Honey these last few years. Last I heard, she supposed to be taking care of her sister's baby. Child got into a little trouble with the law, here back. Can't rightly remember her name, though."

"Is there anybody else I can talk to? Do you have any more family around here?"

"It's been my experience it don't matter where you go, somebody always know some of your peoples or somebody know somebody else that know 'em. That ain't the problem as I sees it, 'cause everybody know it's a small colored world." He winked at me, and pulled together the frayed smoke jacket that he wore over two shirts and a cable knit sweater.

I tried another approach. "Tell me about that killing in sixty-four."

"Ain't nothing to tell. One man got killed, t'other went to the pen. Babies left without daddies, left to get grown and keep up the mess. Folks fight'n and feud'n, and Honey right there in the middle of it all."

I'd finally gotten Mr. Rollie on the track I wanted, but I was having a hard time dividing my attention between him and what was going on outside. I'd heard something; I just wasn't sure what it was. It could have been the bogeyman, or the pattyrollers, or maybe just the storm relentlessly dismantling the little house. I believe it was then when I decided that country living wasn't for me. I couldn't wait to get back to the streets—of suburbia.

Oblivious to his competition outside, Mr. Rollie continued, "When John Henry got out and went 'round apologizing to folks like they taught him in that steppin' program in the pen, I thought things was finally smoothing out. But, naw, that only kicked up more sand."

You know that feeling you get when a sneeze is building, when it's just a vague sort of tickle? A vague tickle fluttered at the outer edges of my mind. Something Mr. Rollie had said was causing the tickle. I couldn't put my finger on it. I couldn't ask him to repeat it, because I didn't know what it was. If I could have held still and concentrated it might have come to me, but the storm made me jumpy. I had settled in listening to Mr. Rollie when a blast of light hit the house, illuminating every crack, and turning Mr. Rollie's eyes into gorged-out holes. I choked off a scream.

Mr. Rollie sighed and said, "Them boys again."

"What boys?"

"From over in Corcoran. They call theyselves devil worshipers. Come round here stealing stuff from the graveyard." He sighed again, and went back to his story. "John Henry came here apologizing for taking some girl from me near on fifty years ago," Mr. Rollie said. "I told him, man I don't even remember no Ethel Lee, much less begrudge anything y'all had going. I can tell you one thing, if she'd a been mine, she'd a stayed mine. Ain't no doubt that. But them babies, they grown now, Mason's babies, they the ones you should be apologizing to. I said it straight to his face; you owes Quinton Anthony Mason's babies some apologies too."

The light hit us again. It was like some alien craft had locked onto us with its tractor beam. I could almost feel the little house shudder. I lost it then, I rolled off the recliner, landed on my knees, grabbed my purse, and was at the door. I had to get out of there. I said, "I'm sorry Mr. Rollie, but I have to go."

"I don't think you want to chance going out there, not less you got one of them SUV things. The mud's about a foot deep by now. You best wait till morning."

I didn't care about the mud. I didn't care about the rain. I didn't care about anything but getting as far away as I could from Pit Pat, devil worshipers, and mysterious lights. And I certainly wasn't going to spend the night with Mr. Rollie, no matter how dapper he was in his smoking jacket, and no matter how much Lipton's tea sweetened with molasses he plied me with. I found my keys and bolted out the door. The rain hit me full-face. I didn't care. I stepped off the porch and sunk up to my knees in mud. It sucked at my legs and wouldn't let go. This time I screamed. I was wearing my brand-new ankle-high Pilner boots, and when I thought about what the mud was doing to them I tried not to weep.

Cooing to me like I was a baby who'd taken a little tumble, Mr. Rollie helped me inside. The mud had sucked off one of my boots, and I hobbled in, making squishing noises and trying not to whimper. I cleaned up the best I could, using the washpan of water Mr. Rollie heated on the kerosene stove. He gave me a pair of sleeves cut from a sweater, old-fashioned leg warmers, and an old pair of overalls. I gladly accepted both and immediately put them on. I reclaimed the recliner and allowed Mr. Rollie to cover me with a quilt he said his mother had pieced before he was born. He pulled a hassock up to his chair, put his feet up, and covered himself with another quilt. "I must apologize for the facilities," he said, "but if nature calls . . ." He blushed and nodded toward a molasses bucket in the corner. I assured him that if nature did call, I wouldn't answer. We watched the hot stove's rosy glow in the darkened room, dozing off now and then. By the time morning came, Mr. Rollie had told me a story of murder and redemption and a man who only wanted to apologize.

"Mother will you listen, please. I told you the rain, dirt roads, I got stranded."

"You could have called. I was worried sick."

"I tried, but I couldn't pick up a signal. Will you just listen? What is Toni's last name?"

"What good is that phone if you don't use it?"

"Mother, this is important. What is Toni's last name?"

She told me, and everything just fell into place. How could I have missed it?

"Mother get over to Toni's house, now. I should be there in an hour, but you've got to get there right away. Call an ambulance and have them meet you there. Mother, you hear me?"

She'd already hung up.

Forty-five frantic minutes later, I pulled up in front of Toni's house and parked behind Mother's car. If the ambulance had been there, it was now gone. I climbed the steps and beat on Toni's front door. I got no answer. I beat some more.

"Goodness, gracious child. Will you cut out all that racket?" I tuned to find Mother standing on the porch next door.

"What are you doing over there? And where is Sister Venable?"

"Aren't you forgetting your manners? Don't you think you should speak to Mr. Leroy before you go putting me through the third degree?"

Mr. Leroy wore a blue flannel shirt this time. He said, "Leave that child alone, Lorraine." Then to me he said, "Sister Venable's at the hospital, baby. No need for us to holler back and forth like this. Come on over here and tell us what you found out."

"First off, Quintelle and Toni are half-sisters," I said. "Quinton Anthony Mason was their father. He was the man who got killed, not John Henry Clay. I think Miss Annie Mae got the names mixed up, which is why we were mixed up. The second thing, Sister Venable is their aunt.

"What does that have to do with poor Venable laying up in that hospital all dehydrated and everything?" Mother was seated on the sofa awfully close to Mr. Leroy. He took her hand and squeezed it. "There, there, Lorraine. I'm sure she'll be alright." I swear Mother simpered.

"That bit of information is key to . . ." Mother's head was on Mr. Leroy's shoulder, now. I stumbled on. "You know how some girls dream of growing up to be like Harriet Tubman or even Halle Berry? Quintelle and Toni grew up in Pit Pat, steeped in the folklore of their father's murder and dreaming of the day they could kill the man who killed him."

It looked like Mr. Leroy was nuzzling the top of Mother's head. I stopped and watched them, transfixed and horrified. Mr. Leroy said, "Go on, baby." It took me a moment to figure out he was talking to me.

"John Henry Clay was called to preach while in prison. He also participated in a twelve-step program. When he got out, he combined the two, traveling about the country preaching and trying to make amends to anybody he ever harmed. Because they were so young when their father was murdered, Quintelle and Toni didn't know what John Henry Clay looked like. They could have walked right past him and not have known him, which is what they did when he started preaching on K Street Mall. That's why when they got word that he was preaching up this way, they dragged poor Sister Venable downtown to see if she'd recognized him. Of course they didn't tell her what they were doing. It was kind of like a street corner line-up, without either of the parties being aware of it. Mr. Clay didn't have long to live after Sister Venable caught one glimpse of him and ran off. Quintelle and Toni saw to that."

Mother lifted her head from Mr. Leroy's shoulder and shook it sadly. "That's a shame. I never did like that Quintelle child."

Mr. Leroy said, "Ladies, I still don't understand how Sister Venable come to be in the wrong house."

I looked at Mother. "You go ahead," she said. You tell him." She nudged Mr. Leroy. "I told you she was smart. Just listen to her lay it all out."

I cleared my throat—performance anxiety—and resumed my narrative. "Sister Venable was terrified that John Henry Clay was coming after her for sending him to prison. That's why she tried to get arrested. Quintelle and Toni didn't tell her that they'd killed him. When they packed frantically, and left taking her car, Sister Venable was certain John Henry was on his way to get her. But Sister Venable is a tough old sister. The only weapon she had was her walker, so she took it and hobbled over to Toni's house to hide. I supposed she thought she could at least make it difficult for him to find her."

Mother nudged Mr. Leroy again, "See, I told you she was smart." Mr.

Leroy nodded in agreement. Then she fixed me with her I-feel-an-urge-to-get-into-somebody's-business look and said, "I wonder if there's a reward for Quintelle and Toni's arrest. I hear that they have people in Jefferson City, Missouri, and Duxbury, Massachusetts."

My phone rang just then. I checked the caller. It was Ada Perkins. I was almost glad.

# BETTER DEAD THAN WED

*Gar Anthony Haywood*

"You see that?"

"I saw it."

"That has to make what? Three times in the last half-hour?"

"It makes four. But who's counting?"

"I am. He's gonna kill that woman at this rate!"

"No, he isn't. He isn't hurting her, he's just bullyin' her. But even if he wasn't—"

"Joe—"

"Close your eyes, Dottie. Try to get some sleep. That's a private matter, and you know it."

It was sound advice, I knew, but I couldn't take it. Tired as I was at 3:30 in the morning, the longhaired, Stetson-wearing cowboy in the blue Dodge pickup two car-lengths ahead of us had my blood boiling too vigorously for sleep. My husband, Big Joe, and I had been lagging behind him for a little over forty minutes, his truck and ours apparently locked on identical cruise control settings as we pushed north on Interstate 15 toward Salt Lake City, and four times now the big man had taken his right hand off the Dodge's wheel to reach over and slap at the face of the woman sitting in the cab beside him. The first time it happened, I thought

I'd imagined it, but then the hand went out a second time, and I heard Joe mumble a curse under his breath, and I knew he'd seen it, too.

"We have to do something, Joe," I said, fighting to keep my eyes open. I was only an hour relieved from a six-hour shift of driving, and my tired old bones were begging for sleep.

"Woman, be serious."

"I *am* being serious. Look at how he's treating that poor girl!"

"I don't have to look. I've been watching it, same as you. But you don't see that shotgun in 'back of that boy's window? What do you think would happen if I pulled alongside 'im, tried to object to the way he treats his woman?"

It was a fair question to ask, and one I had no answer for. Obviously, were Joe to attempt such a thing, I'd likely be a widow—if not a corpse—before the next sunrise.

"If I thought she were in serious danger, I'd take the chance," Joe said, growling. "But she's not. That doesn't make what he's doin' to her right, but . . ."

"It isn't worth getting shot over. No. You're right, baby, it's not." I sighed. "I guess we'd better just stay out of it."

And with that, I closed my eyes. More to keep from witnessing any more mayhem in the Dodge than to try and drift off to sleep.

About fifteen minutes later, I emerged from a restless doze to find our truck and Lucille, the Airstream trailerhome we keep hitched behind it, parked in the lot of a dimly lit public rest stop.

"You need to go?" Joe asked, his hand already opening his door. Obviously, he did.

I gave the question a little thought and nodded, then pulled myself upright and got out of the truck to join him. One thing life on the road teaches you quickly is, more so than "when you gotta go you gotta go," given the opportunity, you had *better* go before you *need* to go. Otherwise . . .

The other thing the vagabond life of the roaming, sixty-something retiree teaches you is, highway rest stops are rarely the most cheerful of places. The facilities they offer are often a godsend, but other than that, most of them are dreadful in broad daylight and just downright terrifying in the wee hours of the morning. This one was a prime example.

Like most of them, it was fronted by highway and had an undeveloped wasteland at its back. Behind the two small mortar block buildings in which the rest rooms and ubiquitous soda machines resided, dry brush faded into pitch black night, giving not a clue to what perils might lay in the distance. Adding to the spooky ambiance of the place was an almost unearthly silence. I hadn't really paid much attention to the parking lot upon leaving the truck, but it hadn't been empty; there'd been at least two big rigs sitting there, and one, maybe two other passenger vehicles as well. Yet Joe and I seemed to be the only living creatures moving about the grounds.

It all made for a scene I wanted to put behind me as quickly as possible.

And I almost made a clean escape. I was hurrying out of the ladies' room, my business done in record time, when the cowboy's woman stumbled in, sniffling and wiping her nose on the back of one wrist. We met in the doorway and all but collided with each other. I hadn't seen the big woman's face before now, but I recognized her all the same. Through the back window of the Dodge pickup, I'd caught glimpses of the checkered blouse she was wearing, and the long, dirty blond hair that ran halfway down her back, just like her man's.

"Pardon me," I said.

The cowboy's woman just nodded, red-eyed, and stepped quickly past.

Now, here is where my story could have ended without incident. This was my opportunity to simply turn and walk away, leave the lives of two strangers to whatever God's plan was for them. But Dottie Loudermilk has never been one to miss a chance to meddle. As Joe has grown fond of saying, I boldly trample in where others fear to tread.

"You shouldn't let him treat you that way," I said, regretting the words even as they were traveling the short distance between us.

She looked at me for a moment, not at all sure she'd heard me right, and said, "What?"

"We saw him hitting you. My husband and I. We couldn't help it, your truck's been right in front of ours for the past thirty minutes."

She didn't say anything.

"I don't know your situation, so maybe I have no right to speak, but if I were you—"

"Yeah, I know. You'd leave 'im." She almost laughed when she said it, the idea was so outlandish to her.

"Yes. I would."

"Well, then. It's a shame you *aren't* me, isn't it?"

"Please. I didn't mean—"

"Lady, if I had somewhere else to go, I'd be there. But I don't. Okay?"

"I'm sure you think you love him. And that he doesn't always treat you that badly. But even so—"

"You don't know what you're talking about. He *does* always treat me that badly. Sandy's a twenty-four hour jackass, all jerk, all the time." She was angry now. "But there ain't nothin' I can do about that, 'cept try and run away again and get myself killed. Is that what you want me to do?"

"No, of course not. I just—"

"You just wish I had more respect for myself. Yeah, I know. That makes two of us."

She barely got this last out before she broke down completely, fled into the nearest stall, and closed the door behind her before I could say anything more.

I thought about going after her, tapping on the stall door to further plead with her to save herself, but I knew that would only be compounding an already monumental mistake.

So I just said a hushed, "I'm sorry," and left.

"What happened?" Joe asked me when I returned to our truck. I wasn't going to say anything, but he hasn't needed to be told when there's something bothering me for a long, long time.

"Nothing. Let's go," I said. "Please."

Now I could see that Sandy the cowboy's truck had been parked under a dark lamp post several spaces from us all along. And it was empty.

*"Corrine! Hurry up in there, damnit, we gotta go!"*

He was standing right outside the ladies' room door, all but sticking his head inside to bellow at her. He sounded like he was furious, but then, I had sense he always did, at least when he was talking to Corrine.

"Jeez Loweez," Joe said sadly, disgusted by this sorry display of boorish manhood.

"Please, Joe. Let's go," I said again, not wanting to be there when the cowboy's woman finally found the will to obey him.

We weren't gone thirty minutes when I awoke to Big Joe shouting:

"Hey! What the—"

I looked up to see him struggling with the wheel, fighting to keep our truck and Lucille aimed in a straight line. His face was a study in pique and concentration.

"What happened?" I asked, working to sit up straight.

"The damn fool almost hit me, that's what! I hadn't seen 'im coming and pulled over . . ."

"Who?" I peered out the windshield at the dark highway ahead, trying to follow my husband's gaze.

"Our spousal abusing friend in the cowboy hat again, that's who. Crazy sonofagun's gotta be doin' eighty-five, at least!"

And sure enough, he was right. There the familiar Dodge pickup was, wobbling from side to side as it rapidly shrank into the distance before us.

"Oh, my God. I wonder what happened," I said, suddenly wide awake.

"I don't know. But . . ." He didn't complete the thought.

"But what?"

Joe glanced at me, wearing the face he usually reserves for only the most dire occasions. "It looked to me like he was alone. At least, if his woman was with 'im, I didn't see her."

"Oh, Lord, no. You don't think—"

"Get the binoculars out of my bag, Dottie. I'm gonna see if I can't catch 'im before he disappears completely."

While I retrieved his gym bag from behind our seats as instructed, Joe stepped on the gas, urged our Ford pickup to haul us and Lucille down the interstate with even greater urgency. It was only a matter of time before the two-truck race we'd just started came upon more northbound traffic, after which the cowboy's Dodge would almost certainly lose us for good, so I knew we had only seconds to steal a look into its cab before it was too late.

"Now, Dottie, hurry!" Joe said. "He's just come up on somebody, he's gotta slow down!"

And it was true. The other truck's taillights glowed bright in the distance as the driver applied its brakes, and it was now only twenty or so car-lengths ahead of us. I took Joe's field glasses from his bag and brought them quickly up to my eyes, spinning the focus controls madly to bring the Dodge into some measure of sharp relief. It wasn't in view for more than fifteen seconds before it used the shoulder of the road to spin around the car ahead of it and, just as Joe and I had feared, escape our reach for good, but that was long enough. Long enough to see that the cowboy in the Stetson hat and fur-lined jacket was alone in the cab now, and that his woman, Corrine, wasn't the only thing his truck was missing.

The hunting rifle that had been mounted outside its rear window was gone now, too.

"Oh, my God, Joe, what have I done?" I asked.

"What do you mean? You didn't—" He stopped when he saw my face, understanding immediately that I'd done something inadvisable yet again. "Oh, no. Don't tell me. Back there at the rest stop . . ."

"I had a few words with her in the ladies' room. As I was going out, and she was coming in. I didn't mean to upset her, but . . ."

"No! Tell me you didn't!"

"All I said was that she should leave him. That she should find a way to get away from him, that's all."

"Aw, Jeez Loweez, Dottie! You went and stirred the poor child up! Two-to-one, she went back out to that man's truck and gave 'im some lip! Either got herself stranded back there, or . . . or *worse!*"

He was right, of course. I could see it all happen exactly that way in my mind.

"We have to go back, Joe," I said. "We've got to make sure she's all right."

"What?"

"Don't. Don't argue with me about this. Just turn this truck around right now and go!"

It took us a little over fifteen minutes to reach the rest stop again, and it looked the same way now as it had when we'd last seen it: dark, desolate, and as creepy as a fog-enshrouded moor. There were still a few sixteen-wheelers parked in the darkest corner of the lot, but ours was now the only passenger vehicle around. If this had been a hot dog stand rather than a rest stop, its owners would have been forced into bankruptcy long ago.

There was no sign of Corrine anywhere.

Predictably, Joe stepped out of the truck and told me to stay put. The thought of being left there alone to imagine I could see all kinds of horrible things lurking in the shadows was unnerving, but I was too tired to join him, even if I had wanted to. I'd been awake now for over nineteen hours, and at the tender age of sixty-one, adrenaline can only take a girl so far. Nodding my head and watching Joe start off toward the ladies' room with only one of two eyes open was the absolute best I could do at this point.

"Hello! Anybody home?" Joe called out, standing just outside the door of the women's rest room in the same way Corrine's cowboy had done earlier. Receiving no response, Joe called again, and still no one answered back. My eyes drifted closed for a moment. I caught myself and sat up abruptly, just caught sight of my husband disappearing inside the bathroom.

I watched and waited for him to exit again.

And waited.

And waited.

How much time went by, I'll never really know. My guess now is that it wasn't much more than three or four minutes. But that was all the time my poor eyes needed to grow bored, flutter closed again—and stay that way.

The next thing I knew, I was snoring. Head tilted back, mouth agape, body propped up against the passenger-side door. Had I not snorted myself awake, I might still be asleep today.

"Oh, my Lord, Dottie," I said.

I scanned my surroundings desperately, searching for Big Joe, but he was nowhere to be found. I was sure I had only been out for a minute or two, but the damage had been done. Four parking spaces to my right sat the cowboy named Sandy's blue Dodge pickup, its passenger cab as empty as the truck bed behind it.

He'd come back while I was dozing.

I leapt from the truck and started running as fast as I could toward the ladies' room, giving no thought whatsoever to slamming the truck's door closed behind me.

"Joe!"

I entered the bathroom and found myself alone; neither Joe nor the cowboy was there. I went to the men's room next, just bolted straight in without warning, but again, the room was vacant. All the stalls were empty and silent.

I was now completely terrified.

I sprinted outside, spun around like a top looking for some sign of my husband, but there was no such sign to see. It was as if he had vanished into thin air.

"Joe! *Where are you?!*"

And then I realized where he had to be: out there in the black void behind the rest stop's boundaries, where Corrine's cowboy would have surely chosen to take her if, as Joe and I had feared, she'd said or done something, thanks to me, to finally make a murderer out of him.

I went around to the back of the two mortar block buildings and studied the black, irregular horizon. They were next to impossible to see, but they were there: one human figure advancing on another, the latter a good fifty yards away. The one in motion was wearing a cowboy hat; the other, whose silhouette was almost certainly that of my husband, was not.

And the one with the hat was carrying a rifle.

"Joe! *Look out!*" I screamed.

I started running even though I knew it was hopeless. I would never reach him in time on this old woman's legs. As I closed in on the pair, I could see that a body lay in the brush at Joe's feet.

"Dottie, no!" Joe called back.

But it was too late. The cowboy with the rifle turned toward me just as I lost my footing and fell, slammed to the cold, hard earth like someone who was already dead. I heard the crunch of footsteps as they rapidly approached, looked up to see what I was certain would be the last human face I would ever gaze upon.

"Hey, are you all right?" the woman named Corrine asked.

. . .

"I swear, woman, I don't know how you do it," Joe said several hours later. He was almost laughing, but not quite.

"What?"

"Bring us both so close to death without actually killing either of us. If the kids knew what you keep puttin' me through out here . . ."

We were Salt Lake City bound again, Joe back at the wheel, me fighting sleep right beside him. Corrine was in a Utah jail cell somewhere, and the boyfriend named Sandy she'd coldcocked to land herself there was in the hospital, trying to remember the serial number on the rifle butt he'd been clobbered with. Which shouldn't have been too difficult, I thought, considering the fact it had been attached to his own rifle.

The state troopers who had cleaned up the mess at the rest stop afterward thought it was funny, how Corrine had not only brained the abusive cowboy she'd finally—and somewhat "mysteriously"—had her fill of, but taken everything he owned as well, right down to the coat off his back and the hat on his head. They even got a laugh or two out of the cold feet that had brought her scrambling back to the scene of the crime. But myself, I couldn't find much humor in the situation at all, and neither could Big Joe. Mistaking the similarly built Corrine for her beloved cowboy after she'd fled the scene of his assault had, after all, cost my husband and me a great deal of grief. And maybe a few years off the ends of our already well-advanced lives, abject terror having that alleged effect on people.

But, hey. No harm was really done in the end. Corrine learned to stand up for herself, and I learned to save my advice for women who ask for it.

And Big Joe and I have yet another great story to worry our five children with.

We look forward to collecting many more.

# THE WEREWOLF FILE

*Hugh Holton*

The murder victims were discovered aboard the *Viking Warrior* tramp freighter on January 18. The freighter, which plied its trade throughout the Great Lakes waterways, had gone to sea with a complement of eight sailors and two officers on January 16. The freighter had sailed from South Chicago's frozen harbor out onto Lake Michigan. Its destination was the port of Milwaukee, where it was scheduled to unload a cargo of copper ore and pick up a load of scrap iron.

Nothing was heard from the *Viking Warrior* after it cleared the 95th Street drawbridge. The ship never made it to Milwaukee and was discovered adrift twelve hours after departure less than a mile off of Navy Pier on the shores of downtown Chicago. The Coast Guard was summoned and, shortly after the grisly discoveries were made on board, the police were called.

January 18 was not only a bitterly cold night, but also the day on which the Reverend Doctor Martin Luther King Jr.'s life of service and sacrifice to his country is commemorated. The *Viking Warrior* was tied up at Navy Pier, and bright floodlights illuminated its rusting sides. Coast Guard personnel and Chicago police officers moved rapidly up and down the gangplank. The news media was on hand, and reporters, fighting the subzero temperatures, attempted to get a statement from anyone at the scene. However, no one was talking. At least not yet. The story of what had occurred aboard the *Viking Warrior* was as chilling as the bite of the frosty January air and could frighten the very marrow of the most hearty human soul.

On board the *Viking Warrior* a conference was being held on the bridge. Present was a Coast Guard lieutenant commander, who was there merely as a courtesy to the maritime agency that had discovered the murders. The rest of those present were Chicago police officers.

The ranks and functions of the cops varied, but the focus of everyone present was on three detectives—two active and one retired. They were in charge of the investigation, as well as the investigations of the other murders that had been committed with the same MO as those on the *Viking Warrior*. And the three detectives were terrified, not because they were the attention of such intense scrutiny from the cop brass that had come out on this cold night, but because they knew who was responsible for all of the murders that had been committed. Murders that brought the number of violent deaths to a total of twenty since the first of the year.

Such knowledge should have given the detectives some degree of joy or possibly even relief, but it did not. This was due to them being aware that the perpetrator of all of these horrible crimes was going to come after them next. The additional dawning factor was that this murderer was not human, but a werewolf.


"Their throats were ripped out," said Detective Esmeralda Montoya, a beautiful Hispanic woman whose unnecessary use of heavy makeup made her partner, B. J. Jackson, derisively refer to her as "the Joker."

It was New Year's morning, and B. J., a thin black man with wavy hair, a café au lait complexion, and a penchant for wearing pastel-colored striped suits with matching derbies, had a hangover. In response to her comment about the crime photos she was viewing, he said, "That'll happen at least a hundred more times in this town before the year is out."

"But these victims weren't slashed with a knife, B. J. Their throats were literally ripped open. Look."

On this New Year's morning, Detective Jackson was wearing a lime-green double-breasted suit with the obligatory matching derby hanging from the hat tree inside the homicide office squad room entrance. When Esmeralda was displeased with B. J., she referred to him as "the neon Stan Laurel." Now as she extended the grisly photos to him, B. J. turned a sickly shade comparable to the color of his suit and said, "Esmeralda, please don't."

She smiled and was about to begin tormenting him unmercifully for all those "Joker" cracks he had made about her over the three years of their partnership, when a sound carried to them from the homicide C.O.'s office, which made her turn a shade of sickly green similar to that of her partner's. It was their boss calling them, and he didn't sound pleased. As if going to the gallows, they went to find out what had the homicide lieutenant so displeased.

As they drove through the six-inch accumulation of snow across Chicago to the Washington Park Boulevard neighborhood, Detectives Esmeralda Montoya and B. J. Jackson were puzzled. On the orders of their commanding officer, they were going to see a retired detective named Thomas H. Hogan. Esmeralda and B. J.'s lieutenant had told them that this Hogan was going to be an "unofficial" consultant on the triple homicide case that they had been assigned to investigate that morning.

Hogan lived in a three-story, multi-unit apartment building on Indiana Avenue at 62nd Street. After consulting the lobby directory, B. J. moaned, "Why has it always got to be on the top floor?"

Esmeralda scolded, "If you spent more time in the gym and less in gin mills, a little stair-climbing wouldn't bother you."

He gave her an evil glare, but didn't respond. As they slowly ascended the steep steps, he was gratified when he noticed that her breathing had also become labored.

At the door to apartment three south, they knocked. A peephole opened, and a suspicious eye carefully examined them before a deep male voice challenged, "What do you two rejects from the Barnum and Bailey Circus want?"

The detectives bristled and in tandem flashed their badges. A moment of silence ensued, which was followed by a chuckle from inside and a quite audible, "I don't believe it." Then numerous locks were undone and the door finally swung open.

Retired Detective Thomas Hercules Hogan was seventy-six years old, stooped and white-haired. On this New Year's Day he had been retired from the Chicago Police Department for twenty years. Esmeralda and B. J., who both had less than ten years on the force, had heard of Hogan's exploits from some of the old-timers. However, most of these tales were a bit on the tall side, to say the least.

Tom Hogan had worked on a special squad out of the chief of detectives' office at police headquarters. The only cases he was ever assigned were of the "bizarre and unusual" variety, whatever that meant. But the strange thing, from what Esmeralda and B. J. had been able to find out about Tom Hogan, was that he never made any arrests, but had an unheard of 100-percent clearance rate.

There was one more unsettling element about the fabled detective that Esmeralda and B. J. had heard from an old sergeant. Supposedly, in his day, Detective Tom Hogan was considered more of an exorcist than a cop.

The retired detective's apartment was nicely furnished but as dated, in Montoya and Jackson's estimation, as he was. The furniture was sturdy, but would have looked more natural in a circa 1900s turn-of-the-century Americana history museum. Then there were the books.

Every available space in the apartment was loaded with books. They overflowed the floor-to-ceiling shelves, were stacked on every surface that would hold them, and covered the floors. There were so many books and the apartment was so cluttered that Montoya and Jackson were forced to stand. Stand under the amused scrutiny of their host.

"My, my, my," he chuckled, "the department has changed quite a bit since I left." He pointed at B. J. "I guess you'd call that 'Kermit the Frog' outfit you've got on conservative business attire."

As B. J. glared at Hogan, Esmeralda laughed. Then the elderly detective turned his humorous criticism on her. "And how long does it take you to put that face on in the morning, dear? You know, you look kinda like that character that Jack Nicholson played in *Batman*. What was his name?"

Before Esmeralda could explode, B. J. stepped forward and said, hurriedly, "The lieutenant wanted you to take a look at these crime scene photos. He said you'd be able to give us a hand with the case."

Hogan shoved a stack of books off the couch, took a seat, and opened the envelope. He became so involved in the crime scene pictures that he forgot about his still standing guests. Finally, he mumbled, "You two have got a bonafide werewolf on your hands."

Detectives Montoya and Jackson exchanged glances which transmitted quite clearly that they were certain that retired Detective Thomas Hogan belonged in a lunatic asylum.


"Is that your area of expertise?" Esmeralda asked. "I mean, like, werewolves?"

"Oh no, my dear," Hogan said, returning the crime scene photos to the envelope and standing up to begin rummaging around in one of the bookcases. "In my day, I handled it all . . . vampires, werewolves, even an occasional alien intrusion." He found the volume he was looking for and pulled it down, causing a cloud of dust to rise into the air. "But you could say that I am one of the few remaining lycanthropists in the world."

B. J. had retreated to a corner of the living room where he stood against the wall cradling his head in his hands. Tom Hogan had made his hangover worse, and he groaned.

Hogan merely glanced at Jackson before saying, "Now there are some folks who believe that werewolves are strictly a European creature. Well, I'm here to tell you, Detective . . . uh . . ."

"Montoya, but everybody calls me Esmeralda."

"A beautiful name," Hogan said. "Was the name of the Gypsy girl in *The Hunchback of Notre Dame*, right?"

She was less than pleased about the comparison, but managed to smile. "So werewolves come from other parts of the world?"

"Dear me, yes. There have been documented sightings in China, South

America, Africa, the Middle East, and Asia. Incidents caused by human beings shapeshifting into werewolves and ripping out their victims' throats, leaving wounds exactly like the ones in your crime scene photographs."

"Wait a minute," B. J. said, pushing himself off the wall and straightening his derby. "Couldn't the incidents you're talking about have simply been caused by an actual wolf, a very large dog, or even a human with an exotic weapon?"

Hogan frowned. "So you don't believe in werewolves, Detective?"

"You can call me, B. J., Tom, and as a matter of fact, I don't."

"Well, B. J., you can call me Detective Hogan, and I'm going to make you a believer before this investigation is over. Now, shall we go take a look at the crime scene?"


The first three murders had taken place in the parking garage of a Loop hotel. Three New Year's Eve revelers, a woman and two men, were found dead with their throats ripped open.

Hogan, Montoya, and Jackson stood in the garage examining the positions in which the bodies were discovered. Although the remains had been removed hours ago, the places were marked with chalk and the entire area cordoned off with yellow barrier tape. B. J. had sufficiently recovered from his hangover to speculate as to what had occurred. Clad in a green overcoat which matched his suit and derby, the detective intoned, "The woman and the first guy were together at a party in the grand ballroom of the hotel, which has been verified. They were both a little tight when they left the party at about one A.M."

Esmeralda interrupted with, "Look who's talking."

Ignoring her, B. J. continued, "Their car was parked down here. On their way to it, the perpetrator confronted them, probably for a robbery, and then killed them both. The death of the other guy is still a mystery, but he was killed in the same fashion."

"The death of the third victim is fairly obvious," Hogan said. "He was killed because he came across the werewolf in the act of killing the first two. His body being found over there indicates that he was running away and the monster pursued and caught him. Now the question we have to ask ourselves is, why did the werewolf come after the partygoers?"

B. J. rolled his eyes and muttered, "There he goes with that werewolf crap again."

"Let me see those crime scene pictures, Esmeralda," Hogan said.

She handed them over.

After sorting through them he pointed to a photo of the dead woman. "Her dress was ripped. Do we have any pictures of the couple while they were at the party?"

"We can check," Esmeralda said.

An enterprising photographer was found who had taken a picture of the couple before they were murdered. The three detectives huddled together and examined the photo.

"What is that?" B. J. asked, pointing to a pin on the ground next to the dead woman.

"It looks like a star," Esmeralda said.

"It is," Hogan said. "A pentagram, the sign of the werewolf."


A careful examination of the backgrounds of the three victims only revealed that they had gone to a New Year's Eve party, which had resulted in their deaths. The female victim's relatives and friends were interviewed in an attempt to determine where she had obtained the pentagram-shaped pin that had been ripped from her dress during the attack. But no one could remember seeing it prior to her death.

A search of her credit card records for recent jewelry purchases also proved negative. But it was there that Esmeralda noticed a pattern. During the late morning and early afternoon of New Year's Eve, she had made four charges at stores in the area of Clark and Diversey on the north side of the city.

On the morning of January 2, the trio of detectives stood at the busy intersection of Clark and Diversey. B. J. Jackson, clad in a pastel gray derby with matching suit and overcoat, said, "First we'll split up and check the stores that the dead woman made her credit card purchases from. Then we'll begin canvassing every store within a mile of this intersection in all directions. If we don't come up with anything then—"

"Who died and left you in charge?" Esmeralda bristled.

Before an argument could blossom, Hogan stepped between them. "We must stay together. It will take us longer to complete the canvass, but we will be able to maintain some degree of safety."

"Now what are you talking about?" B. J. demanded.

"You way not yet believe in the werewolf, but it is aware of you. So as we hunt it, it will be hunting us."

Their eyes locked for a moment, but finally B. J. relented. "Whatever you say, Detective Hogan. After all you are the consultant on this investigation."

They began to canvass stores in the area.


That night the werewolf struck again. The victim was a homeless man, who died in the same fashion as the first three victims. However, this time there was a witness.


The homeless man had been collecting cans in the alley behind the 2400 block of North Lincoln Avenue when "something" attacked him. An elderly woman confined to a wheelchair had been sitting next to a window overlooking the alley and saw the entire thing. By the time Hogan, Montoya, and Jackson arrived, she was close to going into shock. She had a thick accent, which her daughter, who was sixty, explained to the detectives was due to her native tongue being Romanian. The old lady kept repeating one word, which the daughter translated. That word was "werewolf."


On the morning of January 16, which dawned bright, sunny and cold, B. J. Jackson and Esmeralda Montoya arrived at Tom Hogan's apartment. The retired detective had set up a map of the near north side of the city in his cluttered living room. On it were nine red pins, each indicating the location where the werewolf had struck in the last two weeks. Now, after a

number of eyewitness accounts of what had caused the deaths of the previous nine victims, Esmeralda and B. J. had become believers.

"Look at this," Hogan said, pointing to the red pins in the map.

B. J., who was clad in a bright blue derby with matching outfit, said,
"That's the location where each of the bodies was found. We already
know that, Tom."

"Look closer," the retired detective said, exercising the patience he
was always forced to display when addressing the derby-wearing cop.

B. J. did look closer, but was unable to see anything but the pins. However, Esmeralda discovered what Hogan was getting at. Removing a black
eyeliner from her purse, she began tracing lines between the pins on the
map.

"It's a star," she said, stepping back and admiring her handiwork. "Or
at least almost a star. Part of it is missing."

"Very good, my dear," Hogan said. "It is a pentagram. And the last
missing point is . . ." He took her pencil and completed the figure.
". . . right here."

B. J. stepped forward and squinted at the map. "That's a little side
street off Halsted near Wrightwood. There's nothing there but a few old
apartment buildings and a couple of secondhand shops."

"What we have here, my dear fellow partners in crime solving,"
Hogan said, "is a message from the werewolf. In its arrogance the monster
is either telling us where the next murder will occur or where we can find
it in human form. Shall we go?"


The short street looked like an alley. It was rundown, shabby, and wasn't
well traveled. There were a few ragged tenement buildings, most of which
were abandoned, a trash-strewn vacant lot and two storefronts. One of
the stores was occupied by a used plumbing supply company and the other
was the Pentacle Antique Shop. The Pentacle sign was written in white
Old English script on a black background. Beneath the lettering was a
pentagram.

"Are you sure we should go in there?" B. J. said, his voice trembling.

Hogan and Esmeralda turned to look at him, "Have you got a better idea?" the retired detective responded.

"Big fraidy cat," Esmeralda goaded.

B. J. was the last one through the door.

The interior of the Pentacle Antique Shop was as cluttered and dusty as Tom Hogan's apartment. There were all types of antiques on display from handmade furniture to ancient weaponry. A glass case ran the length of the shop. Inside was an odd assortment of costume jewelry, most of which was no more than junk. However, one piece in particular drew their attention. It was a jewel-studded pentagram exactly like the one that the female victim had been wearing before she was murdered on New Year's Eve.

"I've got a bad feeling about this," B. J. moaned.

The woman's voice came from behind them. "Good morning. I am Lucretia Talbot, the proprietress of this establishment. May I help you?"

The three detectives were so startled by her sudden appearance that they spun around and backed up so abruptly they almost knocked over the display case.

Lucretia Talbot was tall, thin, and dressed completely in black. She had black hair worn in a boyish cut and features that could only be described as sharp. Then there were the eyes. They were as black as a pit in hell, and when her gaze swept over them, they felt like prey being examined by a predator.

Hogan managed to find his voice and made introductions. "We were, interested in this unusual pendant in the display case."

Without moving, she said, "Do you want to purchase the pentagram?"

"Perhaps," Hogan managed. "Do you know what it symbolizes?"

She smiled displaying perfect teeth. "In some cultures it is reputedly the sign of the werewolf, if you believe in such things."

"Where did you get it?" Esmeralda asked.

"I really can't recall. I've had it for years, in fact, recently it was stolen from me and then mysteriously returned."

"How was it stolen?" Hogan asked.

"Apparently a shoplifter made off with it. She was a well-dressed woman with a wallet full of credit cards. She came in on New Year's Eve, saw the pentagram and said she had to have it. But I only deal in cash, which she didn't have enough of, so no sale. I thought she had left, but while I was in the storeroom in the back, she returned and took the pendant from the display case."

Hogan handed her the photograph of the female murder victim, which had been taken at the New Years' Eve party. "Is that her?"

Lucretia Talbot took the picture, glanced at it, and replied, "As a matter of fact, it is. And she's wearing my pentagram. How interesting."

Hogan took the photo back. "Did you report the theft to the police?"

She smiled again. "No, but since the three of you are here now, I won't pass up the opportunity."

"We work homicide," B. J. snapped.

"Then I can assume that the shoplifter is dead, Detective Jackson?" she said.

B. J. and Esmeralda tensed, but Hogan remained calm. "Thanks for your time, Ms. Talbot. We'll be going now. Have a nice day."

She watched them walk to the door. "Do be careful, B. J. And remember, Detective Montoya and Detective Hogan, the streets out there are dangerous."


They ran to the police car and locked the doors. Esmeralda and B. J. were shaking uncontrollably, but Hogan appeared as if nothing had happened.

"We should bust that broad, Tom," B. J. said with false bravado.

"For what, B. J.?" Hogan retorted. "Scaring the red corpuscles out of three cops?"

"You were scared too, Tom?" Esmeralda asked.

"You're darn tootin'. And she was merely toying with us. Now we can anticipate the next murder being something a great deal more spectacular than the ones she's committed so far. It will also involve a body of water."

"Why water?" B. J. and Esmeralda asked as one.

"Because female werewolves like to swim."

On the night of Mr. Martin Luther King Jr.'s birthday, the murders aboard the *Viking Warrior* were discovered.

.   .   .

It was dawn when they got back to Hogan's apartment. Esmeralda sat down on a stack of books, and B. J., in his black and white pin-stripe ensemble, simply collapsed on the floor. Hogan shuffled into a bedroom in the rear of his apartment and returned with a small cardboard box. He sat down on the couch and opened the box.

"What's that?" Esmeralda asked.

His fingers shook noticeably as he held two objects in his hand. He held one up for her to see.

B. J.'s eyes went wide. "Is that a silver bullet?"

Hogan nodded "They are chambered for a .38 caliber revolver, and all I have left is these two."

"But we carry nine-millimeter semi-automatics," Esmeralda said.

"I don't see as good as I used to, so one of you will have to use my gun." He removed a rusty four-inch barrel police special from his holster. "Which one of you is the best shot?"

B. J. pointed to his partner.

Lucretia Talbot, in her werewolf form, came for them fifteen minutes later.

The front window of Tom Hogan's living room was thirty-five feet above the ground, and the building facade a wall of solid brick, but she managed to climb it with ease. They were unaware that the she-wolf was there until her shadow blotted out the early morning light. B. J., still seated on the floor, saw her first. Shouting a warning, he leaped to his feet and pulled his Beretta pistol an instant before the werewolf smashed through the glass and bounded into the living room.

Esmeralda attempted to raise Hogan's revolver containing the silver bullets, but the sight of the monster froze the female cop in place.

The werewolf stood upright on her hind legs. She was covered with a thick coat of jet black hair, and canine ears rose on each side of her head. The menacing black eyes, which had frightened the cops back at the Pentacle Antique Shop, were now the blood red orbs of a beast gone mad. A muzzle extended from the center of the face, and the mouth, spewing saliva, was open, exposing razor-sharp, flesh-rending teeth. Her arms and legs were muscular, and the hands tipped with inch-long talons. Then, with a roar that shook the very foundations of the building, she attacked.

B. J. reacted. Taking dead aim at the monster's chest, he fired nine rounds in rapid succession. He was certain that he hit her each time, but the lead bullets not only did no damage, they didn't even slow the werewolf down. It did cause the beast to make him the focal point of her attack.

With one immense, black hair-covered hand, the she-wolf knocked the smoking weapon from B. J.'s hand and grabbed him by the throat. He was lifted off the floor to dangle impotently from her grasp. In an instant it would have been over for the detective, but Esmeralda finally snapped out of her terror-induced trance. She raised the rusty .38, took aim, and fired. The bullet struck the she-wolf in the shoulder, and she howled in pain.

Releasing B. J., she turned on Esmeralda. Now blood was visible, flowing heavily from the wound made by the silver bullet. As she advanced, her red eyes flared with a fury that froze the blood in Esmeralda Montoya's veins.

Hogan had not moved since the attack began. Now he shouted, "You've got to hit her in a vital spot to kill her."

The she-wolf ignored the old man and continued to advance.

The detective trembled, as she lined up the front and rear sights of the revolver. Esmeralda waited until the beast's terrible presence filled her entire field of vision before she squeezed the trigger. The gunshot echoed through the apartment.

Detectives Hogan, Jackson, and Montoya watched the ambulance crew remove the body of Lucretia Talbot from Hogan's apartment.

"How are we going to explain killing that woman?" B. J. moaned. "She looks like a normal human being again."

Esmeralda, who had fired the last silver bullet and hit the she-wolf between the eyes, responded, "We'll simply tell the truth, B. J. That . . . thing came up here and attacked us. We should also be able to connect her to the other murders that have occurred since the first of the year."

"We can't tell the truth," Hogan said, solemnly. "No one will believe us. The homicides in this case will have to be classified like all the others I have handled like this—mysterious deaths from undetermined causes."

It was the day before Easter when the homicide commander called Esmeralda and B. J. into his office. On a beautiful spring morning, the pair of detectives, Jackson dressed in a chautreuse derby with matching outfit and Esmeralda made up like a Gypsy fortuneteller, drove to Tom Hogan's apartment.

When the retired detective opened the door he asked. "What is it now?"

"Would you believe a vampire?" B. J. said.

# DÉJÀ VU

*Geri Spencer Hunter*

The only two jobs I've ever done in my entire life that meant a damn to me were bartending and writing. The first I did as a young man, the second when I got older. So, I always figured I'd end up in some alcoholic haze, strung out on Coors, writing stories, and giving death a run for its money. That's been my pattern, and I have no desire to change it. It suits me just fine. I sell enough stories to keep me housed, clothed, fed, and slightly under the influence. I have a car. I'm in damn good health, mental and physical, and I have access to all the sex I can manage.

I'm up by five-thirty, doesn't matter if it's cold, hot, wet, or foggy. I'm up. By six I've had my shower, drinking my first cup of coffee, reading the papers and half listening to the news. I'm at my computer at seven, staring at a blank screen, willing clever thoughts to form in my head. Damn way to make a living, I know, but I'm lucky. The words usually start flowing, mixed up at first, but slowly falling into place making sense, creating tales of woe.

That morning started like all the others, up at five-thirty, showered by six, drinking coffee, and half listening to the news when the phone rang. *Who the hell's calling at this ungodly hour?* I wondered, picking up the receiver.

"This better be damn good," I said trying to sound civil.

"Billy?"

"Mary Ella!"

"Amazing, after all these years, you haven't forgotten my voice, Sugar."

How the hell do you forget evil? I thought, feeling the old anger and desire welling up inside and trying to stop the images forming in my mind. My God, how long had it been? Years, more years than I cared to remember. It didn't matter. I could never quite forget that voice, and I tried, hard, but it stayed in my mind, occasionally haunting my thoughts. And it hadn't changed, still sounded soft, whispery, sexy.

I first heard it in the early fifties, when I was eighteen still living with my mama in a Midwest city that was really a town, just wanted to be a city. Kinda like me, a boy wanting to be a man. I was in The Rainbow Club drinking beer and trying to look older than I was. Mr. Johnson, the owner, hired me to help out around the place, washing glasses, mopping floors, and scrubbing down the toilets. He knew I was under age, but ignored it cause he knew I was a hard worker, needed the money, and was in a big hurry to be grown. Some days, he let me hang out like a paying customer and have a beer or two under the table, as long as I behaved and didn't draw attention to myself.

It was Saturday. The place was packed shoulder-to-shoulder. The jukebox blared, and the tiny dance floor was so crowded people were dancing between the tables. Her soft whispery voice cut right through all that damn noise. I laughed, it sounded so put-on and fake. Nobody talks like that, I thought, watching her work the room. She was a woman, wasn't no doubts about that, long and lean, with just enough meat on her bones to give her some eye-catching curves. Her black skin was smooth and velvety and flawless, her cheekbones so high they almost brushed up against her huge brown eyes. She was the prettiest lady I'd ever seen, and I wasn't into ebony ladies. I preferred coffee-with-cream or just cream-colored period, until I saw her.

"You like what you see, Sugar?"

I wasn't surprised she felt my eyes on her cause I was staring so hard. I opened my mouth but no words came out.

"What's wrong, cat got your tongue?" She laughed showing perfect teeth, flung her head back, causing her long black pressed hair to sway, and stared right back. "You sure a pretty boy," she added in her fake voice and laughed again.

People were looking, beginning to get nosey. I tried to move away. I didn't want to piss off Mr. Johnson, and I sure in hell didn't want to lose my job. Besides she was embarrassing me.

"How old are you?" she asked sidling up to me.

"Eighteen," I managed to mumble.

"You a man yet?" she asked, rubbing her fingers up and down my arm.

I didn't know what to say. I wasn't quite sure what she meant. I felt hot and sweaty, and my skin tingled.

"Leave the boy alone, Mary Ella." Mr. Johnson's quiet voice said, lifting her fingers from my arm and moving her away from the bar.

Mary Ella! Strange name for a black-black woman I thought.


When I was nineteen, things turned serious. She was still black and still pretty, and her voice sounded exactly the same. I was still at The Rainbow Club, still the handyman, and still in a hurry to be grown.

"You must like hanging out around here," she said, teasingly.

Obviously, I thought watching the bartender pour a shot of Johnny Walker Red from her personal bottle. It was like that back then. You purchased your liquor from a state-owned liquor store and brought it to the club or left it there. The bartender sold you a set up and poured your drinks.

She swallowed it neat, didn't even blink, sat her glass on the counter, and pushed it slowly toward him, again. He refilled it and pushed it back.

"How do you do that?" I asked, impressed in spite of myself.

"Takes a whole lot of practice, Sugar."

"My name's not Sugar," I managed to grumble, annoyed. That sounded childish and I was trying to be a . . . man.

She stared at me. "So what's your name?" she finally asked.

"William Sude Jr.," I said, proud to be carrying my daddy's name. "But around here, they call me Billy."

"Around here, I'll call you Sugar," she responded, a smile on her full lips.

"My name is Billy."

"Damn, Billy it is. I don't argue with no 'man' about what he wants to be called." She downed her drink.

We got on good after that. She became a regular, and I became her . . . puppet. All she had to do was sweet-talk me with that voice and look at me with those eyes, and I'd do practically whatever she wanted. I became the laughing stock of the place. Everybody but me knew I was no match for her, even though I suspected it.

"Boy, you need to leave Mary Ella alone," Mr. Johnson told me more times than I cared to count. "She's way too much for you to even think about handling."

"We're just acquaintances, Mr. Johnson," I said unable to look him in the eyes. "She's educating me."

"About what, stuff you too young to know?" he grumbled. "Hell, she's out of my league, and I'm old." He chuckled, but I sensed the worry in his voice. "You be careful, you hear boy?"

"Careful about what, Mr. Johnson?"

"Careful she don't get you into something you can't get out of."

"Why would she do that?"

"Cause she can."

I ignored him. Just a silly old man, I thought, wishing she'd pay him some mind.

She was paying me plenty, flaunting her sex around like a second skin and whispering about what she was going to do to me making my pale face red with embarrassment. The patrons started keeping track, betting how long it would take her to seduce me. Actually, she already had with her voice, her eyes, and her body.

The first time she did me, I mean really did me, I was helpless. I'd never had sex-sex before. I was always kinda shy, awkward with girls, and nobody had told me shit about sex. The guys I hung out with bragged and scoffed amongst themselves, but the truth was, they didn't know any more than I did, hadn't done much either, kissing mostly, and pressing up real close against girls when they danced. That was about the extent of it. So when Mary Ella made her move, I was beyond scared. But I wanted it, God, how I wanted it.

We did it at her place since I didn't have a place of my own. I paid my mama a little bit of rent to continue to live in the house she raised me in, not an ideal situation to carry on a sexual encounter. So we did it at Mary Ella's. She lived in a grand old house, which surprised me. I assumed she stayed in a boarding room or one of the hotels downtown. I wondered how she could afford all that luxury since she didn't seem to have a job and there was no talk of a husband. But that wasn't foremost on my mind, so I didn't dwell on it.

She opened the door, that day, dressed in lace and satin and smelling of lavender. She kissed me lightly on the lips and led me up a curving staircase. If she noticed my body trembling she made no comment. In fact, she didn't speak at all, just pulled me into a softly lit room with a big bed and drawn blinds. She pushed me gently down on satin sheets and started undressing me, slowly, one piece at a time. She undid the small buttons down the front of my shirt and eased it off my shoulders, licking my fair skin with her tongue, sucking at the soft hollow space at my neck. I twisted and turned, moaned with pleasure, felt the hardening of my manhood. I reached out and grabbed her trying to draw her closer. She brushed my hand away, undid my pant button, slowly slid down the zipper, tugged them over my hips and down passed my ankles. She untied my shoes, pulled them off, then my socks, sucked at my toes before slipping the pants over my feet letting them fall to the floor. My erection filled my shorts. She pulled them down, freeing it, and took me in her mouth. I exploded. She ignored my embarrassment, continued teaching me slowly, exquisitely, about pleasure, leaving her imprint all over my body and soul, marking me for life.

From then on, I could hardly eat or sleep, kept a hard-on, swore I was in love. She was on my mind constantly. She owned me. And she knew it, but she continued to work the room, flirting, dancing, and talking in that soft whispery, sexy voice, making me crazy.

"Boy, I got something I want you to do," Mr. Johnson said one Friday as I was focusing all my attention, as usual, on Mary Ella.

"Yes, Sir," I said, still trying to watch her making a fool of me.

"Come on now." His voice was stern. He led me to a back room full of boxes and closed the door. "Billy, you need to think about finding another job," he said, staring at me.

"You're not satisfied with my work, Mr. Johnson?"

"Naw, it's not that, Son. It's Mary Ella. She seems to have gotten your nose in a joint. You're sniffing around her like some dog in heat. I'm afraid she's going to make you hurt somebody, and that would be real bad for business."

"I ain't going to hurt nobody, Mr. Johnson, honest. I love her that's all."

"Boy, you don't even know what love is. Don't let a little pussy, I don't care how good you think it is, fool you in to believing it's love."

"She said she loves me too."

"So, why she always sucking up to every man in here? You think that's what a woman in love does?"

"She's just having fun, Mr. Johnson, that's all. You know she likes being the life of the party."

"I know what a fool she's making of you, that's what I know, and when you get tired of it, what you going to do then?"

I didn't answer, cause I knew he was too close to telling the truth.

"All I'm saying, Billy, if you can't concentrate on your work, I'll have to let you go. I don't want to do it, but I will. You understand?"

"Yes, Sir," I said, knowing he wasn't playing. Mr. Johnson didn't threaten nobody. He told you what he was going to do and did it.


"You love me, Billy?"

We were in bed, together, at her place, our bodies still wrapped around each other, and our scent still engulfing the room.

"You know the answer to that."

"I want to hear you say it," she said, hugging me tighter.

"I love you," I whispered, kissing her lips, her eyes, and behind her ears.

"Enough to kill a man?"

My breathing almost stopped, making my chest feel like it was bursting. I opened my mouth wide, gulping in air and moved out of her arms. Mr. Johnson's words flashed in my mind.

"Cat got your tongue, Sugar?"

"Don't call me Sugar," I said. "I ain't killing nobody for you."

"Guess that 'love you, Mary Ella' is just bullshit, hum?"

"I love you more than anything . . ."

"Just not enough to kill . . ."

"I ain't killing nobody!" I shouted, jumping up and struggling into my clothes. I ran down the stairs, praying I didn't trip on my untied shoestrings, and kept going right out the front door.

"Don't bring your sorry ass back here no more, you hear me!" she screamed at my retreating back.


I didn't know what to do or where to turn, but I knew I wasn't going along with what she'd asked. I wanted to tell Mr. Johnson, that's what I wanted, but I was too embarrassed. He'd warned me about her. I could hear his I told you so. And Mama? What would Mama say? I didn't raise my son to be a killer for no black bitch. Telling Mama was definitely out.

But, I couldn't get her out of my mind. I was like an addict on some damn drug. She dominated my being. She continued to show up at the club, occasionally, flaunting herself. I went to the back room, trying to ignore her.

"Something bothering you, Billy," Mr. Johnson finally started asking.

"No, Sir," I lied.

"Just wondering. Your woman don't come in so much anymore, but when she does, you spend your time in the back rooms."

"You told me I needed to stick to my work, Mr. Johnson."

He chuckled. "Hmm, hum."

I stayed away as long as I could and, when I couldn't stand it any longer, I showed up at her house banging on her door and shouting her name. After numerous attempts, she opened it wearing lace and satin and smelling of lavender, and let me back in.

"Who do you want dead?" I mumbled, caught up in her embrace.

. . .

I didn't really want to know nothing, his name, what the hell he had done to piss her off, nothing just how and when she wanted it done and where I could find his ass. Of course being Mary Ella, she told me anyway. His name was Munson Taylor, some guy she claimed was out to get her, cause she had some bad stuff on him that could send him away for life. She slipped a sepia picture out of her robe and handed it to me. He was light-skinned, like me, with straight hair and light eyes. She's sure into white-looking men, I thought, staring at his handsome face. Bet he dropped her for another woman. That's really why she wants him dead.

"He still looks like this?" I asked, trying to memorize his face.

"Did the last time I saw him."

"How long ago was that?"

"Last week."

I handed back the picture. "Why don't you call the law?" I asked, leery about what she was telling me.

She gave me a look, shook her head, and slipped a smile on her lips. "You'll learn about 'the law,' as you put it, when you been around a while longer, Billy. I stay as far away from those bastards as I can. They ain't nothing but trouble."

Hell, I already knew that. I was just trying to feel out my options, hoping to get myself out of this mess. I should of stayed away from her, cause trouble was what she was turning out to be.

"You changing your mind?" she asked, seeing through me.

"I said I'd do it, didn't I? I'll do it."

She got up from the bed and sauntered across the plush pale carpet, her satin robe flowing sensually around her slim legs. She went to a beautiful mahogany dresser sitting against the far wall, turned, and stared at me.

"You know how to use a gun, Billy?" she asked in that soft, whispery, sexy voice.

I shook my head and felt my breathing acting funny again, cutting off my air, making my voice high and squeaky. "No."

She smiled. "It's real easy," she said, "you just aim and pull. You know how to aim and pull, right Billy?"

I shook my head again.

"That's all you gotta do, Sugar."

I ignored her damn label. "Where am I going to get a gun?" I asked like a fool.

She opened a dresser drawer and pulled one out. Don't ask me what kind. I didn't ask, and she didn't tell me. Maybe she didn't know either, although I doubted that. My whole body started trembling. This was some serious shit. I watched her cradling it between her hands and caressing it with her long fingers.

"Where'd you get that?" I asked, pressing my body back against the headboard of the bed.

"You don't need to know," she said. She pointed the gun in my direction placing a finger in the hole and pressing the trigger.

I watched in horror. I couldn't move, just waited for that bullet to slam into my chest. At least I'd be off the hook, I was thinking, anticipating pain and blood, my blood, splattered all over her satin sheets. It took me a while to realize nothing happened. There was no noise, no jolt, no pain, and no blood, and she was waving the gun up and down laughing hysterically . . . at me.

"What the hell's so funny?" I shouted, scrambling off the bed. Damn bitch was crazy.

"It's not loaded, Sugar," she said, trying to control her laughter. "I was just showing you how easy it is to aim and pull. Think you can do that?"

"I told you I'd do it." I was still shouting. I needed to get away from her. She was scaring the shit out of me. Why hadn't I listened to Mr. Johnson? "When and where?" I asked, no longer interested in anything else except just getting the job done and never laying eyes on her again.

"Friday night," she said, placing the gun on top of the dresser.

Good, I thought. The sooner the better before I lost my fucking nerve.

"He'll be at that juke joint on First Avenue below the railroad tracks."

"I know the place."

"He's there every night like clockwork. He drinks too much and gets into fights over money and women. He'll be falling down drunk. All you have to do is follow him out. He'll be an easy target."

I knew that was a lie. There couldn't be nothing easy about killing somebody. If he was as slick as she claimed, and I suspected he was, he'd never get so drunk that his second sense wasn't in high gear.

"Anybody know you're here other than the nosey neighbors you attracted banging on my door?"

I shook my head.

"Good. Take the gun and the bullets," she said, moving around the room. "After you kill him, get rid of it . . ."

"Where?"

"Do I have to tell you every little thing?"

"You do if you want it done. I ain't never killed nobody, and I don't know nothing about a gun."

"Just throw it in the damn trash," she said, her voice losing some of that whispery softness. "It's untraceable, and you'll have on gloves, so there will be no fingerprints. Whatever you do, don't show up here. In fact, stay away from me and go back to your usual routine."

"It's going to be real hard acting calm and collected."

"There won't be that much fuss, Sugar. He's a small-time crook the police will be glad is out of their hair. They won't spend much time trying to find his killer. They never do with blacks, especially black men."

I was ready to go. I needed to think, and I couldn't do it with her around. Where was I going to hide the gun and the bullets? And what kind of gloves was she talking about, and where was I going to get them? I wasn't about to ask her. I'd figured it out later.

She showed me how to load the gun, talked about the safety, and suggested not putting the bullets in until I was almost ready for the kill. She rubbed the gun down with a soft cloth and put it in a small leather case, the cloth still wrapped around it. She put the bullets in a separate container and put it next to the gun. She pulled a pair of leather gloves out of the dresser drawer, placed them on top, and closed the case. I heard the soft click of the lock. She held it toward me. I stared at her awhile, finally reached out and took it. She drew me close and kissed me hard on the mouth, then grabbed my hand and guided me down the stairs to the door.

"Been nice knowing you, Sugar," she said, her voice soft, whispery sexy again. She smiled, pushed me out the door, and slammed it shut.

I managed to drive home, still struggling to breathe, locked the case in Mama's old chest with all the hidden compartments, and fell into bed.

My days and nights were torture. I was aloof and on edge. I cursed Mary Ella in all the ways I knew with all the words I could think of, then I cursed myself. I avoided Mr. Johnson as much as possible. If he noticed, he didn't say anything. I was almost relieved when the time came.

Munson Taylor was right where she said he'd be, bullshitting the ladies, talking mess, and throwing money around. He was bigger than I expected, tall, and I'd guess close to two hundred pounds, but not fat, and stylish, in a pinstriped suit, a bold tie, a black-brimmed hat, and alligator shoes. I ordered a Coors, took a seat at the bar, and watched him from across the small, dim, smoky room. I tried not to stare, didn't want to draw any attention to myself. Damn, I was jumpy. I couldn't concentrate, couldn't even talk trash to the women who sauntered up to the bar. I was constantly aware of the gun and the skintight leather gloves weighing down my inside suit pocket. I fought the urge to keep tugging at them. The longer I stared, the more I realized I couldn't do it. I wasn't a killer, and I wasn't going to become one for Mary Ella. If she wanted him dead, she was going to have to find some other sucker or do it herself. Hell, she had the balls. And I was no longer a love-struck boy. My eyes were finally wide open. I didn't want her ass no more. The truth was, I wanted to get as far away from her as possible. What was she going to do? Who was she going to tell?

As soon as I decided not to do it, I could breathe again. I stayed and finished my beer, still watching Munson Taylor. He was drinking heavily, but he sure didn't seem drunk. I eased off the stool and felt the weight in my pocket shift, sway gently against my chest. Damn it! What the hell was I going to do with the gun? I decided to keep it at least for a while. I hadn't killed nobody with it, and she said it was untraceable. I took out the bullets and packed it all back exactly as she had it and returned it to its hiding place.

I overslept and woke to the smell of Mama's cooking. It was Saturday, so I knew it was sausage, eggs, and biscuits, her standard Saturday morning breakfast. I dragged out of bed, half washed, and walked into the kitchen. Mama was at the round Formica-topped table, sipping coffee that looked like mud and reading the paper.

"Why black men always killing each other?" she asked, not looking at me and not expecting an answer. She always commented out loud when she was reading the paper. I'd learned she didn't expect a response and didn't really want one. She was just airing out her thoughts, as she put it.

"Somebody got killed last night?" I asked, curious, but not too interested.

She handed me the paper. I almost dropped it. Munson Taylor's face stared at me. I tried to keep my hands from trembling. What the hell happened? I couldn't read the story fast enough. It was confusing, didn't make no sense. He'd been shot in the chest leaving the juke joint on First Avenue. The place had been crowded with customers, but nobody was able to recognize the shooter. One thing I knew for sure, it wasn't me.

I kept up with the story, reading every word and listening to the radio reports. Mary Ella was right. He was a small-time crook, into all kinds of shit, with a long police record. According to the papers, a lot of people wanted him dead. Had she known that? His killing slipped off the front page after several days and out of the news completely within the month. Mary Ella was right about that too. And as far as I know, nobody was ever charged with the murder. I wondered if Mary Ella actually thought I'd done it. She'd stopped coming to the club, and I never tried to get in touch with her, so I didn't know, and to be honest, I didn't give a damn.

Mr. Johnson brought her name up every now and again, trying to get a reaction out of me, I guess, but I refused to take the bait. Finally he told me he was glad I had turned her loose and never mentioned her again. When his bartender moved on to bigger and better things, he gave me the job. And several years later when he decided to slow down, he gave me his. I'd been at that club so long it was my life. The neighborhood was changing fast. New businesses, new housing, new folks were popping up all over the place. The club was thriving. Mr. Johnson decided to get out while the getting was good. He gave me first dibs on the place, but I didn't have the cash. I probably could have gotten it, but I was ready to move on too. I was tired of the Midwest, and California was on everybody's lips. What the hell? I invited Mama to come along, but she wasn't about to leave her roots. Sadly, I kissed her good-bye, put Mary Ella out of my mind for good, and hit the road. On my way out of town, I dumped that damn gun and bullets in one of the trash compactors that littered the numerous construction sites.

I ended up in the capital. Sacramento suited my fancy. It was a city that felt more like a town, with hot summers and not too cold winters. And no snow, just rain that didn't bother me much, and fog that sometimes drove me crazy. I settled in a small house on Broadway in Oak Park. I was tired of living in somebody else's space. I needed my own. I got hired as a bartender in a club on Stockton Boulevard and soon got into the rhythm of the city.

Six months later I met my wife. Her name was Stella. She was short, slightly chubby, my age, but more mature, and my color, with black wavy hair and dark eyes. She was so outgoing I felt like I'd known her forever. She was a writer, a poet really, performing readings in the club's lounge. Her voice was lyrical like magic, drawing me right in. When I wasn't busy, I'd sneak and listen. I started offering her water to soothe her throat and trying to make conversation. I was surprised we got along so well. She was a California girl, born and bred, had no desire to live any place else. She was a teacher by profession, but wrote poems on the side. They were good, and she wanted to share them with others. She asked the owner if she could read them to the customers on weekends. He was skeptical. He thought there would be little interest and it might even lose him some business. She persuaded him to give her a chance, just a onetime read, before saying no. He did. She packed the house both nights. She eventually opened it up to other poets, encouraging them to come read.

I figured I didn't stand a chance in hell with her. She was way beyond me in all kinds of ways. But she was friendly, as I said, never acted like she was better than me. The first time I asked her out, she smiled and said yes.

It was down hill after that for both of us. I knew about her. I told her about me, even about Mary Ella, but not about what she'd wanted me to do. I just felt it wasn't necessary to drag that out, especially since I hadn't done it. Stella listened intently, told me I sure had a way with words, said she could just see Mary Ella's sashaying movements and hear her sassy voice.

After we married, Stella continued telling me I had a way with words. She kept saying I should try my hand at writing stories. I laughed my head off. I'd never written anything besides my name on nothing. I had good learning though. That was one thing about the Midwest; their schooling was the best. But I hadn't kept up with it. She was stubborn, my Stella, kept talking, suggested I go to one of the local junior colleges and take some writing classes. I continued to laugh, but the more I thought about it, the better it sounded, and when she mentioned I could get paid if somebody liked my stories, it sounded even better. So I did it. I hated it, but she was right about one thing, I did seem to have a way with words. They came easy, and the more of them I wrote, the less I hated doing it. Before long, I was addicted. I wrote all the time anywhere and everyplace. Unbeknowst to me, Stella was sending my stories out, and lo and behold, someone was foolish enough to buy one. Didn't pay a whole lot, but it paid. I eventually quit the bartending business and became a full-time writer.

Man, Stella and I were some team. She writing and reading her poems, and me writing my stories, just the two of us, no kids. We were enough for each other, didn't need anything or anybody diluting our love. We never regretted that decision neither. Only after Stella died, did I long for a part of her to continue to love.

Stella. She was probably turning over in her grave 'bout now, me talking to my past and she thinking what a great story had just dropped in my lap.

I pressed the receiver tighter against my ear. "You still there, Mary Ella?" I asked hoping she wasn't.

"I ain't going nowhere."

"Where you at, anyhow, and what the hell you want?" I asked. The thoughts of Stella had me teary, and I didn't want Mary Ella picking up on it, thinking it was because of her.

"I'm close," she said, "San Francisco, thought I'd take a chance on re-connecting. We go way back, you and I."

"How'd you know where to find me?"

"Easy. You're famous," she said.

I ignored her bullshit. "What do you want?" I asked again.

"You still love me, Billy?" she asked in that whispery, sexy voice.

Her image popped into my mind, black and lean, with high cheeks and big eyes. I sighed and concentrated, hard, on Stella. "No," I whispered.

"Liar," she whispered back.

"No," I repeated, loud and clear.

"I thought you went through with it, Billy," she said still in that whis-pery, sexy voice, ignoring my denial, "thought you aimed and pulled just like you said you would."

That caught me off guard. I felt that old familiar funny breathing be-ginning in my chest. Damn her.

"Thought you not only proved your love, but also that you were a man, you hadn't turned tail and run."

I didn't respond.

"Cat got your tongue, Sugar?"

"Don't call me that."

She laughed. "Still gets a rise out of you after all these years."

"I didn't kill nobody," I said, wanting to slam down the receiver, but I needed this over. All these years, and I hadn't quite managed to push it completely out of my thoughts.

She didn't say a word, but I could hear her breathing. It sounded kinda funny, now, like mine. What the hell was she up to?

"You hear me, Mary Ella," I shouted, "I never killed nobody." I was tired of the conversation. None of it mattered anymore no how. It had been way too long, and we were both too old to be playing cat and mouse games. And it sure in hell wasn't worth having a stroke over. I glanced at my watch. She was cutting into my writing time. "You finished?"

"I haven't answered your second question."

"Say it or forget it. I need to get on with my day."

"You asked why I was calling. That's a legitimate question that deserves an answer." She sighed. "Like I said, Billy, I actually thought you'd killed him."

"How the hell . . ."

"Hear me out. When I asked you to kill Munson Taylor, I wasn't serious, and I sure in hell didn't expect you to go along with it. I expected a good cursing, maybe even a slap or two before you stomped out. But, you were so cute, Billy, so ready to prove your love, so . . . vulnerable. See, I knew it wasn't really me you were in love with. You were in love with love and sex and becoming a man, like so many boys your age. So instead of running away, you called my bluff, and I got caught in my own trap."

"What are you saying, woman? You didn't want him dead?"

"That's right," she whispered. "Munson was an old lover. He hadn't done a damn thing to me, and I had nothing on him. And it was no secret he was a crook. Hell, the whole town knew that, including the cops, especially the cops."

"Why . . . ?"

"I always challenged my lovers. That was part of the game. How far would they go to keep my . . . love. You were special, Sugar. I was falling for you, and that was never part of the plan. You were just a . . . you were a very young man with nothing to offer. I couldn't afford to love you, so I thought I'd challenge you with murder, which I knew you'd never do, and drive you away."

"You led me on, knowing . . . ?" I felt sick all over, weak and dizzy and lightheaded. At that moment I hated her with such fury, if she'd of been there in front of me, I would have killed her with my bare hands. "What if I'd gone through with it?"

"I didn't think you could do it, Billy. I counted on that. That you would get cold feet and not do it."

"You had days," I shouted, "and you never even tried to contact me, call it off, tell me it was just some fucking sick joke."

"I had to save face, Billy, and I knew you couldn't do it."

"Stop saying that bullshit," I shouted. "You don't know what a man will do for the woman he . . . thinks he loves."

She was crying, loud retching sobs, which were having no effect on me, none. I eased into a chair and closed my eyes and tried to stop trembling.

"When I read about his murder in the papers," she finally continued, "I wanted to scream. I couldn't believe you'd actually done it. I was on pins and needles, panic every time my phone rang. I was crazy. I kept thinking if you could kill somebody you didn't even know, how hard would it be to kill me, the one who had fooled you into it? I waited for you to confess and name me. It never happened. That's when I realized you hadn't done it, cause if you had, you'd told somebody. I was relieved. I wanted to hunt you down, tell you I was sorry, and beg your forgiveness. As you know, I never did. I figured the cops concluded Munson was killed by one of his crime buddies and the darkie got what he deserved. I thought the same thing. And you hadn't done it, so your conscience had to be clear. I just hoped, actually prayed, you had gotten on with your life, married a woman who deserved your love, and was living a long healthy happy life. That's why I'm calling, Sugar, hoping you don't hate me too much and begging forgiveness."

The quiet was so thick I could've cut it with a knife. I didn't want to forgive her, damn it. She'd almost made me a killer. But, I had to be honest. She hadn't done anything, not really, just brought the shit up, and I, William Sude Jr., had made my own decision. As much as I wanted to hate her, had just hated her, I couldn't continue. Hell, it had been too long and we were too old and time was moving too fast and life was too short . . .

"I don't hate you, Mary Ella," I finally said, "and forgiving you feels about right." I heard her damn sobs and funny breathing.

"Just one last question, Sugar."

"Only one."

"Did you find a woman worthy of your love?"

"Yes," I whispered and felt Stella's presence.

"What's her name?"

"That's two."

"I never could count, Sugar. What's her name?"

"Stella," I said. "Her name . . . is Stella."

# SURVIVAL

*Dicey Scroggins Jackson*

A Woman's Place had changed a lot in the last year. On this chilly November morning in the nation's capital, it was still not really home to any of the women who found shelter here, perhaps not as unwelcoming as before, but still an unwelcome place to be, even temporarily. Anyway, young women were no longer disappearing, had stopped being swallowed up whole without a trace. And Bernetta Bennett, the B to me, had decided— with just a little help from her friends—to move on, to bring joy to some other unsuspecting souls. The board of directors of A Woman's Place could not recommend her for other work. How exactly do you word a recommendation for someone who has run a hellhole and lost other people's children in the process? The board did, however, give her a big send-off: No gold-plated watch, no severance package, no vacation or additional sick pay. But also no jail time. And she was a criminal. The city is finished with her; I am not.

Every dime the government of the District of Columbia had ever paid Bernetta Bennett was, in fact, sick pay. She was sick, she spread her sickness freely within an already ailing system, and she was paid well for her effort.

Her stench—her legacy of neglect and disrespect—took a while to remove from A Woman's Place. It was sandblasted from the building's redbrick exterior and sandpapered from surfaces tagged with generational graffiti, but it can still be found in crevices of distrust. And, although flowerbeds have overtaken squares of dirt that once subbed as trash bins on both sides of the front door, flowers have seemed uncertain whether it is safe to bloom there, thanks to the B.

It took exactly two months and four days to dethrone the B. The fact that she offered no explanation for the disappearance of a child—mine—or for the return of a runaway to an abusive foster home was damaging. But scrutiny of the organizational accounts proved fatal. Poor handling of money did the job, where cruel, perhaps criminal, handling of people had not.

Taywanda Hammill, who seemed to be everything that the B was not—caring, efficient, human—replaced her as director. In her first interview, she had claimed the job with on-target responses, well-developed plans for improving the shelter, and thoughtful questions. The fact that she maintained direct eye contact and Janice Scott's enthusiasm for her tipped the scales in her favor. Janice, a resident at A Woman's Place who had become the intake administrator, had no official role in the selection process, but I asked her to sit in on the interviews, because she understood resident needs so well.

The only thing weighted against Taywanda was her name, but her neatly trimmed, unpermed hair offset that. Although I really couldn't blame her, because her mother and father—both of whom, she explained, had abandoned her at three months old—thought themselves creative and probably could not spell, I wondered what they had been smoking, snorting, drinking, or mixing when they'd decided to combine their names—Taylor and LaWanda—to create hers.

Nine months into her two-year contract and into the transformation of A Woman's Place, she E-mailed a two-sentence resignation:

I resign from my position as director of A Woman's Place, effective 5 November. I will be on annual leave until that date.

The note, sent on November 3, was copied to all board members but addressed specifically to me, then-president of the board. She wasted no time on salutations, niceties, or even a hint of her reasons for leaving. After a momentary flash of anger and disappointment, I thought about offering her a few tips on not burning bridges. Washington is a relatively small, decidedly Southern, city, even as it sports an international, cosmopolitan veneer, and there are not six degrees of separation here. Anyway, it would be difficult to write a recommendation for Taywanda after such a huge gap in professionalism and courtesy.

I waited two minutes before calmly walking down the flight of steps to her office on the second floor. I am practicing patience. After knocking on her door once and suppressing the urge to pound on it, I yanked it open without waiting for a response.

Taywanda and everything she'd brought with her were gone, and the office was spotless. Nothing was left, except donated office furniture and equipment that appeared to have been wiped clean and a trace of lemon-scented Pledge.

In the hallway outside her office, I picked up a pink message slip, glanced at the numbers on it, and dropped it in the trashcan near the stairwell.

The next day, by unanimous vote of the board—that is, by default—I became the interim director. The position was hotly contested; nobody wanted the job, and I protested least vociferously. I still feel a strong connection to the place, a physical and emotional pull toward it. This is where I believe Amani last slept, was last seen.

My first week as interim director of A Woman's Place began with a meeting in a small windowless room in the basement of a library.

"Ms. Bell, please address Mr. Jordan's concern about loitering," James Palmer, the very pompous, very round ANC president, said. "Actually, it's obvious that if you expand, loitering will increase along with undesirable foot traffic."

"Although the number of women in the neighborhood will increase, the increase will be relatively small," I said, while making nonconfrontational eye contact, first with James and then with Lenwood Jordan, his tag team partner. "We will increase—"

"Could we have some numbers?" James said.

They want answers, but they want the appearance of having to drag them out of me.

"As I had begun to explain, the most viable plan is to expand to an adjoining house that will contain fifteen additional beds. Over the past year, we have increased services, providing job search and skills workshops, career fairs, GED classes, and enrichment activities. Additionally, women no longer stand on the street waiting to sign in. All have resulted in reduced loitering and—"

"But wouldn't the increased number of beds return loitering to the previous level? More of these shelter women coming into the neigh—"

Now, it was Lenwood's turn on the mat.

"The women are all residents of this city, not *shelter women*. Many were prematurely released from St. Elizabeth's, some are the working poor, others are current or recovering addicts, and still others are people like you—Lenwood—and me who have simply lost their jobs and have no cushion or family to assist them."

"I stand corrected, but back to the original question . . ."

*You stand stupid and obnoxious.*

"Obviously, women will have to make their way to A Woman's Place, that is, walk through the streets of this community. So, yes, more women will come into the neighborhood. But, since our services have expanded, there is increased engagement and less idle time. Surely you do not object to the women simply walking down public streets. And, we haven't had one incident of shelter-related vandalism, violence, excessive noise, or vagrancy in the last six months."

"Well, I'm not sure about your statistics, but—"

"They are not my statistics. They came from the D.C. Metropolitan Police Department last week. Do you have more current data?"

Neither James nor Lenwood acknowledged the question. They busied themselves shuffling papers on the only table in the room, perhaps looking for new statistics, perhaps steaming because they had none.

A tall angular woman stood and raised her hand tentatively. She hand-pressed the lapels of her black blazer and offered apology by way of her bowed head even before she spoke. "Well, I don't mean to be uncharitable, but, well, do we have to shelter every homeless woman in the whole city?" Her soft Southern voice, typical of elderly Washingtonians, quivered; this was not easy for her. "Why can't they expand into Georgetown or on Capitol Hill? I don't mean to sound uncharitable . . . I'm a Christian."

She probably was, but I am always suspicious of people who feel the need to tell me.

"Yeah, I agree with Miss Margaret." She gave him a puzzled look. "And we will do whatever we have to, to stop shelter expansion. I'm not sorry for wanting to protect my property value and my family," a very dark, very handsome man said, holding a firefighter's helmet in strong-looking hands. The small group of residents, seated in two rows of metal folding chairs, nodded in unison and mumbled in agreement. James pretended to try to bring order to the meeting, and the handsome man looked disproportionately proud of himself.

I wanted to ask his name, his politics notwithstanding . . . for the record.

And the meeting continued.

One would think women who find themselves in a shelter want to be there, that they pencil into their life plans a nice long stay on a narrow cot in a shelter. Nobody really wants them housed in their community. The haves simply are not having homeless people wandering aimlessly or even with purpose through their neighborhoods. And the almost-haves have worked too hard to become homeowners to be charitable.


At 11:15 A.M., twelve days into my tenure as interim director and within a block of A Woman's Place, Melba Johnson—Mel to her friends, whoever and wherever they were—was found face-down and already stiff on very cold, cracked concrete. She was dressed in a navy fleece jacket and skin-tight blue jeans, open at the waist. Dead, apparently of blunt-force trauma to the head, was the preliminary finding of the first resident of A Woman's Place on the scene.

Mel was a petite woman, with sad brown eyes and full pouting lips. While others played cards or checkers in the intake room of A Woman's Place, she usually sat on the floor, propped up by her soiled yellow backpack, reading tattered paperback novels of all sorts. I could see no pattern to her taste in books—except that she liked the poetry of Paul Laurence Dunbar—and noticed no friendships.

Although I'd had only one conversation of any length with her, at the end of it, she had asked me to please call her "Mel" like all her other friends. She said that she had once held a "good government job" at the Environmental Protection Agency, didn't have much family, and expected to be out of shelter by the end of November. She also said that she'd met a nice man who treated her "like somebody."

When the news of Mel's death arrived at A Woman's Place by way of one of her sister residents, I thanked the almost-eyewitness and immediately closed the door to my office. I knew there would be much excitement surrounding the rapid spread of the news and probably even an exodus into the street to see just where it had happened. There also might be an opportunity for a little press coverage. "Yeah, I knew her. She was friendly and clean. And, I never had no trouble with her. Never." James and Lenwood would love that—not the death, perhaps, but the press coverage.

Over the new public address system, I could have suggested that residents not go to the scene of the crime, but such a message would have been resented first and then ignored without a thought, except perhaps of "who the hell does she think she is?" It has taken me too long to build trust and respect to revert to Bernetta-like tactics.

The heavy front door opened and slammed shut repeatedly for several minutes as I began to flip through mail on my self-assembled desk.

Occasionally, residents who have moved on to better things, even homeownership, called or wrote to update the staff. A few children of past residents have sent lovely drawings of their new homes, of meadows and horses—favorite subjects although most have never been in or on either— or of their families. When I picked up the manila envelope addressed to me in large squiggly black letters, a smile played across my face. As I retrieved the orange file card hiding in the bottom and read the message, twice, my stomach churned its discomfort. The card contained seven typed words: *How does it feel to lose one?*

I dropped the card, pushed away from the desk, and ran to the bathroom at the far end of the hall. Urinary incontinence, or its onset, is not a funny thing. I'll have to make another appointment with Dr. Marke. The need to pee—three drops maximum—every half hour, especially when I'm excited or anxious, is debilitating. At forty-six years old, it is also outrageous.

After washing my hands and splashing a little water on my face, I walked out of the single-stall bathroom into complete silence, speed-walked to my office, and closed the door behind me without intending to do so.

My desk was a little less cluttered than I had left it. The large manila envelope and orange file card were gone.

"Ms. Bell, ma'am, I mean Gloria, I don't have anything yet. I'm not working the case officially," Officer Shirley Morrison said in response to my request for information on Mel's death less than three hours after her body was discovered. "Officers are still on the scene. I'll see what I can find out, but . . . don't expect too much on this one, ma'am."

I knew better than to expect much, but I didn't like having low expectations officially confirmed. I started to end this phone conversation and call Lew—my almost significant other—to file a preemptive complaint, but then I'd have to listen to his warnings about staying out of the investigation and threats about becoming a guest of the police department if I ignored the warnings. I had heard it all before, when I moved into A Woman's Place to find Amani and got thrown out after complaining about Akua's disappearance. I had helped find Akua, though; she is still in my custody.

Officer Shirley—to all residents—had come forward to write a letter in my behalf during my petition to become Akua's legal guardian. A compassionate twenty-six-year-old who still appeared too small to make height and weight requirements for the D.C. Metropolitan Police Department, she is a mentor and regular visitor at A Woman's Place.

When I told her about the disappearing file card, under the cover of friendship, she asked if I had reported this officially or at least unofficially to Lew. I said I hadn't and didn't want her to either. She didn't respond.

"I know you're looking out for us, Officer Shirley." I knew she was smiling—flashing perfect teeth. I bit my tongue on the "don't expect much" slip. Actually, it was not a slip; she'd just been honest. Mel would not be a priority in any department's caseload—a fact, pitiful, but still a fact.

I reminded her of the Career Fair in December. Several residents had expressed an interest in employment with the police department. One said she'd "like to show the police which way is up." Others were certain they had contacts the department could use badly.

"Ms. Bell, ma'am, there's a dead body on the front steps . . . I think," Rosalee—timidity personified—said, as if she were giving the time. She appeared in the doorway of my office without making a sound, mumbled, and slowly backed away as if she were about to genuflect out of the room.

My lack of response probably matched her lack of self-esteem. It took several seconds for the little gasp and then the whispered "what?" to escape, from me, I guess, since Rosalee was halfway down the hall.

A telephone rang somewhere.

I don't remember moving, but I found myself in the doorway staring down at a motionless figure in a black leather coat. She lay face-down on the steps. A small crowd of women was assembling behind me.

Although it occurred to me that the woman might need medical assistance rather than last rites, I did not rush to touch her.

As I inched toward the woman sprawled at the bottom of the steps with her legs spread at an awkward right angle across the sidewalk, Janice rushed past me to kneel at the woman's head, turn it gently to see the face, and lift her thin brown hand to feel for a pulse. Janice appeared to know what she was doing, was gentle but sure in her handling. By the time I reached her side, she had taken off her thick brown cardigan and was placing it as a pillow under the woman's face. Her badge—Janice L. Scott, Intake Administrator—fell from the sweater and clanked to the sidewalk.

*Good, she is not dead.*

"Someone, please call an ambulance," I yelled behind me. At least five long minutes had passed, and I had not even called for help. I glanced at my watch; it was hard to believe that it was only 4:26 P.M.

"You might want to call the police first. An ambulance isn't going to help Arlene, now," Janice said in the gentle, comforting tones of a funeral directress or someone used to delivering bad news to loved ones.

She noticed it before I did, and her entire manner changed. Now she needed comforting, seemed less relieved than before. A slow stream of blood ran down the steps along the contours of the body, across the sidewalk, and into the street.

I have seen full squadrons, or whatever the police equivalent would be, surround cars of every make, condition, value, and lack thereof, containing young Black men stopped for various traffic violations . . . or just because. A like force descended on A Woman's Place within ten minutes, causing me to wonder who the caller had reported dead.

When Lt. Lew Davis stepped out of his always shiny black Sable and dominated the scene with his presence, I understood the rapid overresponse. He took the nine steps by twos and threes—even at forty-seven, you can do that, when you're six three and fit—locking eyes with me from step two onward.

"Glo, are you okay?" he said without attempting to pretend that this was an impersonal official inquiry. The exchange of looks and the stroking of my hair probably precluded the presumption of impersonality. And, I'm pretty sure that there was a rapid change in temperature. I flashed hot, and I am not menopausal.

I tried not to lean into him physically. I am neither the type of woman who needs or wants a man to fend for her, nor do I have the fragile build to carry that off credibly. However, I leaned into him emotionally—all five foot seven and 140 pounds of me.

"I'm fine, but obviously Arlene is not," I said, not even looking where Janice's sweater still provided visible compassion for the young woman, whom I didn't remember having seen before, although she vaguely reminded me of someone.

"Is she one of yours?" Lew asked in a more detached manner, having regained his official composure.

"One of my what? If you mean one of the women who occasionally

finds refuge here, I think so. I don't remember her, but the intake administrator called her Arlene."

"And did you *know* the young woman killed near the telephone booth
around the corner?"

"Yes."

He asked; I answered. He glared down at me, took my arm as if es-
corting me to the dance floor, and more-or-less-gently guided me into the
building and up the stairs to my office door. The shock of two deaths had
taken some of the fight out of me. I am not easily led anywhere by anybody. If anyone knew that, Lew did.

My office door was closed, although I didn't remember closing it. I
turned the knob twice. It was locked, and I know that I hadn't locked it.
In fact, I had never locked it.

"It's locked, and I don't carry the key," I said.

"How'd you lock the door without a key? These doors don't lock auto-
matically." Lew placed himself between me and the door. "Who has keys?"

"Maintenance workers and Janice." I strained to find an explanation
that had nothing to do with murder, disappearing messages, or self-
locking doors. It was hard to think clearly, with images of Mel and Arlene
playing through my head like a still-frame black-and-white exhibit. Black
and white and red.

We stood for a moment in confused silence. Miss Annie Louise, one of
the oldest and most regular residents, walked toward us, heavily assisted
by a beautiful hand-carved ebony cane from Kenya, she'd once bragged.
She reported that the police had ordered all women present to the intake
room and were acting "Gestapo-like," and she just thought that I should
know. She shot Lew a no-account you-don't-scare-me look. He smiled,
and Miss Annie Louise suppressed a blush.

The three of us joined the thirty or so women assembled in the intake
room. Some were fuming, and others were content to be in the thick of an
investigation in which they were not probable suspects.

I asked Lew if the women were going to be questioned, detained, or
what. He said that they would all be asked to give statements and that
they had been asked to go back into the building so they would not compromise the crime scene.

He suggested that we get the key to my office so we could talk there, but Janice was not in the room or anywhere else on the first floor. Lew frowned and asked the two uniformed officers stationed outside the intake room if the building had been searched. Officer Turner, the older and more fit of the two, said that they had cleared the rest of the building and escorted all women to the intake room. None of the women present remembered seeing Janice after she'd made sure that Arlene's lovely young face was not in direct contact with cement. Wherever Janice was, keys that opened doors throughout the building were with her, hanging from the maroon What Would Jesus Do lanyard around her neck.

With a nod from Lew and just two words—"Go easy"—Officer Turner announced that he would take a statement from every woman in the room. The announcement included words like "please," "ladies," and "we will try not to inconvenience you too much."

By the time the officer asked for the first woman on the list of possible witnesses to come with him into the lounge, Lew was halfway up the stairs to the third floor. He hadn't tried to gently strong-arm me toward his destination or even asked me to tag along. When he reached my office, he stood back and sized up the door, I think, to kick it down. I could see that he was worried and angry. He needed to be able to legally hit something. He touched the doorknob, shoved me into the wall behind him, and shifted into a crouch—in one swift, seamless movement . . .

The *locked* door swung open, and Lew eased into the dark office, gun in hand.

Even after making sure no one was in the office, he walked back in first and surveyed the room. When I stepped in behind him, I knew that I wouldn't be coming back to this room except to pack my things, and then only in the presence of a police officer with a loaded gun drawn. *I love Officer Shirley Morrison, but the officer present would have to outweigh me and look like he or she could really hurt something, if necessary, even without a weapon.*

We sat on a baby blue loveseat, flecked with teal and navy, in front of the only window in the room. After the reign of the B, I had donated it to replace her lumpy, overstuffed couch, which reeked of a perfume that could double as bug repellant and bacon—her scents of choice.

"Are you sure the door was locked? These old doors stick," Lew said with an unnecessary touch of attitude.

"You were standing right behind me. You saw me turn the knob twice," I said. *Just because there was no one in here to shoot for your trouble and your worry, don't take it out on me.*

"I'm just searching, Glo. Just searching. Of course, I saw you try to open the door, and for a girl, you're not exactly a wimp."

I decided not to go feminist on him and instead to take his limp bait and smile, blinking back a response out of proportion to and out of sync with Lew's intent. I then took as much of his large rough hands into mine as I could manage. While this thing with Lew might not be love yet, it was something that felt almost as good.

"You wouldn't be trying to take advantage of my one area of vulnerability would you?" he said looking at my lips. His eyes then drifted to the door, which we had left ajar. "Pleeease, let's hold this thought, but at the moment, I am in the middle of a murder investigation, and you're in danger. Why don't you leave this place, put it behind you? I'm not asking you to leave Amani behind; she is no longer here. Glo, you have made this a better place for these women. Now, go home . . ."

I still had his hands, but I could tell he thought I would be returning them shortly.

"Let's not make this a discussion of my career and housing choices. Two young women are dead."

"Okay, Ms. Bell," he said. "Okay for now. So, tell me what you know, and try not to leave anything out."

I recounted what I knew, which wasn't much. When he asked if anything unusual had happened over the last few weeks, the only thing I could think of was Taywanda's departure.

Then, it was my turn to ask questions. "Do you have any leads in Mel's death? Do you think it's linked to Arlene's?"

"The first woman was discovered less than six hours ago, so the investigation is just starting. Because she died within a few yards of a pay phone, we've requested records of the last calls made. We're also canvassing the area for her belongings, but we haven't found anything yet. Do women ever store things here?"

"Some do, mostly younger regulars. Others like to keep everything they own hidden off-site or with them, even if that means wearing several layers of clothing in mid-July. Mel carried a canary yellow backpack, I think. We log belongings in and out, so I'll check for Mel and Arlene."

Until the streetlight popped on, I hadn't realized how dark the room had grown. Lew looked out of the window behind us.

"The call about the second woman came in during a briefing on the first," he said.

"So, you then ordered every man and woman from the precinct here?" Someone would want an explanation of this resource allocation.

"I ordered an appropriate number of officers to the scene. There is a murderer—maybe more than one—in the area."

Officer Shirley stuck her head in the door, and our hands found their own laps, as if we were guilty teenagers. She stepped into the office and looked at me but spoke to Lew. "Lt. Davis, we just got the phone records, and the last call was made to this building—to Ms. Bell's personal line." She held out the telephone record, and we both reached for it.

"You were bringing this for me, weren't you, officer?" he said, as our hands met on the page and mine dropped. She didn't respond. She was definitely not a liar, and he was her superior officer. "You are now *officially* assigned to these cases. I see that you are off duty, but I'll authorize the overtime."

I had not even noticed that she was in street clothes.

He moved his index finger down the list of numbers. Toward the end of it, he stopped momentarily, and his eyes narrowed, so my eyes shifted to the bottom of it. Only one number seemed vaguely familiar, but I made mental note of the last five.

Just as I tried to see a few more numbers without any overt movement, he folded the list rudely and stood.

"Because you are the director of this place, I will keep you abreast of the investigation," he said. "But, you are not to become involved in it."

When I didn't respond, he frowned and looked at the competent little officer standing more-or-less at attention. "Officer Morrison, you are,

*again,* assigned to Ms. Bell. She may be a . . . material witness. Please, stay
with her until further notice. And, she is never to be alone in this place."
He walked out of the room without looking my way.

If he says "this place" one more time, it's going to be *on.*

By the time he made it to the stairwell, I had written the last five phone
numbers on a yellow legal pad beside the phone on my desk and put the
list in my jacket pocket. The message light was blinking; I had one message, left at 4:20 p.m.

I motioned Officer Shirley to the loveseat while I listened to the messages.

The caller, who sounded like a very young child, left no name or number, only a short message: "How does it feel to be losing other people's
children?" I dropped the receiver and ran for the bathroom, with Officer
Shirley closer than I liked anyone behind me. At this rate, I could be wearing Depends within a week.


I left the bathroom and headed for Taywanda's old office. I couldn't imagine what she or her departure had to do with either death, but it wouldn't
hurt to check the office. And, it had occurred to me after talking to Lew
about Taywanda that, at a distance, the dead woman resembled her, even
to the full-length black leather coat. Maybe Janice had thought so, too. I'd
ask her.

Sitting at the wrap-around-desk—one of the nicer hand-me-downs
from a corporate contributor—I searched each drawer.

"If you're searching for evidence, I have to advise you to stop immediately. You might unintentionally destroy or compromise evidence, ma'am,
I mean, Gloria." Officer Shirley stood in the doorway knowing exactly
what I was doing. My guess is, she didn't want to be in this office with me
going through drawers when Lew returned. I'd try to make sure neither of
us was.

The desk was wiped clean, but a little dusty now and empty, except a
few office supplies—paper clips and pens mostly, and a pink message pad.
I had picked up a pink slip from a message pad in the hallway the day

she'd resigned, and I was sure that the number on it would match one of the phone numbers on the pay phone record.

I am not good with numbers, that is, manipulating them, but I rarely forget ones that have or follow a pattern of any kind. The last four numbers on the pink slip were 2-4-1-2, and 24 is 12 times 2.

I found a match with the second number from the bottom of the list I'd copied. I dialed the number using my cell phone and after five rings got an answering machine. There was no mistaking the officious voice on the recorded message. It belonged to the B, Bernetta Bennett. I hung up.

I stood to leave the office, and my cell phone rang, displaying the B's number.

"Hello?" I said without disguising my voice or my hatred.

"Glo? Is that you?"

Lew's question was rhetorical, so I hung up without answering and cut off my cell phone.

The questioning was well under way when I walked past the lounge. Lew had not returned, but his orders were still in force.

"Yes, Miss, you do have to give your full name," Officer Turner said to the elderly resident standing before him with her hands on her ample hips.

"No, sir, I don't. Them parents of that poor *JonBenet* child didn't have to give the police nothing but their high-priced lawyer's business card 'til they wanted to." She removed her hands from her hips and stuck her arms out, wrists together. "So you gon' arrest me, now?" She didn't seem worried and wasn't playing for the crowd.

"No, Miss, I'm not. I'll just list you as Jane Doe," he said, as he pressed a pencil against his pad so hard the lead broke.

"Oh no you won't! That's for dead folks with no name. My name's Annie Louise Jones, and I don't know a thing to tell you. I walked up when you drove up. Don't know her and ain't never seen her but once, God rest her young soul."

"When did you see her before?"

"First and onliest time I ever saw her was today on the steps, dead.

That was the once." She put her hands back on her hips and waited for another question.

Miss Annie Louise had warned me of the Gestapo tactics and clearly wasn't having any of it. Officer Turner's top lip quivered; his patience was probably wearing thin. And, he probably was finding that the women here knew the law and the D.C. Code better than some lawyers he'd encountered in court.

Native Washingtonians and transplants are news and politics junkies. So, even at A Woman's Place, the most popular daytime television shows—except perhaps for soap operas—are news and court TV.

I felt a little sorry for Officer Turner when he returned to the lounge with Etta Jenkins, a former elementary school teacher who had lost her husband, two children, and, she said, her cat in a DWI accident and "just couldn't deal with family stuff and other people's kids after that." She was sharper than a tack and loved word games. They, or at least she, would have fun.

It was clear that most of the women assembled were not particularly frightened. I was afraid for them and for myself, but many had lived in cars and in rat-infested abandoned buildings and had seen people after the blunt-force trauma of a bullet and in violent psychotic rages. And, they had often been the objects of other people's rage—ordinary people who did not like being reminded of their existence.

I needed an Advil or some other legal painkiller, so I asked Officer Shirley to get my purse. It was hanging on the chair in my office. I did not intend to go back into that office. She hesitated, but I assured her that I would be fine. Two officers were stationed in front of the building to protect the crime scene, and two were inside.

Officer Shirley headed upstairs, and I turned toward the kitchen to make tea, perhaps not a good choice, considering my bladder problem. The back of the building was dark and empty. I bumped into a side table in the hallway just past the lounge, so I turned on the light in the dining room-turned health center every Tuesday. The center contained no drugs, OTC or prescription; the physician's assistant brought them with her. I could have waited for Officer Shirley, but the building has been searched, sort of, and I could be sipping tea in the four or five minutes that it would take for her to return, if I microwaved the water.

My hand hit the kitchen light switch just as the outline of someone crouched in the corner beside the refrigerator came into focus. *If the crouching figure is the murderer,* I thought, *I hope he or she is still going the blunt force route.* In the instant that the light came on and immediately blew, I saw someone racing forward, with something in her hand, shaking her head.

By the time it registered that the person was Janice and I heard, "Please help me, please," I'd already turned to run toward Washington's finest. I hesitated for just a moment, thinking she might be hurt or in danger. She grabbed my arm and yanked hard enough to spin me around to face her.

She pointed a gun at my forehead.


Officer Shirley would be looking for me soon, but she probably wouldn't start in this stuffy little pantry, where Janice and I stood facing each other—her back to the door, mine to canned goods. The only break in the darkness came from a flashlight Janice cut on and placed on a shoulder-level shelf, near her. My eyes were locked on the gun. The air was heavy with powdery stuff, and I hoped for a good strong sneeze.

Nothing that Janice had said since directing me into the pantry and locking the door from the inside had seemed unbelievable, especially the part about the B befriending her and then using her. Although Janice said she did not intend to hurt me, just didn't know where to turn, she also did not put the gun down. While I wanted to be on her side, it is difficult to maintain compassion for a person pointing a presumably loaded gun at your head.

"I know Bernetta is involved in these murders," I said. "But, how are you involved?"

"I been hiding in here since they found Arlene and the police came. When you came by, I was trying to leave. Gloria, I didn't kill anybody," she said in a shaky version of her sad voice. "People are getting killed. And

I been in trouble before. I can't get caught with a gun with my fingerprints all over it."

"I don't think either woman was shot, and you'd be a lot more convincing without that gun pointed at me," I said.

She didn't even seem to hear me.

"And today when I saw Arlene on the steps, I thought . . ."

"You thought she was Taywanda." At least one part of the puzzle was becoming clearer. "You almost knocked me down to get to her."

"Bernetta said they'd hurt her if I didn't keep quiet . . . I had to protect her, 'specially after I did so bad by her before. They scared her into leaving." She leaned against the wall and cried, but she still kept that gun pointed at me, now considerably lower than my head.

Someone else must hear her wailing.

"Taywanda is your daughter, isn't she?" I said. The question was rhetorical.

"Bernetta knew, said she wouldn't hurt her if I helped them with keys and stuff. No killing, never. You lost a child, maybe she ain't dead, but she's lost to you, so I thought you'd understand."

"Janice, put the gun down. Bernetta . . . or somebody forced you to do whatever you've done to protect your daughter, but I know you haven't killed anyone, so this can be fixed."

"They said I'm a accomplice and Taywanda, too, because we knew something was going to happen when they sent Taywanda threat'ning notes. I didn't know anything about anybody getting killed." Janice was talking fast, for her, but was calmer.

I wanted to know the details but could wait until the gun was down.

"If you haven't hurt anybody, Lt. Davis will try to help you and Taywanda, too." The gun was still in her hand, but it wasn't really pointed at me until I mentioned Taywanda.

"You can't bring Taywanda into this. She didn't know anything but to leave or get hurt . . . her and her real mother . . . the one that raised her. Bernetta promised not to tell even when Taywanda wouldn't help . . . I don't want her to know." She'd begun to ramble.

"Know what?"

"That I'm her mother, a woman like me . . . 'specially now. I just don't want her to get hurt or get in trouble."

"Trust me, Janice. If you've told the truth, I'll help you, and Taywanda will not get hurt. I trusted you and gave you a job and responsibility, when no one else would. Trust me, now."

Janice leaned off of the wall and tried to smile. "I bought this gun from a boy all the way up Ridge Road. I don't even know if it works. I haven't used it. I never used a gun," she said as if the thought of her doing so were crazy.

She put the gun on the shelf by the flickering flashlight and whispered, "I didn't kill anybody, but I let those girls get killed, didn't I?"

We talked for a few minutes without the gun between us.

She was just a mother trying to protect her child, and I did understand.


Officers Shirley and Turner were outside the pantry door with guns drawn when Janice and I emerged, me first.

Officer Turner grabbed Janice, threw her against the wall, and handcuffed her, while Officer Shirley kept a gun trained on her. I had intended to omit the gun from my reporting of events. When they asked for it, I went back into the pantry and retrieved it from a huge canister of generic Cheerios.

I promised Janice that I would come to the precinct as soon as possible, but I had something else to do first, with any luck before Lew returned and got protective. Janice would be okay. The "go easy" order was still in force.


The door to the left of the pantry led to the basement. I used the key that Janice gave me to unlock the door; she didn't have the padlock on. Even with the lights on, the basement was dim, so I took two flashlights from a junk drawer before heading down. On the narrow unlit stairwell, I used the high-beam MegaLite to light the way down and to warn anything that crawled that people were coming down. Officer Shirley put her gun in the shoulder holster under her vest and took the pinpoint flashlight. She warned me again about tampering with evidence but was not about to leave me alone again. She could come along or not; I didn't care.

Before going to the basement, I had checked the storage log that Janice kept. It listed a canary yellow backpack belonging to Melba Johnson that was placed in Resident Storage Area 4 the previous day. If she left anything behind that might help to find her killer, it would probably be in her backpack. She had nothing else.

Janice and a few of the other women had recently reorganized the basement to store more residents' belongs. Except for a few randomly placed stacks of bricks donated for a small renovation project, everything was in a bin or a partitioned cubicle, and typed 8½ x 11-inch signs hung from partitions, indicating what they contained. Unfortunately, I didn't know the new layout.

At the bottom of the steps, I pulled a string to turn on one of several bulbs hanging from the ceiling.

The basement was filled to overflowing, but orderly in the way that a maze is.

"Are you looking for evidence, again?" Officer Shirley asked, with just a touch of exasperation in her voice.

I turned to the right. I had heard the first warning. "I'm looking for a canary yellow backpack. I'll take the right side; you can take the left. A light hangs from the ceiling about ten feet from the steps."

I was tired and sweaty, and I don't like musty places. I also knew that we still had mice. So, while she didn't have to take orders from me and I really shouldn't have been giving any, I wanted to get this over with. I'd apologize later if she didn't piss me off with another warning.

She stood at the bottom of the steps surveying the area. Her right hand was on her gun, and she shined the flashlight around with her left. By the time I heard her move, I had pulled another string to light the right side of the basement and had cut off the MegaLite, which was beginning to flicker.

I moved quickly from one cubicle to the next, passed Books and Educational Material, Donated Clothes, and Lingerie and Personal Items. *No woman wants to wear another woman's throwaway panties, so I stopped keeping such donations.* I stumbled over something in the middle of the path and dropped the MegaLite. It rolled to the left just out of reach. With my right foot, I pushed the box of files that had fallen in the aisle. I picked up the MegaLite and turned the corner at Resident Storage Area 1. Area 4 was one cubicle down on the right.

Mel's backpack was easy to spot on top of a four-shelf bookcase. I sat on a rusty gray folding chair next to a large cardboard box labeled "Do Not Tuch My Stuff" and opened the backpack. It contained five paperback books, a Race for the Cure T-shirt, a black sweat suit, three matching sets of embroidered silk panties and bras wrapped in red tissue paper, a small bottle of Jean Paul Gaultier wrapped in the same paper, and a framed 3 x 5 photograph of Mel beaming, while the man beside her appeared to intentionally look away. If he had not made himself so hard to ignore at our earlier meeting, I might not have recognized him here. I really should have asked his name.

The zippered front compartment of the backpack was empty except for her EPA employee identification card, a wallet-sized high school diploma, a flyer from Prince George's County Community College, and a handwritten card containing the address and telephone number of John and Maybell Johnson—her parents I assumed.

All I could do for her now was cry and be angry. What could have brought her so far from home?

"I have it. Res Storage 4, the last cubicle on the right," I yelled while carefully returning Mel's life to her backpack and reclaiming my voice. There was no response or movement in my direction. "Shirley?" Again, no response.

There are only two ways out of the basement. The stairwell and door were not an option, and the one window was at least six feet high and many inches too narrow for this body to squeeze through. Besides, I couldn't leave the basement without making sure Officer Shirley was okay.

I knew I'd have to wait for him to come to me and prayed. I put the backpack across my left shoulder, stooped in a corner diagonally across from the entrance, and gripped the MegaLite so tightly my fingers ached.

Only one thing in sight and reach had major weapon potential. When I heard steady movement toward Area 4 and bulbs breaking, I dashed for the fire extinguisher just as the basement plunged into darkness.

With one hand, I frantically felt along the wall for the extinguisher. I wanted to cut on the MegaLite but was afraid of lighting his way and of draining the remaining battery power. I'd need a fully functioning flashlight if he found me before D.C.'s finest did.

Partitions crashed, and movement stopped. It started again, but I didn't see the pinpoint light.

When I turned from the wall, my eyes had adjusted to the darkness a little. I could feel his presence, hear labored breathing. He was in the cubicle. Suddenly, I was facing him, close enough to reach out and touch his chest. Something—blood, I hope—ran down the middle of his face. He raised a hammer. I lifted the MegaLite in my right hand, pointed it at his face, and cut it on. He dropped the hammer when he covered his eyes. The light flickered, so I dropped the flashlight, stepped out of his reach, and—with both hands—lifted and aimed the fire extinguisher for his eyes, waiting for him to drop his hands. He did; I pressed hard.

*I hope this stuff can dissolve a face. He won't be looking so pleased with himself anymore.*

He stumbled backward. I raised the extinguisher and hit his right temple. He staggered toward the entrance, then turned back toward me and lunged forward. Backing out of his reach, I felt the top of the cardboard box for my back-up weapon. My hand found it—rough and rectangular—as his hands reached for my throat. This was my last chance to get out of there alive. I kneed him. He doubled over, and I prayed my scripture of choice, "Jesus wept," before hitting him for Mel and for Arlene.

I don't know when or why I lost consciousness. But, when I opened my eyes, Officer Shirley was kneeling at my side holding my hand. She had a very nasty bruise on her forehead.

"Did he get away? Where is her backpack?" I tried to get up.

"No, he didn't have a chance." She smiled. "And your head is resting on the backpack."

She looked to the left, where he was lying face-down. Since he was handcuffed, I assumed he was alive.

"What happened? He grabbed my throat or tried, I think, and I hit him with something."

"A brick, ma'am. When I got here, you were pounding him with it.

Then you just collapsed on top of him. I came as soon as I could, but you really didn't need my help. He grazed my head with a hammer. The last thing I remember is falling backward. I guess he thought I was dead."

I tried to stand again, and she gently pushed my head and shoulders back on the backpack. "You're not standing until an ambulance arrives. Lt. Davis will have me suspended if anything happens, anything *else* happens to you." She smiled but didn't decrease the pressure on my shoulders.

While waiting for the ambulance, I told her what I knew and turned the backpack over to her. I wasn't sure why Arlene was murdered, but I was pretty sure about Mel. Mel must have known too much, and Arlene probably knew absolutely nothing.

At 9:00 P.M. when Officer Shirley dropped me by the precinct, the B had been languishing in a holding cell for three hours. She had been arrested as a result of Janice's statements and Lew's anger. I hoped she was making friends. Mel's camera-shy boyfriend had arrived a bit later after receiving several stitches. Unfortunately, I hadn't done any real damage.

Janice LaWanda Scott was ensconced in a conference room on the second floor, with a uniformed guard outside.

I waited for Lew in his spartan office.

"I will continue to have officers stationed at A Woman's Place, at least for the next few days. And, there will be additional arrests," he said upon entering the office, kissing my cheek, and sitting behind his desk. "Are you okay, Glo?"

"I'm fine. When can I see Janice?"

"In the morning, after she meets with a court-appointed attorney and gives an official statement. She's asked for you. I'll let her know you came."

"What is she likely to be charged with? All she did was try to protect her child."

"She held you against your will at gunpoint, and she withheld evidence that could have saved one or both women. She knew something bad was going to happen at or near the shelter, and she only warned one person—her daughter. I can't ignore that even for you . . . but she is cooperating."

I had given a complete statement to Officer Shirley after refusing any treatment that the paramedics could not give at A Woman's Place.

Now, it was Lew's turn to tell me all that he knew.

Apparently, as soon as Bernetta saw John Holland—Mel's camera-shy boyfriend—being brought into an interrogation room across from hers, she began to sweat profusely and asked for more time with her lawyer, who then began to negotiate a plea bargain.

The interrogating officers now know everything but her real weight. She admitted coercing Janice to deliver the manila envelope and to paying a child to read the message left on my answering machine. Neither incident had anything to do with the real crimes. She'd just taken the opportunity—the murders of two young women—to get even with me for dislodging her from A Woman's Place. Janice supplied access and information in exchange for Taywanda's safety and Bernetta's silence about her parenthood.

Bernetta also volunteered that John Holland worked for a development company planning to build a pricey condominium development in the neighborhood. The deal was contingent on A Woman's Place closing, so he used poor Mel to get information, hoping to find something to discredit staff at the shelter. The company wanted the property and barring that, wanted to stop the expansion. He had intended to have her plant drugs at A Woman's Place, if necessary.

Also according to Bernetta, two days before Mel's death, Mel overheard a telephone conversation in which John Holland talked about his progress in closing A Woman's Place and then ridiculed his two inside connections: Bernetta and Mel. Mel told Bernetta because they had formed a mother-daughter relationship. They had met through Janice. The morning she died, she confronted John Holland and threatened to expose him, so he killed her, dumped her body by the pay phone near A Woman's Place, and then called my office to ensure that a connection was made. Bernetta said that she thinks that he called her number as well from the pay phone, so she is quite angry. He denied calling her number. She has not explained why he was so forthcoming with so much incriminating information except perhaps to implicate her.

Instead of sitting back and waiting for the D.C. Metropolitan Police Department to do its investigative job, John Holland decided to put icing on the cake—his words according to Bernetta—by having another woman killed and dumped on the steps of the shelter. Arlene's was a random killing to ensure a strong connection to A Woman's Place and lots of negative press. Arguably, Mel's death might not have been linked back to the shelter, but a death on the steps the same day definitely would.

When John Holland discovered that Mel had taken, from his apartment, the only photograph of them together, he came to A Woman's Place looking for her backpack—the only place that she would have kept it. Not knowing that a student who volunteers at the shelter had given Mel a new canary yellow backpack the day before, he was looking for a soiled gray one.

Both of these disgusting creatures claimed the other was responsible for the actual murders. Bernetta even claimed that she'd had no idea that John Holland would kill anyone and that, when she found out about the murders, he'd threatened to say she was an accomplice if she came forward. She was not quite able to explain how she managed to taunt me simultaneously with the murders occurring if she only became aware of them after the fact.

John Holland contended that he worked within the Advisory Neighborhood Commission and other community mechanisms to influence change. He also said that the expansion proposal was providing sufficient community opposition to the shelter and that he'd had no reason to work outside of the law. And he doesn't have a clue why Officer Shirley and I attacked him. He was just looking for his girlfriend's belongings. On last report, he was still waiting for the development firm to arrange for his legal representation.

I'm not sure how he will explain the hair and other DNA evidence on that hammer with his fingerprints all over it.

John Holland stood to earn several hundred thousand for his time and effort.

Bernetta stood to earn $25,000 for hers and to get revenge on me.

## EPILOGUE

I will do more for Mel than simply cry and be angry. I will do one other thing—make sure the monster who'd bought her expensive perfume and sexy underwear and then killed her, pays.

And, I will make sure he pays for Arlene being the icing on his cake.

Bernetta Bennett, aka the B, is still on my list, and now, she is on Lew's and the federal prosecutor's as well. Handcuffs had gone nicely with her Barney slippers, and she is sure to meet at least one woman in lockup whom she mistreated at A Woman's Place.

# WHEN BLOOD RUNS TO WATER

*Glenville Lovell*

He had come up from one of those islands in the Caribbean, Jamaica it was, leaving behind a girlfriend, a mother, three sisters, and cracked airless land. He came brimming with confidence, with expectations heaped on him by family and friends; by people who didn't even know him. That didn't matter because he was going North. To the big city. Countless others had made promises to come back rich. To send money. Countless others had forgotten their promises. But he made no such promises. His only promise was to himself. Don't be a sucker.

He was barely twenty-five, when he got here. Broad shoulders. Lean. Swift hands. Swift dick. Swift dick like his father. A dick swift enough to fly him to New York.

It took four months in Edmonton and two weeks in Toronto to secure passage to New York. Beautiful as it was, Canada was not in his plans, but he'd felt obligated to stay briefly with the woman who got him there, a pretty blond from Edmonton, with laughing blue eyes and fluffy marshmallow skin. Toting a smile as white as her skin, she turned up at Fisherman's Club in Negril with her policeman boyfriend one night. In his four years as the barman at Fisherman's Club he'd seen many near-perfect smiles. But hers was perfect. She sipped cognac; her boyfriend wolfed down rum and cokes as if it was lemonade; by closing he was drunk.

Jeffrey drove them back to their condo on the beach and helped put her boyfriend to bed. She was drunk and beside herself with disappointment; seducing her that night was easy.

For the next week he shadowed the two of them, showing up just when her boyfriend was ready to pass out, having drunk himself into a near stupor. Once the policeman was safely tucked in, Jeffrey would help her live her fantasy of romance under a Caribbean moonlit sky her boyfriend had promised but failed to deliver. When she returned to Edmonton she dumped her boyfriend, and sent him a ticket.

There was no way a woman could be more accommodating, more deferential to a man. His plan was to stay three weeks, but the lifestyle she allowed him—from her condominium in town grandly furnished and decorated with paintings and antiques, to the presents and uninhibited sex—was more seductive than a story from Sheherazade, and he almost changed his mind. In the end, his mother's voice restored his resolve. One Sunday morning while his girlfriend was at church he boarded a plane for Ontario.

He landed in Mississauga, where he had a friend who once worked with him at the Fisherman's Club. His stay there was short. Unhappily married, his friend was not at all happy to see him; his wife of five years, a producer at CBC, drank too much, and was an incorrigible flirt.

After two weeks of searching, he found a woman who said she could get him across the border for a fee. They left after midnight, and four hours later he was in Buffalo, where he boarded a Greyhound bus to Manhattan later that morning.

The picture in his wallet of his three-year-old daughter, Karina, was taken when she was six weeks old. What did she look like now? More like him than her mother?

Several times he tried to get a visa to visit; he was turned down each time. What guarantee do we have that you will not stay in the United States? the consul officer wanted to know. *All I want to do is see my daughter.* The consular officer was unimpressed with his paternal yearning.

Karina's mother, Maria, had not returned to the island since that summer of '95. In one of her letters she declared that the only reason she didn't get an abortion was because of God. She was a good Catholic girl from Queens.

Why weren't you thinking of God when I was fucking you? he wrote back.

That was the last time he heard from her until the picture came. He cursed himself for being so swift. Dick too swift. Mouth too swift.

On the corner of Forty-second and Broadway he took out his tiny black book. He leafed through sea-water-stained leaves, halting at the page with his father's Brooklyn address. Cars, trucks, and buses pounded the air about him, creating a jungle of noise at decibel levels he'd never before experienced.

He stared at his father's address with surreal intensity, unmoved by the army of passersby who jostled him on their way to the subway or the bus. The logic of what he was about to do finally releasing a bubble of doubt in his stomach. The only memory of his father was of a tall bald man leaning against a beat-up Vauxhall car, with a wide white woman at his side.

"That's your father over there." His mother hissed. "You see, he married a white woman, so him got nuff money. Go ask him what him bring back from America for yuh?"

He was nine. His father, who'd been a myth up until then, had brought nothing. Only harsh words.

*Who tell you I am you father? Tell the woman me say she lie. You don't look like me.*

Was the address for the man his mother called Jockey correct? He'd gotten it from his cousin, who'd gotten it from her grandmother, his father's aunt.

With the help of the African cab driver he found the house on East Forty-seventh Street. He thanked the driver and stepped backward on the sidewalk to watch the yellow car drive off. His stomach suddenly felt hollow, as if some evil spirit had invaded his body and scooped out his intestines. The flat gray sky seemed to rise and drift off like a heavy balloon.

What if it was the wrong address? What if Jockey denied him like he did that time back in Jamaica? Like water on his brain, those words still floated in his head. Where would he go? Where would he sleep?

Contrary to his friend Nail's opinion, this trip was not about his father. There was nothing there. It was too late to make up for the pain. All he hoped for was a spot of kindness. A place to sleep for a while, until he got his stake in the big city. He didn't expect love. Love had always been a luxury to him. He'd never been capable of following love's narrow path. But his mother never let him forget who his father was. *You look just like your father. Don't let nobody fool you, Jockey is your father.*

Slowly he started up the steps with his suitcase, which contained a few pieces of clothing, three pairs of shoes, and his CDs. Music was the liquid in which he bathed his soul, drowning the nightmares he'd had since he was a child, and he never went anywhere without his music.

He rapped on the door and waited. Presently a tall bald man with a thin gray mustache peeped through Venetian blinds at an unwashed window.

"Yes?"

"Jockey?"

"Who want to know?"

"Jeffrey. Your son."

The long pause brimmed with confusion and deliberation. Jeffrey breathed deeply, the heavy November air, and strained to hear the other man's thoughts.

The man left the window; then the front door opened slightly.

"You coming in?"

Jeffrey knuckled his way through the crack between the doorjamb and the gaunt man.

"You get tall, boy," the man whispered.

Now standing in a dim hallway opposite his father he wanted to say. *I'm twenty-five. Hardly a boy.* Instead he grinned nervously and said, "Tall like you."

Jockey grunted and closed the door. "Come in and sit down. You want a beer? I got some Bacardi rum. It ain't Appleton, but it gets you drunk the same."

"No thanks. Me nah drink," he lied.

"You don't drink? What kind of man are you? Boy, you ain't my son if you don't drink."

"Me don't care about being your son. Me just want a place to stay for a little while."

Curtly spoken and laced with anger, these words were born sixteen years ago and had been laying in the grass of his shame, coiled, aged, ready to strike.

The older man swayed like a palm tree in a high wind, then shrugged and crawled back into his aloof skin, drawing his lips tight around him. His eyes closed briefly, as though he was about to fall asleep on his feet. Then he stumbled backward.

Jeffrey, already beginning to curse his swiftness, realized the man was drunk. "I'm sorry."

His father fell into a chair and sat like a straightjacket staring dead ahead. The sultry silence blew up a storm of soul-searching for memories that didn't exist.

Jeffrey picked up his suitcase.

"You can stay. Stay as long as you want. It's a big house. Three bedrooms and a finished basement. Nobody in it but me. Gets lonely as hell sometimes."

"Me don't expect to be here long."

"Look, boy, I know you must be angry with me. I wish things was different. But them ain't. I wish we had some memories to joke about. If that's what you come up here for . . ."

"Me nah come up here for you," Jeffrey blurted.

Jockey twisted around to face him. "What you come up here for, if you ain't come looking for the past?"

"The past maybe, but not yours. My own. Me here to find my daughter."

"You got a daughter?"

"Three years old."

"You got any pictures?" There was a drip of excitement in the man's voice.

Jeffrey scooped the tattered picture from his wallet. He handed it to his father and saw the man's body relax, saw a sudden transformation in his face; the eyes suddenly opening wide enough to engulf an eclipse, his smile exploding into a grin.

"White woman?"

Jeffrey nodded.

"You like them white women?"

Jeffrey wondered if his father was trying to make fun of him. "They like me."

"Yeah, I think I know why."

"It ain't what you thinking."

His father chuckled. "What I thinking?"

"Me know what you thinking. And it ain't what you thinking."


Maria had written three letters. In the first letter, she loved and missed him and wished she could've stayed longer on the island. By the next letter, she had found out she was pregnant and cursed him for being so careless. That was when she declared herself too good a Catholic to have an abortion. She did not respond to his letter until nine months later. That last letter contained a picture itemized on the back with the baby's name and weight at birth. His first week in New York he tried calling the telephone number she'd given him, but nobody ever seemed to be home.


It irked him every time his father posed as the concerned grandfather.

"Where this grandchild of mine?"

Why didn't you ask for me like this? he wanted to reply. Instead, he would feign temporary deafness.

Fifteen years divorced, his father never remarried and had no other children. From the look of things he received a decent pension from his retired post office job. The untidy house sat in the middle of a well-kept block in a neighborhood of single and two-family homes, mostly owned by West Indians. The expanse and energy of the city thrilled Jeffrey, and he tried to ignore his father's slovenliness while trying to figure out a way to find his daughter.

New York's well-publicized reputation for violence and crime didn't intimidate him. In his mind he was born for the big city. It didn't take him long to find the West Indian clubs. The Cave on Rutland Road was one such joint. There he ran into Tallabo, someone he knew casually from the nightclub scene back home.

He'd first seen Maria in Tallabo's company and concluded that she was much too pretty for him. Being the bartender it was easy to strike up a conversation with Maria, and before the night was over he had all the information he needed: where she was staying and her room and telephone number. The rest was easy. Tallabo didn't have his looks, his style, didn't have a job, and didn't have a car. He picked Maria up the next day in his Honda and took her on a tour of the island. That night they ran into Tallabo in a club. After a juvenile attempt to intimidate him, Tallabo accepted that he'd lost Maria and took up with her traveling companion.

Over rum punch in the Cave they joked about the *life*.

"Them was some nice day," said Tallabo. "The pussy was flowing, and them touristwomen was some freaky bitches."

"Remember that short fat chick you picked at Golden Sands? She was traveling with a dark-haired, fire-in-her-eyes beauty name Maria."

"Yeah, the Maria you stole from me."

"That was the life. The big dog gets the big bone. What was Shorty's name again?"

"Samantha Seltzer."

"You ever tried to contact her when you got up here?"

Tallabo was a big dude, broad at the hip and shoulders, with a square ridge for a forehead. He traced a circle on his forehead with his fingers and cracked a block of ice in his mouth. His eyes flickered like damp fire. "Why would I wanna do that?"

"You got her number? Me wanna call her."

"No. And if I did I wouldn't give it to you."

"Man, what's your problem?"

"Me nah have no problem. Everything cool."

When he got home he called information and got numbers for S. A. Seltzer in Brooklyn and Samantha Seltzer in Queens. He called both numbers. Neither party was home, and he left his number.

The next day Samantha called. She seemed genuinely excited to hear from him. Riding this wave of good fortune, he asked about Maria.

"There's something you should know about Maria."

"What," he asked. There was a long pause. "What's the problem? She dead or something."

"I don't want to talk about it on the phone. I have an idea. Do you want to get together for a drink tomorrow night?"

His father found him in bed the next afternoon reading *Sports Illustrated* and smoking a Winston.

"Wanna go around the corner and have a drink with me?"

He looked up from the magazine. The man's eyes were crimson. How did he see? The dingy blue T-shirt he was wearing seemed too small and was frayed at the neck. The armpits were dark with sweat stains. Jeffrey took a deep drag on his cigarette, flicked ash in the tray on the floor.

"Me can't. Going out later." He flipped the page of the magazine and exhaled slowly, trying to delay having to breathe the sour fermented smell of sweat and alcohol released by his father.

"When you going to bring that granddaughter of mine to meet her grandfather?"

"How many times me gotta say me nah find her yet?" He closed the magazine and got up to dump the contents of the ashtray into the garbage bucket in the kitchen.

"You nah find her? What you mean you nah find her?" His father trailed him, just off his right shoulder.

"Jeffrey spun sharply. "That's what I mean. Me nah find her."

"Maybe you ashamed to bring her here to meet me. Is that it?"

Jeffrey stepped around Jockey and sauntered back to the bedroom, with his father at his heels like a faithful puppy.

"I wasn't always like this, you know," murmured his father. "Before I get fire from my job . . ."

"Me thought you say you retire?"

"I was forced to retire. To me it's the same shit. If you black they think they can do anything to you."

"Who's *they*?"

"Don't play stupid, boy. Who you think run this fucking country?"

"Look, me nah really wanna hear this."

"You think you got the answer to everything, eh? You just land, and you is fucking Socrates. This ain't Jamaica, boy. This bloodclaat country will wipe your ass with a razor and laugh."

Jeffrey picked up a pair of jeans from the floor by the bed and started to get dressed. He hadn't expected love to blossom between them, but he'd hoped they would get along. The man's bitterness and his perpetual drunken state made it impossible to entertain any emotion but pity. He couldn't even hate him. He pulled on his boots, took a shirt from the rack in the closet, and grabbed a brown leather bomber hanging on the bedroom door.

"Me nah finish with you yet," said Jockey.

"Save it for your buddies around the corner. I got places to go."

"Wake up, boy. You better off forgetting 'bout that child."

"Like you did me."

"I left your ass back there, because your mother was a whore."

"Shut your drunken mouth."

"You think you tough Mister Know-It-All? Then deal with the truth. I wasn't the only man swimming in that ocean. Your mother was a fucking whore!"

Jeffrey's reaction was swift. Too swift. The right hook landed flush on Jockey's jaw. The man sagged to the floor. Jeffrey swung the flimsy wooden door open and went out into the clear evening.


He rode the number 2 train to Brooklyn Heights and walked to the promenade. Sitting on one of the green benches he watched as the setting sun tore the sky to shreds and cursed his swiftness.

Mouth too swift.

Hands too swift.

*Like it or not the man is your father. Striking your father is against God's law.*

Feeling sorrow canoeing in his chest he got up to go apologize to his father. Then he sat down again. Perhaps it was better to wait. His father might not be too forgiving right now. He'd take a bottle of rum home later and work up to it over a drink.

He cursed himself double for showing his mother Karina's picture. He could still hear her admonishment: *Boy you go let that little girl grow up and not know her father? You go be just like your father Jockey?"*

Samantha lived in Park Slope. He arrived early and sat on the sofa while she set her face. They took a cab to Banana Boat, a cozy tropical theme bar on Flatbush Avenue where the drinks were mixed to taste.

Sitting at the bar he ordered two piña coladas.

"Remember the piña coladas I mixed for you at Fisherman's Club?"

She laughed. "How could I forget? Got me in big trouble. That was the last night I wore panties on the island. I know you don't believe me, but all I came down there for was to get some rest. I wasn't looking for sex."

Jeffrey sipped from the large glass. "I believe you."

"No you don't. Not with that devilish grin on your face. After those piña coladas the word *no* had lost all meaning. And the truth is I would've rather said yes to you."

He smiled. Samantha was a large woman, not really his type. Her round blue eyes sparkled too brightly to be natural. She had short frizzy hair, blond on top with black roots. Short with a large sensuous mouth, her perpetual smile, with just a blush of laughter and relaxed way of talking, could be seductive though. Perhaps. It'd been a while since he had some.

"Do I look the same?" she asked.

"Better."

"You're just saying that. When we met you didn't look my way twice."

He laughed. "You had your eyes on somebody else."

"No, I had my eyes on you, but your dick was already hard for Maria."

He laughed nervously. "What's the story with Maria?"

She sighed. "I don't know where to begin."

"Begin with where she living."

Samantha touched his right triceps and let her fingers linger, caressing them gently. "Look, Maria was only nineteen when she got pregnant. The pregnancy was very hard on her. And her strict family didn't help. They practically disowned her. The poor girl had a nervous breakdown. I don't know what you did to her in those three weeks, but she claimed she loved you."

"I want to see her."

"You're too late."

"What about the baby?"

"Karina?"

"Yes. Karina is my child."

A voice boomed behind him. "Why don't you shut your bloodclaat mouth telling people Karina is your child?"

He spun around at the force of the question. Tallabo stood over his right shoulder, sullen as a Voodoo priest.

"This ain't got nothing to do with you, fool," Jeffrey said.

Samantha tightened her grip on his arm to calm him down.

Jeffrey breathed deep and sighed. He stood up to take his wallet out. "Let's get out of here."

"Who the hell you calling a fool?" Tallabo growled.

"What's your problem, man?"

"You're my problem. You need to get Karina off your bloodclaat mind."

"Don't do this here," Samantha said.

"You shoulda stayed where you were," Tallabo said.

Jeffrey put ten dollars on the bar. "Maybe you're the one shoulda stayed back there. Acting all backward like an idiot. Karina is my daughter."

"Maria is my wife. And Karina is my daughter."

The words banged off Jeffrey's head, then floated back, hovering around before trickling into his mind slowly like syrup.

He looked at Samantha. "What's this fool talking about?"

She bowed her head and rimmed her drink with her pinkie.

He turned back to Tallabo. "You're talking gibberish. Maria would never marry a monkey like you. Go get a towel and wipe the drool from your mouth."

"Fuck you!"

The shove Tallabo gave Jeffrey wasn't even hard enough to make him rock on his heels. But Jeffrey's reaction was swift. A hard straight right to Tallaboo's face. The man flopped to the floor.

Taking Samantha by the arm, Jeffrey started for the door. He didn't expect Tallabo to get up. Not after taking his best punch.

No one had time to warn him. Perhaps no one wanted to. In an instant the knife Tallabo wielded was buried in his neck.

Jeffrey stumbled outside. It was raining. People rushing past, hoping to disappear before the police arrived. Samantha screaming. He wanted to tell her to stop, but his mouth wouldn't open. His equilibrium was disappearing fast. For a flash his father was in front of him. He took a step, then he fell, his head resting gently against an empty St. Ives bottle; ten inches of steel rising from his neck like a silver obelisk. A face flashed before him. Maria? Or was that Karina's face? He'd come all this way just to see that face. The streetlight charged the silver strip on the bottle's edge, sending a crackle of light bouncing off his wet cheek. How quickly does a body go cold when blood runs to water on a rainy street?

# A SMALL MATTER

*Lee E. Meadows*

Garrison Brock stared nonchalantly at the digital images being broadcast across a secured network onto his flat screen monitor. The clock located at the bottom of the screen confirmed the middle of the nighttime that signaled him from a restful sleep. Though the sight of a grisly crime scene at that time of the morning was not an unusual occurrence, it was not the academic, scholarly solace he demanded after agreeing to remain "available." It wasn't the first time his supposed retirement was interrupted by an unusual crime. His first thought, as the videotaped images moved slowly around the room, was to focus on the peculiar aspects of the crime scene. Like so many other crime scenes he had experienced across a career in various investigative agencies of the United States Justice Department, the images said more about the killer than the victims. Force of habit, years of being a field operative and his unique talent combined like a single laser beam moving slowly across the monitor, looking for the little things that others miss.

"What do you think, ten?" the audio voice asked through the speakers connected to the computer monitor.

"Where'd you get these?" Brock asked already certain of the answer.

"Just fooling around out in cyberspace, Doc, it just happen to digitize onto my hard drive."

It was the answer he expected from the only criminal for whom he'd called in a lot of favors to keep out of jail. Working in a remote location with a state-of-the-art information system financed by leftover tax dollars, Brian Botcher, was a legend among his peers. The best hacker to have ever been captured by a federal agent, he now availed his talents as an unclassified "information accessor" for the United States government, complete with a six-figure salary, a government-subsidized home, and the red government vehicle.

"Things don't just appear on your hard drive, Botcher. You've been peeping into somebody's system."

"It's what they pay me to do, Doc." He replied matter-of-factly. "So what do you think?"

Brock leaned closer to the screen. "I'd put both victims in their early twenties. From the position of her body, I'd say she must have been coming down the steps, most likely surprised whoever was in there. The man had obviously fallen asleep on the couch when the shots were fired."

"What makes you think . . ."

"Look at the contents on the coffee table," Brock said. "The remote is lying on the floor next to his hand. There are three empty bottles of beer, a half-eaten bag of tortilla chips, an empty cup of salsa, and the channel number on the cable box is consistent with channels that run pay-per-view movies."

"Coroner's report shows the time of death being between one and one thirty in the morning."

"He'd probably been asleep for a least an hour. As far as he knows, he's still asleep." Brock leaned back from the computer screen, smiled to himself, and rubbed his eyes. "Let the local authorities do their job, Botcher. I have a report to finish for the institute."

"You're the only staff member, Doc. Why are you writing a report that no one is going to read? Besides, if it's anything like those journal articles you write, the readers won't stay awake long enough to finish."

Brock yawned, choosing to ignore the comment. "There's nothing unusual here, Botcher."

"I could download all the information they've gathered so far," Botcher replied, having sensed Brock's pretended indifference. "What's the harm? Besides, you know artists like us have to keep our skills sharp."

"If you're about to download information to me that you obtained by illegally going into a city's computer system, then I'd say your skills haven't diminished one bit."

"Those antiquated systems they use should be on display at the Smithsonian, right next to the wheel."

"Don't you ever sleep?" Brock asked.

"The places I have go into are most vulnerable at night," he replied.

"You know local authorities don't like outside interference."

"You are a USA-10, Doc, and that gives you all the authority you need."

Brock smiled at the thought of Botcher being the only person of his background, and to Brock's knowledge, to hack deep enough into the United States Information System and find the obscure 1960s legislation that created the USA category. A United States senator had cleverly attached the funding for the category on the back of several budget requests for building maintenance and restoration. Over the years, the category continued to be a little-known, seldom-discussed budget line item buried beneath the yearly requests that Congress and the Senate typically rubber-stamped. The unassigned special agent status was only awarded to experienced federal agents whose talents or skills were so unique that they would be considered a threat to national security if their talents were used elsewhere. Garrison Brock was the tenth person to be assigned that status since the category had been created, and the first African-American. He retired after twenty-five years of government service that had taken him to more countries than he cared to visit and more people than he cared to know. His special talent kept him available, though not always willing.

"It's moments like this that I wished I had let you go to jail," Brock said.

"I just would have created more like me," Botcher replied. "Imagine how much fun that would have been for you and the limited number of agents trying to catch all my criminally cyber creations.

"Send me what you have, and I'll give it one more look."

Brock watched as the blue line moved quickly across the bottom of his monitor and disappeared, quickly signaling that the download was complete.

"You must have found something interesting, or you wouldn't have brought it to my attention," Brock said.

"It's my way of staying sharp, Doc. Had I not gotten so arrogant, you would have never caught me."

"I didn't catch you because you were arrogant, Botcher." Brock said stifling another yawn. "I caught you because you got lazy."

"Probably explains why I'm up most of the time. Later, Doc. The agency wants me to look into some bookkeeping being done by a revered insurance company."

"Unofficially, of course," Brock said, not waiting for a reply.

Botcher logged off. Brock opened the file attachment from the double homicide and began reading through the reports. Scanning reports into computer systems made for easy storage, but proved less than a challenge for people with Botcher's skills. He made a habit of peeking in and out of systems using his God-given talents and a 70-million-dollar-satellite-supported information accessor. Mostly, he'd just look around to see if there was anything the agency needed to know, but every now and then, something would trigger his interest.

Brock spent just under an hour reading through the reports. The investigating officer had done a decent job of reporting what he'd seen. A number of interviews had proven interesting, but not insightful. The victims were Liddia Moore and Franklin Dempsey. Both had previous records for small-time offenses, but nothing to warrant a double murder. Both were killed with an easily obtainable and equally disposable twenty-two caliber. The murder weapon still had not been found.

"Drugs were ruled out, and it wasn't random," Brock muttered.

Liddia was found lying on the floor between the stairs and the living area, wearing a black see-through robe that Brock concluded she must have thrown on because an unusual noise brought her downstairs. She had been propelled backwards by the three bullets fired into her. The report indicated that she'd been hit three times in the chest. The left hand had been nicked by one of the bullets.

"That's her only defensive wound," Brock said.

Frank Dempsey had taken one in the right temple as he slept. He'd consumed too much beer and snack food, late at night, stretched out on the couch while watching a pay-per-view channel. Other than a small black birthmark on the ring finger of his right hand, there was very little that stood out about his physical being.

Brock read the coroner's report. "He got it first, doesn't necessarily mean he was the target."

He turned his attention to the digital view of the crime scene. His computer was programmed so he could zoom in on particular images, sharpen the focus and change the point of view. He reread the witness statements, believing that there was something said that was missed. The parents of the victims were equally shocked, and their interviews reflected their emotional grief and frustration with not having any answers. Liddia's sister, Lena, essentially went into a prolonged depression, and Frank had no other siblings to grieve his departure. Garrison leaned back in the custom-made, leather high-back chair and stared up at the ceiling as if all the information he'd been given was painted up there in a crude mosaic.

Finally, he said. "No doubt, she was the target."

Wiltshire Commons was a small enclave inside Detroit's borders, having spent its first one hundred and six years as an upscale community that was home to descendants of the city's first robber barons. They spread their wealth and influence throughout the poor structures of Detroit's growing automotive presence, but restricted participation to a small group of wealthy Wiltshire residents. This wasn't the same community that Garrison Brock drove through on his way to keep a ten o'clock appointment with Wiltshire Park's chief of police. What remained was a total devastation of homes and lifestyle left abandoned as the third generation of Wiltshires took their wealth and influence north on the I-75 freeway to the more affluent areas of Troy, Auburn Hills, and other modern-day tributes to wealthy isolation. The main street leading through Wiltshire Commons was a mixture of one-level businesses and fast food eateries. Behind the economic devastation, on the side streets where people took a stab at living, many of the homes were adjacent to boarded up or burnt down dwellings. The people up and out at that time of the morning looked as if they'd gone forty rounds with Satan's evil twin. Life had beaten them up pretty bad, only they were too proud to fall down.

Brock parked in front of the white stucco building, not surprised by the lack of patrol cars in the area. After studying the police reports, he'd gone out in cyberspace and pulled up the most recent articles written about Wiltshire Commons. Living in Detroit had made him aware of the problem facing this city that was on the brink of being taken over by the State of Michigan. He knew as much about Wiltshire Commons as he cared to know. The city had become one more joke being told by comedy club stand-ups, hoping for that big break on Jay Leno. When Wiltshire Commons was unable to pay its water bill to Detroit, a rash of fires left the few remaining firemen with little choice but to keep people from wandering too close.

"I have a ten o'clock appointment with Chief Martin," he said to the burly desk sergeant. "My name is Garrison Brock."

Through half-lid eyes, the sergeant barely looked up while pushing a button on a phone and telling Chief Martin that the ten o'clock appointment was waiting in the lobby.

"The Chief will be right with you," he monotoned. "Have a seat over there." He pointed to a row of unmatched wooden and steel-legged chairs.

He walked over to the corner where the chairs were lined up; backs turned to a large plate-glass window with a view of the main street. Brock chose to stand and watch the human traffic find reason to hang on for another day.

His concentration on what was taking place outside of police headquarters was suddenly interrupted. "Dr. Brock?" a voice asked.

Garrison turned and smiled at the medium-height, dyed-red-haired woman, with brown eyes and Hershey chocolate skin, proudly displayed in police uniform blue. "I'm Andrea Martin."

"Hello, Chief Martin," Garrison replied.

"Andrea."

"Garrison."

"Let's take a ride," she said.

Chief Martin strolled past the front counter, whispered something to the desk sergeant, and motioned for Brock to come along.

"We'll take my patrol car," she said.

Out a side door and into the adjacent parking lot, Chief Andrea Martin's gray unmarked patrol car occupied a reserved spot close to the building. A wire fence stretched around the entire parking lot, which could only be accessed by way of a security card-controlled gate.

She rubbed her security card against a small pad, and the gate slowly slid open.

"So what kind of doctor are you?" she asked as she pulled onto the main street.

"Criminology," Brock replied. "I did my doctorate at Georgetown."

"Never had an interest in getting a Ph.D.," she said. "After I did the masters in public administration, that was enough for me. So, you're teaching?"

"I did for a minute," he said. "Then I was asked to run this 'think tank' called the Beacon Institute."

"And that means what?" she asked.

Brock smiled. "It means I get paid to write papers about aspects of criminality that are interesting to me. Along the way, I get to give out a few grant dollars here and there."

"Well, we could use more than a few dollars," she said as she made a left turn onto a narrow, one-way residential street. "After you called this morning, I had you checked out. Seems your institute has been quite generous to certain police organizations."

"Just trying to help," Brock said.

"How'd a telecom multimillionaire like Carter Tessing happen to pick you to be executive director of the Beacon Institute."

"He read one of my articles, liked what I had to say, and offered me the job."

Martin smiled. "Or maybe he owed you a big favor. That point on the top of my head is from a bad hair day, not because I'm a dunce. However, I will accept your explanation as a polite way of saying 'mind your own business'." Before Brock could reply, she said, "Here we are."

She parked in front of a two-level, gray brick home of boarded windows, with "No Trespassing" notices stapled in several areas. Chief Martin opened the driver's side door, stepped out, and came around to the passenger side, as Brock stood looking at the house.

"Now, Garrison, perhaps you'll tell me what is so interesting about an unsolved double-murder case that would bring you here asking questions five years after it happened."

"I'm doing research on unsolved double-murder cases," Brock said.

"And there aren't enough in Detroit?"

"I prefer the quiet of a small town."

Chief Martin shook her head. "There's nothing quiet about a town in poverty."

They both stood inside the very vacant crime scene area. Five years of neglect and abandonment had taken its internal toll on the last stop for Liddia Moore and Frank Dempsey. It had become a place for the homeless to hide at night.

"Why did you want to come here, Garrison?" Chief Martin asked. "There's nothing to see except more reminders of how much more the city needs."

"I just wanted to check out a couple of things I might have missed."

"You've been here before?"

"In a way," Garrison said, suddenly remembering the images on his computer screen that he wasn't suppose to have. "Sometimes going back through an old crime scene can reveal things you might have otherwise discarded." He moved around the rubble and debris, being careful not to disturb the makeshift sleeping area.

"Chasing them out requires more manpower than I currently have."

"We do what we have to do, Chief," Garrison said while pointing to an area on the floor. "This is where Liddia was found."

He walked around the floor, glancing first at the steps, then over to the former living area. "Frank had fallen asleep, and there was no sign of forced entry."

"Everyone we could find was questioned, and no one had a clear motive," Chief Martin stated. "We ruled out robbery, drug hit, and crime of passion. There didn't appear to be a revenge angle, and former boyfriends, girlfriends, and passing acquaintances all had credible alibis. We concluded that the killer either had a key or the victims had left the door unlocked."

"Unlocked seems unlikely, given the neighborhood," Brock said.

"And the most likely people with a key, didn't have one," Chief Martin replied.

"Is the sister, Lena, still around?"

"Yeah," Chief Martin said. "Poverty has a way of immobilizing those with the best of intentions."

Lena Moore's basement-level apartment offered little in the way of social advancement and reflected the hard-bitten life that plagued Wiltshire Commons. A more rounded version of her dead sister, her slumped shoulders and tired walk suggested that the slightest effort was a physical pain. She invited both visitors to sit, after she removed several toys from the couch.

Listlessly, she asked. "Any word on what happened to my sister, Chief Martin?"

"Nothing, so far, I'm afraid. Dr. Brock and I are going over the evidence once more just to see if we missed anything. Trying to give it a fresh look." She paused. "How are you holding up?"

"I'll do. Baby Antonio is a handful, but we're getting along."

"Where is he?"

Lena pointed. "Outside playing with Marion's boy."

"Miss Moore," Brock began. "I was just wondering if you could tell me something about Liddia that maybe you hadn't thought about since her death."

She sighed. "I've been over this so many times. Liddia wasn't bad, just wild. She always did what she wanted to do and never thought about how someone else would feel. You know the kind of trouble she got into, Chief, and getting together with that no account Frank didn't help at all."

"Did you two get along okay?" Brock asked.

"She was my sister. I loved her. I didn't always love what she did. I tried to help her as best I could. She was always running out of something or needing to borrow something. Her body was her paycheck and Frank was just one more person trying to make a deposit."

The slight turning of the front door knob interrupted the flow of Lena's conversation as an energetic little boy, bounced his way into the room, oblivious to the guests sitting on the couch.

"Ma, I'm hungry," he said.

"Honey," she retorted. "Mind your manners and say 'hello' to these people."

Garrison stood up and extended his hand. "Hello, young man, my name is Garrison Brock. I'll bet you must be Antonio."

Antonio nodded and shook Garrison's hand. It was a strong hand-shake from such a small person. Clearly present were the high cheekbones, brown eyes, and cinnamon complexion features that Lena had clearly passed on to him. He continued his introductions with Chief Martin and then returned to his earlier statement.

"I'll get you something in just a minute, honey. I'm talking with Mr. Brock and Chief Martin right now."

"Don't give it a second thought, Miss Moore," Brock quickly stated. "In fact Chief Martin and I will be leaving now."

"We are?"

"Yes, we are, Chief. Thanks for your time, Miss Moore. We'll see our way out."

Once they were seated and moving through traffic, Chief Martin asked. "You want to tell me what happened back there."

"Nothing, I just realized we were wasting time. Besides, I don't enjoy opening old wounds. She has enough to think about and deal with, so why bring up bad memories?"

"Anybody else you want to question?"

"No, I think I have enough. I'll take what I have and combine it with other similar cases, and it should generate an interesting journal article."

"I have a hunch there was more to this than just a journal article. But, with the hope that this time we spent working cooperatively will lead to some kind of grant allocation. There are a lot of things I need here, Dr. Brock."

Garrison smiled. "Cooperation duly noted, Chief Martin, I'll mail you a grant application."


During the drive back to his restored three-level brick Tudor home in the old Ferry District of Detroit's east side, Garrison reflected on the events and whether or not he should have confided in Chief Martin. She clearly was a competent and overburdened colleague who could use a case closing, but in the end was it worth it?

Garrison had suspected Lena after picking up on the prolonged depression that seemed to carry on beyond the birth of Antonio. Her alibi for that night was plausible, though there was no concrete proof. She said she was home watching television, having turned in early because she was tired from a doctor's appointment. Liddia and Lena argued, but no more than the average sibling rivalry as noted by the investigating officer. She may have been probed further by the economic downturn that abruptly hit Wiltshire Commons, resulting in the layoff and termination of several city employees. It became an old case left hanging by an investigating officer who found employment as a senior investigator for a mid-size town in west Texas.

Lena had killed her sister. It was as clear as the growing birthmark on the right ring finger of Antonio Moore that Garrison noticed when he shook hands with the young five-year-old offspring of Frank Dempsey.

# MORE THAN ONE WAY

*Penny Mickelbury*

Boxer burrowed deeper under the covers, trying to ignore the growing and pressing need to pee. The sound of the wind bouncing frozen rain pellets off the windows telegraphed a certain reality: He'd freeze his ass off going to the bathroom. He'd worn just briefs and a T-shirt to bed, doubting the forecasters' prediction of a winter storm coming. It was still November, but the wind howled like it was January. He inhaled, flung back the covers, and hobbled to the chest of drawers. He grabbed a sweatshirt, sweat pants, and socks and scurried down the short hall to the bathroom, grateful he'd bought the pretty, fake Persian rug and runner on sale at that linen store last month. Not only did it make the bedroom feel warmer aesthetically, it meant not having to walk on bare hardwood floors.

He had the sweatshirt on by the time he got to the bathroom. He peed, then stepped into the sweat pants and pulled the socks on. He wasn't warm. But he wasn't shivering. On the way back to bed, he pulled another blanket from the closet and spread *it* out over the other blankets and down quilt covering his bed. He got the heating pad from the bedside table drawer where it waited, plugged in and ready to bring soothing warmth to any one of the many places on his fifty-six-year old body, which ached almost constantly. Now, however, he turned it on and shoved it under the covers, down near his feet, and wondered how much longer he could last without turning on the heat. Wondered how much longer he could last without money.

"Don't worry, be happy," he muttered, pulling the covers up to his ears.

He shot straight up, snatching himself out of the dream before it became a nightmare. They came just at dawn these days, which was better than at two or three the way they used to, and periodically was better than all the time. After thirty-some years, it finally was getting better. He swung his feet onto the floor and sat still for a moment to calm himself, then he got up, went to the bathroom, brushed his teeth, and headed for the kitchen. He turned on the oven and opened the door. At least he'd be warm while he drank his tea, ate his toast, and read the paper. Dry toast. He had eaten the last of the peanut butter yesterday, the last of the butter and marmalade the day before. "I like dry toast," he said, talking to the cat, forgetting that the cat was gone. A fully endowed male, of course he was gone, and Boxer missed him. "But at least I don't have to worry about not being able to feed you, too."

The phone rang, startling him. He looked at the clock on the stove: 7:15. He trudged through the living room, down the hall to his office. "Charles Gordon," he said into the phone, and flinched when he heard, "Boxer Boy! How ya doin'" yelled into his ear.

"You're up early, Kenny. You changing your stripes in your old age?" Boxer pulled out the desk chair and sat down.

"Not changing, Boxer, worrying. I need you. You got some time today?"

Boxer hesitated only briefly. "The sooner the better, Kenny. You know where I am." He hung up the phone and leaned back in the chair, putting his feet on the desk. He'd have to get a rug for the office, too; the floor was freezing, even through the thick socks he wore.

He'd met Kenny Schuster in Vietnam, and because they were "home boys," they'd connected, but he hadn't really liked him then, didn't like him now. Yet he had to acknowledge the man's positives: He kept in touch, he always was ready and willing to help, and he'd been there for Boxer at the worst times in his life: when his baby daughter died; when Sharon left him, taking their son; when the police department retired him on disability. Kenny was there with the pat on the back, with the encouraging words, with the food he made Boxer eat to keep his strength up. Kenny had helped him move from his cabin in the woods to this apartment three months ago. So why didn't—couldn't—Boxer like the man?

"Because he's loud and he's a bully."

Braggadocio was commonplace in Vietnam; perhaps in all wars. Men had to do something with the terror, and pretending that it didn't exist was as good a thing as any. But Kenny went further. He killed children and old people and raped women—young and old. He burned villages and rice fields and enjoyed the misery that brought to the people. Boxer thought that was wrong then, and he knew it was wrong now. He knew he could never forget the things Kenny had done any more than he could forget Vietnam. And what Kenny did in the present also bothered Boxer. Though he had no proof, he believed that Kenny was a dealer. One of his wives had thought so, too, and had once tried to use Boxer's cop connections to jam Kenny. He'd been reluctant to go along with that, finding it sneaky and underhanded. But if a man's wife suspected he was a drug dealer, then he probably was.

He shivered and got up, went to the hallway, and turned on the heat. It was one thing for him to freeze his balls off, quite another to freeze a guest. Even one that he didn't like. He shaved, showered, and dressed, then ran out and down the corner for a pint of half-and-half and a dozen doughnuts. Kenny liked doughnuts and coffee, and he'd done enough for Boxer that the least Boxer could do was spend a quarter of his last ten dollars on coffee and cream and chocolate-covered doughnuts. He zipped his jacket up to his chin and pulled the hood over his head. It still was spitting ice pellets.

"Damn good coffee, Boxer Boy," Kenny said, draining his second cup and going for a refill. Boxer had made a whole pot, knowing that Kenny would drink it all.

"Comes with the training."

"You still the only Black private eye in Buffalo?" Kenny said, biting into another doughnut.

"I still haven't taken a survey, Kenny, so I still don't know. What's got you so worried you're up and at 'em this time of morning?"

"Linda. I don't know where she is."

Boxer didn't say anything, just studied the man across the table from him. Kenny Schuster weighed exactly what he'd weighed in Vietnam thirty-odd years ago, wore his hair the same way, though the blond was generously flecked with gray now, and lines crinkled at the corners of his mutable blue eyes. And he still was a pussy hound; Linda Stone was his third wife, a barely-thirty beauty who'd fallen for Kenny's charms and spotted the darkness and the wildness only later. She'd divorced him a year and a half ago. Kenny hadn't been happy about letting go.

"I didn't know you still kept tabs on her."

Kenny's face reddened and clouded, then quickly cleared. "I'm not, Boxer Boy, I'm just trying to stay in good with the courts. See, I'm late with this month's alimony check, and I don't want her to report me, which she's done before. I wanted to let her know that I wasn't stiffing her, that I'm gonna pay her, just late, you know? And anyway, she doesn't need my money."

Boxer heard the bitterness. "Maybe that's what's bothering you?"

"You know me pretty well, don't you?"

Boxer waited. He knew Kenny well enough to know how his bullshit sounded when it rolled off his tongue.

"OK, here's the deal: She's dating this guy from Rochester . . ."

"I'm not gonna spy on Linda and some guy from Rochester, Kenny, not even for you. I don't do that kind of thing."

Kenny held up his palms defensively. "I know you don't. Boxer Boy! I'm not looking for you to spy. What I think is she's gone off with him, maybe even married him, and if that's the case, I'm off the hook for four bills a month."

"And you've called her?"

"A bunch of times, and left messages. Sent her faxes and E-mails, even dropped her note in the mail asking her to get in touch. No response at all."

"Over what period of time?"

"The last ten, twelve days. That's why I think she's gone, man. Flown the coop. Gone off to Rochester with her college professor."

Boxer let that slide; he'd ask later how Kenny knew who Linda was dating and that the man was a professor from Rochester. "And you want me to do what, exactly?"

"Find her. And if she's gone, if she's married, get me proof so I can go to court and get out from under this weight." Kenny got up to get another cup of coffee.

Boxer looked down at the legal pad on the table in front of him on which he'd written not a word. He pushed the pad and pen toward Kenny as he resumed his seat. "Write down her full name, address and phone number, place of employment, her parents' names and addresses, her date and place of birth, social security number . . ."

Kenny started writing while Boxer ate a doughnut and thought of more things he could ask for. "The names of a church or a gym if she belongs to one, the make and model of her car and the tag number if you know it, and I'll need a photograph if you've got one . . ."

"I know it. And I've got one." He seemed to know everything Boxer had asked for. The pen sailed across the paper, then he grabbed an envelope that was sticking out of his shirt pocket and slid it across the table to Boxer. "That it?"

"For now," Boxer said, opening the envelope to find an image of Linda Schuster staring back at him. "I can get started with this. Now, when exactly was the last time you saw Linda?"

Kenny shifted uneasily in his chair, and his eyes danced about, looking for a place to land that wasn't Boxer's face. "I haven't seen her to talk to in a while, maybe four or five months, I guess."

"But you've seen her." Boxer said, not making it a question.

Kenny nodded. "I drove by her place a couple of weeks ago. Saw her going in the building with . . . her professor."

"Linda have any enemies you know about?"

"Yeah, me."

"Other than you."

"You know, Boxer, everybody liked that girl. And I do mean *everybody!* Perfect strangers would tell her their life stories. Her friends would make appointments to see her, just to spend time with her. And the guys! Including you! Hell, you didn't even like your own wife, and you liked Linda!"

Boxer pulled the legal pad over and looked at what Kenny had written, thinking that he hadn't known his wife's social security number or her parents' address when he was married to her, to say nothing of a couple of years after the fact. And he *had* liked her. He stood up, paced a few steps, and ended up leaning against the refrigerator, still holding the pad. "You have any reason to believe anything's happened to Linda?"

Kenny's eyes got big. "Anything like what?"

"Nothing in particular, Kenny, just asking. I'll get started right away, and hopefully, three or four days, I'll have something to tell you."

Kenny pushed back the chair and got up, reaching deep into his jeans pocket. He pulled out a roll of bills. "Two hundred a day plus expenses, right? This is a week's worth."

Boxer couldn't answer for a second, then recovered himself. "I wasn't looking for money from you, Kenny."

"I know it, and that's why I'm gonna pay you Boxer. After all, you *are* a private investigator, and finding people *is* what you do."

"You've done me lots of favors. I owe you."

"A favor is helping somebody move or lending him a sawbuck. I'm asking you to do your job, I should pay you." He thrust the money at Boxer. "You gonna take this?"

Boxer took the money, hoping the relief and gratitude didn't do a tap dance all over his face. "Then lemme draw up a contract for you . . ."

"Get it ready, and I'll sign it when I see you again. I don't have time to wait right now. Got to get to work, whether I got to pay Linda or not."

"What're you doing these days?"

"Short-haul trucking. Just in New York state. I leave today, drop off a load in Jamestown, go over to Albany tomorrow, pick up a load, bring it back here next day. Piece of cake," he said with a wide grin, stalking out of the kitchen like a man relieved of a terrible burden and grabbing his jacket, which he'd hung on the antique coatrack in the living room. "The place looks good. Boxer. Real classy. Looks like you been here a few years instead of just a few months."

"Yeah, it's beginning to feel like home," Boxer acknowledged.

"But you still miss the old place?" And when Boxer nodded, he said, "Well that's why you rented it out instead of selling it, in case you ever want to go back there."

Boxer nodded his head some more but he knew he'd never live in the cabin again. He'd probably sell it come spring. God knew he needed the money. The rent on the place only covered the mortgage, the taxes and a fund for repairs, nothing left over for him, and his pension and what little he made as a PI barely covered his apartment rent and the alimony and child support he owed Sharon every month. And here comes Kenny Schuster with two thousand dollars. Loud, rude, boisterous Kenny Schuster had saved his ass again. Maybe he ought to try liking the guy. Kenny said something, but Boxer missed it and had to ask.

"I said you're looking pretty good, too. Been punching the bag, sparring?"

"Punching the bag couple of times a week, but not much sparring. Those young guys would kill me in the ring, Kenny, fast as they are and slow as I am. I'm old enough to be their granddaddy, some of 'em."

"My ass. Bet you've knocked at least one of 'em down, haven't you? Come on, fess up. Tell Uncle Kenny the truth," he prodded, and when the slow grin lifted a corner of Boxer's mouth, Kenny really revved up. "I knew it! Come on, tell!"

So Boxer told him about the nineteen-year-old who pranced around the gym talking shit and messing with people, especially with Boxer, whom he called Old Mother Fucker every time he spoke to him. Boxer had ignored him until he couldn't ignore him anymore and suggested that they step into the ring. The young guy, whose name was Franco, danced and ducked and bobbed and weaved and taunted, all while Boxer shuffled from side to side, looking for the boy's rhythm. And when he found it, he delivered a roundhouse right, just as Franco moved his head into it. "He dropped like a concrete block," Boxer said, laughing gently. "Took two vials of salt to bring him around, and you know what he said? 'Where am I,' like he was in some kinda movie."

"There's more'n one way to skin a cat!" Kenny said with a gleeful laugh. "Next time you see him, tell him you still hold the record for the most KOs in Uncle Sam's army."

"After all this time? No way."

"So what!" Kenny punched him on the arm and sped out the door, slamming it so hard the Manhattan skyline on the adjacent wall shimmied.

Boxer cleaned up the kitchen then went to his office, sat at the desk, and counted Kenny's money: two grand exactly, half in hundreds, half in fifties. He could buy groceries, a new battery, and new tires for his truck before the weekend's predicted solid freeze and flurries, a rug for his office, maybe even a pair of bedroom slippers. And he could leave the heat on. Turned down low, but on. And have money left to reopen his savings account. More than one way to skin a cat indeed, he thought, disliking the expression for the image it conjured up, but appreciating its meaning.

He looked at Kenny's written notes. Linda was his favorite of Kenny's wives, and she wasn't a flighty woman, not the kind to pick up and leave without a word. She'd worked the same job at the county hospital since graduating high school, up the ladder to the position of billing supervisor; had worked her way through night business school; and was working on a commercial real estate license. He took a pen from the cup on the desk and wrote at the bottom of the page: *Professor's name? Best friends?* He could have asked Kenny, but he knew one of Linda's friends, and he'd find the others through her. And he'd ask them about the professor and if they knew him, knew about him, then they'd know if Linda was with him. If she wasn't, and if she wasn't at home and really hadn't been at home for more than a week, then Boxer would agree that Kenny was right to worry. Right now, he would approach the situation as if Kenny were being a jealous, overbearing jerk, overreacting because his ex-wife didn't jump when he said jump. And as grateful as he was for the money in his pocket, that's what he wanted to be the case. Otherwise he'd have a missing person on his hands, and those almost never ended well. He should've told Kenny that, he thought to himself. He'd started to tell him then stopped himself; but he should have started preparing him for the worst. And missing persons always were pretty close to the worst. He looked at the photo of Linda—red hair cut short, green eyes sparkling, freckles dancing across her face—and started preparing himself for the worst.

The difference the new battery and tires made in the twelve-year-old Bronco was miraculous; and it helped that he may have picked up a new client at the automotive store—the manager wanted to hire somebody to run background checks on prospective employees. Boxer felt good as he parked at the restricted curb in front of central police headquarters. The front and rear bumpers of his truck still bore the FOP emblem, and the sheriff's star was in the front windshield. He wouldn't get a ticket. He hustled to the front door and inside, to the duty desk, like he still belonged.

"Heads up, Dugan," he called out, and let fly a jumbo Baby Ruth. The desk sergeant, a central casting cop on the job since Buffalo opened a police department, caught it with the one hand he had, and with the help of his teeth, ripped open the candy bar and bit it halfway down.

"Look what the cat dragged in."

"How're ya doin', Dugan?" Boxer asked as he placed the bag with the extra large cup of Irish coffee on the counter. Dugan had been drinking on the job since he trained Boxer more than twenty-five years ago and seemed no worse for the wear.

"Shitty, as usual. Whaddaya want, Boxer?"

Boxer took a piece of notepaper from his pocket and handed it across the desk. "Missing person filed on her in the last couple of weeks?"

Dugan put the coffee on the shelf beneath the counter and took the paper to a desk with a computer on it and one-handed typed faster than Boxer did with two hands and was back in three minutes. "No missing person, no wants or warrants, nothing from traffic."

"Will you keep an eye out?"

Dugan nodded, Boxer thanked him and left. He stood in the lobby waiting for a break in the rain so he wouldn't have to run to his Bronco, thinking through what he'd learned so far: County Hospital, Downtown Sales and Leasing, and her parents all said that Linda was on a spur-of-the moment vacation. He'd run the missing person angle just in case. He'd met her parents one Thanksgiving when she and Kenny had a big dinner. He was a mess that year, and Kenny, worried, had bullied him into coming to dinner. Linda's parents remembered and were glad to see he was OK. They weren't glad that Kenny was looking for Linda and didn't believe the reason why. "The man's a liar," Jim Stone said. "He hasn't ever paid alimony on time. He's just mad she went off and he doesn't know where."

Boxer went to a one-hour photo shop and got copies of Linda's photograph. Then he went to her church and her gym where she was recognized but had no connection close enough for anybody to know where she was. Driving home, Boxer thought Mr. Stone was probably right, but just to be sure, he'd eat dinner and then spend the evening on the computer, running Linda's credit card numbers and out-of-state checks on her tags. "Which I wouldn't have to do if I could get in her building garage," he muttered. But he couldn't. Linda had moved into a high security building to get away from Kenny . . . so how did he see her going in the building with the professor? Was he stalking her again? He'd done that for a while after she first left, and it had taken all of Boxer's persuasive powers to convince Kenny to leave her alone. "Dammit, man, why can't you grow up?"

Boxer stared at the bank computer screen, hesitant to spend the money to run all the checks he needed. "You've got the expense money, use it!" Instead, he got up from the desk and paced a bit, trying to fix a few things in his head, one of them being the wisdom of calling Peggy Brown. She was one of Linda's closest friends, and she didn't think much of Boxer, though he didn't really know why. Kenny and Linda had tried to fix them up; they were the only Black people either of them knew, and they thought they'd be perfect together. They weren't. But Peggy and Linda lived in the same building. If Linda was on vacation, Peggy would know. If Linda's car was in the garage, Peggy would know. If Linda were secretly married to a professor, Peggy would know.

He sat back down at the computer and typed in the codes to access the information he needed. It had been so long since he'd worked a job that required the kinds of checks he wanted to do that he had to refer to the manual to remember how to do it. He needed to work more, and not just for the money. He couldn't let himself sink back down into self-pitying depression. He *wouldn't* do that. He was a good investigator, trained by the army and seasoned by the Buffalo PD. He was just on his own now, no shame or harm in that. Not his fault that a thief's bullet had finished the work Vietcong shrapnel had begun years earlier. He probably could have stayed on the job, doing desk duty like Dugan, but he hadn't wanted that. He was a field investigator. "So investigate, already."

He worked the computer for the next two hours, turning up no more on Linda Stone Schuster than he already knew, and he checked under Linda Stone, Linda Schuster, and Linda Stone Schuster. If she went on a trip, she didn't pay for it on her own credit cards, nor had she bought gasoline or booked a hotel room. So, the professor's footing the bill? He consulted his manuals, typed in some more codes, and was in Canada. He ran the same checks and got the same nothing. Then he had a thought and checked Niagara Falls; maybe they'd eloped. People still eloped to Niagara Falls. But Linda hadn't.

How long did a "spur-of-the-moment" vacation trip last? He recalled his conversation with the acting billing supervisor at County Hospital: "She just jumped at the chance to get away for a few days." To Boxer that meant three or four days, not almost two weeks. And what had her mother said? "The poor girl needed a little time away." To the average forty-hour-a-week American, two weeks is more than a little time; two weeks is the year's allotment.

He knew where Linda lived, because he'd been to Peggy Brown's for dinner.

Once. The building looked like an old, stone castle. It sat back from the street, inside a circular driveway, and it was impossible to see the front door from the street, and the garage entrance was at the rear of the building, where he was now.

"Who is it?"

"It's Boxer Gordon, Peggy . . ."

"Yes?"

"I'm looking for Linda . . ."

"What do you want with Linda?"

"There's a line of cars behind me, Peggy," he lied again. "Could you just buzz me in and I can tell you what I want when I get upstairs?" It was several seconds before the iron gates guarding the garage began to slide open. Boxer sped in and up to the second floor where he knew Linda parked. He'd spot her classic Cadillac Seville if it were in its assigned space. It wasn't. Boxer found a visitor's parking space and limped to the elevators.

She opened the door to his knock, then stood aside. "Thanks for seeing me, Peggy," he said, sliding past her into the living room that had made him drool the first—and only—time he'd been here. Peggy herself had made him drool, too. She was mid-forties, beautiful, smart, and artistic enough to be a decorator, though she was a nursing supervisor and teacher by profession. It was her Persian carpets—real, not fake like his—

and apparent haphazard blending of the classical and the contemporary that inspired Boxer in his own decorating choices. He found himself wishing again that the chemistry had been better between them.

"What do you want with Linda?" Peggy asked again.

"I'm selling my cabin. I'd planned to wait until spring, but I need the money now. I know commercial real estate is Linda's thing, but the cabin'll sell quickly and since somebody's got to make the commission, I'd rather it be her that some stranger. I've been trying to reach her, but no luck, so I took a chance that you'd be in."

Peggy gave him an appraising look. "That's decent of you, and I'm sure she'll appreciate it. She likes that cabin a lot. She even had a fight with dumb fuck about wanting to visit there more often."

That caught Boxer by surprise, and it must have shown, because Peggy's voice changed, softened a bit. "Don't worry. He accused every man she talked to of wanting her, and her of egging them on, his best friends included. She really likes you, and that really pissed him off."

Kenny's words replayed in his head: *You didn't like your own wife, and you liked Linda.* Shit. "I didn't know . . ."

"I told you, don't worry about it." Then, looking pensive, said, "I wish I could tell you when Linda's coming back, but I don't know."

"Where is she?"

"I don't know that, either, and I'm getting a bit worried, to tell the truth."

"I know I don't know Linda as well as you do, but that sounds, well . . ."

"Not like Linda."

"And I thought you two told each other everything."

"There was an E-mail when I got home one evening two weeks ago . . ."

"An E-mail? She sent you an E-mail?"

"Which makes it even weirder. I don't care how 'spur-of-the-moment' her decision was, she'd have told me about it, in person."

"Maybe . . ." Boxer said, and hesitated, generating the desired result.

"Maybe what?" Peggy jumped right on it.

"Well . . . a guy, maybe?"

She gave him a derisive snort. "The last 'spur-of-the-moment' decision she made about a guy was marrying that fool Kenny Schuster. No, when it comes to guys these days, she takes her time."

"Nobody she cares about enough to spend a few days with?"

"Oh, sure, there's somebody she cares about, but he doesn't know where she is, either. He's why I got worried, he called me looking for her."

Boxer paced a few steps, then turned back toward Peggy. "I don't want to upset you, but I don't like how this sounds, Peggy. Have you talked to her parents? Maybe even the police . . . ?"

Now it was Peggy's turn to pace. "I thought about it, but I don't want to scare her parents. And the police . . . but . . . could you do something?"

Boxer hesitated. This is what he'd wanted when he came here, this is how he'd planned this scenario last night, but now he wasn't so sure. "Not legally . . ."

"But as a friend?"

"I'd be on shaky ground, nosing around in what could be a police matter," *I'm also on shaky ground not revealing that I've got a client who's paying me to do this,* he thought, and didn't feel the slightest remorse.

"What would make it a police matter?"

"If she's missing. And if some harm had come to her." Boxer tried to soften the words, but it didn't work. All the fear that Peggy had been holding bubbled up to the surface.

"You've got to do something, Boxer! Please!"

"You have her keys? Apartment keys and car keys?"

She ran from the room and was back in a flash with a key ring. "But her car's not here. I thought she drove wherever . . ."

"We need to check her apartment. You need to let me in, just in case . . . so I can't be accused of breaking in."

They walked down the hallway and rode the elevator down three floors in total silence. Peggy used two keys to open the door. The apartment was neat and orderly, as sterile as Peggy's was plush, and it didn't feel to Boxer like the place from which a pretty young woman had embarked on a lark. "Follow me and don't touch anything," he said, as he walked around the living room into the dining room, into the kitchen, down the hallway, into the office, and finally into the bedroom. Nothing looked out of place. Boxer wanted to do a full search, but not with Peggy Brown watching him. "Does anything look out of place to you?"

She shook her head. "Can I look in the closet?"

Boxer stuck his hand in his jacket pocket and opened the door. Neat to the point of obsession, he thought, but Peggy seemed to be looking for something. "What?"

"I don't—I'm not sure. It doesn't feel right."

Boxer trusted feelings like that. He'd solved more than one crime with no more to go on than the feeling that something wasn't right. "Any place else you want to look?"

"The refrigerator," she said, halfway to the kitchen. She used her shirt-tail to open the door. The smell of sour milk and rotting vegetables wafted out. Peggy backed up, her hands to her face, and she wasn't hiding from the stink. "She'd never have left food to rot, because she'd never had wanted to come home to this. Something's wrong, isn't it?"

"When, exactly, did you last see Linda?"

"Let me check my calendar. I can tell you."

Back upstairs, she went into the kitchen. Boxer heard her fill the teakettle, "Black or green?" she called out.

"Black," he answered. It was the one thing they had in common—a love of tea. That and AA.

When she returned, she carried a teak tray with a Chinese teapot, two mugs, a plate of ginger snaps, cream, and sugar. The kitchen wall calendar was tucked under her arm. She put the tray on the table, and they fixed their tea. Then she gave him the calendar. "Wednesday the 13th. We saw a movie."

He looked at the calendar square. *Movie, U, Linda* was written in red, "What's 'U' mean?"

"U Buffalo. They show old movies on Wednesday nights. You know Linda and old things. She likes to call it 'classic,' but a lot of it's just old. This was a classic, though: *The Landlord . . .*"

"Diana Sands and Beau Bridges! That's a great movie!"

"I'd never seen it, but you're right, it's something special."

"And when did you get the E-mail about the vacation?"

"When I got home from work Friday night. I was off Wednesday and Thursday and worked 3-to-11 Friday. I usually wind down from the night-shift playing at the computer. When I saw her E-mail, I picked up the phone and called her right away, but she was . . ."

Boxer was on his feet. "Shit!"

"What?"

"The phone. The answering machine. Where does it live, in her office?"

Peggy nodded, and Boxer picked up the phone. "What's her number?" Peggy told him and he pushed the numbers. After one ring, Linda's voice answered: *"Sorry I missed your call, but please leave a message, and I'll get back to you as soon as I can."* "Testing 1, 2, 3, 4, 5," Boxer said into the phone, and hung up. Then he looked at his watch. Peggy wrote the time on the calendar in the square for Wednesday the 27th, the current day and date. "You saw the movie Wednesday the 13th and got the E-mail Friday the 15th. Any contact on Thursday?"

Peggy's brow wrinkled in thought. "I went to my niece's school play that night, and I remember being a bit surprised that Linda's car wasn't in the garage when I got back. It was after 11, which is late for her."

"Did you delete the E-mail?"

Peggy nodded yes, Boxer put a whole ginger snap into his mouth, thinking he'd stop and get a box on the way home. He really liked them. Then he drained his cup and stood up. "Thank you for your time, Peggy, and for the tea."

"You think something's wrong, don't you?"

"You think something's wrong, and that's enough for me."

"Can you do something?"

"I need to spend some time in Linda's apartment, preferably during the day when people are gone. I need to listen to the answering machine. I need to find her car. And I need to talk to whoever else she's close to."

Peggy hesitated. "There's a guy she's been seeing, from Rochester . . ."

"The one who called you looking for her?"

"He's the only person that I know of that Linda would call, and if she didn't call either of us . . ."

"What's his name, Peggy? How do I find him?"

"Sam Bennett. He teaches in the business school at Rochester."

. . .

Boxer got up the next morning going to Rochester. Subconsciously he'd been avoiding this trip; Sharon and his almost eighteen-year-old son were there. Rochester was her hometown. He let the sadness come. He shouldn't have married anybody back then, especially sweet, gentle Sharon. But that's what attracted him, what he thought would save him. Then their baby, Sherry, died. After a few years they tried again and had a boy, and Boxer couldn't shake the feeling that he was destined to grow up just to go to war. His obsession frightened Sharon; then it embittered her. And now the boy was almost eighteen, and that fool president rattling sabers. "OK, enough of that."

He parked illegally, hoping his FOP emblem would have meaning to the campus cops, and limped into the Business Administration building. The pain journeyed slowly and constantly between his right hip joint and ankle: cold, damp weather and sitting for a couple of hours in the truck had done their work. He groaned when the building directory put Bennett on the third floor. A female academic about his age noticed his limp and put him on the faculty elevator.

Bennett's door was open; it was his office hours. He was a very average man of about forty, distinguished by rimless eyeglasses, a Caesar haircut, and a goatee streaked with gray. He was halfway through grading a stack of papers. Boxer knocked and had his ID in his hand when entered the office.

"My name is Charles Gordon, sir. I'm a friend of Peggy Brown and Linda Schuster . . ."

"What's happened?!"

"Peggy's concerned that Linda hasn't been in touch, and she asked me, as a friend, to . . ."

"That bastard!"

"May I close the door, sir?"

Bennett looked at his watch and shook his head, so Boxer walked close to the desk and almost whispered, "Do you know something?"

"She was terrified of him." Boxer must have reacted, because Bennett said, "I can tell by your age . . . Vietnam?" And when Boxer nodded, he said, "He used to tell her the things he did to women and children over there."


Boxer sped back to Buffalo and directly to the long-term parking lot at the airport. He drove every aisle of every level looking for Linda's car. Then he went to her apartment. He used the garage code Peggy had given him, parked in a visitor space, and rode up, praying that Linda had aspirin— preferably something stronger. He'd take his chances with a tampering with evidence charge; and he was feeling a lot like this was, or would be, a criminal case.

He took two Percodan with tap water cupped in his hand, pulled on latex gloves, and went to work, starting with the answering machine. There were thirty messages; the tape had run out two messages after his countdown the previous night. Three messages were from her parents; four each from County General and Downtown Leasing; one each from him and Peggy; three from Stan Bennett; five from friends checking on lunch or dinner dates. The rest were from Kenny. He wrote down the time, date, and duration of each call, then turned his attention to the computer. It was off. He turned it on, easily bypassed the setup and went directly to her E-mail. The last sent message was Friday the 15th, and there were five of them: to Peggy, Sam Bennett, her parents, and both jobs. He checked the inbox: six messages from Kenny. Boxer shut off the computer and went to the bedroom. He checked the drawers and the closets; useless, but he did it anyway. He didn't know what she owned, so he wouldn't know what was missing, but he was certain that a police investigation would re- veal missing clothes and luggage. He rode the elevator down to the lobby and with the mailbox key he'd gotten from Peggy, he opened Linda's box. The mail spilled out onto the floor. Boxer sifted through it, found three let- ters from Kenny, and stuffed the mail back into the box.

"You motherfucker." He had just proven for Kenny Schuster that all signs pointed to Linda being on vacation and that he, Kenny, had been looking for her for almost two weeks. There would be no Kenny finger- prints on the computer even though Boxer was certain that Kenny had typed the E-mails explaining Linda's hasty departure. "You mother-fucker."

Boxer went home and prepared a statement for Kenny—four days' worth of work and expenses—and wrote a check for the balance of the money Kenny had given him. Then he paged him and waited for a call-back, giving up after an hour and making himself some dinner. He was eating when the door buzzer sounded, and he knew who it was. He punched the entry code, opened the door, and waited.

"Hey Boxer Boy!" Kenny blew into the room, snowflakes sticking like dandruff to his jacket. "Got your page and decided to answer in person. You got good news for me?"

"If no news is good news. Linda seems to be a ghost. Told everybody she was going on vacation, then disappeared. No trace of her car, no use of credit cards." He went to his office and came back quickly with an en-velope for Kenny. "Here's my report and your refund."

Kenny scanned the pages, folded them, and stuffed them into his pocket, then ripped up the **CHARLES GORDON INVESTIGATIONS** check. "You earned the money. This is good work. Boxer Boy, thorough, just like you." He looked at his watch. "Gotta go." And he was gone. Boxer looked at the check pieces on the floor and saw Linda, saw Sharon, saw his dead baby daughter, Sherry. "There's more than one way . . ."

A week later, he rang Peggy Brown's doorbell at the appointed hour. She opened the door so fast she had to have been waiting. "Did you see the news?!"

"No, I just left the gym. Why?"

She pulled him in, waited while he removed his snow-caked boots and put them on the mat, took his coat to hang in the bathroom, then pulled him into the den, where the TV was on. "The story is over, but they ar-rested Kenny for dealing drugs! Called him a kingpin! He had five million dollars in cash and some huge amount of kilos of cocaine and heroin, all stashed in a cabin in the woods, out there near your place!"

Boxer sat down, eyes on the TV screen. "Linda told me once she thought he was into something like that."

"And you wouldn't do anything about it?"

He shook his head. "I couldn't, not the way she wanted me to."

Peggy sighed. "Yeah, I know. You said it felt underhanded, sneaky." She shook her head. "She never understood why you were friends with Kenny. She said you were principled and decent . . ."

"What is it, Peggy?"

"I filed the missing person report last week like you said, and talked her parents into doing the same thing—they found her car today." Tears streamed down Peggy's face. Boxer fished for a handkerchief for her. "In a field in St. Catherines. There was blood in it." She wept, and Boxer held her.

"I'm sorry," he said. *So sorry, Linda. So sorry, Sharon. So sorry, Sherry.*

# BOMBARDIER

*Walter Mosley*

Tempest was working at a restaurant on Broad Street down in the Financial District. When he got off at 2 A.M. I was waiting outside the front door to greet him.

"What are you doin' here?" Tempest asked me.

"I wanted to continue our talk. "We were going so well I wanted to go on."

"Man, I just don't get it. Here it seems to me that you don't understand a word I'm sayin', and there you are poppin' up in the middle'a night wantin' to hear some more."

"You agreed that you have sinned," I said. "That the reason you were condemned in heaven is because the police ended your life too soon."

Tempest stopped walking and turned to me.

"No," he said. "Heaven misjudged me, and the cops murdered me on behalf of the state. Everybody sins, even you when you wear a body. Man is a sinner but that don't make him bad."

Tempest turned on his heel and walked at a fast clip. I kept up with him, though, happy that I had gotten under his thick skin.

"But you must admit," I said, "the police aren't on trial here."

"The police ain't never on trial," Tempest protested. "And if they are, then the judge and jury are just happy to believe whatever they say. A cop on the witness stand is like you angels up in heaven, nobody questions your words or deeds neither. But me, on the other hand, I couldn't do right if I tried. Nobody believes me. I'm just a lie waiting to happen. After thirty-four years of bein' made into a lie, they shot me down and sent me to you, and you then said I should enter into hell."

"That's not what happened," I said. "You're twisting the events to make it seem like the whole world is in a conspiracy against you."

"And ain't it?" Tempest asked. "Ain't it so? The police ready to shoot me. The courts want me in jail, I'm makin' just enough to keep off the landlord, but food and clothes takin' turns at my wallet. I'm an American, at least I was before I died; a citizen of the greatest, most powerful country in the history of the world. A citizen, mind you, not no slave or visitor or foreigner to this shore. My people been here longer than most, way back over four hundred years. And we built without salary, and we died without our right names. We are part of the stone and blood of this nation. How can it be that we strugglin' like this? Livin' with drugs and prejudice, shot down, dragged down, sat on, and lied to. If it ain't conspiracy, then I don't know what is."

"Nobody planned it this way, Tempest," I argued. "You must admit that."

"Who needs a plan when you shoot us like fish in a barrel? Who needs a blueprint when we don't have a choice where to live? Them cops didn't need to lay in wait for me. They loose and armed in my neighborhood seven twenty-four."

"So your excuse is race," I said. "That and nothing more."

"It's not just race, angel. No, it ain't that only. There's brown skins and yellow skins and white ones, too, that share my fate. It's poor men and angry ones, fatherless and motherless and homeless ones, too. No, it's not just race but still, a black man got a anchor 'round his neck and bull's-eye on his back. Other people's got problems, too, but excuse me if I suffer alone."

"Many, many people suffer." I countered. "Many climb out of the ghetto and other grim circumstances. Thousands from your own generation have been faced with odds greater than you've faced, and they've accounted themselves nobly."

Again Tempest stopped walking. This time he looked angry enough to strike me.

"When I was a boy, there was a nut in my high school," he said in an exceptionally calm tone. "He was a genius, but he was crazy. Liked to play with fire and get stoned. One day in science class he brought in a cardboard box with wires stickin' out all over the place. It was his project, he told the teacher, a time bomb."

"I don't believe it," I said.

"That a black kid would make a time bomb? Or that he'd lie and say that he did?"

"That you were ever in science class. Don't forget I am your accounting angel. I know everything about you."

"Well, you're right about the classroom. I wasn't in there. But I was at school that day. I heard the story like everybody else."

"Then go on," I said.

"This kid, Vincent Moldin, had the box up front. He had never turned in homework or finished a quiz or test, so the teacher thought it was just some retarded joke. Then Vincent said, 'How do you grade a bomb's inside if it blows up to prove it's a bomb?' The teacher got mad and told Vincent to sit down. Then Vincent got mad and grabbed his box. The heck if it wasn't a bomb and it blew up right there. Set the natural gas for the Bunsen burners on fire. Two kids burned to death right in their chairs. A lotta others were scarred and maimed." Tempest began walking again, his thought lost in that long-ago explosion.

"What does Vincent Moldin have to do with you blaming racism for your sins?" I asked.

"Not Vincent Moldin but Harold Gee."

"I thought that it was Vincent Moldin who made the bomb?"

"It was. But Harold was sitting there right in front of him, right in that first row. Vincent was blinded, lost his left hand. Almost every child in that room had a busted eardrum and some kinda concussion and wound. But

Harold came out of it with nary a scratch. When that bomb blowed up, the force missed Harry. He picked up and ran from the room."

Tempest stopped there, shaking his head in sorrow at the pain of his classmates.

"So?" I asked. "What does that story mean?"

"Don't you get it?"

"No."

"You walkin' there next to me in the middle'a the night after I done worked fourteen hours awashin' dishes for change. You askin' me why I ain't like the few that crawled out from the slime, but you won't even hear what I got to say."

"I don't understand you."

"What did Harold do when he found himself whole after the blowup?"

"He ran, you said."

"That's right. He didn't stop to face the fire or drag his friends from the room. He didn't call for the principal or look for Vincent's hand. If he'da done that he would have been caught in the aftershock of the gas that ignited from the flames the bomb made."

"You can't compare running from an explosion with a man or woman educating themselves and rising from poverty," I said.

"I can and do," Tempest replied. "To begin with, no one educates himself. Anyone that says that they did is either stupid or a liar. How can you learn without a book? How can you want to learn without food in your stomach and a mother's love? How can you know you right if every time you say somethin' somebody hits and says to shut up? I don't blame Harold for runnin', but I don't call him a hero for it neither. He was lucky and he was quick. That's all you can ask for in the battlefield of black America. And if you get away, more power to ya. But please don't tell me I should follow your lucky feet."

"You pervert the truth, my friend," I said. "Many people stay. They work in the community, they help the less fortunate."

"If they stay, then they feel the aftershock; you should bet your feathers on that."

We had reached the subway station. It was desolate at Bowling Green. The wary clerk in the token booth watched us closely as we went to wait for the train.

"You must admit it, Tempest," I said. "Some people have made a life for themselves without resorting to sin."

"Have you ever passed such a person into heaven? A man who never sinned?"

"No. But ones whose sins were negligible, ones whose virtues out-weighed their sins a thousand to one."

"Many poor fellahs like that?"

"As many as the rich."

"I don't believe it."

"But it's true," I said.

"You got statistics on that?"

"No. No, but I know human nature."

"If you knew human nature, you wouldn't be here tryin' to convince me of my sins. I'm sayin' that I believe that a poor man has to resort to sin a lot quicker than a man who ain't poor. Just like a man scared for his life don't have time to waste when he's runnin' from a bomb."

"We don't care about wealth in heaven."

"Rich kids never do. How can you care about somethin' when you always had it? It's like skin. You don't value it unless half gets burned off in a explosion in science class."

"Why are you so angry, Tempest?"

"Didn't I just tell you that I'm comin' off a fourteen-hour shift? I'm tired and I got to go to work tomorrow and they won't understand if I say I want a nap."

"So you're going to bed?"

"With Bronwyn," he said behind a wolfish grin.

"But you said you're upset."

"That's what a good woman's for. She take her man's anger in both her hands and squeeze it till it go down."

Tempest knew how to get to me, too. Every time I thought of Bronywn and him I got angry enough to fight.

"You got to blow off steam, angel," Tempest said. "Try to sometime. You might see sin in a whole new light."

The number four train pulled up just then. The doors opened and Tempest stepped inside.

"Ain't you comin'?" he asked.

"I want to think about what we've said tonight."

He smiled and nodded. The door closed on his smile.

As the train bore him away, I wondered, not for the first time, if Tempest was a spy sent from below to test the resolve of heaven.

# A FAVORABLE MURDER

*Percy Spurlark Parker*

By the way of a definition, I've got a kiss ass job. I'm Walt Johnson, and my official title is manager of the Tower Grocery and Spirits Shoppe. My store is one of fourteen in the Burkley Chain, all located in high-rise buildings in the Loop, or Near North areas of downtown Chicago. I'm the one black in the chain's management team. We have one Hispanic, one Korean, two women, and one guy who's open about his alternative lifestyle. However, we all agree on the job description.

I do an adequate, if not above average job of maintaining store appearances, stock conditions, and profit margins. I get a good buck for that end of the workload, which I justly deserve, if I may say so. But I've never been able to put a price on all the bowing and scraping I have to do.

About ninety-eight percent of the customers we serve are tenants of the buildings where our stores are located. In my case, they're either condo residents who occupy the top thirty floors, or the occupants of the various offices, which are housed on the remaining five. Not all the people I deal with are jerks. It's just that those who have that distinction certainly make up for the rest.

Case in point, Charles W. Vanders. Rude, arrogant, snobbish, and those are just a few of his better qualities. Cheap would be another of his attributes that endeared him to my deliveryman. The times we've made deliveries, and there have been a number of them, whether it was a bottle of milk or a bottle of champagne, a "thanks" was something to rave about. I won't mention the times I've had the personal pleasure of dropping something off to him.

Vanders was a whale of a man, with a tangle of red hair that was fading fast, and an extremely pale complexion. He wasn't much more than six-one, but he was surely pushing the hell out of three hundred and fifty pounds. He did have a great tailor though, his suits doing a fine job hiding his bulk. I guessed if I had to say something nice about him that would be it. Even when Royce told me Vanders had been found in his condo shot to death, I wondered if he'd gotten any blood on the gray gabardine I'd seen him wearing earlier.

"Cops up there now," Royce said. He was one of the uniform security people for the building, a black kid in his early twenties with about three hairs above his upper lip that served as a mustache. I've got enough years on me to be his old man, and I guess we've got that kind of relationship. He's asked for my advice from time to time, and I've enjoyed hearing about his antics.

We were standing in the hall just outside the entrance to the store where he'd beckoned me to fill me in on all the gory details.

"I got a good look before they booted me out. I swear it looked like he had three eyes, one right in the middle of his forehead all red and swollen. Must've caught him by surprise. There was a bottle of champagne on his coffee table. And he was in his robe sitting in the corner of his sofa, holding a half empty glass."

"Did you only see one glass?"

"That's all he had in his hand," Royce shrugged.

"No, I mean, was there another glass by the champagne bottle?"

"I didn't notice. Why?"

"Just being nosey," I said. But I had another reason for asking. I was pretty sure it was the same bottle of champagne I'd delivered a couple hours ago. Only it had been Catherine Lake who'd answered Vanders's door. I was surprised and irritated by her being there.

She's one of the few sisters who live in the building. I'd never given it much thought, but I guess it was logical they knew each other. They lived on the same floor. Her condo was across the hall and two doors south of his. While her condo looked onto the building's mini-park atrium, Vanders's more expensive unit offered the expanse of Lake Michigan.

Okay, so I'm just hired help, but hired help has a right to their likes and dislikes. In what limited contact I've had with Ms. Lake, she had been a pleasant and even fun person to talk to. She wasn't a raving beauty, but she was pretty damn close. Shoulder length black hair, cool brown eyes, and always a wide friendly smile on her full lips. Another time and place, if I was younger, or if I had a bigger bank account, who knows? But as things stood now Catherine Lake was a person I liked, and Charles W. Vanders was a person I didn't.

And unfortunately, it could very well be that Ms. Lake had put an end to Vanders's miserable existence.

"Earth to Walt. Earth to Walt," Royce said.

"What?"

"I thought you left me there for a while, bro."

"Sorry, Royce, got to drifting. Cops say anything about who couldn've done it?"

"I didn't hear it if they did."

"Murder in the Tower," I said. "Well, I guess if you think about it, it's not a real big surprise. Seeing as how large this place is and how many people are packed in here."

"Sounds about right," Royce added. "Hell, we've had just about everything else here. I guess a murder was next in line. Wonder if the guys are getting a pool together on the time it takes the cops to wrap this up."

"If they are, put me down for thirty-six hours. High-profile murders always gets the police moving a little faster."

I got back to doing what I was paid to do. Being Wednesday, a heavy receiving day, there were orders I had to check, and invoices I had to file for payment. I'd been at it for an hour and was in the canned food aisle checking dates on our shelf stock, when Catherine Lake approached.

She could've been doing a fashion layout in Ebony. She wore tan slacks and a dark brown cardigan turtleneck sweater. Her hair was gathered in the back by a bow that matched her slacks. And her earrings were dainty, yet quite brilliant diamond clusters.

"Mr. Johnson, may I speak to you for a moment, please?" She glanced about the immediate area. We weren't especially busy, but there was a couple in the next aisle. "In private," she added.

"Sure, Ms. Lake, we can use my office."

I lead the way, opening the door when we reached my modest cubicle, allowing her to enter first. The scent of her perfume lingered lightly in the air as she passed. I wasn't sure what she wanted, but whatever it was the answer was yes.

"Coffee?"

"No, no thanks," she said. We sat down, and she fumbled with a paper clip on my desk before looking over to me.

"Mr. Johnson, I'm sure you've heard about Mr. Vanders by now?"

I nodded. "I'd guess the whole tower has."

"I suppose so." She paused. "I need to ask you a favor." She hesitated again. "The police are going to be asking a lot of questions. Could you—kind of forget you saw me there?"

"Well, Ms. Lake, I—" I hadn't thought about running to the police with the information, nor purposely withholding it from them.

"I didn't have anything to do with his death."

"I never thought you did," I said, perhaps too quickly.

She smiled. "Thanks. It's nice to have someone on my side. But if the police find out I was there, they've made their case. I'm off to jail and that's that."

"You can't be sure that'll happen."

"Trust me."

"I believe that's what you're asking me to do."

She almost smiled again, an ironic little gesture this time. "I didn't do it, Mr. Johnson, I had no reason to. Charlie was one of my best clients."

I guessed my expression must have changed. I know the implication of what she said had me looking at her more intently now.

She took a deep breath. "I've been a pro for the past six years. I'm independent. I work mostly by referrals. When you brought the champagne up, Charlie and I were just capping off a little early evening session."

I've been flirting with an ulcer and began to get a burning sensation in my stomach. I'd rather she'd said she was at Vanders's trying to sell him a year's subscription to the *Watchtower.* The thought of her and Vanders in a sweaty embrace wasn't something I wanted lingering in my mind.

"We cut the evening short because he said he was expecting someone. He was alive and in a good mood when I left him."

A part of me wanted to believe her. My practical side didn't want to have anything to do with the whole mess. What did I really know about her? She had a friendly smile, and a great pair of legs.

Terrific assets, but who the hell was this woman?

"I know I'm asking a lot. But can you just help a sister out? Could you just forget I was there?"

She didn't offer herself to seal the bargain, and I somehow took that as a point in her favor. I told her if the police came by, I was simply a store manager and that's all I knew.

I should have said, maybe.

It wasn't a half-hour after she left that a Detective Hooks came into the store. He was tall and thin with graying hair, and he'd missed shaving this morning. He brought the sales receipt I'd left when I delivered the champagne. The register prints the time and date of sale on every receipt and if it's a delivery or a purchase made in the store.

Once he learned I'd made the delivery, his questions were very direct. "Was there anyone with Mr. Vanders?"

"Catherine Lake, she has the condo across the hall a few doors down from him."

"Anyone else?"

"No one that I saw."

"Thank you, Mr. Johnson, you've been a big help."

It wasn't long after that that Royce informed me the police had taken Catherine in for questioning.

I didn't sleep well that night. I'd gone belly-up as soon as the cops approached me. I felt like the biggest wimp around. Could I help a sister out?

Hell, I'd helped her right behind bars. She'd come to me, and I'd deserted her the first chance I got.

"If you think she's innocent, you could look into this thing yourself," Royce said.

"What?" I'd been up half the night browbeating myself and was using Royce as a sounding board over morning coffee at the Micky D's in the building. "Are you out of your mind? That's the craziest idea I've ever heard."

Royce shrugged. "Either jump in with both feet or quit bitching 'bout it. I kind of think the cops may be right. I mean, she was there just before ol' lard ass was killed. You saw her yourself, Walt. But, if you want to still believe her, then try proving it."

"And just how do I do that?"

"I can help. I've been reading a lot 'bout investigative techniques. I could lay it out for you. Show you how to go about it. Maybe do some digging around for you myself."

"I think you've been putting too much sugar in your coffee."

Royce shrugged again. "Put up or shut up, Walt. It's as easy as that, man."

Royce's challenge stayed with me much of the morning. Getting involved in the murder investigation any more than I already had was a dumb idea, yet I couldn't shake the thought. Here I am a forty-eight-year-old store manager. I'd done a stint in the Army, been divorced twice. My only child, my daughter from my second marriage, was a month away from making me a grandfather. Nothing in my past had ever presented me with the opportunity, or desire to try to solve a murder. Could I actually do it?

And hell, what made me think Catherine Lake was innocent, anyway?

The phone rang. Betty, the cashier up front caught it, then called over the P.A. for me to pick up line one.

"Hello?"

"Mr. Johnson? This is Catherine Lake."

"Yes, er, Miss Lake, I . . ." I said, trying to think up an excuse for what I'd done.

"I'd like to see you if I could, Mr. Johnson. Could I get a few minutes of your time?"

"Well, er, sure." Central Police Headquarters was on Roosevelt and State, maybe fifteen minutes by cab. "What time is visiting hours?"

She laughed, the richness of it not diluted by the phone. "The police let me go hours ago. I'm back in my condo. I'd appreciate it if you'd come up as soon as you can."

"I'll be right there," I told her.


She was wearing a simple skirt and blouse when she answered the door. The top two buttons of the blouse undone, peek-a-booing the lace underneath. Her dark skirt draped her casually, yet didn't hide the shape of her rounded hips and thighs.

"Mr. Johnson, please come in."

I'd never seen her wide smile any warmer, and some of the nervousness I felt as I rung her doorbell began to subside. She was barefoot, her toenails and fingernails the same lust red. Her thick piled carpet muffled our steps as she escorted me into her living room.

We sat at opposite ends of the sofa. There was a bottle of white Zinfandel and two long-stem glasses on the cocktail table. One of the glasses was three-quarters full, with lipstick smudges on its rim. I begged off her offer, and she refilled her own glass, then settled back, tucking a leg under has as she sat. I've seen some men sit like that, but I've always viewed it as a totally feminine gesture. A very attractive one at that.

A gentle breeze flowed through her open balcony doors. To compensate for not having a view of the lake or the rest of the city, the inner condos had balconies that looked down onto the floral atrium below. It really wasn't much of a balcony, standing room only. The double doors opened outward, abutting the four-foot-high wrought iron fencing.

She took a sip of her wine, started to say something, paused, then, "Mr. Johnson, I asked you up here to apologize. I really had no right to ask you to lie to the police."

"Maybe I should be the one to apologize."

"No. You did nothing wrong. I shouldn't have put you in that predicament. I was really confused and a little frightened. I didn't know what to do. And I tried to take advantage of you. I'm sorry."

"Well, okay. But everything must have worked out. The police let you go."

"I got a good lawyer." She chuckled slightly. "Former client, actually."

I let the former client part go without comment, mainly because I didn't know what to say. "If the police felt you were guilty you'd still be behind bars, wouldn't you?"

"They may still think it, they just didn't have enough proof. I'm not out of it yet."

"But, you didn't do it."

"Thanks for the vote of confidence. If the police really look at this, they've got too many people to choose from to bother with me. You've dealt with Charlie, you know at times he wasn't the nicest person. He must have had a number of enemies."

"One for sure," I said.

She nodded her agreement.

"Did the police give you any idea they were looking elsewhere?"

She shrugged. "They said they were continuing their investigation. I told them everything I knew about Charlie. He was into gambling pretty heavy, you know. He was generous with the tips when he made a big score."

"Had he been winning lately?"

"The police asked the same question." She put her glass down and slid closer to me. "I don't think so. Why?"

I hadn't had the chance to check out Royce's investigating techniques. But, it seemed to me that if Vanders was a gambler and he was in debt, then the most likely murder suspects were the people he was in debt to. I ran that by her.

"Makes sense," she said, scooting closer, her breasts jiggled slightly in the V of her blouse. "Police ask me if I knew who Charlie gambled with. Maybe they don't believe I had anything to do with it after all?"

"It's possible. What did you tell them?"

"Not much really. I only heard him talk to some Joey over the phone once or twice."

"Any idea if this business he had to take care of yesterday was with this Joey dude?"

"None," she said, getting closer, a hand on my shoulder now.

There were probably a hundred bookmakers in the city named Joey. The police should know the ones who would be willing to commit murder to satisfy a debt. If in fact it was Joey. It could just as easy be a Lefty, or Mugs, or Spike.

I stood; I'd been up here too long. "Well, maybe the police will get this thing wrapped up pretty soon."

"I hope so," she said, standing also. She touched my shoulder again. "You know, I usually don't have this much trouble apologizing to men."

She was pressing herself against me, her body warm, soft. Her perfume enveloping us in a light cocoon. She kissed me, or I kissed her, I'm not sure. I tasted her lipstick, the tart sweetness of the wine she'd drunk. The room seemed to swirl. It would be easy to get lost in her passion. I pushed back slowly.

"What's the matter?"

"You don't have to do this," I said, knowing my body was telling my mouth to shut up.

"Have to do, no. Want to do, yes. I'm not used to being turned down."

I took a breath. This wasn't something I wanted to rush through. "This evening, when I get off from work."

"Promise?"

I kissed the tip of her nose. "Promise."

At the elevator my body was still telling me to turn around and run back to her. There was a time in my life that a quickie would've been just fine, another notch on the ol' pole. But lately I've been going for quality. A sign of maturity or senility, I wasn't sure which.

I didn't have to wait too long for an elevator; one arrived a second or two after I'd pushed the down button. The doors slid opened, and the man who stepped out was about my height but considerably more muscular, a fact easily detected from the bulges under his dark blue suit coat. We passed each other with darting glances. As the elevator doors closed, I wondered if he was a policeman continuing the investigation, or a client Catherine had scheduled for a morning romp. Then I called myself a jerk; I'd gotten on the up elevator and had to travel three more flights up before I could get it going back down.

Royce was passing by the entrance to the store as I approached. "Playing hooky!"

"No. The cops let Catherine Lake go. I was just up to her place."

"Say what? My man, go on with your bad self."

"Get your mind out of the gutter, Royce. She invited me up to apologize."

"Whatever you say. Nice shade of lipstick."

"It was just a thank you kiss," I said, wiping my lips with my handkerchief.

"Works for me," Royce shrugged.

I was thinking it would probably take a jackhammer to get the grin off his face when we heard the screams. Something bad was happening in the atrium area.

Royce broke into a run, putting in a disturbance call on his two-way. I tried to keep up, but his longer, younger legs increased the distance between us. Down the hall, through the revolving doors of the atrium, a small crowd was gathering on the lawn near the rose bushes. Royce waded in, ordering them to move back. The crowd slowly complied, I was right behind him by then and through the crowd's thinning ranks I first saw a bloodied hand protruding through the crushed roses, then a foot, then what was left of a face.

Maybe the world stopped then, I don't know. I got nauseated, felt as if I was in a huge spinning vacuum and the thump of my heart seemed to vibrate my whole body. The bloody tangle in the rose bushes didn't want to stay in focus. I guess I didn't want to believe what I was seeing. I turned and ran. I thought I heard Royce call to me as I hit the revolving door, but I didn't stop to find out.

I caught an elevator right away, but it seemed to take forever to get to Catherine's floor. It wasn't much better going down the hallway to her condo. I felt like it was all happening in slow motion, although I know it wasn't.

She answered the door on my first ring. Her hair was just a mite ruffled, and she was breathing heavy. "Off work so soon?"

I brushed by her not answering and went directly to the balcony. Twelve floors below the crowd in the atrium had gotten larger. Two other building security people had joined Royce and were preventing the onlookers from getting too close to the body. The body. It was the man I'd passed at the elevator; the one I'd guessed was a policeman, or another of Catherine's clients.

"He tried to kill me," she said, as I turned to face her.

I felt glass crunch under my shoe. A long-steam wine glass lay broken on the balcony floor in a small puddle of clear white wine. I looked at the cocktail table where the bottle of Zinfandel still sat, along with Catherine's lipstick-smeared glass, the mate to the broken one at my feet.

"He poured the wine himself," she said. She must have been following my gaze, thinking one or two steps ahead of me.

"He was a pretty big dude. How'd you do it?" I looked around the room for any heavy base statue or ashtray that could've been used as a weapon. "What'd you do, hit him with something when his back was turned then helped him over the railing?"

"I said he was going to kill me. What else could I do?"

"The police are better equipped to answer that."

She rushed up to me, taking my hands in hers. "No, no police. They don't have to know he was up here. There's a couple of dozen balconies he could've fallen from."

She had my fingers up close to her mouth; I felt her warm breath flowing across the back of my hands. Her eyelashes batted ever so gently as she looked up to me.

"I must have 'DUMMY' stenciled on my forehead."

She flung my hands away, turning from me. "Okay, okay," she said, walking into the middle of the room. She paused. "I'll tell you the truth." She turned back, ran her fingers through her hair. "Tate, the guy down in the atrium. He hired me to set Charlie up. Only I didn't know he planned to kill him. Said he had a very important business matter to discuss and Charlie kept ducking him. All I was supposed to do was get him in a good mood, then let Tate into the apartment and leave. I didn't know Charlie had ordered more champagne. I thought you were Tate when I went to the door. When I found out Charlie was dead, I knew you could place me in his apartment so I went to you for help, but I couldn't tell you the whole truth then."

"And inviting me up here earlier . . . ?"

She shrugged. "Insurance, kind of. I guess I wanted somebody on my side. I like you. You're good people. You were always nice to me when I came into the store."

"What about this Joey?"

"A name I threw at the cops to get them off my back."

"So Vanders wasn't into gambling?"

"He couldn't've been. He was into something that got him killed. The only thing I know for sure, when Tate showed up here today, he was here to tie up loose ends."

"So you killed him?"

"I had to defend myself. I didn't have a choice."

At that point, I didn't either. I told her to clean up the broken glass, close her balcony doors, and try to stay calm. "With any luck the cops won't even look in your direction for this."

"You do believe me, don't you?" she asked, coming up to me.

I took her in my arms. "Getting to know you better hasn't been dull." I kissed her lightly. "Yeah, I believe you. Don't worry, we'll get through this. The police won't hear anything from me."

It would be the second time in two days I'd broken my word to her. Only this time I wasn't saddled with any remorse. I still had Detective Hook's business card on my desk in my office. I tried to get in touch with him but learned he was on his way out here to investigate the body in the atrium.

I intercepted him when he came into the building and told him about Catherine and her confession.

We went up to her condo together along with two uniform cops, but apparently Catherine didn't hold much in my ability to keep her confession to myself. Her condo was empty.


Two months later I got word from Detective Hooks that Catherine had been found off a back road in Indiana. Gun shot. She'd been dead for several weeks. Reprisal, more loose ends being tied up, or something altogether unrelated? Chances are we would never find out, Hooks said. It wasn't a satisfying solution but one he was forced to accept.

As for me, I counted myself as being pretty lucky. This whole mess could've gone any number of ways, and I would've been the worst for it. As it turned out, I didn't get any mention in the media about my involvement in the murder investigation. And after a little buzz around the building; things pretty much got back to normal.

Oh yeah, my daughter had a boy. I passed out cigars for a week.

"Hey, Walt," Royce called as he hurried down the paper goods aisle. "Did you hear what happened up in twenty-three twelve? Old man Huvack was found in bed with a big ass knife sticking in his chest. Nobody knows where his wife is. You haven't seen her have you?"

I'd bumped into Mrs. Huvack this morning in the basement-parking garage. Her purse had hit the floor, spilling among other things an airline ticket to Canada.

I didn't know what time her flight was scheduled for, she could be in Canada by now, or sitting at the airport waiting to depart.

"No," I said, and it felt like a pressure valve was being released. One murder was more than enough for me. "Come to think of it, I haven't seen her for about a week."

# BEGINNER'S LUCK

*Gary Phillips*

Chainey awoke with a headache. She smacked her lips and wiped at the side of her mouth wet from drool. She sat forward and felt woozy. Then a bolt of nausea lanced through her and for a moment, it seemed she might vomit. That, the throbbing beneath her skull, and the rising heat bearing down compelled her to sit back and slump down. She squeezed her eyes shut and tried to assemble chunks of random memory into sequential events.

A door slammed. A car door.

A man shouted her name. No, he didn't yell, he'd spoken in a tone as if he was a friend or at least knew her in some way.

Close, he stood close, smiling, conversational.

Turning, sunlight glinting off a polished hood, the man before her, asking her a question quietly.

Then a burning mist fogging her eyes. Bastard sprayed her with pepper spray? No, something else, something nastier.

Sky upside down, sun behind her eyes. Mooch, what about Mooch?

A cell phone jingled. Chainey sat up again, aware that she was on a bus bench, traffic going along. Pedestrians walked by, used to drunks or druggies sleeping off their highs in public. Anything goes in Vegas. Then the cell phone went off again. The drowsy woman realized it was in her jeans' pocket and removed the instrument.

"How do you feel?" The man asked pleasantly.

"Like shit. I'd appreciate the opportunity to return the favor."

His chuckle was mirthful, suggesting a person of expansive humor. "At another time, Ms. Chainey. But right this minute, you have a more important task to perform."

A CAT bus chugged up, and Chainey waved it on. "And what would that be?" Her annoyance was quickly becoming anger, and it was dulling the hammer blows inside her temple.

"That envelope-sized accordion folder you were supposed to deliver to a certain party in L.A."

"If you know about that, then you must also know it's in the safe." Anxious, she chewed her lip. She had a bad feeling what was coming next.

"Yes, about that," the man on the other end said. "Mooch is a stubborn cuss."

There it was. "I want to speak to him."

"Your boss is unavailable at the moment, Martha. So you see, it falls to you to obtain that envelope for me and deliver same not to the city of oranges and palms, but to me."

His tone had remained upbeat, but the implication behind his words were clear. "Only Mooch has the combination," she said.

There was a gulp as he drank. "Yes, well," he said, clearing his throat, "as I mentioned, Mr. Maltizar is determined to be noncompliant on this matter, and really, there's little time or patience I can ill afford to waste."

"Look, there's nothing I can do unless you release Mooch."

"Oh, don't be so modest. I know a little something about you, and you're plenty resourceful." He paused to take another sip. Fucker was probably having his morning latte, Chainey reflected.

"And you don't have much choice. None at all if you don't want what could happen on your pretty head."

Chainey was up and walking around. "Let's say I can get the envelope, and I'm not promising that."

"But let's say you can." The voice lost part of its casual veneer.

"Where do I deliver the package and get Mooch back?"

"You're in no position to demand a goddamn thing, missy. What you better do is get that sweet ass of yours in gear and back to your office to get my money."

"Why aren't you at the office? You had the drop on both of us." She'd been in the parking lot below the second story set of offices that Ira "Mooch" Maltizar maintained as Truxton, Ltd., a licensed and bonded courier service. And though the company, named for a racehorse owned by the seventh president of the United States, Andrew Jackson, did generate decent revenues conveying such freight as law firm's briefs to the courthouse or the occasional platinum watch to the showgirl from the smitten sharpie, it was Truxton's "off the books" endeavors that had earned the company its real swag.

"Quite observant of you, Chainey," the man replied. "That's why you're needed."

"Who's watching it?"

There was that laugh again. "I can't for one hundred percent say who, but if you press me to lay odds, I'd wager one of the men on duty is a good-sized gentleman, six-five or six, head like a four-slot toaster, chest like the back end of a Peterbilt."

No use complaining, it wasn't going to change anything. "You've got to give me time to work this out. It's Sunday, and—"

"Sorry my dear, but the clock is against us. You will have to be at the McDonald's on the food court floor of the Excalibur by one forty-seven this afternoon. Be at the table with the 'MC' carved into it."

Her watch read three minutes after eleven. "Hey, you're the one that needs this file, man. Seems to me setting an unrealistic timeline is counterproductive. Might lead to mistakes."

He sighed. "I realize haste in a situation such as this is fraught with unpredictability, but so be it. My time is not my own, and neither is yours, Chainey. For the moment, you hustle when I blow the whistle for the good of Mooch. You can dispense with the cell phone you're using as there will be another one waiting for you at Mickey-D's. Just in case you have the ability to trace these things." The line clicked off.

Chainey didn't waste time trying to figure out who the asshole was.

That would come later if she completed the job. It didn't matter to her what was in the file. For all she cared, it could be Long John Silver's lost treasure map.

The problem was that at least one large individual representing another interest baby-sitting her office. She assumed that he would at least have somebody with him. But what about the chump who was making her jump through hoops? Did he have help? Did he have a partner too?

Chainey was on Fort Apache Road near the twenty-four-hour Albertson's. She walked across the street to the store and hailed a cab. Two blocks from the unpretentious mall where Truxton was located off the Strip and not far from North Vegas, black Vegas, she got out and paid the cabbie. Her enemy was unknown to her, and she had no way of gauging if he would truly hurt or kill Mooch. If, she chillingly amended, he were still alive.

Walking closer, she tensed as she passed a van but there was nobody in it, at least not in the front seats. But she didn't think a couple of gunmen would be hunkered down in a family van, but you never knew. In the lot of the strip mall where the office was, six cars were parked. As this was Sunday, only Kleopatra's Nails and the video store were open for business. Technically, Truxton didn't have set hours, the need to move unreported monies demanded twenty-four seven service.

Chainey had come to the office because Mooch had called her. Over the phone, he'd mentioned that a matter had come up suddenly, and he needed her on the double. And it was a sad testament to the current fallowness of her love life, that she was available this morning.

Two of the cars on the lot she could ID. One was her late model T-Bird, the other Mooch's Cadillac Eldorado. The others, strangers to her, could belong to anyone. She watched from across the street, alongside a narrow passage beside the closed Cosmic Cube comic book shop.

A woman with two small children left the video store and departed in one of the cars on the lot. Chainey had focused on a shiny Jaguar S-Type tucked in the far corner. From this distance, she couldn't tell if anyone was in the vehicle, but then her hunch was confirmed. A hand came out of the passenger window, flicking ash from a cigarette.

Okay, that's the players. Time to get busy. The design of the mall was such that the steps and storefronts all faced the parking lot. There were rear service entrances on the backside of the shops, but only on the ground floor. There was only one way to the second story.

One option was to draw the men in the Jaguar out of the car or distract them long enough for her to sneak into the office. It happened that Chainey was acquainted with several working girls, as they were always good sources of underworld information. She could rally a few of them, work out the price, and have them show up and descend on the occupants in the Jag. They could offer all manner of sexual favors. Of course, she concluded, that would probably result in one or more of the women getting punched in the face. And if the cops rolled up, they might haul everybody down to the station to straighten out the mess, and she could get in the office unbothered.

It was thirteen to twelve. She needed a better plan. Chainey walked the long way around the back to avoid being seen, hopped her six-foot frame over the rough hewn wall behind the mall with the aid of a plastic milk crate, and went along the narrow path. She hoped she counted the doors right and knocked. She put her face in line with the peephole.

"Martha?" Jenny Giap, the owner of the nail salon said when she opened the door.

"Too long to explain, but you mind if I come in?"

"No, come on." As was customary, her fifty-plus body, her stocky legs still shapely and toned, was clad in a mini.

Chainey entered. There were only two customers inside the shop. One was at the nail table that Giap, in her rubber gloves and face mask around her neck, had been working on. The other woman, her foot in a cast, had her chipped vermillion toenails sticking out. She idly leafed through a *Vogue*. An oldies soul station was playing "Hollywood Swinging" by Kool and the Gang on the radio.

The watch on Chainey's wrist felt like a hundred pound weight dragging her down to the bottom of a depthless sea. She didn't want to look at it nor the cat clock on the wall, with its eyes that shifted back and forth ticking far too loudly.

"I need a favor, Jenny. No questions, but there's four hundred in it for you."

"You've just said the magic words, girlfriend. What I gotta do?"

Less than fifteen minutes later, Jenny Giap was waving her arms wildly above her head, hollering incoherently and trudging onto the parking lot in her platform clunkies. A firetruck had also arrived silently. The crew drove it onto the lot at an angle, blocking the Jaguar.

"The car, the car is on fire," Giap pointed nervously at the Jaguar. "This ruins business. I can't have them burning up my store."

"Now hold on, ma'am," the firefighter who'd alighted from the truck said. "Calm yourself, what are you talking about?"

"Smoke, smoke was pouring out of it." Giap took two steps back from the Jag as if afraid it might combust at any moment.

"What, from the engine?" The firefighter looked dubiously at the car.

Jenny Giap said, "All I know is I've seen smoke, and that means fire, don't it?"

"What, is this dizzy broad talking about?" The man, the big one the kidnapper had described, had unlimbered himself from behind the wheel. He was in his forties, dressed in a dark suit and thin dark tie with a clip.

"We're trying to determine that sir," the firefighter said.

"Well, move your fuckin' rig and work this out somewhere else, huh, pal?"

"Be cool, Hal," his partner in the passenger seat advised.

The two other firefighters alighted from the truck.

"Why don't you cooperate, sir?" This firefighter was a sizeable blond man with a tackler's shoulders. He drifted toward the belligerent Hal.

"Okay, look," the tall man began, "I'm sorry for any misunderstanding we might be having." He pulled out his wallet. "This is for the fireman's fund, okay?" He flashed a hundred dollar bill.

"Maybe we should check his car," the third one, a tawny haired woman said.

"You're not cops, so stop trying to sound tough," Hal sneered.

"It's no problem to get them here," the first one mentioned. "No problem at all."

"Hey, how about you move your truck and let us out?" Hal's buddy, a brown skinned man with white hair in a Hawaiian shirt was now out of the car. "We're late and need to get going. Or maybe your captain would like a call from our lawyers?"

The one who'd talked to Giap took a cursory look around the Jag and did a modified push up to look below it too. "Okay. Sure," he said.

"I tell you it smokes, whoosh," Giap said, throwing her hands back in the air and muttering to herself as she returned to her shop.

The firetruck backed up, and the Jaguar tooled out of the lot.

"That was great, Jenny." Chainey said, heading for the front.

"It's all good," her friend cracked. They knocked fists.

At the door Chainey added. "Those motherlovers will be back in a few once they figure the fire department has bounced. Just to play safe, close up for the rest of the day, alright? I'll tighten you up on the dinero this week."

"Shit, a couple of chumps like that don't scare me," Giap retorted, dropping the stilted English act she'd put on for the suckers. "I got something for 'em if they want to jump bad." She snickered.

"Jenny," Chainey implored.

"Fine, for the sake of my customers."

Upstairs at Truxton, Ltd., Chainey hoped that since Mooch Maltizar was past sixty and enjoyed his afterhours Cuba Libres, rum and coke, with his cigars, he would have written down the combination to the safe in case he forgot. But as it was now almost twelve-thirty, she was trying to be methodical and not just rushed in looking for it. That the numbers would be in Mooch's office was a given. So at least the area she had to search was knowable.

The phone rang, and she let the machine get it. Nobody spoke on the other end, so it had to be the two hitters calling on their way back to check if anyone had come in. And the third party, the one that had engaged Mooch, was no doubt going to be pissed that their goods weren't going to reach them. But, Chainey reminded herself, one set of worries at a time.

Fortunately, the blinds hadn't been opened yet by Mooch in his office, as the morning had been overcast and the sun had come out late. She started her hunt in his office with occasional breaks to peek through a slat for the return of the watchers. And she hoped none of the other couriers of the company had any business that required them to come in today.

Less then ten minutes later, the Jaguar returned. The tall man, Hal, got out, and Chainey observed him as he walked up to the shops on the ground floor. After a few moments, having no doubt confirmed that the nail salon was closed, she heard his footsteps on the concrete stairs. She remained motionless, one of the office guns, a 15-shot Glock 20, ready at her side.

The door handle jiggled. Chainey hadn't reset the alarm. It had been off due to Mooch having been hustled out of the place, probably with a gun in his ribs. The tall man's heavy footfalls echoed on the balcony as he prowled back and forth in front of the office. The window shuddered. Chainey figured the frustrated hood had pounded the pane. His footsteps then receded.

It took Chainey longer than she would have liked to find the safe's combination. The crafty old player had secreted the numbers, typed out on his Underwood circa Horace Greeley, on a little sheet of paper he'd cut to a sliver, and taped to the underside of the back padding of his executive chair. In the corner of the office, the safe squatted. The thing was a Defiant, a free-standing '50s-era floor model old battle hull of a mother that had been there before Chainey came on board.

She dialed the combination and opened the heavy door. Inside were all manner of items ranging from bundled bills to jewelry boxes. The accordion file had an object wrapped in white sheeting on top of it, and she had to remove it to get what she wanted. Curious, she unwrapped the cloth to reveal a weathered machine pistol that had Japanese lettering stamped on the stock. She shrugged, replaced the piece, and shut the safe. Now came the hard part. She had to get to her car.

At the entrance she took a deep breath, mentally ran through her plan, shaky as it was, and stepped onto the landing. Chainey had reset the alarm and walked toward the stairs, but not fast. This part called for icy nerves to resist running.

Hal, who'd been standing in the parking lot smoking, was striding quickly to the foot of the steps. "Hey, I want to talk with you," he demanded, his long legs brining him up two steps at a time.

Chainey made sure she stopped halfway down. "Who the hell are you?" She tried to sound unaware.

"Don't you worry about that, sweetness." His hand was inside his jacket, locking on the piece she was sure he kept there in a shoulder rig. "What ya got there, huh?" He asked, referring to the file. They were now both in the middle of the stairs, separated by less than an arm's length.

"Oh, this?" She produced the Taser she'd taken from the office and shot the two probes into his chest and juiced him.

"Fuck," Hal hollered as the volts charred his kidneys, causing his legs to buckle. But he was strong and held on to the rail, the piece slack in his gun hand. "Fuckin' bitch," he slurred, dropping the gun and making an anemic grab for Chainey.

"Nice meeting you too." She jabbed an elbow into his face, and the tall man fell ass end off the stairs. His pal in the Hawaiian shirt was out of the Jaguar heading toward them, but Chainey had scooped up Hal's gun, an old-fashioned Smith & Wesson revolver, and leveled it. The Glock stuck out of her back pocket.

"Now, look, baby—"

"I ain't hardly your baby. Face down," she ordered.

"I'm sure we can—"

"You want to try me to see if I know how to use this thing?"

"I guess I don't." He complied.

Hal groaned as Chainey gained the lot and patted down the man in the flashy shirt. She took the gun he had on his belt and walked to their car.

"We can work this out you know," Hawaiian shirt said. "Money is the great communicator."

Chainey ignored him and got the hood of the Jaguar open. She pulled out a few electronic pieces connected to the engine, hoping that would incapacitate their car.

"This is only a minor delay, Miss. We've got time and resources."

"Aren't you special." Chainey got in her car and as she backed up, Hawaiian shirt was helping his stunned partner to his feet. Hal was bleeding from the nose. She zoomed away in the T-Bird.

At the Excalibur, Chainey bought a cup of coffee at the McDonald's in the food court. She was ahead of schedule and walked around the tables. Given the hour of the day, the place was full, and it was hard getting a full view of the tabletops because of food trays, extra large cups of soda, and what not. Because she didn't want to look too suspicious, she walked in and out of the section. It would do no good to have security show up to escort the lady making the kids nervous away. She wasn't having any luck spotting the table with the carved letters. It was now 12:43.

She kept circulating. A man with straggly shoulder-length hair, in a T-shirt with the rock band Creed's logo on it, sat at a corner table slowly munching on his Big Mac. Fries were spread out before him like pieces of a chic jigsaw puzzle. He had the baggy-eyed air of having pulled an all-nighter at the tables and come up short. Way short. He looked up as Chainey cruised past.

"You showgirls think the world owes you the driver's seat of life, don't you?"

Please, she told herself, let this fool be talking to himself. She kept going but, naturally, he was going to get her attention.

"Gonna ignore me, huh? Spend my money in this pussy trap, get the toothy smile and the free drinks as long as I'm feeding the slots." He was starting to squeeze his hamburger. "All of you are worthless cunts."

The people around him did their best to continue talking and eating amiably, hoping that indifference would make him shut up or at least return to gambling elsewhere. Chainey looked back at the table now that he'd shifted his arms. Sure enough, her initials were etched there. It was 12:46.

She came closer. "Why be so unfriendly?"

One of the man's orbs was shrunk to the size of a dot, the other pushing and engorged, seemingly contaminated with brain fluids that had leaked into that side. "You know why." He held onto his Big Mac with both hands, the veins rigid on his thin forearms. Pinkish sauce embedded with bits of chopped onion dribbled across his fingers.

"You know," he said again, taking another bite, smacking loudly.

The cell taped beneath the table chimed a tune, and Chainey had to sit next to him to reach for it.

"Okay, yeah," the goof bobbed his head agreeably. "All you chicks eventually come around to the dude. Don't milk my lizard too hard, baby." He cackled like a hyena.

Chainey withdrew the phone and clicked it on. She tried to get up, but her new boyfriend had put an arm around her shoulders, staining her shirt with gooey stuff.

"I got your package."

"Good," the voice on the other end said.

"Let me talk to Mooch, or I burn what's in it now."

The goof leaned toward her. "I love black women. You know how to treat your men."

"What?" the kidnapper said.

Chainey stomped her boot heel on the clown's tennis shoe-clad foot. He didn't yell as she expected, but his face and upper body twitched convulsively, like a man attacked by hornets. She rose.

"Quit fucking around. I don't know if Mooch is breathing, dead, or incapacitated. But this goes no further until I talk to him." She had to bank on his greed or desperation, or both. "Go ahead, drag this out. How long do you think before Hal and Mister Hawaiian stud catch up to you, asshole?"

"They follow you?"

"Yeah, I'm that stupid."

"Hold on." There was the fumbling of the phone, the scuffing of feet, and inaudible conversation. Then her boss said in his thick Cuban accent. "I'm here, chica. *No preoccupado. No se—*"

"No Spanish," the kidnapper ordered, snatching the phone back. "Okay, you had your little pow-wow, now you do as I say, and everything will be just swell."

The goof was again occupied with her burger.

"It better be. Now where do we finish this?"


The rear side window looked like a dry riverbed crisscrossed with parched lines then imploded, and hundreds of tinkling pieces rained down. Chainey crawled forward in the dirt and squeezed off two shots from around the T-Bird's tire. She didn't expect to hit anyone, just let that joker handling the shotgun know she was still kicking.

That done, she pulled her body back and got up on a knee.

It didn't help matters that the sun was now up high and that there wasn't much in the way of shelter in Tender Oaks—there wasn't much of Tender Oaks in general.

The plan had been for Nevada Power to build a coal-burning plant in this desert section east of Boulder City butting up against the Arizona border. The rest of Nevada might be static in its growth, but Vegas was sprouting like wild weeds. And as the city and environs expanded upwards and outwards, the beast of a million neon signs had a need to gobble up more and more electricity. The Tender Oaks power station was to be a pristine example of public and private capital working together for the common good and commerce.

Only the transmission lines were blueprinted to travel over sacred Indian burial grounds. A court challenge was a mounted by the Shoshones to block the development. And during the process of discovery by the attorneys, funny addition had been revealed. The private sector developer, Rene Hillibrand, had disappeared, and the project was stalled in suits and countersuits.

"Come on, let's join forces. We have the same objective in mind," Hawaiian shirt yelled to Chainey. He was crouched behind large spools of cable, nearer to the Nevada Power maintenance shed.

"Let's ask Hal," she quipped.

"Fuck her and Fraizen." The tall man and his shotgun were on the far side of the Tahoe SUV they'd screeched to a stop in minutes after Chainey.

"He's just blowing off steam," the one hiding behind the spools said. "He's really a big ol' teddy bear."

"Well I'm not hugging him," she muttered.

"Chainey," the man in the Hawaiian shirt said, "there's got to be a reasonable way we can come to terms. We want Fraizen, and you want your boss back. They're both in that shack. And Fraizen's a punk. Gun or no gun, he's not going to be a problem."

He knew her name. They worked fast. "And the file?"

"That's our property, you devious skank," Hal bellowed. "You ain't getting it."

"Shut up, Hal," his partner advised. "I'm trying to work a deal here."

"No," he answered in a tone like a defiant teenager. "You can't trust her. She'll cut you down first chance she gets."

Hawaiian shirt asked, "So now what? Wait here until a police chopper flies overhead and we all go to the pokey?"

From where she was, Chainey was pinned down by Hal. But if Hawaiian shirt stepped out toward the shack where this Fraizen and Mooch were, she could tag him.

Fraizen appeared at the window of the shed again, half his face showing as it did when Chainey had first arrived. "Ramos, I got something to trade for my life."

Ramos, the one in the bright shirt, called out. "You suckin' hind tit, Fraizen. Like you been doing all your lousy life."

"The old man, he's got all kinds of shit in that safe. I know they move money for the casino owners."

"Oh, you stupid," Hal began.

"Yeah," Ramos cut in, "that sounds good, Fraizen. Real good. You bring him out, we sweat him, and we all go home rich."

Chainey shook her head. Hal and Ramos were pros. They knew better than ripping off the cold cash belonging to the types that Mooch delivered for. They weren't going to bring that kind of heat down on themselves. But Ramos had to be hedging that Fraizen saw no other way out, and believed his foolish offer had weight. They were going to kill him and Mooch, too, in the process, if he was in the way.

"Nothing happens to Mooch," she said from her cover.

"Things have a way of working themselves out in these funky trickbags, Chainey."

Ramos addressed Fraizen, "Come on out."

"Take care of her first," Fraizen said.

"She won't shoot with Maltizar in tow," Ramos answered.

"That's right, Fraizen," Hal added, realizing what his partner was up to. "Besides, she pokes her head up, I'll take it off."

Incongruously, a jack rabbit suddenly bounded into the shooting area. He sat back on his haunches, aware that everyone was suddenly transfixed by his furry presence. The animal twitched its nose then bounded away.

The door to the shack creaked open, and Mooch was shoved out first, Fraizen behind him. The older man's hands were tied, and there was a clot of drying blood alongside his face where Fraizen must have pistol-whipped him. Fraizen, a beefy man in expensive slacks, had one hand on Maltizar, the other pressed into his back. They stopped about a yard beyond the shack.

"He's told me the combination, Ramos." Fraizen said, laying out his insurance policy. He kept Maltizar in front of him, facing the man in the Hawaiian shirt. This exposed his flank to Chainey.

"You pointing him in the wrong direction, slick," Ramos chided.

Fraizen cocked Maltizar toward Chainey and walked sideways, heading over to the grouping of giant spools.

"You're almost there, Fraizen," Hal goaded. "You're almost home free, baby."

When Ramos took care of Fraizen, he was going to have control of Mooch, but there wasn't much Chainey could do at that the moment. The file gave her something of a bargaining chip, but a live body was the ultimate trump card.

"We're going to work this out, okay, Fraizen?" Ramos said soothingly. "Money is the great comforter."

Fraizen and Maltizar were at the edge of the spools.

"Okay, Ramos," Fraizen started. "Let's you and me go get the money. Hal keeps the girl pinned down, then we come back and take care of her." Maltizar was positioned in such a way that he was now between Fraizen and the still-crouching Ramos. Part of the heads and shoulders of the kidnapper and her boss were exposed to Chainey. Even if she could make the shot and take Fraizen out, Mooch was still Ramos's prisoner.

Suddenly Mooch slumped and said, "Oh God." He sagged against his captor, knocking him back a few steps.

"You old bastard!" Fraizen screamed, "don't you have a heart attack on me now." The dead weight folded against him, and Fraizen let the body drop. Having a clear shot, Ramos shot him in the gut. Reflexively, Fraizen shot back.

"Ramos," Hal called out. "Hey, man."

"Motherfuckers," Fraizen said. He staggered backward, away from the spools. "You lying motherfuckers." Spittles of blood flew from his mouth. He had one hand pressing his breached stomach, the other clutching his gun. His pant legs were soaked in crimson, and he was colorless as old parchment.

"You're bleeding out, Fraizen," Chainey said. "You need a doctor."

"No he doesn't," Hal had stood up, and the blast from his Mossberg semi-auto took most of Fraizen's face off.

Chainey had also popped up quickly, and her round caught the tall man up high on his torso. He spun around then went down to the ground. She knew he was alive and wasn't going to rush the spot behind the Tahoe.

After a moment, Hal said, "So where does that leave us, girly? The ones we cared about are dead."

"Fuck you to hell."

"I'm sure that day will come." She heard movement and chanced to look up from the top of the pickup's bed. Hal was inside the Tahoe and had started the engine. The vehicle was driving away as she ran to where Mooch Maltizar lay. She stood over his still form as the SUV's motor receded into the distance. Ramos died in a sitting position, his legs straight out, his back against one of the spools. Fraizen's bullet had punched a hole in his heart. Quite a shot for an amateur. Beginner's luck.

"The bad men say bye-bye, chica?"

"You goddamn faker." She wiped the wetness from her eyes and helped him to his feet.

"It wasn't that much of a bluff." He was shaking and unsteady, but he was alive. "I was about to, *come se dice,* stroke out, *que no?*"

"Whatever," she said smiling, helping him to her car. Chainey never did get the full story from Maltizar about the relationship of Ramos and Hal to Fraizen. He hadn't survived since the days of running numbers for Moe Dalitz by being chatty. Though he did bestow a sizeable bonus in her bank account for saving him to enjoy more Cuba Libres.

Her friend, Rena Solomon, did an in-depth piece in the *Las Vegas Express,* the alternative biweekly, where she was a staff investigative reporter. From that and a few segments on the local news, Chainey learned that Fraizen had been the attorney for the missing developer of the Tender Oaks project, Rene Hillibrand. In her piece, Solomon pointed out that Hillibrand and Fraizen had lived lavish lifestyles but had come up bust in both investments in the dot-com fever awhile back, and the more recent downturns in the stock market.

There was also, Solomon wrote, allegations that some of the operating capital for Hillibrand's business originated from less-than-Fortune 500 sources. The sort of folks for whom lawsuit might as well be Sanskrit for all the meaning it had for them. They believed in the direct approach in getting their monies back.

Maltizar and Chainey had to provide statements to the police and the accordion file—containing cashiers checks made to bearer totaling some four million dollars—was turned in. The story she and Mooch agreed to beforehand was that the file of checks was with Fraizen all the time. That he'd kidnapped Maltizar in a deranged effort to force him to get Chainey to deliver those checks to a boat off shore in Baja. Sure, the story was flimsier than a politician's promise, but who was around to contradict them?

Hal never turned up. And Chainey knew better than to persist in asking Maltizar who she was supposed to have delivered those checks to originally. About three and a half months later, a bit of stink was raised, as the checks disappeared from the police evidence locker. This on a weekend when Mooch Maltizar had gone to Scottsdale to relax, he'd said.

And later, Chainey noted a small item in the *Review-Journal* that a man vaguely answering to Rene Hillibrand's description was spotted boarding a transpacific plane at L.A. International Airport.

# GOD OF THE POND

*Charles Shipps*

"We're going to sweat the bastard out," Detective Sgt. Robert Loomis swore with a vengeance.

The head of the special task force to investigate Internet-based crimes frowned as he studied the faces of his team; two county sheriffs and an FBI agent. A second detective, Paula Douglas, had not yet arrived. Nothing of vital significance could happen until she did. Where the hell was she, and what was she doing?

Loomis was out for blood. His vanity would be pleased with nothing less. It had taken months of endless on-line sessions to draw out the target. The days and hours he had committed to this case had escalated into countless nights away from home.

The possible consequences of his steady absences were not a predominant worry. Another kind of man—a less self-absorbed man, in a far more passionate relationship might worry, with just cause—but Loomis did not. The swivel chair he leaned back in protested his weight with an oppressive squeal.

His pager buzzed.

It was the duty sergeant from headquarters. "How's it going down there?"

"What's up Tommy? Tell the boss that he need not be so concerned; we're going to get him this time. The Glitch was an arrogant-ass, hanging around hacker's chat rooms, bragging about his little scams. Paula and I will have him hardwired faster than a shockwave can cap a browser. The trace is ready to go."

"Your boy is a smooth talker."

"As smooth as snot on a windshield," Loomis agreed.

"We got a call a few minutes ago from a man who identified himself as a Detroit Police Department detective. He talked the talk and knew all the right things to say. He wanted us to bring him up to speed on the SWAT team operation of a hacker that's supposed to go down tonight."

"What? Nobody but us knows."

"Obviously somebody else does," the sergeant said. "He wasn't guessing. We didn't give him jack after he said he was you."

"Holy Madonna," Loomis whistled.

"Bob," His friend's tone wavered. "There is one other thing. Your wife called."

There was a weighty silence.

"Did she leave a message?" He asked. There was no sense in trying to avoid her any longer.

"She sure as hell did," Tommy said.

"A bit edgy, huh?"

"You know it. She said you'd better turn on your cell phone or stop ignoring her pages."

"Did you remind her that I'm in the middle of a damned important operation down here?"

"I got the impression that she understood that."

"When did you get this urgent call of hers?"

"About ten minutes ago. Just before the other one."

"Thanks again, Tommy—"

"Bob, I just promised that I would get the message to you."

"Don't sweat it," he told Tommy. "No foul, no harm."

He began reflecting on his wife the instant he disconnected. It would be better he thought, if he beat her to the punch and called her now.

"Oh thank God," she said. "You've got an extra suit and tie there, don't you? You still have time to meet me at the theatre if you hurry. I'll leave your ticket at the box office."

"I can't Judith."

"Can't or won't?" She fumed. "Robert, I should have known better. If you had a heart or mind, you'd stop whimpering and try something different like keeping a promise for a change."

"I never—"

"Oh yes you did," she challenged. "You were just oblivious to my wants and needs, as usual."

Now he was growing impatient and getting angry. Something about her tact had taken on a more blatant and demanding characteristic than usual. His mouth constricted in sudden fury. The harsh implication in her words made him consider the prospect that a drink or two had loosened her tongue. He denied himself any overt reaction and exhaled to check himself before speaking.

"All right, we need to talk, but it will have to be later. I have to go now."

"So do I."

"You're not listening to me. I'm not sure you ever have."

"You had better listen to this. If you don't come now, whenever you do decide to come home, I won't be there."

The line was silent.

Though she had threatened before, Judith's disquieting tone made him feel uneasy. Nothing would come of it, he thought, nothing ever did. Lately the extent of their communication rarely amounted to little more than a series of thinly disguised conversations that quickly escalated into squabbles. The quarreling had gradually evolved into a ritual. They'd had more disagreements in the past few months than they had experienced throughout their entire seven-year marriage.

A barren Judith had once wanted children. Robert would never have had the time. She teased him about his dedication to his job and accused him of making her bargain for every minute of time they did spend together. Maybe a child would have been a good preoccupation for her. Maybe he had not appreciated her as much as he might have. He resented the insinuation that something might really be wrong, far less than she probably resented his lack of presence around the house. She had found a friend on the Net at one time, but obviously she did not feel like that kind of mingling tonight.

Quickly dismissing any implication that he might be lacking, Loomis convinced himself that he was a better detective than he was a husband.

Tonight he would triumph over the menacing hacker known as Deadly Glitch, a computer security specialist who had written software security programs. Glitch was the worst kind of electronic shoplifter and con man in the virtual universe.

Loomis knew that it required nothing less than his own tenacity to trap this cyber punk—a trap that was firmly in place tonight, with or without modification.

Through a small tinted window, Loomis observed the dark avenue, speckled with rundown buildings and shelters. The Cass Corridor was the home of the destitute. A man with an unkempt beard slowly pushed a rusty shopping cart full of bottles and other discarded gems.

What kind of game was Deadly Glitch playing, and why had he lured the detectives to skid row?

Detective Loomis looked at a laptop screen with a pervasive hunger in his impatient eyes. He stared at the blinking white cursor. His own background had yielded little indication ten years ago when he had gotten into law enforcement, that he would end up in a weather-beaten mobile command post with deceptive Water and Sewage insignia, complete with a dozen rack-mounted computers, in a cyber surveillance stakeout in a virtual room, where they became actors enticing strangers to give up their secrets. The anonymity of going undercover on the Internet made it easy for anyone to pretend to be somebody they weren't. He loved the pursuit and playacting almost as much as he loved fishing. That was the only other place that he wanted to be—sitting near the warm water with a cold beer.

Three mild taps against the tarnished vehicle startled the school of fish in his imagination, drawing everyone's attention to the back door, which sat in close proximity to an open manhole flanked with bright orange cones. The door opened. Detective Paula Douglas, a six-foot-four-inch brunette, came inside.

"Sorry for the delay," she smiled. "I thought they told you that I was to take a bus over from headquarters so I'd look like a civilian."

"Thirteen hundred Beaubien is less than two miles from here. So what happened?"

"The bus driver got a bit flirty."

"Flirty enough to ignore his schedule?"

"So, I've got charisma," Paula smiled with self-approval. "I didn't stop traffic all by myself. By the way, it looks like they've already shut the street lights out about an eighth of a mile in all directions of our target to help the SWAT team sneak in."

Paula picked up a clipboard from the dashboard and faced the other team members.

"He's using a cell phone radio transceiver with his computer. We're picking up the electronic high-five with scanners. I'm going on-line to hold his attention long enough for us to track him. He's also got a program that can monitor me any time he suspects we're not on the up and up."

"Wouldn't it be simpler to hit up his Internet provider with a court order to give up what we need?" Agent Chase, assigned to the case at the last minute, had a limited knowledge of the Internet.

"He's using false headers in his E-mail; the provider couldn't give us anything but the bogus name and address." The Glitch was an Internet shoplifter, Loomis thought. He had access to corporate trade secrets worth billions. He was a cyber safecracker, the kind who could read your will and personal diary without your knowing he had been there. He had hacked and seized control of a Michigan phone system and wiretapped the authorities that searched for him. That made him a threat to national security.

"What makes you so sure that he's here?" Agent Chase inquired, with a strong suggestion of skepticism in his tone.

"Our boy just social engineered the desk sergeant," Loomis told him.

"I'm nobody's mooch." Paula smiled. "I can be incredibly persuasive when it comes to reverse engineering."

"Paula," Loomis said, "I'm from Missouri, it's show time. We need all the time we can get to trace. The second he bites, snatch that hook up in his jaw like he was a fat corn-eating catfish."

"I think I can keep him engaged long enough."

"We tossed enough ground bait in that chat room to choke a snake. They're going to be like leeches, so move fast."

It was hot, and Paula's sunburned skin glistened with sweat. Loomis put his hand up and glanced at her. He wondered with growing curiosity if he could revive an old and brief affair with her. Almost short of breath, he had a yearning to feel her damp body next to him.

The only passion Paula shared with Loomis now was the inimitable passion to trap Deadly Glitch as bad as Loomis wanted to.

"You're a very naughty boy." She winked.

Loomis glanced at the FBI agent.

"You do your job," Agent Chase said. "My support unit will take him. All you have to do is find him."

Paula positioned the laptop across her legs, caressed the keyboard with her fingers, and logged on as Trixie, just as she had the same time every night for more than a month. As she watched the other geeks in the chat room, she felt like a hooker on a street corner, waiting for Deadly Glitch. There was no sign of him. Within minutes she opened a dialogue. Several irrelevant conversations with curious computer geeks drew short and unconcerned responses from her. Loomis began to wonder if Glitch was on to them.

The computer suddenly shrieked like an alarm. The scanner locked on to a special call. There was the familiar static crackling sound of the modem connecting. A miniature box popped up on the upper right corner of the screen, which displayed the call data and the number dialed.

"Sweet Jesus," Loomis's faint grin blossomed into a full smile of delight. "We've got activity," he shouted. "He's coming out to play. Start that trace, now."

A flurry of activity flooded the command center. All eyes were on the computer monitors. Everyone knew their assignments. One techie rotated a small directional antenna, while another punched the keys on a second keyboard, entering the frequency data of the Internet connection they were trying to seize.

With the touch of a button, Loomis put the scanner in an automatic trap mode. Little lights flashed as it skipped from one channel to another.

Loomis signaled to the driver. They began to move slowly. The strength of the signal became stronger as the Cellscope got closer to the location of the target.

Typing feverishly, without error, Paula communicated with The Glitch.

Trixie: Hi guy.
Deadly Glitch: What's going on?
Trixie: I need your help with something.
Deadly Glitch: Eavesdropping?
Trixie: That's positive. You rock dude.

The Mobile Command Center made a left turn at the end of the block. The signal began to drop.

"Wrong direction," Loomis screamed. "It's the other way." He was as much a cyber dog as Glitch. He knew how to sniff out a hot modem and where to backtrack. In this instance he was certain it was somewhere in a six-block radius. "Make a left here," He ordered.

They cruised by a four-story brick and wood building. The signal jumped. The decibel readings bounced. The red LED blinked fast at nine o'clock.

Deadly Glitch: Have you been lurking?
Trixie: I was waiting on you. Can we talk?
Deadly Glitch: You mean—alone?
Trixie: Please.

The cursor blinked for a very long moment.

Deadly Glitch: Join me in the green room for a more private chat.

Paula and Loomis looked at each other. "What can I give him?"

"Give him whatever it takes to buy us a few more minutes," Loomis replied.

Paula depressed a button. A small box appeared in a corner of her laptop screen. The others would no longer see what she and The Glitch typed to each other.

Deadly Glitch: Where are you?

Trixie: Why?

Deadly Glitch: Curious.

Trixie: In the Sunshine State, Clearwater, near the Gulf of Mexico. Where are you?

Deadly Glitch: In the Windy City. Pardon me. I need to attend to something.

Deadly Glitch typed JAM, which meant Just a Minute.

"Think he suspects something is wrong?" Loomis asked.

"What do you think he's doing?"

Paula shook her head.

"He's probably checking. I'd guess he has Hacker Tracker."

"That means he can pull up a map and see where this connection is coming from. We're running out of time. You better hurry."

Deadly Glitch: What's cooking?

Trixie: It could be my hard drive before long.

Deadly Glitch: Somebody in your house?

Trixie: Major unauthorized invasion.

Deadly Glitch: So you went to sleep and left a door unlocked, huh?

Trixie: I'm no guru—I thought I'd had all my ports closed and my firewall was secure, but somebody got in my shit, man, and they're screwing around with me.

Deadly Glitch: You have a secret love, the kind of shy guy that likes to talk dirty—without a response. Don't worry. He'll run out of wind and sail himself into a boring little corner before long. It'll pass.

Trixie: No I can't risk the wait. It's more than that—much more.

Deadly Glitch: For instance?

Trixie: I'm in trouble with the law. I'm on the run.

Deadly Glitch: A fugitive with a computer?

Trixie: It's a laptop; it's all that I have left. The cops tried to pick me up for some pretty big bad checks I wrote.

Deadly Glitch: So be cool and lay low.

Trixie: That's kind of hard dude, not being able to contact my family and friends.

Deadly Glitch: I doubt if they care to track you down for checks.

Trixie: That's just it. I feel like a marked woman. You know I'm not too sure they haven't sent this person to mess with my E-mail. I know somebody's reading it, and making little changes.

Deadly Glitch: You're being paranoid; the police don't work like that. If I intended to hurt someone, I mean really mess with an enemy's mind, I'd get in his pocket. The bank is a very vulnerable institution. So are wives and their secrets.

Loomis touched Paula's shoulder. "You've got to keep him on-line, just a few more minutes. He's so damn close I can smell him." In a low voice, as though someone on-line could hear him, Loomis instructed the driver to make a right turn at the next corner. The shift in direction confirmed his suspicion. The fading signal gathered strength again. The techie pointed the antenna toward a set of buildings in a single block. They passed right by what looked like the hot spot. The signal faded again.

"Go back," Loomis ordered.

They turned and doubled back.

"Slow down a little and hang a right at the next corner. OK. Drive, drive. He's here," Loomis said. The Cellscope left no doubt. The meter jumped like an out of control Geiger counter. The LED pointed toward a building. The Glitch was less than a thousand meters away. "This is it." Loomis said, "This is the place."

Loomis beamed with confidence. It was the Crescent, a dilapidated transient hotel on the skid row strip.

"Well, all right then." Agent Chase chuckled. "That's a real cute little gadget you've got there, Jelly Belly."

Because neighborhood spectators had seen many drug raids, which they likely assumed this was, they did not draw a crowd of thrill-seekers when several marked cars, transportation, and surveillance vehicles quietly converged on the building minutes later.

The SWAT teams were deployed and ready for action.

Agent Chase spoke into a headset microphone and clicked a switch. "This is Bravo leader to Charlie, testing."

"Bravo leader, I hear you loud and clear." Gary Noble, in charge of the designated tactical team going in, responded, flak-jacketed like his troops in bulletproof vest and full gear.

"Take care of the preliminaries."

Detectives Robert Loomis and Paula Douglas exchange looks. The Glitch had not made a move.

Agent Chase contacted Noble again. "Bravo leader to Charlie. We have to move on this right now, what's the setup?"

"It's an old four-story building with thirty units and a fire escape. No back doors on the ground level and no entrances on the sides. The desk clerk says a computer man checked in yesterday, early afternoon. He's in room two-eleven, but he hasn't seen him today."

"I guess not, he's on-line right now, Charlie. You got a name?" Agent Chase countered.

"Joseph Giordano from Chicago is the name on the registration, which is probably bullshit. He's not driving, either. A woman dropped him off in a black Navigator. No bags, just a weird-looking phone and a couple of computers. One is a laptop."

"Secure the perimeters and evacuate the guests on that floor."

"The building is surrounded," Noble said. "The second floor is vacant, and my people are ready to go."

"Outstanding job, Charlie. It's time to rock and roll. Lock and load," he ordered Noble.

Loomis panicked and grabbed Agent Chase's headset. "What the hell, we want to arrest this guy. He's a cyber thief, not John Dillinger. You're getting ready to go in like a bunch of paratroopers."

Agent Chase held his hand up like a traffic cop. Any amity that existed between them vanished with the gesture. "Listen up. We both know he has intent to commit a wrongful act. That act could become an extremely aggressive one upon discovery. He's relying on our ignorance. If he makes any kind of move against my boys, I'm going to throw down and take him and his hot-ass modem out."

Loomis stared at Chase.

"What you people fail to understand, Loomis, is that the FBI has the support of the president, and anybody, anywhere that attempts to obstruct my orders will face serious consequences." Chase turned to the mike and barked instructions to Noble, "Charlie, move sledgehammers into position."

Inside the hotel, Gary Noble gave a hand gesture that directed ten SWAT troops to creep up the stairs. They secured the rooms on both sides of two-eleven. Two men positioned themselves direction in front of the door with a heavy black metal ram. The others lined up in perfect formation, crouched on either side.

Across the street in the mobile command post, Loomis questioned Chase.

"Is this necessary?" he asked.

"Yes, is the long and the short of it." Agent Chase explained. "It's better to bust the hinges off in case he has deadbolts."

Deadly Glitch: Have the pony soldiers arrived yet?
Trixie: What are you talking about?
Deadly Glitch: You're spinning my wheels.
Trixie: I don't know what you mean.
Deadly Glitch: You know perfectly well what I'm talking about. Take
    a look out the damn window. What do you see?
Trixie: Palm trees? What are you trying to get at?
Deadly Glitch: Poverty. You see poverty, don't you?

Suddenly Paula was not sure what to type.

Deadly Glitch: Still there? You don't have to answer. I see what you
    see, and it doesn't look like Clearwater to me. The gig is up, as
    they say. There's nothing further for either of us to gain by in-
    dulging in this boring dialogue—Detective Douglas.

Loomis and Paula were stunned. Paula's fingers were as idle as the blinking cursor. Loomis's knees stiffened. A surge of anxiety flickered on his lips.

Deadly Glitch: You're not in Florida.

Trixie: And you're not in Chicago.

Deadly Glitch: No, actually I'm not.

Trixie: What do you say we have a little face time?

Deadly Glitch: Should I prepare something special?

Trixie: That won't be necessary, Glitch. Besides you don't have the time.

Deadly Glitch: I'm afraid that it's you who has run out of time, detective. I have to run along now. By the way, I planned something very special for Detective Loomis. I'm sure he's standing by. Ta, ta.

"Ten seconds, Charlie." Chase panted. A surge of tension swept through him as though he were there. "Three, two, one. Go, Charlie, go." He commanded, giving Paula the nod to let it go. Paula Douglas typed a final sentence.

Trixie: Stand clear of the door; I don't plan on ringing the bell.

Inside there were three loud hits against the door. The men stormed into the room. "Federal agents!" one of them bellowed. There were screams and crashes, and the whole room plunged into pandemonium.

They checked, in the closets, behind the beds, and under the cabinets. Deadly Glitch was gone. Nothing moved in the wide and open space of the room except the little active light on the front of a lone computer.

Once the search was completed, Agent Chase followed up with Officer Gary Noble. "Charlie, did you get him?"

"Nobody is home, Bravo."

"What? He has to be there, we can see that he's still on-line."

"Negative, Bravo, there's nothing here but a computer with no monitor that has a little blinking red light, hooked up to a cell phone near the wall."

"Kiss my ass. Are you sure there is nothing there but a fucking computer hooked up to a telephone?" Agent Chase shouted in a breathless rage. "Go to hell!"

"Don't touch it!" Loomis gasped.

Agent Chase shook his head and looked at Loomis. "Too late, he says he just picked it up a second to look at it."

"Oh my God." Loomis pounded his fist on a nearby desktop. "Run now!" Loomis screamed. "Get everyone out of there, now!"

Wide-eyed and baffled, Chase ordered Noble to clear out fast. Inside, grim-faced troops dashed and dove for cover. As the last man cleared the door, there was an explosion.

The scent of smoke, chalk dust, and sizzling electronic components carried as far as the mobile command center across the street where Loomis reacted in a savage rage. "Damn it to hell!"

"How did that bastard manage to get us running after our own tails?" Agent Chase howled.

"He used a roaming number to deceive us." Loomis explained. "He was doing the same thing we did, but he did it in a different way. Modem numbers and calls to roamer access numbers are like a dead end."

"Then we never traced him all the way?"

"No, he blocked us. He fooled our equipment into thinking what he wanted us to think." A pale Loomis shook his head in utter disbelief. "This is bad, very bad. It can only mean one thing."

Agent Chsae stared intently.

"He has root."

"He has what?"

"Root access, the ability to take control of the account owned by the system administrator," Loomis said. "It's like having the master key in a hotel. You can go in any room and do whatever you want. Change passwords, read files, or delete everything on the hard drive. He's the God of the Pond."

Loomis felt drained as he shook his head and looked out a window. The birds began to chirp, and the last gray hints of a long night gave way to the first hint of morning. He looked up at a cloudy dismal sky. His perception of the distance and the seemingly unlimited depth of the sky was much like being at sea, staring across an endless ocean.

His personal cell phone buzzed. He looked down at a familiar number. It was Judith. She was probably worried.

Loomis had already decided to change his habits. Yes, he had the ability to change. There was nothing he wanted more, and he was going to start by rearranging his priorities. Deadly Glitch had given him the slip, and he had no intentions of spending another night at work. He was going home to a wife that he was going to make love to, after a long sentence of unaffectionate nights. There was still hope. He had to try. Maybe he would start by taking some flowers with him. It was time to call a truce. He was ready to reconcile with her.

He held the phone to his ear. "Hello."

"Mr. Loomis," a deep velvet voice churned a shudder of shock through the essence of Loomis's soul. "It was not my intention to take all of your money, but your wife will need a little spending change."

"What the fuck."

"Oh, I'm so sorry, I haven't properly introduced myself. You know me as Deadly Glitch. Nice to put a voice to a name, isn't it?" The Glitch delivered his final declaration of revenge in a chilling tone. "Things change, don't they?" He said with a grin in his voice. "What a difference a day makes. I made her feel appreciated again. She fell right into my plan. A witty exchange of dialogue, a few Internet rendezvous, and presto, like magic, I create a business trip to Detroit and we meet for that definitive act of intimacy."

"Fuck me!" Loomis screamed in a furious rage.

"Yeah, I suppose we have done just that."

No children, no money, and no wife. Loomis thought; only a few hours ago, he had felt secure and hopeful. It was all over now. He felt like crying, but what good were tears? He was literally out for blood now. There was nothing left for Loomis to think about but murder.

"You're going to die, you motherless bastard," Loomis promised.

"Aren't we all, someday? Judy, Judy, Judy." He concluded. "No one's to blame. She actually suspected that you knew all along, but you were so busy detecting everything but her affair, you never had a clue. You simply had a Glitch in the computer."

# About the Authors

**Frankie Y. Bailey** is a faculty member in the School of Criminal Justice at the University at Albany. Her area of research is crime and culture focusing on two areas: crime history and crime and mass media/popular culture. She is the author of the Edgar-nominated *Out of the Woodpile: Black Characters in Crime and Detective Fiction*. She is the coeditor of *Popular Culture, Crime, and Justice*. She is the coauthor of *"Law Never Here": A Social History of African American Responses to Issues of Crime and Justice*. She and Donna C. Hale are the coauthors of the forthcoming book, *Blood on Her Hands: The Special Construction of Women, Sexuality, and Murder*. As a mystery writer, she is the author of *Death's Favorite Child* and *A Dead Man's Honor*, featuring criminal justice professor/crime historian Lizzie Stuart. Bailey is a member of the Mystery Writers of America, Sisters in Crime, the International Association of Crime Writers, and Romance Writers of America. Her most recent work is the third Lizzie Stuart mystery, *Old Murders*.

**Jacqueline Turner Banks** currently has two series of novels: one of young adults novels and one of adult mysteries. Her work has appeared in several anthologies, and her screenwriting work has won her honorable mention for two separate scripts. Her videoscript *Black People Get AIDS Too*, won numerous awards, including the Bronze Award for best documentary at the National Film Festival and an honorable mention at the Black Filmmakers' Hall of Fame. The film was also screened as an award presentation at the American Film Institute in Los Angeles. Her young adult novels have received many awards as well. Her fourth novel in the juvenile series, *A Day for Vincent Chin and Me*, is nominated for the state award in Oklahoma and North Carolina. She is currently marketing an adult fantasy series.

A Chicago-based writer and lawyer, **Chris Benson** has worked as a city hall reporter in Chicago for an area radio station and as Washington editor for *Ebony*. His articles also have appeared in *Jet*, *Chicago*, and *Reader's Digest* magazines. In addition to his journalism experience, Chris has worked as a promotional writer and as a speechwriter for several Washington, D.C., politicians, including former U.S. Representative Harold Washington, and as press secretary for former U.S. Representative Cardiss Collins. As an assistant professor of journalism at the University of Illinois (Urbana-Champaign), he taught magazine article writing, with an emphasis on literary journalism—using the best techniques of fiction, including character development, descriptive narrative, and theme, to add depth and texture to nonfiction writing. Chris is coauthor of *Death of Innocence,* Mamie Till-Mobley's story about the life and death of her son, Emmett Till, and the love that helped her survive. Chris also has written *Special Interest,* a Washington-based suspense thriller, and is at work on the sequel, *Damage Control.* In "Double Healing," the short story included in this anthology, Chris wanted to play with the compression of time and space to intensify the suspense. The story unfolds in roughly a thirty-minute time span on a gritty urban street in Little Beirut, as the protagonist considers everything that led to yet another bloody murder, hoping that nobody—the legal gangbangers, the police—will figure out what really brought him to that spot on the block.

**Eleanor Taylor Bland** says, "I just completed the eleventh novel in the Marti MacAlister mystery series. I always have material for at least three more novels floating around inside my head and dozens of characters waiting to get out and be given a voice. Marti is a joy to write about, the perfect protagonist. I never feel any constraints. I can write a novel that is cozy or suspenseful, a puzzle or a thriller. I can include social issues that are important to me. I can depict Marti's family life as wholesome and caring, while allowing family members to be their less than perfect selves. They are a stable contrast to the central plot, which generally depicts families that are dysfunctional and villains who tend to be sociopaths or psychopaths. Many of you know my son, Anthony Bland. He has been traveling to fan conventions with me since he was four years old. Anthony is fifteen now. He was twelve when the nonfictional elements of "Murder on the Southwest Chief" took place. He's been keeping travel journals over the years, and his jottings, recollections, and somewhat sinister mind provided major contributions to the story."

**Patricia E. Canterbury,** is a native Sacramentan and holds BA/MA degrees from the California State University in Sacramento. Patricia is the assistant executive officer for the State of California Board for Professional Engineers and Land Surveyors and is a political scientist, award-winning poet, award-winning short story writer, and novelist. As a political scientist she was a member of the 1985 United Nations Women's Conference in Nairobi, Kenya. Her speech, "Women and the Family Farm" is part of the permanent United Nations archives. *The Secret of St. Gabriel's Tower* is her first published novel, the first of the proposed Poplar Cove Mysteries series. Her great-grandfather was a merchant in Sacramento the day that gold was discovered. Patricia won the 1989 Georgia Poetry Chapbook contest for her collection of poetry *Shadowdrifters, Images of China*. She is married to Richard Canter-bury, a short story writer, and they live in Sacramento with their pets: three cats, a red Doberman who thinks he's a cat, one fresh-water and one salt-water aquarium, and a vicious parakeet named Spike. She has been published in numerous poetry journals throughout the United States and is hard at work on the next Poplar Cove Mystery.

**Christopher Chambers** is a Washington, D.C., native who served four years as an attorney with the U.S. Department of Justice, before turning to teaching commu-nications at Queens University in Charlotte, N.C. His critically acclaimed debut mystery-thriller novel, *Sympathy for the Devil* (Crown, 2001) has been followed by *A Prayer for Deliverance* (Crown, 2003). He's served on panels with such masters as Donald Westlake and Stuart Kaminsky; he is active with the National Association of Black Journalists and the Mystery Writers of America. He resides in Maryland with his sweetheart, Dianne.

**Tracy Clark** is the author of two as-yet unpublished novels, *Hard Promises* and *Bor-rowed Time*. She is currently working on her third novel, *Into Temptation*. She lives and writes in Chicago.

*Publishers Weekly* says, "**Evelyn Coleman** knows how to keep the pages turning in her inventive, funny, assured debut thriller, *What A Woman's Gotta Do* from Simon & Schuster." Optioned by the Academy Award–winning producer of the movies *The Peacemaker* and *Deep Impact*, *What a Woman's Gotta Do* is now in paperback from Dell. Coleman also has two highly praised juvenile mysteries with the Pleasant Company's American Girl History Mystery series. Coleman is the past president of Mystery Writers of America, SE, the 2002 Georgia Author of the Year in Children's Literature, a King Baudouin Cultural Exchange Fellowship recipient, and a former winner of the Atlanta Mayor's Fiction Award. Coleman was also the first African-American in North Carolina Arts Council's ten-year history to win one of their fic-tion fellowships.

**Grace F. Edwards** was born and raised in Harlem and is the author of the Mali An-derson mystery series. She is a member of the Harlem Writers Guild and currently teaches creative writing at Marymount Manhattan College. Her Harlem-based mys-tery series has been adapted for television at CBS, featuring Queen Latifah as the in-trepid sleuth.

**Robert Greer,** author of the C.J. Floyd mystery series *The Devil's Hatband, The Devil's Red Nickel, the Devil's Backbone, Limited Time,* a medical thriller, and a short story collection, *Isolations and Other Stories,* lives in Denver, where he is a practicing surgical pathologist, research scientist, and professor of pathology and medicine at the University of Colorado Health Sciences Center. His short stories have appeared in numerous national literary magazines, and two recent short story anthologies showcasing Western fiction. He also edits the *High Plains Literary Review*, reviews books for National Public Radio, and raises Black Baldy cattle on his ranch near Steamboat Springs, Colorado. His fifth novel, *Heat Shock,* was published in 2003.

The first book in **Terris McMahan Grimes's** Theresa Galloway series, *Somebody Else's Child,* garnered an unprecedented double Anthony Award for best first mystery and best paperback original, as well as an Agatha Award nomination for best first mystery. She also won the Chester Himes Black Mystery Writers award. She began her career as a feature writer with the *Sacramento Observer* newspapers. Her current projects include a coming of age novel set in 1964 Oakland, California, a memoir, and a Negro Leagues baseball-themed novel. A native of Tucker, Arkansas, Terris grew up in Oakland, California—the home of Ebonics—and graduated from McClymonds High School. She attended Coe College in Cedar Rapids, Iowa, and graduated with a degree in English from California State University, Chico.

**Gar Anthony Haywood** is the Shamus and Anthony Award-winning author of nine crime novels: six featuring African-American private investigator Aaron Gunner; two recounting the adventures of Joe and Dottie Loudermilk, Airstream trailer owners and beleaguered parents of five grown children from hell; and *Man Eater,* which *Publisher's Weekly* called "The best Elmore Leonard ripoff since Elmore Leonard." He has also written for the *Los Angeles Times* and the *New York Times,* authored scripts for television dramas, including *New York Undercover* and *The District,* and has cowritten two Movies of the Week for the ABC Television Network. He is a former president of the Mystery Writers of America's Southwest California chapter.

**Hugh Holton** (1947–2001) was a captain in the Chicago Police Department and the author of seven novels featuring CPD Detective Larry Cole. He did not just try his hand at straight police procedurals, however, but incorporated science fiction or fantasy elements into his books as well. The only son of a police officer, he grew up in Woodlawn, and attended nearby Saint Anselm Elementary School and Mount Carmel High School. In July 1964, Holton joined the police department's cadet program, which had been launched to encourage young college students to join the force. Two years later he enlisted in the army for a three-year tour of duty, including a seven-month stint in Vietnam. By March 1969 he'd returned to Chicago and joined the police academy. As he was moving up in the department, he began to get interested in writing, after a lifetime of reading authors such as Ian Fleming, Robert Ludlum, Mickey Spillane, and Sir Arthur Conan Doyle. He enrolled in the writing program at Columbia College and the summer program of the prestigious Iowa

Writers' Workshop at the University of Iowa, and later placed his first short story in *Detective Story* magazine. Once he began writing, he also contributed a monthly column on the police for *Mystery Scene Magazine*. His book *The Left Hand of God* won a Readers' Choice award at the Love Is Murder conference in Schaumburg, Illinois, in 1999. He passed away on May 18, 2001, just eight days after his eighth novel, *The Devil's Shadow*, was released.

**Geri Spencer Hunter** is a native of Mashalltown, Iowa, and a graduate of the University of Iowa's College of Nursing. She is still active in the nursing field, working as a public health nurse. Her first novel, *Polkadots*, was published in 1998, and her second novel, *Mother's House*, was recently published as well. She is a member of the Zica Creative Arts and Literary Guild and is currently working on numerous projects in various stages of completion. She's married with children and grandchildren and lives in Sacramento, California.

**Mary Jackson Scroggins** is an eclectic writer, who has published essays, articles, and short stories—literary and mystery. Her writing focuses on the unseen, underrepresented people who populate her life and on family—what constitutes one and what does not. She writes about strong, resilient, family-oriented working women and the strong but not overshadowing men with whom they partner. She is also a women's health advocate and is on the board of directors of Haiti Lumiere de Demain, a nonprofit organization that provides books for children and promotes literacy in Haiti, and on the advisory board of Washington Independent Writers, the largest regional writing group in the country. The story that appears here is an extension—not the completion—of "Dreams of Home," which appeared in the anthology *Women on the Case*. As Dicey Scroggins Jackson, she is completing two novels, one featuring Gloria Bell in the search for her teenage daughter who disappeared from a homeless women's shelter. She lives in Washington, D.C., with her husband/best friend, Kwame.

**Glenville Lovell** is the author of *Too Beautiful to Die*, published by Putnam, a noir mystery set in New York, starring Blades Overstreet, a black ex-cop with two white siblings, who is trying to win his estranged wife back as he maneuvers through the minefield of his dysfunctional family in his attempt to solve the murder of an FBI agent. His other two novels are *Fire in the Canes* and *Song of Night*.

**Lee E. Meadows** is the author of the Detroit-based mystery series featuring Lincoln Keller, Private Investigator. Both *Silent Conspiracy* and *Silent Suspicion* have received critical raves. Meadows is currently working on the third Lincoln Keller novel, *Silent Rage*. "A Small Matter" starts the adventures of his latest protagonist, Dr. Garrison Brock.

**Penny Mickelbury** is the author of seven novels in two successful mystery series: the Carole Ann Gibson mysteries, featuring the first Black female criminal defense attorney in the mystery genre, and the Mimi Patterson/Gianna Maglione mysteries, featuring the first Black female investigative reporter in American Mysteries. Her short stories have been included in the anthology *Spooks, Spies, and Private Eyes,* and *The Mysterious Naiad.* She has contributed articles to several mystery magazines and publications and is a frequent guest lecturer at colleges and universities across the country. Also an accomplished playwright, her work was chosen by the California African-American Museum to be presented as part of its Radio Theater Program. Her novel *Night Songs* was nominated for the 1995 Lambda Literary Award, and *Paradise Interrupted,* her fourth Carole Ann Gibson book, won the 2001 Golden Pen Award, given by the National Black Writers Alliance for the best mystery novel of the year.

**Walter Mosley** is the author of twelve books and has been translated into twenty-one languages. His popular mysteries featuring Easy Rawlins and his friend Raymond "Mouse" Alexander began with *Devil in a Blue Dress,* which was made into the film of the same name, starring Denzel Washington and Jennifer Beals. Others in the series were *A Red Death, White Butterfly, Black Betty, A Little Yellow Dog,* and *Bad Boy Brawly Brown,* a prequel to the Rawlins mysteries, *Gone Fishin',* and a series of short stories collected in *Six Easy Pieces.* His other character, ex-con Socrates Fortlow, lives in Los Angeles, infusing his episodic tales with ethical and political considerations. Excerpts from his collection *Always Outnumbered, Always Outgunned: The Socrates Fortlow Stories,* have been published in *Esquire, GQ, USA Weekend, Buzz,* and *Mary Higgins Clark Mystery Magazine.* One of these new stories was an O'Henry Award winner for 1996 and is featured in *Prize Stories 1996: The O'Henry Awards* edited by William Abraham. In 1996 he was named the first artist-in-residence at the Africana Studies Institute, New York University. Since that residency, he has continued to work with the department, creating an innovative lecture series entitled "Black Genius," which brings diverse speakers from art, politics, and academe to discuss practical solutions to contemporary issues. Designed as a "public classroom," these lectures have included speakers ranging from Spike Lee to Angela Davis. In February 1999, the collection was published with the title *Black Genius,* with a Mosley introduction and essay. This past year, Mosley returned to the mystery world with the debut of a new series. *Fearless Jones* is now available. Set in 1950s Los Angeles and introducing secondhand bookstore owner Paris Minton and his best friend, war veteran Fearless Jones, the novel is already garnering early praise. In November 2001, he published *Futureland,* an episodic view of the near future with Warner Books. HBO has already optioned three of the stories.

**Percy Spurlark Parker** has been a member of the Mystery Writers of America for over thirty years, and a member of the Private Eye Writers of America since its inception. For MWA he has served as Midwest chapter president, regional director, and treasurer. For both organizations he has done his stint on writing panels and on writing committees to select best works in past years. His tally so far is one novel and more than fifty published short stories. A transplanted Chicagoan, he and his wife, Shirley, now live in Las Vegas.

**Gary Phillips** is the winner of the 2003 Chester Himes award for writing. Currently, *Bangers*, a novel about corruption and power set in the underbelly of Los Angeles, is on the shelves. He has written two books about the 6-foot heartbreaker Martha Chainey, *High Hand* and *Shooter's Point*—both set in and off of the Strip in Las Vegas. "Beginners Luck," the tale in this collection, is his first short story with the character.

**Charles Shipps** presently works for the Department of Transportation in the city of Detroit, where he lives with his wife and sons. He published a volume of poetry, BLACK NEMESIS. A local radio station produced and aired two plays based on his early short stories. After graduating from Martin Luther King High School he attended Highland Park Community College, Central Michigan University, and majored in Mass Communications at Wayne State University. His numerous life experiences include clothing salesman, word processor, hotel telephone operator, a reproduction engineer in the manufacturing department of a major auto maker and projectionist in an X-rated theater. Mr. Shipps has completed a mystery novel that his agent is currently shopping to publishers.